A BROKEN WOMAN

Laura & Eric
Thanks for reading!
Dharma Kelleher
5.9.24

A BROKEN WOMAN

A JINX BALLOU NOVEL

DHARMA KELLEHER

eBook ISBN: 978-0-9791730-8-0

Print ISBN: 978-0-9791730-9-7

Library of Congress Control Number: 2019917473

Cover design by Damonza.com

Dark Pariah Press

www.darkpariah.com

ACKNOWLEDGMENTS

This book, and the entire Jinx Ballou series, would not exist were it not for my lovely wife, Eileen (not an alias). She is my first reader, head cheerleader, and holder of my heart. She came up with the idea of a bounty hunter and is always willing to let me bounce ideas off of her, no matter how ridiculous.

I would also like to thank the fantastic editing team at Red Adept Editing, most notably Angela McRae and Kristina Baker. They help debug my manuscripts and are always teaching me something new about grammar and style.

Thanks to Kevin Bales and Ron Soodalter, authors of *The Slave Next Door: Human Trafficking and Slavery in America Today*. A big thank you to Adam Richardson for sharing his expertise on police procedure both via email and his brilliant podcast, The Writers Detective Bureau. Also to ProPublica and the Center for Investigative Reporting for their coverage of the way some police departments misuse the cleared by exceptional means status to misrepresent their clearance of unsolved rape cases.

Thanks goes to the myriad podcasts who have invited me to blather on about my work and my life including *The Bastard Title*, *A Leap of Doubt*, *Kobo Writing Life*, *Crime Friction*, *Writer Types*, *DIY MFA*, and many more.

To all of you, thank you for helping to make this book

possible and for contributing to the visibility and representation of transgender people in crime fiction.

For my wife, Eileen,
the woman who makes my heart soar

"There is nothing stronger than a broken woman who has rebuilt herself."

— HANNAH GADSBY, *NANETTE*

1

The metal railing on the concrete staircase groaned when I fell against it. A bottle of Cuervo Gold dangled precariously from my unsteady hand. I shivered while a shrill chorus of coyotes pierced the cool night air. One cried out the plaintive melody. The others harmonized, raising it to a crescendo, fading to silence for a heartbeat before the cycle started again.

A lot of people hated coyotes, but their cries resonated deep in my soul. Hunter. Trickster. Solitary and yet still reaching out to connect with others of their kind. I'd been solitary too long. I needed some connection.

I pulled my body up two flights, stumbled along the walk to room 319, and pounded on the door. "Willie, man. Let me in."

"Who the hell is it?"

"Liz. Liz Windsor." Not my real name, but he'd find that out soon enough.

"Never hearda you."

"Frank sent me. Thought we could party a little."

I was trying to keep my mind on my business, but part

of me just wanted to play the role of the drunken whore for a night. Drinking on the job, especially on an empty stomach, was never a good idea, but what the hell. I was a solitary hunter, but I needed to connect. Lately, the nights had been awful lonely.

The door breezed open so fast I almost fell into the room.

"Whoa," I said with a laugh, steadying myself with the doorframe.

The bare-chested man before me looked worse than his mug shot. Three days' worth of beard growth extended halfway down his throat. He smelled of sweat, musk, and weed. A few weeks on the lam will do that to a person.

His name was Wilhelm Penzler. He'd been charged with money laundering and fraud. When he failed to appear at his court hearing, his bail bond agent hired me to pick him up and take his stinky ass back to jail.

"Hey, Willie!" I held up the bottle of tequila and shot Penzler my most seductive smile. "Ya wanna party?"

"It's Wilhelm." His gaze slid down to where my tube top barely covered my breasts. He grabbed the bottle and took a long pull. "Come on in."

I should've cuffed him right then. But I'd been in a funk for the past week. Okay, more like the past few months. Hadn't been laid in forever. I deserved a little fun.

A porno played on the television. Open boxes of Chinese takeout sat on the nightstand next to green glass pipe and a mirror dusted with a white powder. Clothes were strewn across a wood-framed chair, the bed, and the floor. A small trash can by the dresser overflowed with fast-food bags and an empty Entenmann's pastry box.

"Nice place," I said playfully.

"The maid hates me. So Frankie sent ya, huh? Gotta say,

you're better lookin' than most of the skanks he has in his stable. How'd he know where I was, anyway?"

I shrugged. "Didn't say."

Penzler came up behind me and grabbed my crotch. Under normal circumstances, I would've given him a nose job with my elbow and twisted his wrist until the bones popped.

Instead, I moaned with feigned pleasure. Well, somewhat feigned. It felt damn good to be touched. Penzler's hands migrated up to my breasts, squeezing and massaging. *Oh, Conor*, I almost said out loud, remembering my ex-fiancé.

I sat on Penzler's bed, eyeing the glass pipe that lay next to a box of Mongolian beef. "You smoking a bowl?"

"Yeah. Wanna hit?"

"Definitely."

He handed me a lighter, and I indulged myself a little further. The smoke burned my throat, but it helped silence the voice in my head asking me what the hell I thought I was doing. *Yeah, I got a fucking job to do. So what?*

"Shit." I lay back on the bed, releasing a billowy cloud of sweet white magic. My brain felt like an old barnstorming biplane doing loop the loops. I passed the pipe and lighter back to Penzler.

He lay next to me and took a hit. "I know, right? Good shit."

My phone pinged. "Dammit."

I glanced at it. A text from Assurity Bail Bonds' Sadie Levinson read, *You find Penzler yet?*

"Fuck."

"What's wrong?" Penzler asked.

"My asshole boss."

"Frankie?"

"Not exactly." I took the pipe and lighter from him and set them on the nightstand.

"Whaddya mean, 'not exactly'? You're one of his girls, right?" He slipped a leg over mine and started massaging my breast.

I rolled my eyes. I wanted to just lie there and let Penzler fuck me. Instead, I sat up and twirled my finger in the air. "Turn around."

"Why?"

"Just do it," I insisted.

He guffawed but obeyed. "You ain't gonna do nothing kinky, are you?"

"Not kinky."

I took a deep breath to clear my head. Didn't help. I pulled the handcuffs out of my back pocket and snapped them onto his wrists.

"What the fuck?" he yelled.

"Wilhelm Penzler, you missed your court date and violated your bail agreement." I'd repeated these words so many times that, even high as a kite, I could repeat them without missing a syllable. "I've been hired to return you to custody."

"Bitch, take these off me, or I'll fucking kill you. You know who I work for?" He began to buck. I tried to pull him off the bed, but in my impaired state, I lost my balance. I fell on my ass, banging my head on the nightstand.

"Fuck, that hurt."

A loud thud shook the room. I pulled myself up enough to see Penzler slam the door with his shoulder a second time. The doorjamb cracked.

"Dude, chill." I rubbed the goose egg forming on the side of my head.

He charged again. The door smashed open. I heard a

metallic clang and a yelp of fear followed by a sickening thud.

My head cleared with a rush of adrenaline. "Awww...shit!"

I rushed out the door after him and stopped at the metal railing. Penzler lay in a heap on the pavement two stories below. "Shit, shit, shit, shit!"

I raced along the walkway, vaulted down the staircase with moves that'd make Jackie Chan jealous, and rushed over to Penzler's body. In the dim overhead light, I could make out a dark liquid puddling around his head. "Goddamn motherfucker shit."

My official title is bail enforcement agent, but that's just a fancy term for a bounty hunter. Unfortunately, the days of "Bring 'em back dead or alive" were long gone. I don't get paid when my fugitive is in the morgue.

I can just walk away. Or call 911 from the burner phone in the glove box of my car. Then when I've sobered up, I can tell Sadie I found Penzler dead in the parking lot, with no idea how he got that way. Yeah, that might work.

"Hey!" A woman in a flowery dress and flip-flops ran toward me with an ice bucket in her hand. "What happened?"

Fuckity fuck fuck fuck!

"Not sure." My heart thudded in my chest. "He...he pitched himself over the rail."

"He dead?" She pulled out her phone, no doubt dialing 911.

"I think so." I was so fucked.

While Ice Bucket Lady called emergency services, I raced back to Penzler's room and tried to figure out what to tell the cops. Between the booze, the weed, and the adrenaline, my mind was having trouble focusing.

Okay, I was never here. Wait, my handcuffs are still on his wrists. Shit. Even if I remove them without anyone seeing, the autopsy will show his wrists were bound. See, I may be drunk and half baked, but at least I remember shit like that.

Okay, so I was here, and I...I knocked on the door, and he ran out of the room and pitched over the rail. No, that doesn't make sense. Why would he do that?

How about, he opened the door. When I told him who I was, he ran back inside. I chased after him and cuffed him. But he knocked me off balance and busted through the door to escape, only he pitched over the railing instead. Okay, we'll go with that. Wait, who is this we? Shit, I'm so fucked up.

With a ratty towel from the bathroom, I wiped down the tequila bottle, the pipe, and every surface I thought I'd touched. Didn't want anybody to know I was high when I showed up to arrest Penzler. Finally, I called my attorney, Kirsten Pasternak. The phone rang four times before she picked up.

"Jinx? What's up?"

My teeth chattered from a combination of nervousness and the cold. "I'm...in a bit of a situation."

"Can it wait? I'm at the movies with this really charming man. I think he likes me."

I didn't say anything. I just felt stupid for letting something like this happen.

She sighed on her end of the line. "Okay, where are you?"

I gave her the details. She promised she'd be there as soon as she could. "Don't say anything to anyone until I get there."

"I know the drill."

2

Sirens alerted me that the police had arrived. I hated leaving the bottle of tequila behind. I was going to need it after dealing with this shit. But best to leave the wiped bottle for the crime scene techs. I took a deep breath and wandered downstairs to face the music.

As a general rule, the local cops weren't fond of people in my profession, especially after a team of bounty hunters mistakenly stormed the home of the Phoenix chief of police a few years back. I wasn't involved, but it didn't boost our reputation among those sworn to protect and serve.

When a uniformed officer showed up and asked me for an initial statement, I followed Kirsten's instructions and said, "I'm not saying anything until my attorney gets here." Statements like that naturally drew suspicion, but in my impaired state, it would have been way too easy to slip up and say something incriminating. I didn't need to give the cops a win tonight.

I was sitting on a wooden bench outside the motel when Kirsten's silver-blue Mercedes pulled up. We had met years earlier at the Phoenix Gender Alliance. She stood an inch over six feet and wore a black blazer over a revealing white blouse.

"Jiminy Christmas, Jinx. You look like the walking dead," Kirsten said in her deep, sultry voice.

"Gee, thanks," I replied sarcastically. I couldn't stop the shivering, even after I'd grabbed a jacket from my car.

"Look, I'm not trying to be mean. I'm worried about you. You're skinnier than a runway model, and you smell like a frat house after a kegger. You been smoking pot?"

"No!"

She glared at me over her yellow-framed glasses.

"Okay, maybe. Lately, things have just been so...I don't know."

She put a hand on my arm. "You know you're more than a client to me, right? You're my friend. What's gotten into you? Is this because of what happened with Conor?"

Five months earlier, my fiancé, Conor Doyle, had attempted to stop a white nationalist with a truckload of explosives bound for Phoenix City Hall. Conor forced the truck off the highway several miles away from its destination. The driver triggered the bomb, killing forty-three people and injuring two hundred more.

Conor was lauded as a hero until the media learned that the Police Service of Northern Ireland had an outstanding warrant for him, dating back to his teenage years. Reporters hounded me at my house and followed me when I went out, making it impossible to do my job. By the time they had scavenged the last tasty morsel of gossip, I was a broken woman—traumatized, alone, and struggling to reassemble the shrapnel of my life.

"I don't want to talk about Conor," I told Kirsten. "Or about Toni."

"Oh yeah, that corrections officer you were dating. Toni Bennett. Helluva name. I'd forgotten about her."

I snickered darkly. "Wish I could."

She put a hand on my arm. "I'm sorry. But if it's any consolation, Conor died a hero. Had the driver reached City Hall, the death toll would have exceeded a thousand."

It wasn't any consolation. Nor was Conor dead as everyone thought.

"Back to the matter at hand. What happened this evening?" Kirsten asked.

"Wilhelm Penzler skipped on a money-laundering charge. I tracked him here and talked my way into his room. When I cuffed him, he freaked. Busted through the door so hard that he flipped over the railing and fell two stories."

"Were you inside the motel room?"

"Yeah."

"Where'd you get the pot?"

"He was already smoking it when I arrived. Looked like he'd also done some lines of coke before I got there."

"So rather than arrest him right away, the two of you had a little party. How very Hunter S. Thompson of you."

I shrugged. What could I say? Guilty as charged.

"What a mess." She shook her head. "Do you have any drugs on you?"

"Sorry. No. You'll have to get your own." I burst out giggling. Couldn't help it. This was all so absurd.

"Jinx, this is serious. You could be charged with involuntary manslaughter."

That sobered me up a bit. "I didn't bring any drugs other than a bottle of tequila."

"Did he drink any?"

I tried to remember. So many of the details were muddled. "I don't think so."

"Well," said Kirsten, "time to face the music."

Detective Pierce Hardin was speaking with two other

detectives near the staircase, then wandered in our direction when Kirsten waved him over.

Hardin's graying hair contrasted with his dark skin. He'd started growing a beard since the last time I'd seen him. Ten years earlier, when I joined the Phoenix PD, Hardin had been my field-training officer. He was so tough and by the book, he'd earned the nickname Detective Hardass.

My pulse quickened as Hardin approached. I assured myself I wasn't responsible for Penzler's swan dive, but I still felt guilty.

"Detective Hardin," said Kirsten.

"Evening, Counselor." He gave her a brief, polite smile, which vanished the instant he looked at me. "Jesus, Ballou! What the hell's going on with you? You look like shit on a cracker. And you smell worse."

"Pleasure to see you, too, Detective," I said as soberly as I could.

"You mind telling me why this guy Penzler took a header onto the pavement? And why he's wearing a pair of handcuffs, which I'd bet my left nut belong to you?"

Kirsten gave me a nod.

"He failed to appear in court. I tried to arrest him. He went berserk. Charged out of the room like an enraged bull on steroids, hit the rail, and belly-flopped onto the asphalt. If only he'd stuck the landing." A guffaw threatened to surface. I covered my mouth to suppress it.

Hardin's nostrils flared. "You think this shit is funny? A man is dead, Ballou."

"I know. Sorry." I clamped down hard on the urge to laugh, but it felt like riding a bucking bronco. This whole thing was so absurd, it was hard not to laugh at it.

"You realize who Penzler worked for, right?"

I tried to remember, but the details were fuzzy. "Shit, some bar in Scottsdale, I think."

This time, it was Hardin's turn to scoff. "Some bar? Is that all you got? Used to be you'd know an FTA's shoe size and their third-grade teacher's maiden name. Now all you know is he worked at some bar?"

"Why? What's the big deal?"

"That bar is a strip club run by the Volkov crime family." The Volkovs were Chechen gangsters with ties to the Russian mafia.

"Volkov? Volkov's dead. I—" I stopped when Kirsten gave me a red-light look.

"Yeah, Ballou, you killed Milo Volkov. I know all about it. But here's the rub. Milo had a brother, Sergei, who now runs the organization. The tittie bars, the sex trafficking, money laundering, and probably a whole host of other shit we don't even know about. And Penzler was in the middle of all of it. His attorneys had been in talks with the feds and the county attorney's office about a plea deal."

The fog in my mind burned away. Milo Volkov had been a ruthless Chechen mobster running a human trafficking organization. I'd landed in the son of a bitch's crosshairs while pursuing a teenage murder suspect he had kidnapped. When the smoke cleared, Volkov, several of his men, two federal agents, and a fellow bounty hunter were dead.

"Penzler had a plea deal? To testify against Volkov, I suppose."

"So I'm told," replied Hardin.

"Shit, that'd be suicide. Wait, maybe that's why Penzler jumped. If Sergei's anything like his sadistic brother, jumping off a balcony'd be a helluva lot less painful than what awaited Penzler if he testified."

"You're saying he committed suicide?" Hardin didn't look convinced.

"You have any proof he didn't?" Kirsten countered.

Hardin shook his head. "You realize this was one of Special Agent Lovelace's cases? I know you two have a history of butting heads. When she hears you wrecked their case against Sergei, she's going to go ballistic."

"Detective, do not threaten my client. She has had a rough few months. And yet, she's here doing her job. It is not her fault Mr. Penzler skipped his hearing. Nor is it her fault he fell over a railing, whether accidentally or intentionally."

"Unless you're working for Volkov." Hardin's gaze landed on me.

Daggers flew from my eyes. "You know me better than that. I might bend the rules here and there. And I'll admit, I've been in a funk the past few months, but I would never, ever work for the Volkov organization."

Hardin didn't look happy, but the fire in his eyes tempered a bit. "Anything else I should know about what happened here?"

"Nope. But I would like my handcuffs back."

"Too bad. They're evidence." Hardin glared at me. "Now get the hell off my crime scene."

"Gladly." I turned and walked away, with Kirsten beside me.

"And get your act together!" he shouted at my back. "Because if shit like this happens again, I will lock your skinny white ass up and throw away the key. You got me?"

I ignored him. When we reached my car, Kirsten put a hand on my arm. Her face showed concern. "You okay to drive?"

"Yeah, I'm fine. Thanks for tonight."

"Jinx, I'm seriously worried about you."

I yanked my arm out of her grip. "I said I'm fine."

"You look anorexic."

"Oh, so you're going to body-shame me for being slender."

"That's not it, and you know it. I'm concerned. You're not slender; you're emaciated. You're clearly not eating. You're driving and working while under the influence. And if you don't get help soon, situations like tonight or worse are going to happen again. And I may not be able to keep you out of jail. Or the morgue."

"If I wanted someone to play armchair therapist, I'd call up my dad. At least he's the real deal."

"Jinx, I'm only saying this because I care."

I turned away, irritated. "Maybe you shouldn't care so much. Conor cared, and look where it got him." I climbed behind the wheel of the Dodge Charger.

Kirsten started to say something, but I revved the engine.

"What's that? I can't hear you!"

"I said—"

I revved the engine louder and roared out of the parking lot, leaving twin trails of rubber on the pavement. I was a total bitch, and I knew it. But I didn't need anyone feeling sorry for me. Especially her.

3

I arrived home around eleven o'clock to the boundless energy of Diana, my nine-month-old golden retriever. She jumped and yipped with excitement as I closed the front door. Her paws were covered in dirt from digging in the backyard, but I didn't care. With all the shit going on in my life, Diana was my one source of happiness. I'd never thought of myself as a dog person before my brother, Jake, gave her to me as a Christmas present. But now I couldn't imagine my life without her.

"Hey, baby girl." I lay on the floor and let her slather me with slobbery puppy kisses. "How you doing?"

I went to hug her, and she bolted to the kitchen. "Fine. Be that way."

She returned a moment later with her empty food bowl in her mouth. *Shit. I forgot to fill it before I left this morning.* "I'm sorry, baby. Mama was out later than expected."

I grabbed the bag of gourmet kibble from the pantry and filled her bowl. She dug in, tail wagging like a high-speed metronome.

I tried to remember if I'd eaten that day and couldn't

recall anything. The dishes in my sink were at least a couple of days old. The fridge was empty except for a gallon of milk that was turning lumpy. I checked the pantry. A package of ramen, a few dusty cans of tuna, and a box of Rice-A-Roni. I looked at the instructions on the Rice-A-Roni box. It required butter, which I didn't have, unless the sour milk counted. I settled for the ramen dusted with the contents of the "oriental-flavor" seasoning packet. I concluded that if oriental really was a flavor, it shouldn't be.

The old me would have had plenty of healthy food in the kitchen. And it wasn't like I was short of funds. End of last year, I'd brought in two hundred grand for capturing one of the FBI's most wanted. My fiancé, Conor Doyle, had listed me as his beneficiary on his life insurance policy, so when he was declared dead, I'd inherited a sizable sum.

If anything, I was short on motivation. The thought of wandering the grocery store aisles, dodging idiots who paid no attention to where they were going, set my teeth on edge. Last time I was there, I was two seconds away from bludgeoning an old man who'd been blocking the aisle with his cart for five minutes, trying to decide between two brands of canned peas. They were canned peas, for fuck's sake. They all taste like green mush, so just pick one!

Using the wall for balance, I zombie-shuffled down the hall to my bedroom with Diana trailing me. I lay on sheets that hadn't been washed in weeks and stared at the popcorn ceiling. My body craved sleep, but my mind wouldn't shut off.

As Diana snuggled her warm body next to me, I kept thinking about Wilhelm Penzler. Was it an accident? Was it suicide? Either way, he'd still be alive if not for me. A lot of people would still be alive if not for me. In nine years as a bounty hunter, I'd killed nearly a dozen people. Granted, the world was a better place without most of them—drug dealers, human traffickers, rapists, murderers, and a few terrorists.

But each one came with a cost. What made me better than any of them? I didn't solve crimes. I just tracked down people who didn't show up for court and took them to jail. Before you knew it, most were bailed out again. I was useless. A drain on society. A drain with a mail-order badge and a gun.

At some point, I drifted off because the next thing I heard was the garbage truck rumbling down the street. Diana dangled a slobbery leash in my face.

"Hey, puppy." I gave her a head scratch. "What's up?" As if I didn't know.

She dropped the leash beside me on the bed and gave an impatient whine.

"Okay, let's go for a run."

I dragged myself to the bathroom, emptied my bladder, and stared at my reflection in the mirror. Gaunt didn't describe it. Aside from the limp black hair, the pale woman staring back at me looked like a White Walker from *Game of Thrones*.

"Bitch, get your shit together," I muttered.

My phone rang. I glanced at the screen. *Ugh.* Sadie Fucking Levinson of Assurity Bail Bonds. I sent the call to voice mail. She was going to have a shit fit when I told her dear old Wilhelm Penzler failed his first flying lesson.

A text appeared on the screen. "Ms. Ballou, get your tuchus in here."

I was in no mood to deal with her attitude. *It's Saturday,* I replied.

Don't care what day it is. Get here now. Not a request.

I pulled on a mostly clean T-shirt and a pair of shorts, grabbed a Wonder Woman baseball cap, snapped a leash to

Diana's collar, and we went for a run through the neighborhood.

I lived in Phoenix's historic Willo District, near Third Avenue and McDowell Road. The neighborhood was a labyrinth of streets lined with small but pricey brick houses sheltered by maturing shade trees. The area attracted quirky Gen Xers and millennials who sported a lot of ink and had a live-and-let-live attitude.

Up until last December, I'd lived a couple of streets north in a house that my brother had renovated and sold to me for a song after the housing bubble burst.

After Conor was declared dead, I inherited his house, which I'd nicknamed the Bunker. It had twelve-inch-thick brick outer walls, bullet-resistant polycarbonate windows, and steel-reinforced doors. Oh, and there was the underground tunnel that led from the coat closet to the back room of a tattoo shop on McDowell Road. Conor had hardened the place's defenses after a drug dealer he'd returned to jail sent his crew to retaliate.

I'd offered my old house rent free to a few transgender friends who needed a safe place to transition and rebuild their lives. Not everyone had a supportive family like mine.

The cool air buzzed with the droning of leaf blowers, their modulating pitches going in and out of phase with each other. Despite the high temperature hitting the triple-digit mark just days ago, a cool front had settled in, giving the city a temporary reprieve before summer blazed into full fury.

Fellow residents walking with their canine companions waved as we passed. I knew faces and dogs but not names. The petite Korean woman with the Shiba Inu. The older white guy with the pug. The muscular Latino with the Belgian Malinois.

Just as well we never spoke. Who in their right mind

would want to know me? I was a drunken loser who'd been engaged to a man wanted for terrorism. Didn't exactly make for pleasant small talk.

How was your day?

It was great! I got wasted and let a fugitive take a twenty-foot nosedive into a parking lot. How was yours?

Diana stopped to lift a leg next to the tire of a pickup decorated with MAGA and NRA bumper stickers.

"Good dog," I said before rounding the corner back toward home.

After our run, I hopped into the shower to wash off the previous night's shame, got dressed, and pulled my hair into a ponytail without bothering to blow it dry. This was Arizona. It'd be dry in thirty minutes, anyway.

For breakfast, I poured coffee into a travel mug and flavored it with a dash of coconut rum. Or more than a dash. I needed a little liquid courage before I told Sadie about Penzler's recent demise, assuming she didn't already know.

I strapped my ballistic vest over my T-shirt. I hooked my utility belt around my waist and slipped a Taser in the holster on my right hip, a Ruger nine-mil in a cross-draw on my left. Pouches in back held two pairs of handcuffs, a spare Taser cartridge, and a spare magazine of ammo. I hung my bail enforcement agent badge around my neck and slipped on a pair of wraparound shades, followed by a pair of fingerless gloves. Ready for action.

"Okay, Diana. Be good while I'm gone." I topped off her food bowl and filled her water bowl from the RO spout. "Try not to terrorize the feral cats too much."

She responded with a bark, which I took to mean, "Yeah, who are you kidding?"

I hopped into the Charger and cruised downtown for my meeting with Sadie.

4

I drove south a few miles to the Arizona Center, an open-air shopping center that was a mix of trendy restaurants, touristy shops, and small business offices. Assurity Bail Bonds was tucked away on the second floor in the corner of the L-shaped complex. A string of bells jingled as I walked in.

Unlike most bail bond shops, which had all the charm and elegance of a check-cashing joint, Assurity looked more like a cross between a law office and an art gallery. Plush carpeting. Framed prints on the wall. Leather armchairs for clients. Two cherrywood desks separated the waiting area from the rest of the office. One of them was occupied by Sadie, who did not look pleased to see me, despite her urgent texts.

Her wedge-cut helmet of hair was immaculate as always. Her makeup understated and professional. And the scowl on her face all too familiar.

I plopped down in one of the chairs in front of her desk. "Whassup?"

The creases in the corners of her eyes deepened.

"Whassup?" she echoed in a mocking tone. "Are you genuinely asking me that? Where is Mr. Penzler?"

"Well, you see, there was an incident."

She pulled a folded newspaper from the side of her desk and slapped it down between us. The headline read "Mob Informant Leaps to Death."

"Would this be the 'incident' in question?" Her mouth was an ugly slash across her face.

I shifted in my seat. Maybe I should've brought Diana with me. Or that bottle of rum. "Yeah, poor Penzler, huh? Maybe the Volkovs got to him."

"Don't give me any of that mishegas, Ms. Ballou. It's beneath even you. Tell me what happened."

"Look, I tracked him to a motel off I-17 and Northern. Talked my way inside, but when I cuffed him, he busted through the doorway so hard he flipped over the railing. Totally not my fault."

"And were you drunk like you are this morning?"

"Drunk? Who's drunk?" I stood in protest.

"Don't even try! You smell like a tiki bar."

"My point is Wilhelm Penzler either fell by accident or he jumped. Cops said so. At least you don't have to pay out the full bail amount."

"I have a business to run, and Mr. Penzler was a client. In the past three months, I've had more than a dozen complaints against you. Harassment. Assault. Abusive language. One gentleman claimed you broke his wrist."

"That asshole broke his own wrist trying to squeeze out of the cuffs."

"Not what he said." She turned her attention to her computer screen.

"Who you gonna believe? Me or your criminal clients? Besides, a little rough play makes them more likely to show up to court."

"You've got chutzpah. I'll give you that."

"Thank you. I think."

"You're fired."

The words hit me like a gunshot from a sniper. "What?"

"You heard me." Her gaze met mine. "I have no need for someone who lacks a single iota of professionalism. I'm reassigning your remaining cases to Viper Fugitive Recovery."

"What about me? Where am I supposed to go? No one else will hire me."

"Not my problem." She tossed the newspaper in the trash and turned back to her computer.

"I've recovered a ton of fugitives, including some that no one else could locate. Paul Russo. Doug Chang. Shelly Reid. Steve Shaw." I counted each one off on my hand. "Remember Holly Schwartz? Not even Fiddler could track her down. I did."

Sadie leaned back and crossed her arms. "Yes, you used to be an ace bounty hunter. And you'll recall I hired you when no one else would. I didn't care if you were transgender. All I cared about was results. Right now, your results are bupkis. Time you get over Conor Doyle's death and ..."

The mention of Conor's name sent a bright blade of rage slicing through me. "Leave Conor out of this!" I slammed my fist on the desk so hard she jumped. "I bet you're the one who snitched on him to the Northern Ireland police."

"I did nothing of the kind." Her face became a wall of stone.

"Only three people knew about Conor's past. Conor, me, and you. And I sure as fuck didn't turn him in."

"Ms. Ballou...Jinx." She took a breath, and her expression softened. "I apologize for what I said. While I did not care for the man, I kept my knowledge of Conor's past to myself. And I am sorry for your loss."

"I don't need your pity, lady."

"Jinx, listen to me."

Were those tears in her eyes?

She put a hand on my arm. "I respect you. You have the potential to be a top-notch bail enforcement professional. But since Conor's passing, you've fallen apart. Understandable. Grief hits us hard. I struggled after my father passed. But you need to get help. Until you do, you're a liability."

I stepped away from the desk, even as my own eyes threatened to water. I was not gonna let her see me cry. "Fuck you, bitch! I don't need this shit, anyway. I got money. Maybe I'll just hang out at coffee shops and write a novel."

"Do what you like, Ms. Ballou. But for your own sake, get some help. Your father's a psychologist, isn't he? I'm sure he can recommend someone."

I flipped her a single-finger salute with each hand, turned on my heels, and marched out of the door.

On the way home, I stopped at a liquor store and picked up a couple of bottles of tequila. Back in the car, I poured some into a travel cup. Fuel for the road.

Despite my simmering rage, I kept to the speed limit as I drove north up Seventh Street. Not hard to do since there were so many stoplights.

"Go, you fucking idiot!" I shouted at the Ford Explorer ahead of me, going five miles under the speed limit. When I finally passed him, I noticed the Phoenix Police decal on the side of the car. *Fuck!*

I kept pace with the patrol vehicle until it turned west on McDowell, then I floored it. *Fucking slow cop.*

I was feeling better when I pulled into my driveway. Grabbed the paper bag with the two bottles along with my travel cup and shuffled to the front door. Took me a moment to figure out the right key to open the door. When I finally stumbled inside, I collapsed on the couch and turned on the TV.

For the record, daytime television sucks ass. Seriously, it's all talk shows with the worst sorts of people on. And the commercials. Holy fuck me with a spoon! Nothing but ambulance chasers, substandard insurance, and pharmaceutical ads with a mile-long list of horrific side effects. I finally found a punk-rock music channel and cranked it up while I vegged to ponder what a shithole my life had become.

"Hey! Can you turn it down? Some of us are trying to sleep."

I looked up to see an androgynous person in a wifebeater and boxers standing over me.

"Who the fuck are you?" I asked.

"I'm Max, and I live here. Who the hell are you?"

"This is my fucking house!" I tried to stand up, but the room wobbled, so I sank back down on the couch.

"Like hell it is. I've never seen you before. I'm getting Ciara."

Ciara. The name was familiar. Ciara. Ciara Mountains. No, that was the Sierra-something Mountains. Who was Ciara again?

Next thing I knew, a woman with a familiar yet asymmetrical face was standing next to the asshole, telling me to get out of my own goddamn house. Ciara. Now I remembered. I drained my travel cup.

"Jinx, what are you doing here?"

"I'm sitting here listening to music in my house. What are you doing here?"

"I was trying to do some bookkeeping until Max interrupted me."

Max. The asshole giving me shit. "Tell Max to get the hell out of my house, then."

"Jinx, Max lives here. And while yes, technically you still own this house, you live in Conor's old place now. Remember?"

Thoughts flitted against the current of booze lubricating my brain. Shit. I was at my old house. Ciara was... was something...oh yeah, she was the resident manager. Fuck.

I took a deep breath and looked at the asshole. Max. Not an asshole. Or maybe an asshole. Wasn't sure. "Look, man, I'm sorry. I got a little confused."

"Like I don't have enough shit to deal with." Max crossed his arms.

I rolled my eyes. "Whatever. Just sorry." I pulled myself to my feet. The room spun, but I managed to stay upright and hold onto the bottle of tequila. "I'm outta here."

Ciara put a flat hand on my chest. "Whoa. You can't drive home like this. Come on. There's an empty bed in my room. Sleep it off."

I looked at her. Or tried to. Everything was so goddamn swirly and hard to focus on. I was tired. "Yeah, okay."

5

I woke with my mouth tasting of coconut-flavored bile. The bedsheets didn't feel right, though the room was vaguely familiar. The front of my shirt was damp.

"Diana?" I called. Where was she?

"Feeling better?" Ciara stepped in and flicked on the overhead lamp, sending steely shards of light through my eye sockets.

I squinted in the glare. "Oh fuck. Tell me I didn't do anything too stupid."

"You mean like yelling at our newest resident and puking in the bathtub? Yeah, a little."

"Shit. I'm sorry." I rubbed my temples, trying to get the explosions of pain to stop.

"No worries." Ciara sat next to me on the bed and offered a glass filled with something red. "Here, have some of my hangover remedy."

I took a sip. It was thicker than it looked, but it didn't taste bad. "What's in it?"

"Spicy V8, raw egg, parsley, and a dash of lemon juice.

You'll want to drink a lot of water too. That much alcohol will dehydrate you."

"Thanks. You're a good friend."

"You're a good friend, too, usually."

"But not lately."

She shrugged. "You've been in a slump. I get it."

"I...I haven't been myself since Conor..." I was surprised by my openness. I hadn't exactly been forthcoming with my feelings of late, other than rage.

"Can't blame you there. After I was attacked a couple years ago, I had a lot of PTSD. Even now, sometimes I feel triggered looking at my misshapen eye and jaw. The doctors saved my life, but I couldn't afford a reconstructive surgeon."

I felt guilty. I'd experienced a similar attack on my high school graduation night. But I had supportive parents with good insurance. Ciara didn't have anybody but her friends in the trans community.

"You look good, Ciara. Really."

She blushed. "I don't, but thanks."

We sat there as the silence grew awkward. "I should head back to my place. My real place. Thanks for helping me out." I gave her a hug and handed her the empty glass.

"That's what family's for. And if you need to talk, you got my number."

"I do. And I know where you live."

She laughed, and it sounded like sunshine. "You off to capture more bad guys?"

I let out a deep sigh. "I got fired this morning. So, no."

"For being trans?"

"No, for being a drunken bitch."

"You need money?"

I shook my head. "No, I'm good. Just need to get my shit together."

I grabbed my utility belt and vest and followed Ciara to the front door. The sun was riding the horizon, painting the clouds with red, orange, and lavender. How long had I been asleep?

"Take care of yourself, Jinx. Maybe you should look into getting some—"

I cut her off with a gesture. "Don't say it. I know. I need help. When I'm ready, I'll…I don't know. I guess I'll talk to someone."

After a final hug, I walked wearily to the Charger and drove up two streets to the Bunker. A black SUV sat parked in front of the house. With the light bar on top, it looked like a police vehicle. But the gold lettering on the side read Viper Fugitive Recovery.

"Shit." I pulled under my carport and walked down the driveway toward my visitor.

A white guy I recognized as Paul "Deez" Dzundza climbed out of the SUV. I had a vague memory of a recent text conversation with him, though the details escaped me.

Deez stood six-eight, a walking wall of muscle. Even in the fading light, I could see the scar on his neck from when he'd taken a bullet for me three years earlier when we worked together on Conor's crew.

"I's getting worried." His voice was a gentle rumble. "I thought we said seven."

I glanced at my watch. It was seven thirty-five. "Sorry. Traffic."

"No worries." A wave of sadness washed over me when he wrapped me in a tender bear hug. I hadn't seen him since Conor's funeral.

"How's it going, Deez?"

He released me and met my gaze. "Good. How you holding up, girl?"

I shrugged. "Same shit. Different day. How's Tommy Boy?"

"That kid of mine won't quit growing. Just turned twenty-five. He's an inch taller than me now."

"Twenty-five? Shit. Guess that makes you..."

"Old as the hills." His eyes watered. "We've missed you, kid."

"Yeah, me too."

"Sorry about Assurity. That wasn't my doing. I'd never steal work from you. You know that, right?"

"I know." My headache started hammering a little harder behind my eyes.

"I'd love to have you on the team again."

Memories of the day he got shot gutted me with guilt. "Thanks for the offer, but you know, I got my own thing going."

"Well, listen, I have a job I think might be right up your alley."

"Deez, Sadie gave me the boot. She doesn't want me anywhere near her cases."

"This isn't Assurity. It's Pima Bail Bonds in Scottsdale."

"Pima? They didn't want anything to do with me after I got outed a few years ago."

"I know, but this case is different. I've already talked to Maurice about it. He's cool with you taking it."

I narrowed my gaze at him. "Why?"

"It's the James Fitzgerald murder case. You familiar with it?"

"That preacher? The one that got his dick cut off in the sleazy motel? Why does Maurice want me to take the case?"

Deez hesitated a moment. "The client's transgender like you."

I eye-rolled hard. "Oh, I get it. Maurice will hire me if

I'm putting away one of my own. Is that it? Well, you can tell Maurice Begay that I won't be his Judas, all right?"

Deez put a hand on my shoulder. "It's not like that. From what I'm told, this client got roughed up pretty bad in lockup before she was bailed out. Put her in with the men."

My stomach turned. Recent changes in DOC policy dictated that transgender prisoners be housed based on their assigned sex at birth, even those who had had gender confirmation surgery. Many had been assaulted as a result, and one had died. Lawsuits had been filed, but so far, DOC hadn't blinked.

"Shit, Deez, and you want me to put her back in that hellhole?"

"No, but who better to safely return this woman to custody and get her bail reset but someone like you?"

"What'd she do?"

"Charged with first-degree murder for allegedly killing Brother James Fitzgerald."

I shook my head. "That fucking street preacher who showed up at schools, saying women deserved to be raped and calling for queer people to be put to death? We should give her a medal, not lock her up."

"I don't disagree. Nevertheless, she jumped bail. I had Tommy Boy and Rodeo on it, but they hit a brick wall. Pearson's a member of an all-girl biker gang up north. They're not giving her up."

"Not my problem."

"Think about it, Jinx. If you don't take it, Maurice will assign the job to someone else, someone who isn't afraid to get rough."

"How long before the bond is forfeit?"

"Little over a week. You could ask for double the standard rate. Maurice'll pay it. Bail's at three hundred thousand. That'd be a sweet sixty grand for you."

I thought about it, then shook my head. "I appreciate you thinking of me, man, but I can't do it. Maurice had his chance to hire me a few years ago. If the only reason he wants me now is to go after one of my own, he can go to hell."

"I understand." Deez shook my hand and clapped me on the back. "If you change your mind, let me know."

"Yeah, whatever."

"Take care of yourself, Jinx. You're family to Tommy and me."

"Likewise." I trudged back down my driveway.

"Hey!" he called from inside his SUV.

I turned. "Yeah?"

"Let's get a drink sometime."

"Yeah. I'll call you." I wouldn't. Too many fucked-up memories.

Inside the house, Diana jumped up and nearly bowled me over. "Hey, baby! How's my girl?"

I filled her bowls with kibble and water, then plopped down in front of the TV, looking for something on Netflix to help me unplug. Nothing looked interesting.

I pulled out my phone. My best friend, Becca Alvarez, had left a message asking me to call her. No doubt she was worried about me too. Like I needed anyone else's pity.

I tossed the phone aside, opened the other bottle of tequila, and settled in to binge-watch *Dexter*. Something satisfying about watching assholes get what they deserve.

6

I didn't know how long I had been staring at my ceiling—minutes, hours, weeks. Diana lay beside me, her head on my chest. I would have stayed there, but my bladder was so full my back teeth were floating.

I padded to the bathroom and sat on the toilet. The golden glow of morning shone through the window. A clock on the wall told me it was nine o'clock.

What the hell am I going to do now? I had liked working for Sadie Levinson. Sure, she had a stick up her ass, but after I was publicly outed by a local newspaper, she'd given me a chance when no one else would. And now I'd screwed that up.

The thought of taking the job with Pima Bail Bonds turned my stomach. Tracking down a transgender woman to throw her back in jail? I don't think so. Jail's bad enough for cisgender people. For trans people, it's a fucking nightmare. No way would I be a part of that.

I felt lost with nothing to do, nothing to look forward to. Like a sailboat adrift in the doldrums.

I was shambling into the kitchen when the doorbell rang. I glanced at a video monitor on the wall that showed my bestie, Becca Alvarez, and her nonbinary partner, Easton St. Claire, at my front door.

Becca and I had been thick as thieves since we first met in middle school. She now worked as a freelance IT security consultant, whom I frequently hired for skip tracing.

Becca was dressed in a shirt emblazoned with a portrait of Frida Kahlo made up like a sugar skull. Easton wore a cornflower-blue button-down with a yellow tie and matching suspenders.

I pressed the call button. "Hold on a sec."

I ran to the bedroom and pulled on a clean shirt and jeans. Diana started whining, clearly wanting to go for her morning run.

"Gonna have to wait, girl."

She shot me a look of disappointment.

"Hey." I opened the door and welcomed Becca and Easton inside. They each gave me a lukewarm hug and greeted Diana enthusiastically. "Want some coffee?"

"Sure," said Becca in a curt tone she often took when she was upset about something.

They followed me into the kitchen and sat at the antique wooden table that my grandmother Marie Lafitte had given me. She claimed it once belonged to our ancestor, the legendary pirate Jean Lafitte. I filled three mugs with coffee. "How you want your coffee?"

"A little cream," Becca answered.

"Black's fine for me," Easton replied.

I added a dash of cream in Becca's and brought all three mugs to the table.

"What's up?" I said in my most convincing "everything's great" tone.

Becca stared daggers at me. "You don't answer my calls. Don't reply to my texts. Your hair looks like a rat's nest, and you look and smell like something Diana threw up."

Diana glanced up at the mention of her name, her tail wagging excitedly.

"Becks, I've been busy."

"Bullshit! In the years we've known each other, you've never shut me out like this. You didn't go to Pride. You haven't shown up at the Hub since Goddess knows when."

The Hub was a coworking space downtown where we shared a table for our respective businesses.

"I called you to get a location for Wilhelm Penzler," I pointed out.

"And then hung up on me before I could say anything else. Are you even signed up for Phoenix Fan Fusion? Or have you given up cosplaying too?"

"I'm dealing with enough shit without you getting all up in my grill."

Easton put a hand on mine. Flecks of glitter in their nail polish sparkled in the morning light. "Jinx, we're not here to guilt-trip you. We're concerned about you. You look depressed."

"And anorexic," Becca added.

"Don't body-shame me!" I wrapped my arms around my chest.

"I'm not body-shaming you, Jinxie. I'm worried." The angles of Becca's face softened. "You and me, we've had each other's backs since forever. Part of that meant speaking up if the other was self-destructing."

Words caught in my throat. I hated that she was right.

"Remember what I went through when my mom got sick?" she asked. "Between the grief from her death and my chronic fatigue flaring up, I felt like a zombie. You were there for me, even when I tried to shut out the whole world. You helped me get back into my groove. You were at my apartment so much my dad thought we were a couple."

I chuckled in spite of the immense pressure inside me. "I remember."

"With Conor gone, it's understandable what you're going through. There's no set timeline on grieving. But it's easy to let grief turn into something more toxic. Like alcoholism. Anorexia. If this keeps up, you could get fired."

"Too late. Sadie fired me yesterday."

"I'm sorry, babe."

Becca laid her head on my shoulder. Easton side-hugged my other shoulder. I liked being in the middle of this cuddle puddle.

"Guess it's time to quit feeling sorry for myself."

"You have any prospects for work?" asked Becca.

"Deez dropped by yesterday with a job. Not sure I want it, though."

Becca turned and met my aimless gaze. "Why not?"

"The FTA is transgender."

"What's an FTA?" asked Easton.

"Failure to appear," I replied. "She didn't show up to court. She's allegedly the one who killed that douchebag Brother James."

"Holy sugar!" Easton covered their mouth in surprise. "You're talking about Zia Pearson, aren't you? I heard what happened to her in jail. It was horrible."

"Didn't look at the file, but the name sounds familiar."

"She's been on the news," they added. "Apparently, she and Brother James got into a shoving match at a biker festival in Scottsdale. That same night, he turned up dead in a skeevy motel room. Police found her partying at a strip club next door. She said she didn't do it, but even if she did, he deserved it."

"You should take the job," Becca said matter-of-factly.

"What?" I pulled away and stared at her. "Why?"

"Sooner or later, someone will. And maybe they won't be as understanding as you."

I barked a laugh. Unlike the bounty hunters portrayed on TV, I wasn't the type to get all touchy-feely with my fugitives once they were in my custody. "Understanding as I drag her ass back to jail where God knows what will happen to her, whether she's guilty or not."

"And then you can help her get her bail reset," Easton added. "Becca told me you do that sometimes."

"I don't know." The whole idea turned my stomach. "I'd feel like a traitor to the community."

"Doesn't Zia deserve her day in court?" asked Becca.

"Of course. I'm not stopping her. She's the one who failed to appear."

"But by bringing her back," said Becca, "you're giving her the opportunity to clear her name."

My head was swimming. "Let's say I bring her back. What if she's innocent, and they convict her anyway?"

Becca shook her head. "That's not on you. That's on the legal system."

"It doesn't feel right." I buried my face in my arms.

"Fine, don't take the job," said Becca. "What *are* you going to do?"

"About what?"

"Your life."

"I don't know. I don't feel like doing anything. What's the point? Between the reward I got for capturing Barclay Dietz and Conor's life insurance, I'm not exactly hurting for cash."

"This isn't about money, sweetie." Becca cradled my face in her hands, forcing me to meet her gaze. "But you know that."

I saw in her eyes the friend who'd stood up for me when I was bullied in school for being transgender. "You're right."

"Uh, hon," said Easton. "We gotta get to the airport."

Becca glanced at her watch. "Shit. You're right."

"I'm updating some backup servers in Denver," Easton said to me.

I gave them a smile that I actually felt. "Enjoy the freezing weather."

"Thanks!"

I looked at Becca then Easton. "I love you guys, people, whatever."

Easton chuckled. "Right back atcha."

"Love you, girl." Becca gave me a tight squeeze.

I led them to the door. As she was walking out, Becca turned and said, "And for the love of garbanzos, return my calls and texts next time. Maybe show up at the Hub once in a while."

"I will." And I meant it. "Let me know if you need any help while Easton's out of town."

"Will do. See you soon, I hope."

After they drove off, I grabbed Diana's leash, and the two of us went for a run. The exertion felt good, energizing me both mentally and physically, sweating out all the alcohol from the day before. I hadn't yet decided whether to take the job from Pima Bail Bonds, but I needed to get my ass in gear and do something. This pity party had gone on long enough.

I was rounding the corner back onto my street when my phone rang. Caller ID told me it was Deez.

"If you're calling to pressure me on the Pima job, I'm considering it, okay?"

"This isn't about that. It's Conor. He's..." His voice choked on emotion. "He's alive."

I just missed colliding with a palm tree. "What?"

"And he's been arrested."

7

"Jinx? You still there?" Deez's voice sounded like it was in a tunnel.

I leaned my back against the tree as my heart thundered in my chest. "Arrested? I...I don't understand."

"He survived the explosion. Don't ask me how. But the news is saying he ran away to Mexico before turning himself in to the police in Northern Ireland. They're convinced he's really Liam O'Callaghan, a terrorist who was involved with a bombing two decades ago. It's insane."

"I...I can't believe it."

"I know this must be a shock. Here we all thought he was dead."

Guilt and shame pressed down on me with all the crushing weight of an SUV. He turned himself in because I refused to run away with him. Thoughts swirled through my mind so fast it left me dizzy. "I need to talk to him."

"I don't know how. Though I guess he must have a lawyer...or a solicitor or barrister or whatever they call them there. I can have our investigator try to find out."

"That'd be great. And Deez, thanks for letting me know."

"You going to be all right, Jinxie?" The concern in Deez's voice threatened to rip me in two.

"Yeah, look, I gotta go, okay? I'll be in touch about the Pima job."

I hung up. Diana was tugging on her leash. "Come on, girl." I ran home at top speed.

When I got inside, I dug through the junk drawer in the kitchen until I found the old burner phone. I dialed the number saved in the Favorites. It rang three times before a recorded voice said the number was no longer in use. I threw the phone across the room.

An idea came to me. I scrambled through my home office, digging out bits of paper from my center desk drawer until I came across a business card with nothing but an email address and a single name—Tuckey.

Using an anonymizer app on my laptop, I tapped out a quick email and waited. For ten minutes, I stared at the computer screen, waiting for an instant reply. But there was nothing. "Shit."

I flipped on the TV in the living room, and there he was. Conor Doyle being hurried by police officers through a crowd and to a waiting car. The headlines read "American Hero An Irish Terrorist?" and "Piestewa Freeway Hero Faked Own Death."

My stomach convulsed. I made it to the kitchen sink and heaved until I was too weak to stand. I sank onto the cool tile floor. Diana walked in, her claws clicking on the tile, and licked my face. I held on to her and bawled.

My phone rang in the other room. I pulled myself to my feet and shambled into the living room, banging my leg against an end table. I snatched up the phone.

"Conor?" I asked breathlessly.

"Um, no. Ms. Ballou?" asked an unfamiliar male voice.

"Yeah, who the hell is this?"

"Pete Stansfield. I was the claims adjuster for Mr. Doyle's life insurance policy."

Shit. "Yeah? What do you want?"

"It has come to my attention that our payout to you of three hundred thousand dollars was...well, premature. Mr. Doyle, as it turns out, is still alive. I hate to say this, but I'm afraid you will need to return the money."

I hung up without a word and tossed the phone onto the couch.

My insides felt like a colony of ferrets were conducting an MMA free-for-all. I crawled to the pantry and grabbed a bottle of tequila, then stumbled back into the living room, where some news guy in heavy pancake makeup and overly pink lips was asking a panel of talking heads their opinions about the situation, speculating on facts they knew nothing about.

"Fuck you assholes!" I chugged what remained in the bottle. Laying my head on the couch, I spotted the handle of the Smith & Wesson .44 Magnum I kept mounted underneath my coffee table. The empty bottle clanked to the floor, and I slid the revolver from the holster.

The weight of it felt solid, almost reassuringly so. I had said goodbye to Conor twice. The first time, when I thought he was dead. A week later, on Christmas morning, Conor's buddy, Tuckey, hand delivered the burner phone with Conor's new number in it. He had survived the blast with only a broken leg and escaped to Ensenada, Mexico.

When I visited him a few weeks later, he begged me to join him. But I couldn't walk away from my friends and family. Letting him go ripped out what was left of my soul. Was I the reason he turned himself in?

Guilt and sorrow coiled around my chest, smothering

me like a python. I ached to feel him in my arms, his hands on my body, to hear his Irish brogue teasing me about my cosplaying as Wonder Woman at comic book conventions.

I stared down the barrel of the revolver, the long dark tunnel drawing me in. My thumb curled over the trigger. *I'm such a waste of space. A black hole sucking joy and happiness from the good people around me. Maybe it's time I join those I've killed—all of the murderers and rapists and drug dealers and human traffickers. Am I any better than them? I've killed. I've lied. I've broken into places. I've even protected a man wanted for terrorism.*

I squeezed harder on the trigger. *What waits on the other side? Sweet oblivion or hellfire?* I pressed my forehead against the barrel. *Just squeeze and find out.*

A cold, wet nose stuck in my ear, followed by a doggy tongue. My thumb slipped out of the trigger guard, and the revolver clattered to the floor, unfired. The noise was still enough to send Diana dashing away down the hall.

"Fuck." Some angels have fur instead of wings.

"This is what happens when transsexuals are allowed to run free on our streets." I looked up to see some scumbag in a MAGA hat talking to a reporter on the TV. "They should all be rounded up and shot. They're a menace to decent society. Bad enough they're allowed to invade ladies' rooms. Now they're killing men of God? Is nothing sacred in this country? What happened to the Constitution?"

The video footage cut to a woman in shades holding a baby on her hip. "I don't really know. I mean, that preacher was telling people to rape women. That's just wrong. I don't really agree with her lifestyle, but I hope she's proven innocent."

Cut to the anchor in the studio with a photo insert of a black woman with a headful of braids. "Thanks, Mike, for that report. As of right now, Ms. Pearson's whereabouts remain unknown. The courts consider her a fugitive from justice. If you see this woman, do not approach her. She is considered dangerous and possibly armed. Instead, you are advised to call the authorities immediately."

Once I saw Zia Pearson's face, something in me shifted. *Considered dangerous and possibly armed.* They were practically telling all good ol' boys with a gun that it was open season on trans women of color.

Deep in my soul, a small flame ignited. A need. A calling to get back into the fight.

I returned the revolver to its holster under the table and shuffled to the kitchen. My refrigerator was near empty. My freezer was a wasteland of unknown objects coated in a thick layer of frost. With a little digging, I located a Marie Callender's chicken potpie, only two years out of date. Close enough.

I stuck it in the microwave. While it cooked, I filled Diana's food and water bowls. A few minutes later, I was testing my molars on hardtack piecrust and burning the roof of my mouth with magma-hot gravy. It was the best meal I'd eaten in days.

An hour later, I was showered and dressed in a clean collared shirt and cargo pants. My long black hair was braided. My breath smelled only a little like alcohol. I was mostly sober.

The TV news program was still on, this time talking about a professional photographer found stabbed to death in his studio, possibly linked to a serial killer dubbed the Valley Slasher.

I pulled out my phone and called Deez. "Tell Maurice I'll take the job. For twenty percent, not ten."

"I'll make the call. You learn any more about Conor?"

"Not yet," I said. "But I've put out some feelers."

"Keep in touch. I'm worried about our boy."

"Will do."

I hung up and checked my laptop. A reply from Tuckey. "Conor being held without bail in Belfast. Has legal team on board. Will try to learn more soon but security is tight."

"That's it?" I said out loud.

My phone rang. "Yeah?"

"Maurice has agreed to twenty percent. Head on over there, and he'll get you set up with the paperwork. When you've got it, give me a call. I'll give you a rundown of what we've already learned so you don't cover the same ground."

"Thanks, Deez."

I hung up and looked at Diana's face. "You saved my life."

Her tail wags seemed to say, "You're welcome."

"Time to rebuild."

8

I drove the Charger east on I-10 to Scottsdale. Pima Bail Bonds was a block away from the Scottsdale City Jail on Pima just south of Thomas. The office was an old renovated house with faded-yellow wood siding. The letters on the sign out front were peeling from decades of brutal heat.

Last time I'd been here was after the *Phoenix Living* weekly newspaper outed me as transgender and got me fired from the bail bond agency I'd worked for. Maurice was one of the many agents who'd agreed to keep my resume on file but never called. Conor later confirmed I'd been blackballed.

The cluttered office showed the years. Faded pictures, recognitions, and framed thank-you letters competed for space on the scuffed walls. The corners on the wood furniture had been worn smooth in spots. The scent of pine oil hung in the air.

Short, dark hair framed Maurice Begay's round face. He spoke in soothing tones to a frail woman who sat clutching a tissue. "Don't worry, Ms. Lewis. We'll get your son bailed out and home with you. Okay?"

She nodded wordlessly.

He handed her a stack of papers stapled together. "Take this to the Scottsdale City Jail, and they will get him processed out."

Another nod. "Thank you." She stood, and he walked her to the door.

When she was gone, Maurice turned to me. "Jinx Ballou, am I right?"

"So they tell me."

"Come on over." He led me to his desk.

"You were working for Assurity, were you not?" he asked.

Oh, brother. Here we go. "Yeah. About two years now."

"Word on the street is she fired you and hired Viper Fugitive Recovery instead."

"Sadie and I had some...creative differences."

"Creative differences?" He gave me a disbelieving look. "Those creative differences wouldn't be named Wilhelm Penzler, would they?"

"Penzler's death was an unfortunate accident. Maybe a suicide. I understand he had agreed to testify against Sergei Volkov. God knows what Volkov would've done to him if he caught him."

"And you're working for Volkov, are you? Maybe a little wet work on the side?"

"Are you kidding me?" I shot to my feet, sending the wheeled chair spinning away behind me. "Is that what you think? That I'm a hit man working undercover as a bail enforcement agent?"

"I heard you had some involvement with Sergei's brother a while back."

"Milo Volkov was a psycho dirtbag who murdered two feds and kidnapped a teenage fugitive I was tracking. I didn't work for him. I put him in the ground. Or did your research not uncover that little tidbit?"

"Relax. I wanted to see how you'd react." He leaned back and gestured toward the chair I'd vacated. "Sit down."

I did but was not cool with the way things were going. "Look, slick, you need somebody to find your wayward defendant. I'm your gal. If you'd rather play head games, I got better things to do."

"Deez recommended you for this job. Though to be honest, I wasn't expecting someone so...scrawny. This defendant, she's a member of a women's biker gang. You sure you're up to the task?"

"I get the job done. I've taken on drug dealers, murderers, sex traffickers, and domestic terrorists. A few women on motorcycles don't scare me."

He shuffled through some files and pulled out a folder and opened it facing me. "Defendant's name is Zia Pearson. She's a transgender woman who lives up in Ironwood with her wife. Bail's set at three hundred thousand. Deez thought since you're trans yourself, you might have an in he doesn't."

"How long before the bond is declared forfeit?" I asked.

His tan face darkened. "A week, I'm afraid."

"Not much time. I'm gonna have to demand twenty percent."

He gave me a shrewd look. "Deez mentioned you were looking for that. Sure you can't do it for fifteen?"

"With only a week to bring her back? I charge double for rush jobs. Deez already tried and failed. I can get her back."

I let the silence hang between us. He twiddled the pen in his hand. "Very well. Twenty percent." He held out his hand, and I shook it. "Just be sure you deliver Ms. Pearson on time."

"I'll get her." I took the folder from him and headed toward the door before turning back around. "And thanks for the opportunity."

"You can thank Deez for that."

It was getting on to two o'clock when I called Deez from my car. "I got the job. You still available to meet?"

"Absolutely. What's your twenty?"

"Still at Pima Bail Bonds."

"Meet me at Abuela's Cucina in thirty. Corner of Hayden and Indian Bend Road. Byrd and I are dropping off an FTA at the Scottsdale jail."

I found the Mexican restaurant easily enough. The lunch crowd had largely dissipated. No sign of Deez or Byrd.

I grabbed a table and ordered a couple of fish tacos. A small sign on the table advertised their top-shelf tequila. Tempted as I was for a victory celebration, I didn't want Deez to think I was a drunk. Especially after what happened to Penzler. I settled for a Dos Equis instead.

I was finishing off the tacos and my second Dos Equis when Deez and Byrd, a light-skinned African American man, strolled in the door. Byrd had joined Viper Fugitive Recovery after I left to run my own company. I waved them over.

"Jinx, you remember Byrd, right?" asked Deez.

I nodded. "We've met a couple of times."

Byrd shook my hand. "Sorry about Conor."

"Thanks." The mention of Conor's name intensified my craving for tequila. I took a deep breath, pulled out a small notepad, and opened the folder Maurice had given me. "What can you tell me about Zia Pearson?"

Deez snagged a chip from the basket on the table. "Honestly, I'm disappointed Tommy Boy and Rodeo couldn't find her."

Nathaniel "Rodeo" Kwan had been a member of my team until I got blackballed. Despite his loyalty to me, he needed paying work and joined the Viper crew.

"Tommy and Rodeo are good hunters. Some people are just harder to find," I replied.

"And to be fair," added Byrd, "they got close. Missed her by minutes one time. Pearson's got a lot of people trying to keep her out of jail."

"Interesting."

Deez opened up a notebook of his own. "Zia Dominique Pearson, goes by the nickname Indigo. Two prior arrests, one for solicitation, another for possession. Charges dropped on the solicitation, probation on the possession charge. She works for the Lambda Resource Center, an LGBTQ support organization up in Ironwood."

I flipped through the file. "What does she do for Lambda?"

"Serves as community relations with the Cortes County Sheriff's Office. Her boss told Rodeo and Tommy Boy she's on temporary leave. No intel on her current whereabouts."

"Maurice mentioned Pearson belongs to a biker gang. What can you tell me about them?"

"The Athena Sisterhood Motorcycle Club," said Byrd with a dark chuckle. "Some seriously scary chicks."

"Pearson and her wife, Chelsea Tucker, are both patched members," added Deez. "The club's based in Cortes County, though it's not unusual to see them here in the valley. Not technically an outlaw club like the Confederate Thunder or Hell's Angels but still pretty hardcore from what I hear. Had a few run-ins with the law over the years."

I jotted notes as they talked. "Tell me about Pearson's wife."

Deez nodded. "Chelsea Tucker works as an EMT.

Former military medic. Goes by the nickname Savage. Tommy Boy and Rodeo searched their house. Looked like Pearson had pulled up stakes and left."

"Who is this Shea Stevens? The one who put up the bond. Used her house and a fleet of motorcycles she owns as collateral."

"One of her biker buddies," Byrd replied. "Ex-con who did time for grand theft auto a while back."

"She's the co-owner of Iron Goddess Custom Cycles," said Deez. "It's a motorcycle shop in Sycamore Springs that hires a lot of second-chancers."

"Second-chancers?"

"Ex-cons, recovering addicts, and the like," Deez explained.

"Stevens sounds like a real peach," I joked. "Think she's single?"

"Oh, it gets better," Byrd added. "This chick's father was president of the Confederate Thunder biker gang until he murdered Shea's mom about twenty years ago. In 2016, Shea and the Thunder teamed up against a Latino drug gang after Stevens's niece got kidnapped. Things got bloody."

"Shit. Starting to sound like a real FUBAR job."

"You think you can handle it?" asked Deez.

"Oh, I can handle it." I had no idea how, but that never stopped me. "Though I could use a little backup. My guy, Caden, quit the business after he got shot last year. And Conor, well...you know. Maybe you could spare Rodeo, since he used to work for me."

"Rodeo's currently working another case." Deez glanced at Byrd, who nodded. "But my man here can give you a hand, if you need it."

Working with someone new was always awkward. But Byrd was a veteran bounty hunter who knew how to pull his weight or he wouldn't have been working for Viper as long as he had.

"That'd be great." I locked eyes with Byrd. "I appreciate the help."

The server laid down another bowl of chips as I stared at the paperwork. "I'm thinking maybe the best approach is to do this low-key. No show of force."

Deez nodded. "Maybe you being a woman, and a transgender one at that, will yield better results."

"How amenable you think Maurice will be to recommending her bail be reset?"

"I've worked a number of Maurice's cases. He's a reasonable guy. As long as a defendant wasn't violent when we recovered them, Maurice was usually able to get bail reset."

"Good, because that may be my only bargaining chip. Convincing a trans woman to sit in a men's jail through her trial would be impossible. I wouldn't even attempt it."

"Under the circumstances, I'm sure Maurice would consider it."

"Any idea where Pearson's hanging out?"

"Tommy Boy and Rodeo seemed to think Stevens was hiding her. But they weren't willing to risk a shoot-out on a hunch."

The more I thought about the job, the more a feeling of dread crept over me, like I was walking into a deep, dark cave without a light. I felt a strong desire to just get fucked up again. Tequila therapy.

I set down a few bills to pay my check. "Thanks, Deez. I'll let you know how it turns out."

"Good to see you again, girl." As we stood to leave, Deez drew me into a hug. "You hear any more about Conor?"

I shook my head. "Just that he's being held without bail in Belfast."

"Still can't believe the fucker's still alive and didn't reach out. This whole mess about a bombing in Northern Ireland just floors me. The man I knew would never do something like that."

I didn't know how to respond. To Byrd, I said, "Meet me at my place tomorrow morning at eight. Pack a bag in case it takes us a few days. We'll head up to Cortes County in the Gray Ghost."

"That beat-up old SUV that looks like it belongs to a soccer mom?" Byrd laughed.

"She may not be pretty, but she blends in. Perfect for sneaking up on fugitives. Driving around in one of those shiny new SUVs you guys at Viper drive—all decked out with light bars and decals that practically scream 'cop'—I'm surprised you catch anything more than a cold."

"Touché, girl. Touché." Byrd clapped me on the shoulder. "I'll see you at eight."

9

I returned to central Phoenix and cruised into the Hub's parking lot, near Roosevelt Street and Grand Avenue. The large, glass-sided building dated back to the 1940s when it served as a car dealership. It resembled an inverted boat hull with a broad metal beam that jutted from the roof, piercing the sky like a ram bow.

The Hub's interior was raw and industrial. Steel beams rose like spires from the concrete slab floor to the cavernous ceiling. Krewella's song "Alive" thrummed from speakers in the back, the volume turned up just enough to make it recognizable.

Once my eyes adjusted to the dim lighting, I navigated through the maze of folding tables where entrepreneurs—from tech startups to accountants to Realtors—had created a home base for their businesses.

"Hey." I sat in my chair across from Becca.

Mock surprise bloomed across her face. "I don't believe it. Could it be? No way! Not the one and only Jinx Ballou, bounty hunter extraordinaire. She hasn't been seen in these here parts in almost forever."

I smirked. "Funny. And for your information, I took that job I told you about."

"Really?" She rushed over and hugged me. "So good to have my bestie back from the dead."

"Good to be back."

She sniffed. "You been drinking?"

I gave her a look. "Becks, don't start."

"Fine." She pulled her chair around next to me. Her face grew serious. "Speaking of being back from the dead, did you hear about...?"

"Conor? Yeah."

"Did you know he was still alive?"

I held her gaze and knew I couldn't lie anymore to her about it. "Not at first. On Christmas morning, he had a burner phone delivered to me. When I called him, it felt like talking to a ghost."

She punched my arm. "And you didn't tell me? What happened to sisters before misters?"

"I'm sorry. I...I didn't know what to do. For a week, I thought he was dead and then...it was so fucked up. I was fucked up."

"That's why you took that trip right after New Year's. You went down to see him in Mexico."

I nodded. "He wanted me to run away with him. But I couldn't walk away from you and everyone I cared about, not even for Conor. And I loved him so much." Sorrow gripped my throat, choking off my words.

She squeezed me tight. "I'm sorry. But I'm glad you stayed."

"Me too."

"But now he's been arrested for that bombing in Northern Ireland?" Becca was the only other person I'd told about Conor's past. "He was a teenager when it happened, and all he did was phone the local media."

"I know." I took a deep breath. "You forgive me for not telling you he was alive?"

She sighed as she thought it over. "Yes. But no more secrets, all right?"

"No more secrets."

I pulled out the notebook where I had stashed the Pearson folder. "Now, I need you to do your magic and see what you can find out on Zia Pearson. Also her wife, Chelsea Tucker, and Shea Stevens, the one who put up the collateral for the bail bond."

Becca took the folder from me. "Will do."

10

The next morning, Byrd showed up in a red Chevy Malibu at quarter to eight. Diana greeted him at the door with a wagging tail and a few friendly barks. Byrd looked a little wary. "He bite?"

"She," I corrected. I grabbed her by the collar and pulled her back as I let him inside. "And in answer to your question, no. Diana's friendly."

Byrd walked in carrying a gear bag over his shoulder. He wore a heavy leather jacket over a navy-blue T-shirt. "She's cute. My pittie, Peaches, loves people. Not so good around other dogs, though."

"Thanks. She keeps me sane or as close to it as I come." I pointed toward the hallway. "Diana, go lay down." She trotted back to my bedroom.

"You want some coffee?" I offered.

"Naw, just ready to get this show on the road."

I flicked off the coffeepot. "Sounds good to me."

I pulled on the wool-blend winter coat that I'd dug out of the back of my closet. I hadn't worn it in two years, and the shoulders had a layer of dust on them.

I stuffed the Pearson file, filled with printouts of the background info Becca had dug up, into my notebook and tucked it under one arm. With my other hand, I grabbed my canvas go bag, which contained my Kevlar vest, my weapons, extra ammo, clothes, and other essentials. “Okay, let’s do this thing.”

We threw our gear into the back of the Gray Ghost, an eight-year-old Nissan Pathfinder covered in scratches, swapped paint, and a few spots of missing trim.

I hopped behind the wheel. Byrd slid in beside me. I started up the Ghost and pressed Play on the sound system. The Pink Trinkets’ *TERF Whores* album filled the truck with screaming guitars and feminist vocals.

“So this stuff about Conor is something else, huh? First he’s alive. Now it comes out he was a terrorist in his teenage years?”

“He wasn’t a terrorist. His father was a member of the IRA. Conor was just a kid who got caught up in the conflict.” I wasn’t one to open my heart to strangers. But Byrd had worked with Conor for a while now.

“He was a good man. Is…is a good man. A miracle he survived the Piestewa bombing. I saw photos of the carnage. Somebody upstairs was looking out for him that day.”

“Yeah.” I wasn’t much of a believer myself. I’d seen too much.

“You talk to him?”

“Not recently.” It was as close to the truth as I wanted to go.

The miles dragged on as the silence between us grew awkward. We left the city for the long, lonely stretches of scrub desert. Towering saguaros and scraggly chollas eked out an existence among aromatic creosote and brittlebush.

Clusters of green-barked palo verde trees huddled along the washes. Rugged mountains rose in the hazy distance on all sides.

An hour later, the road twisted up in the rocky switchbacks of Sycamore Mountain. Clusters of yucca clung to the craggy mountainside, white blooms rising on stalks above the prickly leaves. Spiny lizards darted from their sunny perches as we passed.

The air was chilly at the top, just barely in the forties, according to my dashboard. A wooden sign welcomed us to Olde Towne Sycamore Springs, a mile-long string of family-owned cafés, antique shops, and a real estate office or two.

"Iron Goddess Custom Cycles" was painted on the plate glass window of a storefront to my right. Five motorcycles sat out front in half-width spaces. Women in full biker leathers, their faces covered with bandanas, stood out front chatting despite the cold.

I pulled into the first full-sized space and surveyed the area.

"Looks like Shea Stevens is doing all right for herself, running a place like this," Byrd said.

"I've been meaning to stop here for some time. Been thinking of learning to ride. I hear Iron Goddess makes some kick-ass bikes."

Byrd shot me a grin. "You're going to take Stevens's friend back to jail and then ask her to sell you a bike? Girl, that is bold."

"You think she'd rather lose her house for defaulting on the bond? You ask me, we're doing her a favor."

"So how you want to play this?"

"Low-key. No weapons, except concealed. No vests. No badges. I'll introduce ourselves, explain we just want to help Pearson get her bail reset so she can stay out of jail until she gets her name cleared."

"You think that'll work with these hard-core biker chicks?"

"Rodeo and Tommy Boy tried the tough-guy approach. Figured it's worth a shot."

"I'll follow your lead, then."

We hopped out of the Ghost and stepped into the shop. The place was bigger than I expected. To our right, motorcycle jackets and leather chaps hung from racks in front of a wall display of helmets. To our left, T-shirts, hoodies, and clothing featured the Iron Goddess logo. Several customers, mostly women, wandered aisles.

On the other side of the sales counter, a dozen or so motorcycles gleamed on the showroom floor. The adrenaline junkie in me gazed longingly at the mechanical beasts, a perfect blend of artistry, engineering, and raw horsepower.

A stick of a woman in her forties with long bottle-blond hair and leathery tan skin sat behind the sales counter, flipping through a magazine. She reminded me of an aging pinup girl. "Can I help y'all find anything?" she asked.

"We're looking for Shea Stevens."

"And you are?"

"Jinx Ballou. This is my partner...Byrd." I realized I didn't know his first name.

The woman behind the counter regarded the two of us for a moment. "Wait here." She sauntered to the back of the showroom and down a hallway.

I caught Byrd staring at her waggling ass, and I nudged him. "Cut it out."

"What? A man can't appreciate God's fine craftsmanship?"

"Oh, please."

"Fine, I'm gonna check out these leather jackets over here."

While Byrd explored the jackets, I wandered among the motorcycles. One look at the price tags and my jaw dropped. These were not cheap bikes. Some were the price of full-size cars. Not that I was hurting for cash at the moment, but still. These two-wheeled beauties were a serious financial commitment.

A display stand showing off several helmets with black, white, and pink designs caught my eye. The top of the display held a photo of Maria "Wicked" Wickham, Victoria "Vicious" Ruiz, and Natasha "Nasty" Johnston from the Pink Trinkets standing behind three pink and black motorcycles. Each helmet on the stand featured a band member's name as part of the design.

"You listen to the Trinks?" Shea Stevens stood a few inches shorter than me, wearing a sleeveless denim shirt. Her sinewy arms, dark-blond pixie cut, and deep, irregular scars criss-crossing her face gave her an intense look that suggested she knew how to handle herself.

"Only all the time." I gestured toward the photo. "You build these bikes for them?"

A flush of pride spread across her disfigured face. "They wanted some bikes to kick off their Singing Mammogram tour."

"Great album. Beautiful bikes. I'm Jinx Ballou, by the way." I offered my hand, and she shook it.

"Shea Stevens. What do ya ride?"

"I don't yet," I said. "But I've been wanting to learn."

I would have liked to shoot the shit with this woman. She had good energy and reminded me a little of my ex-girlfriend, Toni. I caught Byrd's eye, and he wandered over to where Shea and I were standing. "Look, we're here on a more serious matter."

"Oh? And what matter is that?"

"Zia Pearson's bail bond."

Shea Stevens's face turned to cold steel in the span of a heartbeat.

My pulse quickened. *Here we go.*

11

"Shea, we want to help her," I said as pleasantly as I could.

"Bullshit. Y'all wanna send her back to that men's jail. Like I told them other guys, Indigo ain't going back to that hellhole. Not for one fucking minute. Not while I still draw breath."

"I get it. I'm transgender as well. I heard what happened at the jail, but—"

Stevens stepped into my space with fire in her eyes. "But nothing. She ain't going back 'cause she didn't kill that son of a bitch no matter how much he deserved it."

"I'm not doubting you. The last thing I want to do is put a member of my community in harm's way. I can promise you, if she comes along without a fuss, we can get her bail reset, get her court date rescheduled, she'll be home for dinner."

"What chance you think a black transgender woman has with a conservative white Scottsdale jury? Hell, they already got some fabricated DNA evidence against her. Do I really gotta explain what'll happen? One way or another, this is a death sentence against an innocent woman."

Byrd and I exchanged a brief glance. She wasn't entirely wrong. All too often, white cisgender men got a pass for rape and other violent crimes, while women and minorities faced maximum sentences, even when acting in self-defense.

"As a black man, I hear what you're saying, Ms. Stevens. My family's experienced our share of the ugly side of the legal system," Byrd said. "But this case against Zia isn't going away. Don't she deserve her day in court? The chance to put this whole mess behind her?"

"She deserves to be left alone."

Byrd opened his hands in a pleading gesture. "Believe me, if it were within our power to get these charges dropped, we would. None of us wants to send an innocent woman to prison. But we can't do that. But we can improve her chances of beating this by getting her trial back on track."

"Otherwise, the judge'll issue a bench warrant and remand her without bail," I added. "She could spend the next few years in jail enduring hell knows what while her trial drags on."

Stevens sneered at us. "Only if she gets caught."

"You're willing to lose your house and your personal fleet of motorcycles to protect her?" asked Byrd.

"My house. My bikes. My money. My life, too, if need be." Not a hint of hesitation in her voice. "Now you two get outta my shop!" She pointed toward the door as her shout echoed off the walls. Customers stopped their browsing and stared at us.

Clearly the low-key approach wasn't working. "I admire your loyalty, Shea," I said. "But we *will* find her, whether you help us or not. And we *will* return her to custody."

"You can try, but you'll fail just like them other knuckleheads. Don't matter how many bounty hunters Pima Bail

Bonds sends. You'll walk away empty-handed or wish you had."

I laughed. "Are you trying to scare me, Ms. Stevens? We've dealt with people a lot bigger and scarier than you and your biker gang. If Indigo doesn't come willingly...if you or your buddies try to interfere, I will recommend she be remanded. You know what that means?"

"Yeah, it means you're a pawn for the prison industrial complex. You'll have her innocent blood on your hand when she gets murdered in prison for a crime she didn't commit. Now get the hell outta here!"

A bearded black man in an Iron Goddess polo shirt and a Native American woman wearing grease-stained coveralls and swinging a large wrench walked in from the back of the shop and stood on either side of Stevens. Shea lifted her shirt enough to reveal the grip of a pistol tucked in the front of her jeans.

Byrd put a hand on my shoulder and whispered in my ear, "What say we mosey on out of here?"

"Fine," I said to Stevens. "You win. If we can't locate Ms. Pearson, she'll stay out of jail. For now."

"Glad we came to an agreement," replied Stevens.

"Consequently, Pima Bail Bonds will take your house, all your fancy motorcycles, which you won't need anyway since you'll be in prison."

Anger amplified on Shea's face. "What the hell you talking about?"

"After I file my report, the Maricopa County Attorney's Office will charge you with hindering prosecution and with conspiracy to commit murder after the fact. Both major felonies with serious prison time. But hey, I'm sure it's no big deal for you. You being an ex-con and all, it'll be like homecoming. Am I right?"

The black man shot Stevens a nervous glance, but all three held their ground. Time for a tactical retreat.

"Come on, Byrd." I gave Stevens a confident smile I didn't feel and backed away. "Enjoy prison, Ms. Stevens."

They followed us out of the store, shooting daggers with their eyes as we hopped into the Gray Ghost.

"That went well," said Byrd.

I started the engine. "No worries. We'll find her." I peeled out of the parking lot and headed down Sycamore Mountain the way we had come.

"If we're not giving up, then why are we headed back to the valley?"

"Stevens lives at the base of Sycamore Mountain. I suspect Pearson's staying with her."

"Let's hope, because I'm getting a bad feeling about this job. If Rodeo and Tommy Boy couldn't find her..."

"All due respect to Rodeo and Tommy Boy, I've been doing this longer than either one of them. Hell, I've found people Fiddler couldn't find. You remember him?"

Byrd shook his head. "Never met, but heard he was a legend in his time."

"Damn straight he was. But he couldn't find Holly Schwartz."

"That girl in the wheelchair who killed her mama? You tracked her down?"

"I did. Turned out her visiting nurse was hiding her in a cabin outside Prescott."

"Well, all right, girl. Let's go find our fugitive."

As we reached the base of the mountain, the road straightened out. At a weather-beaten sign that read Sycamore Estates, I turned right.

The residential area was nothing like the cookie-cutter neighborhoods in Phoenix. The lots were sprawling, rustic, and rocky. The aroma of manure lingered in the air, suggesting someone nearby kept livestock. Mature mesquite, ironwoods, and sycamores offered shade to a brilliant palette of wildflowers and wildlife. A small ridge ran behind the houses on Stevens's street and up the side of the mountain.

Stevens's house sat second to last at the end of the lane. I backed the Gray Ghost into the driveway.

"Let's gear up." I opened the back of the SUV, and we pulled on our vests, weapons, and walkie-talkies. "I'll hit the front door. You cover the back."

"Roger that. What if no one answers the door?"

I surveyed the area. No one on the streets, but that didn't mean some nosy busybody wasn't watching. "We'll make entry through the back, away from prying eyes. Grab the ram."

By law, we had the right to enter a building without a warrant, provided we had reason to believe that our fugitive was inside. Of course, that left a lot of gray area.

Byrd slung the thirty-pound ram over his shoulder and marched around the house. I gave him a couple of minutes to get into position.

"Any signs of life in back?" I asked into the radio.

"Negative. All quiet back here. No activity through the windows."

"Okay, keep your head on a swivel."

I pounded on the front door and gave the doorbell a few rings, then listened. No sounds came from inside the house. I waited a few minutes then knocked and rang again but without any results.

"Anything?" asked Byrd.

"Nada. Any evidence of a security system?"

"Negative."

"All right. Make entry, then let me in through the front."

"Roger that."

I waited for the thud of the ram and the satisfying crack of the doorframe giving way. It didn't come.

"Byrd? You in?" I heard the distant sound of voices.

"Uh...Jinx, we got a problem. You might want to come around here."

I trudged around to the back of the house to find a petite woman with pale skin and a gray bouffant hairdo, wearing a pale-pink-velvet housedress. A long-haired Chihuahua in her arms was yapping its pampered little head off.

"What are you people doing back there?" she demanded in a voice that was equal parts Catholic nun and Mommie Dearest. "You don't live here."

"Minding our own business," I replied. "I suggest you do the same."

She put a hand on her hip. "And what business would that be?"

A flashed her a confident smile. "None of yours."

"I'm making it my business. I'm Mrs. Collins, Shea's next-door neighbor. We look out for each other 'round here."

"Well, Mrs. Collins, I suggest you leave us to our work and go back to watching *Price is Right.*"

From a pocket in her housedress, she pulled out a cellphone. "I'm calling the cops. We don't take kindly to thugs." She glared at Byrd.

Byrd held up his bail enforcement badge. "Go right ahead, ma'am. We're here to return a fugitive to custody. We always appreciate help from local law enforcement."

Collins's face went blank for a moment, and she clearly was not expecting Byrd's encouragement.

"There ain't no one here! You two are up to something. I'm calling Shea."

Byrd gave me a look that said, "What now?"

I was really hoping to complete this job without violence. But I was not going to let Miss Jane Marple here or Shea Stevens keep me from doing what I was hired to do.

"You interfere with us doing our job, lady, and we'll haul you to jail as well." I pulled out my handcuffs to show her I was serious. To Byrd, I said, "Give me thirty seconds to get around front and then break it down."

"You don't scare me!" She held up her phone while her dog yapped away.

Just as I reached the front porch, a loud crack shook the house. Byrd opened the front door.

"Avon calling," I said with a wry smile, noticing a wooden baseball bat leaning against the wall next to the doorway.

"I suggest we get a move on," replied Byrd. "Got a feeling we're gonna have company real soon."

The front of the house had a large living room with a small kitchenette to the left. The floors were bare concrete slab with a rug in the living room. I pointed at a door next to the kitchen. "Check the garage. I'll search the bedrooms."

"Roger that."

I checked the first bedroom. Queen-sized bed. Minimal decor. A few photographs of Shea Stevens with other female bikers on one wall. A desk sat in the corner. On it lay a sketchbook, which had drawings of motorcycles, and a Mac laptop. A bookshelf on the far wall was filled with service manuals, motorcycle magazines, and some novels by Tammy Kaehler. The adjoining bathroom and closet held nothing of interest. No signs of another adult living here. Only a single toothbrush in the cup by the sink.

I moved on to the guest bathroom and then the second bedroom. A couple of plushies were on the bed with a Captain Marvel comforter. A vase of wilting carnations stood in the windowsill. On one wall, a Dua Lipa concert poster was tacked next to a few others for young male artists I didn't recognize.

A hemp net hung from the far wall, strung through with fairy lights and photographs of a young girl with a family resemblance to Shea. The bond agreement had mentioned Shea's niece, Annie Wittmann, lived with her, though I didn't know the story behind why. This must have been her room. No sign of Pearson anywhere.

Byrd returned to the living room. "Lots of motorcycles in the garage, but no evidence of Pearson."

"Shit. No joy on my end either. Let's get out of here before..."

The air rumbled with the thunder of motorcycle engines. I opened the front door to see four bikers pull up in front of the house and park their rides across the driveway, blocking the Gray Ghost. *Damn, they got here fast.*

Stevens pulled off her helmet and held it in one hand, drawing a pistol with the other. "What the fuck y'all doing in my house?"

The three other women gathered around her, holding their helmets like clubs. All wore matching biker vests with white and pink patches. Byrd and I drew our weapons. I held up my free hand in an attempt to de-escalate the situation.

"This house? The one you put up as collateral for the defaulted bond you signed for Pearson?" Okay, my mouth was clearly less interested in de-escalating.

"You had no right to break in."

"Once Pearson failed to show up to court, we had every right to search any location we believed she might be hiding. But if you tell us where she is or, better yet, get her to come down and surrender, we'd be happy to be on our way." Wishful thinking, but it never hurt to ask.

"And I'd be within my rights to shoot an intruder. This is Arizona, after all."

"Fine. Move your bikes away from my truck, and we'll leave."

"Make us," said a tall Latinx woman with long dark hair.

"Suit yourself." I gestured toward the Gray Ghost.

Byrd kept his pistol trained on Shea as we got in.

I started the engine and rolled down the window. "Last chance. Move your bikes."

"Fuck you, bitch!" said one of the other bikers, who was aiming a revolver at us.

I slammed the Gray Ghost into Drive and floored it, pushing the bikes off to the side. A couple of gunshots behind us made me duck. The SUV lifted up onto two wheels as we turned the corner at speed.

12

"You hit?" I asked as I took a hard right onto the main highway, heading south. I kept glancing in the rearview mirror, but so far there were no signs of our biker friends.

"No. Don't think so." His voice was as shaky as I felt.

I glanced over. Bits of foam rubber surrounded a hole at the edge of his seat that lined up with a corresponding hole in the glovebox. "Wow," he said. "That was close."

"You want to quit?"

"Aw, heck no." He shot me a grin. "It's just getting interesting."

"Awesome, because I really need your help."

"So where we headed now?"

"Ironwood."

"To Pearson's house? Rodeo and Tommy already checked out the place. Said Pearson's side of the closet was cleared out like she was on a long vacation."

"I want to talk to Pearson's employer, the Lambda Resource Center over by the university."

"No offense, Jinx, but Ironwood is back the other way. Why are we headed south?"

"I didn't want to drive up those switchbacks with bikers on our tail. We'd never outrun them. There's a state highway ahead that bypasses Sycamore Springs."

After a mile or so, I hooked a right onto the state highway. The purple and yellow wildflowers lining the roadside reminded me of my ex-girlfriend, Toni Bennett, a corrections officer from Scottsdale. She'd always said wildflowers were her favorite flower. Beautiful and wild, yet still tough enough to bloom in the unforgiving desert.

We'd started dating last February. She was fun and flirty, not to mention a goddess in the sheets. But our relationship didn't last. I was still damaged goods after losing Conor. Toni's attempts to pull me out of my shit failed. I sunk deeper into a funk, ignoring her calls and texts. In the end, she dumped me via voicemail. It was more a relief than anything.

Now I blamed myself for Conor turning himself in. What would happen if he was convicted? Would they imprison him for life? Behead him? Did they still do that in the UK? I had no idea.

The rolling hills rose into steep, forested peaks as we entered the Cortes National Forest. The road twisted through the mountain folds. A recent snowfall had left patches of black ice in the corners, forcing me to focus on the driving rather than my failed relationships.

"I haven't been here since I was a kid," I said, breaking the stifling silence.

"Yeah?"

"My folks used to rent a cabin every summer. I remember playing in streams, roasting marshmallows by campfire, dodging prickly pears that grew among the piles of fallen pine needles. Oh, and the maddening itch of poison oak."

Byrd stared out at the treetops stretching out below us.

"My mama sent me to a Christian summer camp up here once after my dad got killed."

"Shit. I'm sorry. How'd he die?"

"A cop mistook him for a man who carjacked a Toyota like the one he drove. Shot him in the back."

"Geez, that fucking sucks, man." I didn't know what else to say.

Byrd shrugged. "Can't change it. It is what it is."

"So afterwards, your mom sent you to a summer camp?"

"Thought it might help. Gave me some father figures to fill the absence left by my dad."

"How was it?"

"Strange, but cool. It was my first time outta the city. Trees and shit everywhere. Animals, like you'd only see in the zoo or on TV, but just wandering around—bobcats, javelinas, and even a skunk. Oh and elk. They looked like deer on steroids. And the sounds, especially at night. Man! Coyotes howling, owls hooting, and all night long them crickets or cicadas or whatever they were. You'd think they'd get tired after a while, but no, they kept on going all day and all night like the Energizer Bunny."

"Nice to get out once in a while."

"Yeah. Your family still rent a cabin up here?"

"Not lately."

"My church has a thing up here every summer. Never gone, but being here now, remembering that time as a kid, I kinda miss it, you know?"

I nodded.

"You'd be welcome too, if you want. They're always encouraging us to invite visitors."

"Thanks, but I'll pass."

"You Christian?"

Ugh, here we go. "My mom is. Italian Catholic. I used go

to Mass with her, but not since I came out as trans." I gave him a quick look. "You're not gonna try to recruit me, are you?"

He paused for a moment. "Naw, but I'm curious, how do decide between what's right and wrong?"

"Live and let live. Treat others how you want to be treated. I don't need some Bronze Age tome to tell me that. All them Catholic priests raping children. Evangelicals doing everything they can to make life harder for queer people, acting like we're some kind of threat to society when they're the one's brutalizing us. Hell, look at the case we're on. That street preacher carrying signs saying women need to be raped and that queer people deserve to be murdered. If that's what you call morality, you can have it."

"Not all Christians act like that."

"What's your church's position on transgender people?"

He sighed. "Not as enlightened as it should be."

"There you go."

"How'd your folks react when you came out? They freak on you?"

"They were cool when I finally told them. I got to transition young, which is rare." The conversation lagged as we wound through the sun-dappled mountain curves. "You and your mom still close?"

"Yeah, pretty close. She hates what I do for a living. Keeps wanting me to become an engineer."

"Like on a train?"

"Mechanical engineer. Loved math and physics in high school. Got a football scholarship to ASU."

"You played football?"

"Until some guy sideswiped me sophomore year and tore up my knee. End of football. End of scholarship. End of college. So here I am."

"Shit. That sucks."

"Yeah, I think about going back. Got some money saved up. Just got so damn expensive, you know? Tuition's ten times what it used to be. Tried to qualify for a student loan but no luck."

"My mom worries about me doing this job too. Even offered to pay my tuition to law school."

"And you said no?"

"To being a blood-sucking lawyer? Not just no, but hell no."

After half an hour of zigzagging through the forested mountain roads, signs of civilization appeared. First a trading post, then a QT gas station, and finally the trees gave way to the businesses of downtown Ironwood. Cafes, hardware stores, and art galleries. Pickup trucks and cars dusted with frost filled the streets. A few hearty cyclists weaved their way between the vehicles, sending up clouds of water vapor in the chilly air.

We drove east to Ironwood's University District. The art galleries and gift shops of downtown were replaced by bookstores, frat houses, dormitories, and classroom buildings. The students lugging backpacks full of books brought back memories of when I attended Arizona State ten years earlier. My biggest worries then were turning in term papers on time and passing final exams. Now I struggled to stay sober and employed without getting killed.

We found the Lambda Resource Center south of campus on Red Tanks Trail Road. I pulled into the lot behind the small wooden building. In the lobby, rainbow flags and a gallery of event photos hung from the walls. The receptionist desk was empty.

"Hello?" I called.

"In here," came a voice down the main hallway. We followed it.

I knocked on a half-opened door which bore a plaque

that read Director. A woman in a mauve suit and short dark hair looked up with a pleasant expression on her face. A nameplate on her desk identified her as Trina Lantz, Director of Operations. "Hi, can I help you?"

"Yes, we're looking for Zia Pearson. I understand she works here."

Lantz's smile faded a bit. "I'm sorry, she's not in today. My name's Trina. Perhaps I can assist you." She offered her hand, and I shook it.

"I'm Jinx Ballou. This is my associate Jubal Byrd."

Trina's smiled brightened as she shook Byrd's hand, clearly taking her time. "Love your name. So poetic."

"Thanks. I like yours too," he replied. The two of them were having some kind of flirty moment that bugged the shit out of me.

I cleared my throat. "Where can we find Ms. Pearson?"

Trina sighed and straightened her suit jacket. "Judging from your bulletproof vests and badges, I'm guessing this is about that murder case down in Scottsdale."

"She missed her court hearing. We need to find her before her bail gets revoked entirely."

"Have you tried her at home?"

"She wasn't there," answered Byrd.

"Well, I don't know what to tell you. She's on temporary leave from her position here. And...can I be honest?"

"Please," I said with a little more snark than I intended.

"I believe she's being framed. I've known Zia for a couple years now. She has a good heart. She's not a violent person much less a murderer. As vile as that preacher was, I don't see Zia killing him."

"And yet this model citizen is a member of a violent biker gang and has now skipped bail."

Byrd shot me a look that said ease up. I ignored him.

"The Athena Sisterhood," said Trina. "Yes, I know about them. But they're not violent."

"Really? Well the bullet hole one of them put in the back of my SUV would indicate otherwise."

"I can't speak to this bullet hole, but from what I've seen, the Sisterhood is a law-abiding, pro-feminist, pro-LGBTQ club. They've been active participants in several of our fundraisers. And they provide protection to battered women and children. They're nothing like those other biker gangs. I don't think the sheriff's office would work with Zia if they were."

"And yet now she's violated the terms of her bail agreement," I replied. "And the biker club has closed ranks around her."

"Can you blame them?" asked Trina. "After Zia was brutally assaulted in a men's jail? What were they thinking to put her in there?"

"So you've spoken to her since she was arrested?" asked Byrd.

Her gaze hit the floor. "Yes."

"Where can we find her?" I pressed.

"I don't know. That's the truth. She sent me a text a few weeks ago saying she was going on leave for a bit and asking me to hold her job for her. But nothing about where she was or when she would return."

"Who is her contact at the sheriff's office?" I asked.

"Detective Toni Rios. She works in their Violent Crimes Division, but she's also a part of their Community Outreach Division." Trina flipped through a Rolodex on her desk, then scribbled a name, address, and phone number on a scrap of paper. "Not sure if she knows anything, but you can certainly try."

I took it from her and stuffed it in back pocket. "Thanks."

"And if you find Zia, please be gentle with her. She's been through a lot."

"We will, Trina," Byrd replied, taking her hand again. I felt like I was going to barf.

An androgynous person with purple hair knocked on her office door. "Hey, Trina! Sorry to interrupt, but Parker Davies with the Cortes Chronicle is on line two."

I gave Trina my business card. "If you hear from Pearson, call me. Immediately. The longer this drags on, the worse it will be for her."

Trina stared at the card. "Don't know when I'll hear from her. But if I do, I'll let you know." She looked up at me, then at Byrd.

"Thanks for all your help," he said, giving her a wink as I turned and walked out of the office.

"Geez, Byrd, since when is flirting part of the job?" I asked when we finally emerged into the sunlight. "I was half afraid you'd start humping her leg."

"Aw, that wasn't flirting."

"Yeah, right! 'Oh Jubal, your name is so poetic.'" I climbed into the driver's seat of the Gray Ghost, slamming the door shut.

"Hey, that was all her. Not my fault she likes what she sees." He flashed me a blinding white smile.

I started the ignition just to get the heat going as I planned our next move. "Maybe the two of you should get a room, and I'll track down Pearson myself."

"Aw, don't hate the playa, girl."

I rolled my eyes and pulled onto the street.

"At least we didn't get shot at this time," I said, trying to remain upbeat as we returned to Downtown Ironwood.

"You're setting a low bar for success, there, Jinx." Byrd replied.

"We'll find her. Just have to shake the trees till something falls out."

"We shake much harder, and the Athena Sisterhood's going to be putting us in the morgue."

"And here I thought you were a man of faith," I teased.

"Oh, I am. I have faith that the Athena Sisterhood is serious about not surrendering one of their own."

"Let's get some lunch. Maybe we can figure out another approach, one that doesn't involve getting shot at."

"I hear that."

I followed Prospector Avenue into Ironwood's Downtown Square, the heart of the city built around the old courthouse. Normally this time of year, the sidewalks would be bustling with Phoenicians escaping the desert heat. But with temps hitting near freezing at night, most pedestrians were students from nearby Central Arizona University.

I grabbed a parking space and looked along the street to assess our dining options. "Let's see, we got College Burger—very popular among the students. A few doors down, there's a Filipino restaurant called the Manila Grill. And across the courtyard, the Desert Star Saloon in one of the historic buildings. What's your poison?"

"Let's give the Manila Grill a try."

Byrd ordered a pork dish called crispy pata with a soda. I asked for a fried rice dish and a beer. While our server walked away to place our order, I caught Byrd giving me a look.

"What?" I asked.

"You often drink on the job?"

"It's a beer. I think I can handle it, preacher boy."

"I hope so, Miss Jinx. I hope so."

"So what kind of name is Jubal anyway?"

"It's from the Bible."

"I shoulda figured. Jubal Byrd, huh? Sounds like a creature from Greek mythology."

"Oh yeah? How'd you get the name Jinx? Sounds like a bad luck kind of name."

I chuckled. "Bad luck for whoever I'm chasing. It's a mash up of my first and middle names, Jenna Christine. A friend of mine gave me the nickname when I was a teenager."

He nodded just as our server showed up with our drinks. "Well all right, Miss Jinx. How we gonna put the jinx on Zia Pearson?"

I took a sip of my beer. "Not sure.

"Let me see if my skip tracer's got anything." I called Becca.

"I'll be honest, I haven't been monitoring Pearson this morning. I'll see what I can pull up as far as phone logs, emails, and social media, but it may take me a while," she explained. "I'm working on a tight deadline for a security client."

"I'm working on a tight deadline, too. I only have a week to track her down before Pima Bail Bonds has to cough up the rest of the bail money."

"I'll see what I can do."

"Also, pull the phone logs for Shea Stevens, the woman who put up the bail bond, and Pearson's wife, Chelsea Tucker. See who they're talking to. Check for common phone numbers they've been calling."

"Jinx..."

"I know it's a big ask. But who loves you more? Your bestie since junior high or this security client of yours?"

"I'll do what I can. Anything else you need? A massage? Your car washed? The dog walked." She teased, the frustration evident in her voice.

"Naw, Adam and Steve from next door should be

walking Diana. Seriously, though, thanks, Becks! You're the greatest!"

After our food came, I flipped back through the job folder looking for anything that might suggest our next approach. "Pearson worked for the Lambda Resource Center as a liaison with the Cortes County Sheriff's Office. I want to talk with her contact at the CCSO, this Detective Antonia Rios. Maybe she knows how we can reach Pearson."

"Seems like a long shot."

"Every lead is a long shot until it pays off." But despite my optimistic words, I felt the same frustration. After the Penzler disaster, I wondered if I'd lost my mojo. Maybe I should find another line of work, one where people were less inclined to shoot me.

13

When we reached the CCSO's Ironwood Substation, I asked for Detective Rios at the front desk. The desk sergeant made a call, talked to someone, then hung up. "I'm afraid she's away from her desk at the moment. Can I leave her a message?"

I shook my head. "Thanks, anyway."

Back in the Gray Ghost, I called the phone number Trina had given me.

"This is Detective Rios. How can I help you?"

"Detective, this is Jinx Ballou. I work with Pima Bail Bonds down in Scottsdale. I'm looking for an associate of yours—Zia Pearson."

There was a pause at the other end of the line. "I haven't spoken to Ms. Pearson in over a month. I'm guessing this is connected to the homicide she was charged with in Scottsdale?"

"Yeah, she jumped bail. I could use your help bringing her back into custody."

"I'm wrapping things up at a crime scene at the

moment. Meet me at the Ironwood Substation around three o'clock. We can talk then."

"I appreciate it." I hung up. "Now we're getting somewhere," I said to Byrd.

"She know where Pearson is?"

"Didn't say, but she wants to meet in a couple hours. I'll count that as a step in the right direction."

"What should we do in the meantime?"

"We tried Pearson's residence, workplace, and the woman who posted bail. Let's try her attorney, this Rebecca Li."

"Since when have you gotten any information from an attorney about one of their clients?"

"Not often, but right now, all we got are long shots. Besides, attorneys are still officers of the court. Attorney-client privilege does not extend to harboring fugitives."

I started the Gray Ghost and returned to downtown Ironwood. Rebecca Li shared a small professional building on Raven Rock Drive with another attorney. Despite our lack of an appointment, the receptionist escorted us to Li's office.

Li, dressed in a tailored black business suit, stood and shook our hands as Byrd and I entered. The room was small but tidy. Shelves of law books lined the wall opposite a modern desk. A familiar black leather vest with pink and white patches hung on a coatrack behind her desk.

"How can I help the two of you today?" Li asked with a bright smile.

"We're looking for your client, Zia Pearson," I said. "As I'm sure you know, she missed her hearing."

"Ah, I see." Was that a flush of embarrassment I saw for the briefest of moments? "Unfortunately, I don't know where she is right now."

"Really? No clue, huh? Why do I find that hard to believe? Maybe it's that biker vest you got hanging there."

"Ms. Li," said Byrd, "we understand your client had a rough time before she was bailed out. And we're willing to help get her bail reset..."

"No." I cut him off. "No more Ms. Nice Bounty Hunter. We tried being nice to some of your fellow bikers, most notably your client's wife and that crazy bitch who runs the motorcycle shop. After being threatened and shot at, I have zero interest in helping your client reset bail. You and your biker gang are conspiring to harbor a fugitive wanted for murder. If you don't turn her over now, we will recommend you—"

"Don't threaten me, Ms. Ballou." Li's professional demeanor turned dark. "You don't know the law half as well as you think you do."

"You're an officer of the court," I replied. "You hiding her is a conflict of interest."

"If my client is staying with another member of the Sisterhood, I'm not aware of it. There's no conflict of interest."

"Of course not," said Byrd, giving me a look. "We're just trying to return her to custody so she can stand trial and put this unfortunate episode behind her."

"Sounds great," Li replied. "Provided they don't convict her for no other reason than being a trans woman of color."

"Look, we get it," I said. "But sooner or later, she has to face the charges."

"Like I said, I have no idea where she is."

I dropped one of my business cards on her desk. "If you see her, get in touch. We'd hate for anyone to be disbarred for hindering prosecution." I glared at her. "Come on, Byrd."

The two of us stormed out of there. Well, I stormed out. Byrd just followed.

"You sure do know how to make friends," he joked.

"Bite me. All this driving around is making me cranky." I swung open the driver's door of the Gray Ghost, hopped in, and slammed it shut.

"Oh, is *that* what's making you cranky." His goofy laugh only made me more frustrated. "I thought you were this super bounty hunter, capable of finding fugitives even the legends in the business can't find."

"Keep it up, Jesus Boy. You'll be walking back to Phoenix." I started the engine and drove out of the lot.

"All right, all right. That was rude of me. I apologize."

"Besides, I've got a plan to lure her out of hiding."

"If you're planning to use the old 'you just won a new cellphone' trick, don't. Rodeo and Tommy Boy already tried that. She didn't take the bait."

"Huh, that usually works. Anyway, that's not the plan."

He cocked an eyebrow. "No? What is the plan?"

"We need to drive to the hospital."

"You hurt?"

"Nope."

"Then what?"

"You'll see."

I drove north to the upscale Shadow Hills district with its exclusive country clubs, overpriced condominiums, and gated neighborhoods. The Gray Ghost didn't blend in so well here, among the Ferraris, Bentleys, and Porsches. Still, we had a job to do, and at this point, I wasn't planning for us to hide in the SUV.

The Shadow Hills Medical Center's emergency department was on the back side of the building. I parked in the emergency visitors' lot.

I took off my vest and tactical belt, then stashed a pair

of handcuffs in my back pocket. Byrd also disarmed. Even as licensed bounty hunters, we weren't allowed to carry firearms into a hospital. I hoped it wouldn't be a problem.

As we walked through the parking lot and past the sliding glass doors of the hospital, Byrd said, "You're not planning on doing what I think you're doing, are you?"

I smiled mischievously. "Depends on what you're thinking. I just need to make a phone call."

I strode past the check-in desk to where a courtesy phone hung on the wall. I dialed 9 to get an outside line and then Zia Pearson's cellphone number. It rang three times before a voice answered.

"Yes?"

"Hello, is this Chelsea Tucker's wife? A Ms. Pearson?" I asked.

"This is Zia Pearson."

"Good afternoon. I'm sorry to disturb you, but my name is Liz Windsor." It was a fake name I often used. "I'm a nurse in the emergency department at HealthCorp Shadow Hills Medical Center. Your wife has been in a serious accident. You need to get down here right away."

"What kind of accident? Is she okay?" The panic in her voice was evident.

"It's best we discuss this in person. Are you able to be here soon?"

"Y-yes, I'm leaving right now. Just tell me, is...is she still alive?"

"The last I checked she was, but really, you need to hurry."

"I'll be there in about fifteen minutes."

I hung up. Byrd shook his head. "You are diabolical."

"I have a reputation to uphold and a fugitive to return to custody."

We took seats in the waiting area near the door. People

wandered in and out, many looking in pretty bad shape. More than one looked like they had a bad case of the flu, which I hoped I didn't catch. After ten minutes, a team of EMTs brought in a white man on a gurney. I caught a glimpse of blood-soaked bandages as they rushed past. A lot of people were having a bad day.

A few minutes later, a woman who matched the photo in the file I was given rushed in. Dark skin, long braids that looked like they could use some maintenance, and an Athena Sisterhood biker vest. She was a few inches taller than me and probably outweighed me by a good twenty pounds.

"Ding, ding, ding! We got a winner," I whispered to Byrd as we got up.

14

Pearson approached the information desk and gave the elderly volunteer behind the desk her wife's name to look up in the computer.

"Zia Pearson?" I asked from behind her.

I was tempted to snap the cuffs on her right away, but I had to confirm it was her. Otherwise, I risked being charged with kidnapping and a few similar charges. Byrd stood on the other side of her.

She turned. "Yes. Where's my wife, Chelsea Tucker?"

I snapped the cuffs on one of her wrists and was reaching for the other when someone shouted, "Hey! Leave her alone!"

I turned to see three other women in matching biker vests running toward us. "Aw, shit."

Byrd ran to intercept them while I struggled to get Pearson cuffed.

"Zia Pearson, you missed your court date and violated your bail agreement. I've been hired to return you to custody."

She slipped out of my grip, whirled around, and delivered a glancing blow to my jaw. Damn, she was fast! I blocked another punch and tried to get her into an arm lock. Someone grabbed me from behind and dropped me onto the linoleum.

"Get off me! I'm a licensed bail enforcement agent arresting a fugitive."

"Not today you're not," said a deep female voice.

I turned my head in time to see Pearson escape out the sliding glass doors with her fellow bikers. Byrd chased them.

"If you don't get off of me, I will have you arrested for aiding a fugitive. It comes with a mandatory two-year sentence." It was a bullshit threat, but it usually worked.

The woman got off of me. I pulled myself to my feet and glared at her. She was a stocky woman with a squarish face and short blond hair. The words Cortes County Fire and Rescue were stitched on her shirt. With a grim look on her face, she crossed her arms. Goddamn EMT!

"You have any idea who you let escape?" I screamed.

"Sure do. She's my wife."

Suddenly, I remembered. Chelsea Tucker was an EMT. Shit!

"She missed her hearing. I'm trying to help her get bail reset and her court date rescheduled."

"No, you're trying to take her back to the men's jail so she can be raped and assaulted again."

"I understand her predicament. I'm transgender. If I help her get her bail reset, she won't have to sit in jail for the remainder of the trial."

"You tell that prosecutor to drop the bogus charges, and it won't be an issue."

"Unfortunately, that's not within our power," said Byrd, walking up to us. "But we do care and will do what we can to help."

"Sorry. Not interested."

Two men in security uniforms approached. "We received a report of a disturbance."

"Hey, Hank! Dave!" Tucker said to them. "I think we got it under control. Just make sure they leave." She shot us a glance and walked away.

"We're bail enforcement agents," I told them. "Her wife jumped bail. We are here to bring her into custody."

"Not here you're not," said the larger of the two security guards. "This is a hospital. Not a wrestling arena. You're going to have to leave, or we're calling the cops."

I exchanged a glance with Byrd. Pearson was gone. The cops wouldn't do anything about it.

"Fine, we're leaving."

We trudged back out into the parking lot.

"It was a good plan," said Byrd. "Would've worked if she didn't have her friends with her."

"This is looking like it may take a few days. Maybe we oughta check in to a motel before meeting with this Detective Rios. I've been seeing a lot of No Vacancy signs in town," I said.

Despite the late-May wintry weather, many Phoenix residents were already up here in the high country since most years it was already in the triple digits down in the valley.

"Just out of curiosity, who's paying for these rooms?" he asked. "I'm in this to make money, not shell it out."

"Relax, dude. I'll cover the rooms."

We sat in the Gray Ghost while I searched Google for motels in the area. I drove east and pulled into a Hampton Inn. They were full. Days Inn. Full.

After making several calls, I found a little mom-and-pop operation called the Montgomery Family Inn located not far from the Central Arizona University campus.

When I balked at the price of a single-occupancy room, the man behind the counter explained that those were the normal in-season rates. Decent rooms were at a premium.

"We could always double up," suggested Byrd. "Get one room with two beds."

"What would your fellow churchgoers say?" I teased. "You shacking up with a woman you're not married to."

"Hey, I ain't tryin' to get in your pants, Jinx. I'm just offering to save you some Benjamins."

"Fine." I replied and handed over my plastic. "One room."

The room was standard budget motel fare—clean and utterly uninteresting, especially the artwork, which had a theme of desert sunsets. I tossed my duffel bag on the double bed nearest the door and unpacked while trying to ignore the whirlwind of feelings inside of me. I could've used a little something to even me out.

Byrd had stepped into the bathroom when my phone rang. No name on the caller ID, but the number looked local.

"Ballou Fugitive Recovery."

"I think we got off to a bad start earlier," said a husky female voice that reminded me of Jodie Foster. Shea Stevens.

"A bad start? I'd call blocking my vehicle and shooting at me more than just a bad start. I'd call that aggravated assault and attempted murder."

"For the record, I didn't shoot at you. It was one of our younger members who's a little eager with her trigger finger. She's been properly chastised."

"She should be in jail."

"We want to make this right. We understand you're trying to do your job."

"Give me Pearson, and we'll be out of your hair."

I heard another voice in the background but couldn't make out what was being said.

"Let's meet."

"That's the first sensible thing I've heard all day. When and where?" I was intrigued by this sudden change in direction and duly suspicious. I didn't want to be walking into a trap.

"Eight o'clock. There's a bar in downtown Ironwood called Gertie's. Know where it is?"

"I've heard of it. Lesbian bar on the square."

"We'll be at the large table in the back. Can't miss us."

"If you and your biker gang are planning an ambush, I'd advise against it," I replied.

"No ambush. I've talked to Indigo. She wants to come in, but there are conditions."

"Which are?"

"That's what we need to discuss."

On the one hand, it was a public place. There would probably be a lot of witnesses on the square, especially college kids enjoying a last hurrah before final exams. On the other hand, I had a hunch Stevens and Pearson wouldn't be alone.

"See you at eight." I hung up and called Becca, hoping for some intel in case this meetup with Stevens and company turned out to be a bust. "Got anything for me?"

I heard a long exhale. "Jinxie, I'm sorry. By the time I got done with the job for my security client, I was out of spoons. I'm wiped, bestie."

I was frustrated with the situation, but I knew it wasn't her fault. Living with chronic fatigue was tough. "Easton still out of town?"

"Yeah, but they went grocery shopping before they left. I should be okay."

"Don't worry about the skip tracing for now. Get some rest and call me if you need me."

"I should be okay, but thanks. Good hunting, Jinxie. And be careful."

"Always."

Byrd walked out of the bathroom. I filled him in.

"Totally a trap," he said.

"Maybe. Or Pearson is tired of hiding and genuinely wants to turn herself in. Stevens said there are conditions but didn't specify what. If our meeting with Detective Rios doesn't pan out, we'll gear up and try to bag Pearson at Gertie's."

15

We returned to the Ironwood Substation. The same desk sergeant called and confirmed Rios was there. A few minutes later, a Latinx woman barely five feet tall walked into the waiting area. I guessed her to be in her mid to late thirties.

"Jinx Ballou?" she asked with a faint Central American accent.

Byrd and I stood. "That's me. This is my associate, Jubal Byrd."

"Come on back." She led us past the locked door, down a hallway to a small interview room. "Let's talk in here."

After we sat down, she said, "Honestly, all of this came as a shock to me. Wouldn't have guessed Pearson had it in her."

"You think she did it?" I asked.

"In nearly twenty years as a cop, I've learned that anyone is capable of just about anything. I've seen sweet little grandmothers who tortured children. A teacher of the year running a dog-fighting ring. I don't know whether Pearson killed Fitzgerald, but with the hateful rhetoric that *pendejo* was spewing, it was a matter of time before someone did."

"Any idea where Pearson might be hiding out?" asked Byrd.

"Well, if she's not at home, I'd guess she's laying low with one of her friends in the Athena Sisterhood. You familiar with them?"

"A bit," I replied.

"They're not a bad group of women, all in all. Helped us with a major drug bust a while back. Do a lot for the community, especially women in trouble. Just don't cross them. They are rather protective of their own."

Now you tell me.

"Any particular member she might be staying with, if you had to guess?" I asked.

"I couldn't tell you. They have about two dozen members locally. Could be any of them. The Sisterhood also has chapters in LA, Vegas, Denver. At this point, she could be anywhere."

"Would you have a list of names and addresses for their local members?"

"Unless they've got a jacket, which most of them don't, we wouldn't have a record of them. But if you want to wait a bit, I can check with our gang task force, see what they have. Can't guarantee anything, but you never know."

"I'd appreciate that."

"Okay, sit tight. Either of you need anything while you wait? A soda? Coffee? Bottle of water?"

Byrd shook his head. "No, we're good."

When she left, Byrd said, "I'm beginning to see why Tommy Boy and Rodeo couldn't find this chick."

Rios returned twenty minutes later with a small stack of papers. "We have sheets on eight of their members. Nothing recent and mostly minor offenses—reckless driving, possession, a domestic dispute, one with a DUI from six years ago."

I glanced through the printouts. "Thanks, I appreciate it."

We stood and shook hands with Rios.

"Hope you find her. And honestly, I hope she's acquitted. I enjoyed working with her. She was a good liaison with Lambda."

"We'll let you know," said Byrd.

We grabbed dinner at a local diner near the motel, then drove back to the Downtown Square, parking a few doors past Gertie's.

"Gear up," I said as I killed the ignition. "Vests, weapons, and backups. The works."

"Maybe this isn't such a good idea, Jinx. And me being a guy? I'll stick out like a sore thumb in a dyke bar."

"We'll be fine. Just keep a cool head."

Byrd shot me a grin. "Oh, trust me. I'm always cool."

A few minutes later, we walked into Gertie's and immediately drew stares from the patrons. The place was about half filled, including several women in Athena Sisterhood biker vests, sitting at a large table near the back covered with pitchers of beer, shots of booze, and baskets of pretzels.

The smell of alcohol called me like a siren. I only wanted a shot or two. Or three. Just enough to take the edge off. But I needed my wits about me if Byrd and I were going to get out alive.

Shea Stevens sat at the far end, her back to the wall, with Chelsea Tucker on one side of her and Rebecca Li on the other. The rest of the women looked familiar, from either the information Detective Rios provided or our tango at Stevens's house. Zia Pearson was nowhere to be seen.

We sat in a couple of empty seats across from Stevens. A patch on her vest read *Havoc*, her biker name. Under that was another that identified her as the club's VP.

"You showed. I'm impressed," Stevens said.

"Where's Pearson?" I asked.

"Indigo is safe," said Tucker.

"You said she'd turn herself in," Byrd replied.

"She will," Stevens explained, "after you locate the real killer."

"Excuse me?" I almost choked on a pretzel I'd snagged from a basket between us.

"Indigo didn't kill that preacher," Tucker said. Her name patch read Savage. "She shouldn't have to suffer just because the Scottsdale police are too stupid or too lazy to go after the real murderer."

A tall Latinx woman whose biker vest identified her as Fuego, the club president, put a calming hand on Tucker's shoulder. "Indigo's only crime was getting into a shouting match with the guy at Bike Week."

"Someone posted a video of that online," Byrd added. "The confrontation got physical. She made threats."

Stevens shrugged. "So they shoved each other a couple of times. Not that big a deal. No one got hurt."

"Police also got a DNA match," I said. "That's pretty damning evidence."

"Maybe some of her skin got under his nails in the tussle at Bike Week," replied Fuego. "She didn't shoot him or cut off his dick."

"And it was just coincidence that she was in a strip club next door to where the police found his body?" I asked.

"We had no idea that asshole was at the sleazy motel next door," Savage insisted. "The cops targeted her because she's a black trans woman. Kept calling her a tranny and a junkie whore. I wanted to put my fist through their teeth."

"Look, I understand y'all want to protect your friend," I said. "But I was hired to return her to custody, not to work as your private investigator."

"You used to be a cop. And you are licensed as a private investigator," Li said. Her name patch read Dragon. "Yeah, I checked up on you too."

I tried not to show my frustration. "I was a patrol officer for a year, and that was a long time ago. I was never a detective. As for being a private investigator, I only got the license because the bounty hunter I used to work for wanted me to. I've never investigated any cases beyond my capacity as a bail enforcement agent."

"That's the deal," said Shea. "Get the county attorney to drop the charges against Indigo, and she'll turn herself in to you."

"I sympathize with Indigo's situation. I'm a trans woman. I know what it's like to be brutally assaulted and what it's like to be arrested on bogus charges. Which is why I'm willing to help get her bail reset so she can stay out of jail for the duration of her trial."

Tucker held my gaze. "But you can't guarantee that."

"No."

Tucker shook her head. "Not good enough."

"If we got the charges dropped, then we'd lose out on the recovery fee," said Byrd. "Why should we work for free?"

"Exactly." I turned to Li. "You're her lawyer. Hire a professional investigator to track down the real killer."

"I've suggested it." Li looked at Stevens.

"We don't have the money," said Stevens. "We put up all the cash we had for the deposit on Indigo's bail."

"You're going to lose a lot more if Indigo doesn't come with us. You'll lose your whole house and all those pretty motorcycles you have in your garage."

"And *you'll* lose a whole lot more than the bounty if you try to take her by force." Stevens made an upward gesture, and the other members of the Athena Sisterhood suddenly stood and surrounded Byrd and me.

I eased to my feet, my hand resting on the grip of my Ruger. "You all need to back the fuck off."

Adrenaline roared into my system, sending my senses into overdrive. Li, I noticed, had disappeared. Plausible deniability, no doubt.

Well, here we go.

Byrd put a hand on my arm. "Everybody just chill before someone gets killed. It doesn't have to go down like this."

I kept my hand on the grip of my pistol and glared at Stevens. "You try anything, we'll put enough of you down to make you regret it."

"Leave Indigo alone." This from Fuego. "Everybody walks away in one piece."

"Sorry, can't do that. She skipped out on her bail bond. Law says she goes back to jail."

"And y'all get paid your thirty pieces of silver," said Stevens.

I shrugged. "We all have a job to do. No shame in getting paid for it."

"You want to get paid, find the real killer," said Fuego. "We'll make sure you get something for your trouble."

"We'll consider the offer," said Byrd, trying to be all diplomatic and shit.

"Like hell we will," I replied. "We're taking Pearson back to Scottsdale with us, willing or unwilling."

"Ever heard of the Confederate Thunder?" asked Fuego. "They used to rule this area. Tried to shut us down. Didn't want us calling ourselves a motorcycle club. Raped and murdered a couple of our members. So we took them down. They're all dead or in prison now."

I nodded. "Interesting. You ever heard of Milo Volkov?"

A self-satisfied smile curled the corners of Stevens's mouth. "Bastard kidnapped my girlfriend once. I shot him too."

"But you didn't kill him, did ya? I did. Him and several of his goons. And I didn't need a biker gang to do it."

"Enough of this." Fuego shot glances at her fellow bikers, and they put away their weapons. "I suggest you two leave. Now."

"Come on, Byrd. Let's blow this dive." We pushed our way through the bikers, ignoring the stares from the bar's other patrons.

When we stepped out the door, I let go of a breath I'd been holding, sending out clouds of water vapor. "Fuck me."

A chill was growing in the air. A ring of ice crystals encircled the full moon casting a silvery glow on the Downtown Square.

Byrd ran a hand over his close-cropped hair. "That coulda gone better."

"No shit, Sherlock." I shuffled along the crowded sidewalk back to the Gray Ghost.

"So what now?"

"Back to the hotel. Go over the paperwork Rios gave us on the Athena Sisterhood members with a record. Formulate a game plan."

"So you still intend to arrest Pearson?"

"I do."

"And when they come after us?"

"We'll deal with the threat as it comes." I unlocked the Gray Ghost and hopped in behind the wheel.

16

As we cruised out of the downtown area, the headlights of two motorcycles behind us caught my attention. "Looks like we got a tail."

Byrd turned in his seat. "Gotta give them points for moxie."

"Moxie? Geez, what century are you in? Been binge-watching *Mary Tyler Moore*?"

"I like to read. Gives me a rich vocabulary. So what you gonna do about our tails?"

"Nothing for now. The Ghost isn't exactly built for speed. They're probably just keeping an eye on us."

They followed us out of downtown, never more than a couple of cars behind. I drove into the pass-through of a Days Inn. The bikers pulled into parking spaces nearby facing the motel entrance. Neither got off their motorcycle.

"This isn't our motel," Byrd said.

"No, it's a diversion." I turned on my walkie-talkie. "Sit tight and keep an eye on them. If they get off their bikes, hail me on the walkie."

"I don't like this."

"Stay cool, man. You're good at that, remember?"

I gave the biker women a friendly wave and walked into the motel lobby. At the front desk, a white man in his late twenties with gelled animé-style hair greeted me. His name tag read Chuck.

"Do you offer room service?" I asked, knowing the answer. I pulled a brochure from a holder on the counter.

Chuck smiled. "I'm afraid not, but in your room, you will find a directory of nearby restaurants that deliver. Big Daddy's Smokehouse is a popular barbecue restaurant. There's also the Peking Palace, if you prefer Chinese. And the Ring of Fire is a fabulous Mexican-Asian fusion place. Of course, right now, we're all booked up."

I nodded appreciatively. "How far is it to the Grand Canyon from here?"

"Depending on your route, it should take you about two hours."

I asked a few more unnecessary questions, thanked him for his time, and walked out holding the brochure prominently as I climbed into the Gray Ghost. Our escorts were still watching from their bikes. I drove around behind the building. The bikers followed but maintained their distance.

"Why are we here? I don't understand," said Byrd.

"I was hoping they'd assume we were staying here and then drive on. Time for plan B." I jumped out and opened up the back. "Grab your bag."

"Did you get us a room here?"

"Not exactly." I led Byrd to a door at the rear of the building. Unfortunately, the back door required a room key card to open.

"Shit." I glanced through the window. A woman with two young kids was approaching the door from the inside. "Ah, here we go."

The door burst open as the kids raced through playing tag, followed by their haggard-looking mother. I held it open for her.

"Thank you," she said in a tired voice.

I smiled. "My pleasure." We stepped inside and turned down a corridor, out of view of the door.

"Would you mind explaining what's going on?"

I called up an Uber ride on my phone. The app told me the driver would arrive in ten minutes.

"I'm trying to lose our tail. I requested an Uber to take me back to the Square. The Goldstrike Saloon on Prospect Avenue has a rear entrance onto Orange Grove Boulevard. If I'm right, the bikers will follow me in the Uber. I'll lose them at the Goldstrike, and you can pick me up on Orange Grove."

The Uber car arrived shortly. I tossed Byrd my keys, stepped outside carrying my duffel, waved at the women on bikes, then hopped in. As expected, the bikers followed. When I kept glancing back at our tail, the driver, a young man originally from Benin, asked if everything was all right. I shot him a smile and assured him it was.

I hopped out at the Goldstrike and hustled in past the hostess station, saying my group was already waiting for me. Just past the restrooms, I found the back door. The sign had the words Orange Grove Blvd painted on it and a crooked arrow pointed downward. I stepped outside and took the staircase down to the rear parking lot. Byrd flashed the headlights to the Gray Ghost.

He laughed. "I honestly did not think that would work."

"My plans always work. Eventually."

We drove back to the Montgomery Family Inn, with a side trip to a liquor store so I could pick up a bottle of Cuervo. The thrill of losing our biker tail faded, replaced by the tendrils of depression and self-doubt wrapping around my brain. What made me think I could find this chick? For that matter, what was Deez thinking when he recommended me?

People had a tendency to get hurt or killed around me. Teammates, fugitives, and even innocent bystanders. I was a walking disaster. And now I was responsible for Byrd's safety. The more I thought about it, the more I wanted to chase him away so he didn't get hurt.

While Byrd stretched out on his bed and watched the TV, I poured some tequila into a plastic cup.

"Want some?" I offered.

Byrd shook his head. "Nah, I'm good."

"Why? Because Jesus?" I mocked.

"I don't drink when I'm on a case. But you do you, girl."

"Yeah." I was being a bitch. I didn't care. I poured more into the cup, then sat on the bed and dove into the paperwork Detective Rios had given us.

Two of the eight members were Shea "Havoc" Stevens and Zia "Indigo" Pearson. Nothing new there. Two were deceased. That left four others with rap sheets. While there was no guarantee any of those four were hiding Pearson, I figured they were our best bets.

My phone started playing the *Game of Thrones* theme song—Becca's ringtone.

"What's up, Becks. You okay?"

"Yeah, I felt bad about not running those checks for you."

"Geez, girl. You know your health takes precedence over any skip tracing work."

"I know. I just felt bad, so I ran the phone logs you needed. There's been no activity on Zia Pearson's phone. Nothing of interest on her wife's either. No unidentified numbers."

"Not surprising. Clearly laying low. I'd think they would be communicating somehow. No text messages?"

"A few people sent messages to Tucker asking how Indigo's doing. Tucker just responded that she was fine. Didn't elaborate. From what I could find out, most of the people sending the messages appear connected to the motorcycle gang."

"Damn. I was hoping for some direction. We don't have long to find her."

"How are things working out with Byrd?"

I glanced over at him. He was laughing at something on the television. "We haven't killed each other yet. We're sharing a motel room, if you can believe it."

"Ooh, sexy. I want details."

"It's not like that."

"Sure, sure."

"Honestly, sex is the last thing I want." I took a long pull on the tequila. "Kinda wondering if I lost my mojo."

"For sex?"

"No, for catching fugitives."

"Jenna Christine Ballou, you are a badass bounty hunter," Becca said matter-of-factly. "Don't let this rough patch let you forget you've caught a lot of fugitives."

"And a lot of people have been hurt along the way. Caden. Peyton. Rodeo. Deez. Conor. I don't want Byrd to be added to that list."

"It's a rough business. You know that. Byrd knows it, too, I'm sure. Everyone who does that job knows that. And for the record, Peyton's death is not on you. Those racist bastards with White Nation killed him. You'll get your mojo back, girl. Remember, smile."

The word *smile* was like a piercing ray of light into the murky black of my soul. The word was code, a reminder of the first time Becca and I had gone to the movies together as kids. We were eleven years old. I had recently transitioned and was still insecure about going out dressed as a girl, terrified people would laugh or worse.

We'd gone to see the movie *Anywhere But Here*. I was petrified when we approached the ticket taker in the lobby. Becca leaned in close and told me to smile. I did. And instead of mocking me, the ticket taker simply returned the smile and said, "Enjoy the movie, girls."

Since then it had been a code, a magical word that helped me rediscover my strength and courage.

"Thanks, Becca. You're the best. Now get some rest."

17

The next morning, I woke to a scratching sound. "Diana, cut it out."

The scratching continued. "Diana, if you don't stop scratching at that door, I'm gonna..." I realized I wasn't at home. Diana wasn't around. I looked up to see Byrd standing on his bed. The painting that had been secured above his pillow lay flat on the bedspread. Byrd had a pen and was drawing on the wall.

I rubbed my face to wake up. My head pounded, no doubt a result of my indulgence the night before. The bottle of tequila was half-empty. Or half-full. Whatever.

"What the hell are you doing?" I asked.

"SWT."

"SW-what?"

"Secret Wall Tattoo. You create your own art behind the awful pictures they mount on the walls."

"I believe the legal term for that is vandalism. You realize I'm paying for the room, right? I don't want to get charged extra just because you decided to express your subversive creative side."

"Don't worry. No one will know. Besides, there's already artwork on the inside of the toilet tank lid, on top of the bar for the shower curtain, and on the inside of the nightstand, behind the drawer."

I studied the image he was sketching with the ballpoint pen. It looked like a scene from an Avengers movie. "You're good."

"Thanks."

"You into comic books?"

"Marvel mostly for superheroes," he said, focusing on his work. "Though most of the books I read are more indie. I'm currently reading a pulp crime series called *Las Vegas Repo*. How about you? You into comic books?"

"Yeah, more DC than Marvel. I also read *Bitch Planet*, *Peepland*, and *Rat Queens*. Even got a signed first edition of *Tank Girl*. You ever cosplay?"

"Not really. You?"

"Wonder Woman. Sometimes Xena," I said, feeling a little embarrassed.

Byrd stopped drawing and turned to me with interest in his eyes. "I can see that. You'd be badass as Wonder Woman."

My face heated. "Thanks, I guess. So how'd you get the picture off the wall?"

"With this." He pulled out a little tool with a notch in it, then stuffed it back in his pocket.

"Huh." I couldn't think of anything else to say. We were both comic book geeks working as bounty hunters. Weird. "Well, be ready to go in thirty. I really want to wrap up this job today and go home."

"Roger that. Ready when you are."

I took a quick shower and threw on a fresh set of clothes. Just as I was putting on my tactical belt, my phone rang. It was Becca.

"Hey," I said. "Feeling better?"

"A bit. I may have found something."

"Really? What?"

"I was going back over Chelsea Tucker's mobile phone logs," she told me. "There is one number she calls a few times a day that belongs to another member of the Athena Sisterhood—a woman named Helen Butler. Her biker name is Rah-Rah."

"Butler. That name rings a bell. Hold on." I thumbed through the report Rios had printed out for us. "Here she is. Helen Butler. Six years ago, she served three months for a possession charge and having a fake MMJ card. You think she's hiding Pearson?"

"That would be my guess."

"Good work, Becks. Do you have a location for this phone?" I wanted to make sure the address listed in the printout from Rios was still current.

"I pinged it, but the phone seems to be off. No location. The calls seem to be at regular times. Seven o'clock in the morning. One o'clock in the afternoon and nine o'clock in the evening. Like clockwork."

I looked at my watch. It was seven forty. "Guess we missed the good morning call."

"Yeah. I'll monitor it and let you know if it pops up."

"You have an address for Helen Butler?"

She gave it to me. It matched the one I already had, located in Bradshaw City, twenty minutes north of Ironwood.

"Thanks for the info. I have a good feeling about this."

"Be extremely careful, Jinxie. I don't think they'll give up one of their own very easily."

"So I've learned. Don't worry. I got my head on a swivel. Talk to ya later."

I hung up. "Let's go track down our fugitive," I told Byrd.

I spent ten minutes scraping the frost off the windshield with an old Macy's charge card. Never saw the need for investing in an ice scraper. Even in winter, the temps down in the valley rarely dipped below freezing.

On the way to Bradshaw City, we stopped at a QT convenience store. I grabbed a couple of breakfast burritos. Byrd snagged a few power bars. Breakfast of champions.

Once we were underway, I filled him in on what I'd learned about Helen "Rah-Rah" Butler.

"Why they call her Rah-Rah?" he asked.

"Who knows? Maybe she was a cheerleader in school."

"Or maybe it stands for 'rambunctious radical,'" joked Byrd.

"Or 'random razor blade.'"

"Rational radiologist."

I struggled to think of another. "Raging racketballer."

"Weak. How about ravishing rabbi?"

"With a name like Butler, she doesn't sound Jewish. Radiant radish."

"Could be if she's a vegan," he said. "Raucous raccoon."

We continued on, coming up with sillier and sillier explanations for Butler's nickname. Despite a lingering headache from my drinking the night before, I felt hopeful about wrapping things up. For the first time, we had a solid lead. Whether we could bag our fugitive without bloodshed remained to be seen.

Bradshaw City was smaller and more rural than Ironwood. Plenty of used car lots, feed stores, Walmarts, and check cashers. Not many Starbucks or shopping malls. Pickup trucks with NRA stickers outnumbered Priuses with Coexist decals by a ratio of thirty to one.

The terrain in Helen Butler's neighborhood was hilly. Homes were small with single-car garages. Aging vehicles lined the street. Lawns were choked with weeds and wildflowers. The Gray Ghost fit in perfectly.

Three motorcycles sat in Butler's driveway and a few more on the street. Two women stood guard by the front door, and I recognized one of them as Shea Stevens, Ms. Iron Goddess herself.

"Shit." I drove past and parked several doors down.

"What's our strategy?" Byrd asked.

I stared at the house in my rearview mirror. "We go in and get our girl."

"How? They still outnumber us. I really don't want to kill anyone over a bounty."

"Roadhouse rules."

"Roadhouse rules? What? 'Be nice until it's time not to be nice?' Hasn't worked so far."

"Just follow my lead." We stepped out of the truck and geared up. I put a Taser in my right holster, my Ruger in the cross-draw. Walkie-talkies on. I handed Byrd the beanbag shotgun.

"Sneak into the backyard between those two houses over there, then find a spot where you can see the back door. If it's guarded, keep your distance. If not, approach cautiously. If Zia Pearson runs out, tell her to stop. Be nice about it. Use your cool charm. If she doesn't stop, hit her with a beanbag and cuff her. You have handcuffs?"

He nodded.

"If one of the bikers comes at you, tell them to keep their distance. Be nice. Try to de-escalate the situation if you can."

"So the complete opposite of your approach last night."

I sighed. "Yeah. If they keep coming and or look like they're about to hurt you, shoot them. And if you get into trouble, call me on the walkie."

"I'm really not liking this. We should have a bigger crew

for a situation like this. I could call Deez, see if he can spare anyone else."

"No time. We got this." I had my mojo back. I could feel it. "Just keep your head on a swivel. Ready?"

"No."

"Relax. You got Jesus protecting you, right?" I slapped him teasingly on the arm. "Call me on the walkie when you're in position."

He raced like a deer into the backyard of the house three doors down from Butler's. I checked my watch, then kept an eye on the two women guarding the front door. They didn't appear to have noticed us. Yet.

A few minutes later, my radio crackled.

"I'm in position."

"What do you see?"

"No one on the backside of the house."

"Good. Can you see anyone inside?"

"The sun makes it impossible to see in."

"Do you have cover?"

"Yes."

"Hold position for now. I'm approaching the front door."

18

I took a deep breath. Despite the danger, this was the part of the job I loved. The hunt was a challenge, but the take-down was always the satisfying conclusion. I was pumped. I was ready. No one was going to stop me from doing my lawful duty.

When I started crossing over into Butler's yard, both Stevens and the other woman at the door were watching me. Stevens's companion looked more like a cheerleader than the typical biker chick. Slim, athletic build. Hair in a cute chestnut ponytail, perfect makeup. Her biker vest read Rah-Rah.

"You need to pack up and go home," Stevens announced as I approached. Her hand rested on a Glock on her right hip. "We gave you our offer, and you turned us down. You ain't taking Indigo."

"Ms. Stevens, I don't negotiate. I don't play detective. I'm a bounty hunter, pure and simple. Indigo has a chance to get back on track so she doesn't spend the rest of her life looking over her shoulder. Nobody wants to live like that."

"I done told you, you ain't gettin' her."

I placed a hand on the Taser. "Step aside. No one needs to get hurt."

A boom echoed from the backyard, followed by a second. Shit.

Shea went for her Glock. I fired the Taser and hit her in the chest. Her body seized, and she fell to the ground with a strangled cry. Her Glock tumbled under a nearby shrub.

Rah-Rah rushed me, drawing a pistol at the same time. I sent the gun flying with a roundhouse kick. She swung. I blocked and slammed her perfect perky nose with a palm-heel strike. When she came at me again, I dropped her with a boot to her solar plexus. She lay in a heap, gasping for air, blood trickling down her face.

I picked up Stevens's Glock and reached for Rah-Rah's pistol, a Ruger similar to mine. Next thing I knew, I was tumbling off the porch into the hard-packed dirt of the front yard. I rolled to keep Stevens from pinning me.

She came at me with a series of punches and kicks. We sparred back and forth, exchanging blows. She was a ruthless street fighter with fast reflexes—a fair match for my years of training in Krav Maga.

At one point, I had her pinned. Heaving, I said between breaths, "It's not...not worth it. Just stop."

Her weight shifted below me, and she tossed me sideways. I fell hard against a large rock and tasted blood. I blocked a series of blows and kicks, grabbing her boot and twisting her off her feet. I reached my Ruger, but she drove a knee into my eye socket before I got a grip.

As I lay on the ground, trying to clear the cobwebs from my mind, a thunderous boom made my heart skip a beat. Stevens fell to the ground beside me, moaning. Twenty feet away, Byrd stood holding the shotgun.

"Drop it!" Rah-Rah held the Glock on Byrd and her Ruger on me.

Byrd looked at me for instructions. I nodded while still catching my breath. He dropped the shotgun and raised his hands.

I rubbed my throbbing eye socket. The vision was blurred. My face felt swollen. Blood ran down my shirt. My fists were scraped and bruised. Stevens didn't look any better.

"So what now?" I looked up at Rah-Rah. "You going to kill us?"

The guns in her hands trembled. Her expression was that of a frightened child. Someone with less experience might assume she wouldn't shoot. But I knew better. Fear made people do stupid things.

"F-forget about Indigo, all right?" said Rah-Rah. "Just... just forget her."

Stevens pushed herself to her feet, moaning and wincing. To my surprise, she offered me a hand and pulled me to my feet.

"Or take our offer," she said through gritted teeth. "We'll find a way to compensate you if you don't get your bounty."

I didn't like other people telling me how to run my business, especially people protecting a fugitive, innocent or not. But it was clear that with a couple of dozen members on their roster, the Athena Sisterhood had Byrd and me outmanned. And that was just the local chapter. If they brought in help from outside chapters, who knew how many we would face. No wonder Rodeo and Tommy Boy threw in the towel.

"Fine. We'll take your offer," I said reluctantly.

Byrd's eyes narrowed. "Jinx, no."

I locked eyes with Stevens. "But I need every bit of information you and Rebecca Li have about the case. And it has to be the truth."

"We'll give you what we got. I'll have Dragon hook you up."

"Another thing. I have less than a week before the judge vacates the bond and demands the full amount of the bail. If that deadline passes, it's no longer up to me what happens. Pima Bail Bonds will file to take your house. I've seen it happen. The sheriff will show up with a whole lot more firepower than you've got and kick you and your niece out on the street. And your pal Indigo will spend the rest of her life on the FBI's Most Wanted list."

"We'll come down to Phoenix with you," said Stevens. "We'll work together on this."

A bitter laugh escaped my throat, causing me to cough and spit blood. "Thanks for the offer, but I don't work with people I don't know and can't trust."

"You can trust us to help find the real killer. That's what we want."

"I don't need a bunch of outlaw bikers getting in my way. Bad enough I'm playing private eye instead of dragging Indigo's sorry ass back to jail."

"Don't talk about Indigo that way," said Rah-Rah.

"We're not one-percenters," insisted Stevens.

"Whatever that means," I sneered.

"It means, we're a law-abiding club."

"Really? Is that why your buddy's on the lam while you're pointing guns at us?"

"We're working toward the same goal. That's all you need worry about. Or you can walk away."

Every instinct told me to do just that. Who knew what these bikers would pull, all with my reputation on the line.

I looked to Byrd, who shook his head. "Let's just walk, Jinx. No shame in it."

I thought about it some more. It was the sensible thing to do. Tommy Boy and Rodeo couldn't bag Pearson. Why should I risk my life trying? But if I didn't come through for Maurice at Pima Bail Bonds, I might never find work again.

"Fine, we work together." I wiped blood from my eyebrow onto my arms. Byrd's face fell in disappointment. I didn't blame him.

Stevens took her Glock from Rah-Rah and holstered it. "Meet me at Iron Goddess in an hour."

"Agreed." I waved to Byrd. "Grab the shotgun, and let's check out of the motel."

"The shotgun stays here," said Rah-Rah.

"Oh, so you're robbing us now? Is this the trustworthiness you were talking about?" I directed the question at Stevens.

"Rah-Rah, let them take the shotgun."

"But Havoc..."

"I'm club VP. I say give it back. You gotta problem with that, take it up with Fuego."

I held out my hand to Rah-Rah. "And my Ruger."

She looked to Stevens, who nodded. "Give it to her."

Rah-Rah let me take it from her. Byrd picked up the shotgun, and we shuffled to the Gray Ghost. I had no idea how Maurice was going to react to this latest development. But I hurt too much to care.

19

"What happened in the backyard?" I asked when we climbed into the Gray Ghost.

"Pearson ran out the back door with three other women. I hit one with a beanbag round. Tried to get Pearson but missed. The other women started shooting at me as they ran off."

I glanced at him. "You hurt?"

"No, I'm good."

I breathed a sigh of relief. "Glad to hear it." I started the SUV and drove off down the road.

"Jinx, all due respect, I don't like this. No shame in admitting we couldn't find her. Rodeo and Tommy Boy didn't get her either. Maybe Pima Bail Bonds just has to eat this one."

"You want to be the one to tell Maurice that?"

"Not really. But like you said, we're bail enforcement, not detectives."

"I guess there's a first time for everything. If you're not interested, I won't blame you for walking away."

Byrd grew silent, staring out at the passing landscape as

I drove south to Ironwood. I hated this tension between us. I almost wanted him to say he didn't want to join me on this ludicrous mission. At the same time, I wanted someone I could trust to do the right thing.

At the motel, I cleaned myself up and put on some clothes that weren't covered in blood. I tried some concealer and other makeup to make my face look less like an heirloom tomato. But there was no hiding the fact that I'd taken a beating.

"So what's it going to be, Jubal Byrd? You in or you out?"

He let out a long sigh. "I like you, Jinx. And I respect you as a bounty hunter."

Aw, shit, here it comes.

"Honestly, I think you're impulsive and sarcastic. You curse and drink more than I'd like."

"Oh, for fuck's sake, just spit it out. You're bailing on me."

He met my gaze. "No, that's just it. It's because I respect you that I'm willing to do this."

"Huh. Did not see that coming."

We packed up our stuff and checked out. It was nearly noon when we reached the motorcycle shop.

The skinny blonde behind the counter took one look at us, said, "I'll get them," and disappeared into the back. She returned a moment later with Stevens, Fuego, Savage, and Dragon. All four were wearing their biker vests.

"Well, look who shows up again, now that the fighting's over with," I said to Dragon.

Her face was unreadable when she handed me a thick manila folder. "These are copies of documents I deemed relevant from what I received in discovery from the Maricopa County attorney. You'll find crime scene reports and forensics—autopsy, fingerprint, DNA, and trace—as well as statements from my client and other witnesses."

"How do you explain Pearson's DNA on the victim?" I asked.

"The victim scratched Indigo when they got into a shoving match earlier that day. I'm planning to impeach with an expert witness, but I can't count on that. Juries hear DNA, they assume the defendant is guilty. I need more to acquit my client."

"Like I said, you should hire a professional investigator." I thumbed through the paperwork.

"I'm already working pro bono on this case," replied Dragon. "The club has put up all they had for the bail bond, money they'll never get back even if Indigo is cleared. We need your help. Find the killer, Ms. Ballou, and get my client off the hook. She doesn't deserve this travesty of justice."

"We'll see what we can find out." I held up the folder. "This is a lot of information to sort through. Can you give me a highlights reel?"

"That is the highlights reel gleaned from the boxes of information the prosecution sent over."

I felt like I was competing in a marathon and was just leaving the starting block while everyone else was halfway to the finish line.

I looked to Stevens. "So who all's coming on this Quixotic adventure?"

"Just me and Fuego for now. If we need more, they'll be there."

I shook my head. This was going to be such a clusterfuck. "Okay, here's the game plan. I want to get my skip tracer, Becca Alvarez, looking into the victim's background, this Brother James or whoever he is. Hopefully, she can dig up something that will point us in the direction of the killer. If not, we'll check out the crime scene, talk to witnesses, whatever it takes."

I handed the keys to Byrd. "You drive while I get up to speed on these reports."

"I appreciate you doing this," said Savage as we walked to the front of the shop. There was a sadness and sincerity about her that I hadn't noticed before. "Indigo's the love of my life. And she's no killer."

I nodded. "I can't promise anything."

Byrd and I climbed into the Gray Ghost.

"Take it easy on the curves going down Sycamore Mountain. She tends to be a little top heavy."

"Easy on the curves. Got it."

We pulled onto the road. Stevens and Fuego followed on their motorcycles down the switchbacks. Trying to read as we wound down through the curves was all but impossible. I called Becca.

"How goes the hunt for the biker chick?" she asked.

My head still throbbed. "Things have taken a rather unusual turn."

"What's wrong? Are you okay?"

"More or less. Are you at the Hub by chance?"

"Yeah, why? You need me to skip trace more of Pearson's biker buddies?"

"Not exactly. Pearson's biker buddies have..." I struggled for the right word. "Let's just say they convinced me that she's innocent. They want me to find the real killer."

"I thought you always said you're not in the guilty or not guilty business..."

"I'm making an exception."

"Because she's trans?"

"Because Byrd and I are grossly outnumbered. Pearson has promised to turn herself in if I can come up with enough evidence to get her acquitted."

"This doesn't sound like you, Jinxie. Are you being held

against your will? Do I need to call the Cortes County sheriff?"

"I'm fine. But I do need you to research the victim in the case, Brother James Fitzgerald. Personal history, financials, phone logs, social media, anything to point me to someone with the motive, means, and opportunity to murder him. I don't have much time before Pima Bail Bonds has to cough up the full bail."

"Got it. I'll see what I can find out."

I hung up and saw I had a voicemail message. I hit the play button.

"Hi, Ms. Ballou. Pete Stansfield again with Arizona Mutual Life Insurance. I really do need to talk with you about the claim we paid out on Conor Doyle. Please call me."

I deleted it. Dealing with that shit was so at the bottom of my list it deserved a gravestone.

Once the road straightened out, I was able to concentrate on the stack of papers in my hand. According to the crime scene report, Brother James, aka James Fitzgerald, was found dead in a room registered under his name at the Cactus Inn in Scottsdale.

The medical examiner's report listed cause of death as a gunshot wound to the head. The crime scene photos revealed a large man, probably over six feet tall, who looked like he'd lost a fight to a professional boxer, something I had personal experience with. His face was swollen beyond recognition. A trail of blood led from the body to where his severed penis was found in the toilet. A brutal but fitting end to a man who preached such filth against women and minorities.

A member of the motel staff claimed to have seen a tall African American female with long braids running from the motel room and screaming shortly before the body was discovered.

Patrol officers canvassed the area and questioned patrons at neighboring businesses. Members of the Athena Sisterhood had been drinking next door at Naughty's Cabaret. Zia Pearson fit the description of the woman leaving Fitzgerald's motel room.

When questioned by Scottsdale homicide detectives Atkinson and Torres, Pearson admitted to getting into a confrontation with the victim earlier that day at Scottsdale's Wild West event center, which was hosting Arizona Bike Week. Fitzgerald was reported to have been holding up signs that read "Women Deserve 2 B Raped" and "Put Homos 2 Death."

The police report noted Pearson's knuckles and forearms were scraped up, which she explained were due to her attempts to attach a luggage bracket to the back of her motorcycle while at the biker festival.

I flipped to the forensics reports. The room contained fingerprints from dozens of individuals, none matching Pearson's. DNA found under Fitzgerald's fingernails matched Pearson's, but no other corroborating trace evidence was found.

Pearson had two previous arrests, one for possession of controlled substances and one for solicitation. The controlled substance in question turned out to be estradiol, for which Pearson didn't have a prescription at the time. She received a suspended sentence. The solicitation charges were dropped after the arresting officer admitted he assumed she was a prostitute because she was black and transgender.

So if Pearson didn't kill the little hate-monger, who the hell did?

By the time we reached Phoenix, I had read or skimmed

most of the documents in the file. I directed Byrd to go through the drive-through at Tres Leches, a downtown coffeehouse, where I picked up a regular latte for myself, an almond milk cappuccino for Becca, and a regular coffee for Byrd. I thought about getting something for Stevens and Fuego, who waited on their bikes on the other side of the parking lot, but considering the day's events, I wasn't feeling too charitable toward them.

With drinks in hand, I guided Byrd to the Hub's parking lot, having shed our winter coats to enjoy the more spring-like weather of the valley.

"Where are we?" asked Stevens.

"The Hub. It's a coworking space where I rent a desk. Follow me."

I led them through the maze of desks while music from Dead Can Dance played on the Hub's sound system. I pulled up some extra chairs. Becca thanked me for the cappuccino.

"Becca Alvarez, this is Byrd, who's temporarily on loan from Viper. Becca is an IT security guru who handles my skip tracing."

The two of them shook hands.

"And these two"—I pointed at my biker guests—"are Havoc, aka Shea Stevens, VP for the Cortes County chapter of the Athena Sisterhood and the owner of Iron Goddess Custom Cycles."

"You can call me Shea." She shook Becca's hand.

"And this is Fuego, the chapter's president."

"Nice to meet you, Ms. Alvarez." Fuego nodded.

Becca gave me a look that said, "What the hell?"

I shrugged. "What'd you find out about the late Brother James?"

Becca rolled her eyes. "What a piece of work that guy was. I'm surprised nobody murdered him sooner. Officially, he was a licensed minister in the Evangelical Light of the Messiah Church, which is run by Michael Andrew Wilkes, or Elder Michael, as he calls himself on their website.

"Of course, it's less of a church and more of a cross between a psycho religious cult and an extreme right-wing lobbying organization. No location or schedule of services listed on the website. Their 'disciples,' as they call themselves, show up at schools or large public events, spewing their bigotry. The Southern Poverty Law Center lists them as a hate group."

"No surprise there," I said.

"James Fitzgerald joined the organization in 2007. Prior to that, he worked as an elementary school teacher for a private Baptist school. The so-called church pays him three grand a month. He's divorced, no kids officially, though one woman claims he's the father of her special-needs child.

"He has accounts on most major social media. Shortly before his death, Twitter suspended his account for posting hate speech. He received a lot—and I mean a lot—of death threats.

"Late last year, he was charged with raping a teenager, copped a plea for misdemeanor assault. Sentenced to six months probation, no jail time, didn't have to register as a sex offender. He's been sued multiple times for harassment. Won most of those cases. One was settled for twenty thousand dollars, although the settlement remains unpaid.

"He routinely shows up at high school and college campuses preaching hate against women and minorities. He also rents a room twice a month at the Cactus Inn, the same motel where his body was found."

"No doubt getting his holier-than-thou nob polished," Shea replied.

"Makes me sick," Byrd said. "Guys like him give Christianity a bad name."

"A year ago," Becca continued, "he was attacked by a lesbian teen with a two-by-four while he was protesting outside the fence by her high school."

"I remember that," said Shea. "The Athena Sisterhood raised money for her legal bills."

"So what's the bottom line?" I asked. "Who's the most likely suspect?"

"Bottom line is you're probably looking for a needle in a monster-sized haystack. Even in an ultraconservative state like Arizona, there were a lot of people who wanted this guy dead."

"Any of the death threats stand out, like whoever sent them intended to act on it?" I asked.

"Hard to say," Becca explained. "Most of the ones on social media were from accounts that have since been deleted or suspended. All I had were screenshots posted by Fitzgerald and his fellow 'disciples.' A few threats were from Wes Hancock, the father of the girl he raped. But that was last year. Nothing from him recently."

Stevens shook her head. "If Brother James raped my niece and got no prison time, I woulda dropped his ass down an abandoned mineshaft."

"We'll put him number one in the motive category," I said.

"So what's our game plan?" Fuego asked me.

"I want to talk to Detectives Atkinson and Torres, the ones who arrested Pearson."

Stevens scoffed. "Those fuckers wouldn't know their asses from a hole in the ground. They kept trying to get me to roll on Indigo, claiming she had this big criminal past, which we all knew was bullshit." Her face colored with anger. "Talking to them is a waste of time."

Before I could reply, my phone rang.

20

The number on the caller ID wasn't familiar. "Ballou Fugitive Recovery," I said.

"Is...is this Jinx Ballou?" asked a frantic female voice.

"Yeah, who is this?"

"V-Vanessa Colton. Used to be Vanessa Nealey. You... you took my husband back to jail a while back."

It took me a moment, but I remembered. Battered white woman giving me attitude when I showed up at her door, looking to arrest her then-boyfriend. I guessed she married the bastard.

"I remember. What do you want, Vanessa? I'm not looking for Freddie right now. If he's jumped bail again, I suggest you contact his bail bond agent."

"No, I...I need your help."

"*My* help? For what?"

She sobbed pitifully at the other end of the line. "I want out."

"Out of what?"

"Away from him. He...I'm so tired of being his punching bag."

"So why are you calling me?"

"I got no one else to turn to. Most of my friends, they don't want nothing to do with me."

"Oh for the love of bacon," I muttered. "Look, Vanessa, if Freddie's hit you again, call the police. Or get an order of protection."

"I tried all that. That order of protection didn't do shit. He just laughed and beat me up again. And when I called the cops, he was out on bail a day later."

"So change the fucking locks."

"Now that we're married, he says I can't."

"He says? Jesus fucking Christ on a cracker! What do you expect me to do about it? I'm not a bodyguard."

"Last time you were here, you told me to call if I needed help. You gave me your business card."

I didn't remember telling her that. I was pretty sure I hadn't told her that. But clearly that was what she remembered.

"What's going on?" asked Shea.

I put a hand over the mic while Vanessa sobbed in my ear. "Girlfriend of a fugitive I arrested a couple years ago. He's beating her up again, and she wants me to do something about it."

"Where is she?" asked Fuego.

"You still live in the same place?" I asked into the phone.

"Yes."

"Off Northern and Seventh Street," I told Fuego. "Why?"

"Is the abuser there now?" Fuego pressed.

"Vanessa, is Freddie there?"

"He just left."

"He's gone," I told Fuego and Stevens.

Fuego exchanged a look with Stevens. "Tell her we'll be there shortly."

"What? Wait a minute! The deal was you're here to help Byrd and me clear Indigo, remember? Now you want to go galloping off to save this damsel in distress?"

"This is what the Athena Sisterhood does—we protect women," Fuego insisted.

"Besides, you're going to talk to that cowboy Atkinson," said Shea. "Fuego and me had enough of that guy when he arrested Indigo. So while you're playing nicey-nice with the pigs, we'll help out this friend of yours."

"She is *so* not my friend, but whatever." I kicked myself for trusting them.

I turned back to the phone, fuming. "Vanessa, I'm sending a couple of"—I glanced at Shea and Fuego—"colleagues over to your place. They'll be riding motorcycles and have leather vests that say Athena Sisterhood. They'll help you deal with your asshole hubby."

"Thank you," she whimpered and hung up.

I gave Shea and Fuego Vanessa's address. "Have fun rescuing this princess, but don't say I didn't warn you. She's a piece of work."

"Call me when you're done talking to the heat," Shea replied. She and Fuego walked out.

"Jinx, what the hell's going on? You look like you lost a fight. What have you gotten yourself into with these bikers?" asked Becca.

Byrd nodded. "My thoughts exactly."

"I'm an idiot. I admit it. But there was no way we were going to arrest Zia Pearson. So I made a deal."

"And yet they're not holding up their end of it," said Byrd. "All due respect, Jinx, I think this was a mistake."

"Maybe so," I admitted. "No one's saying you have to do this with me. But I don't have a lot of options right now.

Assurity Bail Bonds fired me after the Penzler fiasco. And now Conor's life insurance company is demanding I return the money they paid me, a lot of which I already spent on Caden's medical bills after he got shot while working for me. So if I need to track down the real killer to get Pearson to turn herself in, that's what I'll do."

Byrd held my gaze. I could see the calculations going on in his mind. I almost wanted him to walk away. To tell Deez what a head case and a failure I was. And he wouldn't be wrong.

"Let's see what those detectives in Scottsdale have to say."

"I'll keep poking around and see if I can't find anything more that'll point you to the murderer," Becca added.

I hugged her. "Thanks, bestie."

"I always got your back, girlie."

"Likewise. When's Easton get back from Denver?"

"They fly in tomorrow night. Can't wait. I'm in serious need of some cuddle time."

"Call me if you need help in the meantime." To Byrd, I said, "Thanks for doing this. For a Jesus freak, you're all right."

Byrd let loose a laugh. "I'll try to take that as a compliment."

Back in the Gray Ghost, I adjusted the driver's seat from where Byrd had moved it to accommodate his stilt-like legs.

"Despite walking out on us, it was mighty charitable of them to help that lady out," Byrd said while I pulled onto the I-10 heading east.

"I can't believe that dumb bitch married that asshole. It's a sick cycle with this woman. He beats her up. She calls the cops. They arrest him. She drops the charges and lets him back home. The one time she didn't drop the charges, he jumped bail, and I had to track him down. And then she goes and marries the son of a bitch. What'd she think would happen?"

"I had a cousin like that," Byrd replied. "Her boyfriend abused her, and she kept going back to him."

I shook my head. "No offense, but that's the definition of insanity. Doing the same shit over and over, expecting different results? Absolutely stupid."

"My cousin wasn't stupid. She was a biogenetics researcher. And hella beautiful. She just...I don't know, he was like her Kryptonite. He knew exactly which buttons to push to manipulate her."

"But why go back when he was so abusive?"

"She was convinced that if she loved him enough, he'd come around and treat her right. She was determined to figure out how to fix his abusive behavior, like he was one of her experiments."

"So did she fix him?"

Byrd got quiet. "He shot her in the head and then shot himself."

"Jesus Christ on a cracker! Couldn't just kill himself, could he?"

"I really wish you wouldn't use the Lord's name in vain like that."

"Sorry. It's just that relationships are so...I don't know. Maybe I should be celibate the rest of my life."

A half hour later, we arrived at the Scottsdale PD's main precinct.

"How can I help you?" asked the desk sergeant in the lobby, a woman with a sensible haircut, minimal makeup, and crow's-feet around her eyes.

"We need to speak with Detectives Atkinson and Torres, please."

"And you are...?"

"Jinx Ballou. This is my associate, Jubal Byrd. We're looking into a homicide case they handled recently."

"Let me check to see if they're in." She dialed the phone, spoke to someone, and hung up. "They'll be down shortly."

Twenty minutes later, two men came down the hall, both wearing detective shields on their belts.

Atkinson was a white guy in his late fifties and wore a grayish-tan suit badly in need of pressing. Below his Stetson, his curly hair hung in shades of silver, matching his barn owl of a mustache.

Torres was ten years younger, clean-cut with jet-black hair and penetrating eyes that left me feeling unsettled.

"Howdy, ladies. I'm Detective Wyatt Atkinson," he said in an exaggerated western drawl. "This here's my partner, Detective Marc Torres. How can we help y'all this fine afternoon?" He shook our hands, while his buddy gave us a nod.

I gave them our names. "We're looking into the case against Zia Pearson. You were the lead detectives."

"Are you reporters?" asked Torres.

"Bail enforcement." Byrd held up his ID and badge.

The two exchanged a glance. Atkinson beckoned with his long bony fingers. "Y'all come down the hall, and we can have ourselves a little chat."

Byrd and I followed them to an interview room nicer than most I'd seen. Instead of the typical broom-closet, bare cinder block aesthetic, this one had brightly painted walls, a window, and comfortable chairs. I figured the intent was to put suspects and witnesses at ease to make them chattier. Whether that worked or not, I couldn't say.

"So, y'all are bounty hunters, huh?" asked Atkinson. "I heard Pearson was a no-show at his hearing."

"*Her* hearing," I corrected. "We were wondering about other potential suspects for Fitzgerald's murder."

"Other suspects?" Torres raised an eyebrow.

Atkinson gave me a slow nod. "Y'all are working for the defense attorney, I reckon. As investigators, not bounty hunters. That it?"

"More or less." I shrugged.

"We thought maybe you arrested the wrong person," Byrd explained.

"Ya did, huh?" Atkinson stroked his mustache, like he was petting a bird. I half expected it to hoot. "With all due respect, boy, between Detective Torres and myself, we've been wrangling murderers, rapists, and other wrongdoers for a few decades now. We know how to work a case."

Torres glared at us. "We don't need a couple of two-bit bounty hunters with mail-order badges second-guessing our work."

"I used to be a cop too," I replied.

"Did you now?" Torres's patronizing tone was getting under my skin. "For how long?"

"A year," I admitted without enthusiasm.

"A whole year. Well, then you must have *all* the answers."

"Plenty of people had motive to kill Fitzgerald," Byrd insisted. "Some with a lot more motive than Pearson. Wes Hancock, for instance—the father of the girl he raped."

Atkinson adjusted his hat and gave his bushy mustache a few more strokes. "Well, son, let me set your mind at ease. My partner and I don't turn a case over to the county attorney unless it's solid as granite. I assure you, this Pearson fella's the perp."

"She's not a fella." A vein in my neck twitched.

Atkinson laughed. "No offense, little lady, but bulls are bulls, and heifers are heifers. Never the twain shall meet, as they say. Just 'cause a man cuts off his johnson and puts on a dress, that don't make him a woman."

"And you putting on a Stetson doesn't make you a cowboy," I replied.

The sudden fire in Atkinson's eyes told me my jab hit home. "You best watch yourself, missy. Now I'm trying to be respectful to y'all. Torres and me, we interviewed a lot of folks, reviewed *all* the evidence, and put together a solid case against this Pearson *person*. They had a history of solicitation and drug possession. Not that big a leap to murder."

I was trying not to let these guys get under my skin, but I felt my hands ball into fists. "Those previous charges were bogus. The drug charge was for estrogen, not a narcotic. And the solicitation charge was dropped after the cop admitted it was bullshit. Or is a nonconviction only proof of innocence when it comes to cisgender men?"

"Enough of this nonsense." Torres stood up. "We have cases to solve. You two best leave before you get yourselves into trouble."

"What if we provide proof that someone else killed Fitzgerald?" asked Byrd. "Will you drop the charges against Pearson?"

"No," Torres said without hesitation.

"No?" I got to my feet, and Byrd followed suit. "You'd rather send an innocent woman to prison? Why? Because she's transgender?"

"Or black?" asked Byrd.

"We cleared the case and turned it over to the county attorney's office." Atkinson opened the door and stood there with an expression that said the conversation was over. "Our job is done. You want the charges dropped, talk to the prosecutor."

"And who would that be?"

"Wayne Prather," Torres said with a sneer. "I suppose you need us to give you his number too."

"Oh, would you, sir?" I said in my best Scarlett O'Hara voice. "That would be ever so nice."

"Get out." Torres looked ready to bite me in half. His partner didn't look too much more accommodating.

We got up and left without a word.

"That was a waste of time," Byrd said when we returned to the Gray Ghost. "What now?"

"Talk to the prosecutor."

I'd met Wayne Prather a few times over the years. Decent guy most of the time. If we came up with evidence that someone else killed Fitzgerald, there was a chance he'd drop the case. But it would have to be unimpeachable to counter the DNA evidence against Pearson.

I pulled out my phone, dialed the county attorney's office, and was directed to Prather's voicemail. "Mr. Prather, this is Jinx Ballou. I need to speak with you about your case against Zia Pearson." I left my number and hung up.

"Should we call Shea and Fuego?" asked Byrd.

"Soon. First, I want to check out the scene of the crime."

21

I headed south on Scottsdale Boulevard. Just past Oak Street, I pulled into the Cactus Inn parking lot, which was empty except for a 1990s-model Chevy Caprice and newer Kia Sephia. The paint on the street sign was peeling, giving the lettering a pointy, menacing style similar to the illegible graffiti tags on the sign's posts. A smaller, backlit sign by the front office promised rooms with free Playboy channel and other adult content.

The building's stucco exterior was pockmarked and yellowed from years of relentless heat and dust. Windows were dirty. Trash collected in corners.

To the north was a liquor store. To the south was Naughty's, the strip club where the Athena Sisterhood was hanging out when Fitzgerald's body was discovered.

"What do you hope to learn here?" asked Byrd.

"Not sure. I'd like to know why Fitzgerald rented a room every couple weeks."

My phone rang. Wayne Prather's name came up. "Thanks for calling me back, Wayne. I wanted to speak with you about your case against Zia Pearson."

"Pearson? The Fitzgerald murder, right?"

"That's right."

"You're the bounty hunter who was assigned to pick up Wilhelm Penzler. Isn't that correct?"

"Uh, yeah. But this isn't about—"

"You know he was helping us build a RICO case against the Volkov organization. That is until you got him killed."

"Now hold on a second. His death was accidental."

"Accidental, huh? Funny how anytime someone dares to testify against Sergei Volkov, they die in an unfortunate accident."

"About Zia Pearson..."

"Forget it, Ms. Ballou. I am not discussing that case or any other with you." The line went dead.

I looked at Byrd, feeling like I'd been sucker punched. "Grab the file. Let's see about this crime scene."

We walked into the rental office, a smallish room with a Plexiglass window that separated it from the office proper. The lobby, if it could be called that, held the faint scent of cheap perfume, taco sauce, and stale cigar smoke. I caught a glimpse of a security monitor that showed a camera view of the parking lot, including the Gray Ghost.

A man with a stubble-covered face sat on the other side of the window, eating a football-sized burro. A smear of salsa ran down his Hawaiian shirt. He stared at a computer tablet that was playing a video with cheesy music and a lot of moaning and groaning.

When I dinged the service bell on the counter, he grunted like we were intruding on his precious time.

"Hi, my name's Jinx Ballou." I flashed him my badge and my most charismatic smile. "What's yours?"

"Lenny. What's it to ya?" he asked with a mouthful of burro.

"I need some information, Lenny."

"Try Wikipedia," he replied without looking up.

"I need information on James Fitzgerald, otherwise known as Brother James."

"Never heard of him."

I laid a couple of twenties on the counter in the pass-through at the bottom of the window. "Heard of him now?"

Lenny glanced up at me, then down at the bills. "A fleeting memory. Don't recall no details."

I set down two more twenties. "Better now?"

He grabbed the cash, holding one of the bills up to the light to check the watermark. Like anyone would bother forging twenty-dollar bills. "Whaddya wanna know?"

"We know he rented a room a couple of times a month. We want to know why."

Lenny shrugged and returned his attention to the porno. The moaning was reaching a crescendo. "What people do in the rooms is none o' my business so long as it don't leave a big mess."

"Was he sleeping with hookers?" asked Byrd.

Lenny cast an eye in Byrd's direction. "That'd be illegal."

"Doesn't answer the question, does it?" I asked, matching his snarky tone.

Lenny didn't respond. Maybe he was waiting for me to shell out more money, which wasn't going to happen.

"Did he check in alone or with a lady friend?" asked Byrd. "Or male companion, for that matter."

"Not that I saw." He switched off the video and crossed his arms, glaring at both of us. "Anything else? I'm busy."

"How much for a room?" I asked.

"Forty-nine dollars. Checkout's at eleven."

"How much for just a few hours?"

Lenny tried to look indignant, but the result was more

comical than he intended. "What kinda enterprise you think I'm running here?"

"A seedy motel crammed between a titty bar and a liquor store? But I'm sure the price includes numerous amenities. In-room Jacuzzi, perhaps? Michelin-rated restaurant? Open wine bar? Silk sheets?"

"Well, since you put it that way. For you, a special price. Forty-nine dollars. And I need an ID and a credit card." Lenny wiped his face and hands with a napkin, then dabbed at the spot on his shirt, which only spread the stain wider.

I laid fifty dollars in the pass-through. This was becoming an expensive fishing expedition. "I'm paying cash."

"State law says I gotta get an ID."

I held up a ten-dollar bill. "There's my ID. Hamilton. Alex Hamilton."

He looked at me like I was trying to pull a fast one. Or maybe he was trying to figure out if I was a vice cop. "You have to sign the register, *Ms. Hamilton.*"

I did so, and he grabbed a key and tossed it into the pass-through "Room 219. Upstairs, 'round back."

"I want the room Brother James's body was found in."

"Geez, you people into some kinky shit." He swapped the key for another one. "Room 149. North side of the building near the liquor store." He gestured with his thumb in the direction of the room.

"Thanks."

"Don't mess up the room, or you'll wish you hadn't. That means no physical damage, no bodily fluids on the walls. Or the ceiling. And no smoking. You got me?"

I waved as we walked out of the office.

"Why do you want to see the room?" Byrd asked when we walked around the building. "The crime scene techs would've already gone over every inch after the body was found. And who knows how many times the room's been rented since."

"Probably won't find anything. But maybe we'll luck out. I doubt the dearly departed Brother James was here for a Bible study."

"I was looking through the file Ms. Li gave us and found a photocopy of the motel register. Fitzgerald was signing in under the name Saul Tarsus." He showed me the photocopy.

"Saul Tarsus? Doesn't ring a bell."

"Saul of Tarsus was the name of the apostle Paul before he was converted."

"Well, isn't that clever," I said dryly.

We reached room 149, which had a lovely view of the strip club. I suspected the dancers were supplementing their income by providing more than lap dances to their customers. I inserted the key and had to jiggle it a bit to get the cylinder to turn.

Inside, the room smelled of a combination of mold and industrial cleaner with the lingering scent of decomp. The latter might have been my imagination. The place was small and dark. The floral wallpaper was peeling in spots, stained in others.

"We're not really going to stay here, are we?" Byrd looked a little green.

"Oh, come on, honey," I teased in an innocent yet seductive tone. "I did everything to make our little getaway special."

"What? I...uh...no offense, but I'm...I'm not..."

"What? Am I not pretty enough? Is it 'cause I'm trans?"

He looked like he was about to pass a kidney stone until I burst out laughing. "I'm just messing with you, man. No, we're not staying here."

He let go of a deep breath. “Oh, thank goodness.”

“And lately, I prefer women, anyway. Mostly,” I added.

He raised an eyebrow. “You’re bisexual?”

“Bisexual, pansexual, who knows? After Conor disappeared, I dated this woman for about a month. A corrections officer, no less. Kind of a rebound thing.”

“What was that like?” The curiosity in his voice was palpable. Like he wanted to know but didn’t want to know.

“The sex was fantastic. But I wasn’t in the right headspace for another relationship. I never called her. After a couple weeks of me ignoring her, she dumped me. Not that I blamed her.”

“What did you two, you know, do in bed?”

I clapped him on the shoulder. “A lady has to have her secrets.”

I opened the drawer in the nightstand. One standard copy of the Bible courtesy of the Evangelical Light of the Messiah Church, according to the stamp inside the cover.

“Maybe he really was doing a Bible study.”

I laughed. “Here? Doubt it. But I’m sure God’s name was called upon on multiple occasions. ‘Oh God, that feels incredible. Oh God, don’t stop. Oh God...’”

He was putting his fingers in his ears. “Please stop. I get it. Ha ha.”

I was starting to like having him around. It had been a while since I had someone who was so much fun to torture.

I pulled back the bedcover and examined the sheets. They appeared relatively clean, but one never knew. Certainly not silk.

A cluster of reddish-brown, pinhole-sized dots on the edge of the fitted sheet caught my attention. “Ugh. Okay, I’ve seen enough.”

“Why? What is it? Blood?”

"Sort of." I pointed at the dots on the bedsheet. "That is bedbug poop. They live on human blood."

"Bedbugs? For real?"

"Time to move on." My skin began to crawl, as if I was lying on an ant mound. We hurried out just as my phone rang.

"Jinx Ballou." I tried to ignore the creepy-crawly sensation.

"It's Shea. Where are you?"

"About to leave Scottsdale. How's your damsel in distress?"

"We checked with the domestic violence shelters around town. They're all full up with a waiting list."

"Oh, well, you tried." I should have been more sympathetic, but I still remembered how snotty she'd been the last time I'd seen her.

"We were wondering if she could stay with you."

"With me? Not just no but hell no! I do not need her drama in my life. I'm already trying to help out your buddy Indigo, remember?"

"Well, can you meet us over here? We need to discuss this."

I wanted to tell her there was nothing to discuss, but I didn't. "We'll be there in about half an hour."

22

We took the Loop 202 to the northbound Piestewa Freeway. A wave of sadness hit me like a sledgehammer as we drove past where White Nation had set off a massive bomb last December. The memories and trauma drew me back into the emotional hell I'd been fighting.

At the Dreamy Draw exit, I turned west onto Northern and took that to Phoenix's Sunnyslope neighborhood. The enormous white *S* on Sunnyslope Mountain gleamed like a beacon against the dark green-gray of the craggy hillside. It was after four in the afternoon when we arrived at Vanessa's house. I parked behind Shea's motorcycle.

"Let's gear up," I said, "just in case Vanessa's husband shows."

Byrd nodded, and we pulled on our weapons and vests.

I pounded on the front door. From inside came the yapping of a small dog.

Shea opened the front door. "Glad y'all are here. You learn anything from those good ol' boys in Scottsdale?"

I shrugged. "No, but if you want me to exonerate Indigo,

we need to work together. I don't need to be sidelined with this nonsense."

Shea nodded, guilt written on her face. "I know."

She led us through the living room to a small kitchen, where Fuego and Vanessa sat at a table that looked like a garage sale reject. One corner of the tabletop was broken, revealing layers of particleboard.

Vanessa looked much like the last time I'd seen her. Face swollen and bloodied, arms covered in a patchwork of purple, green, and yellow bruises. Then again, I wasn't looking much better.

She wore a pink Cinderella T-shirt, her hair a ragged mess. A Yorkie with a pink bow atop its head sat in Vanessa's lap, yapping its damn head off at Byrd and me.

"Don't mind Jasmine. She barks at anyone she doesn't know," Vanessa said with a self-deprecating chuckle.

"So what's the deal?" I asked Fuego.

Fuego glanced at Vanessa. "All the local shelters are currently at capacity. Vanessa left a voicemail for a friend of hers but hasn't heard back. We were hoping Vanessa could stay with you until her friend calls her back."

I barked out a laugh. "Are you shitting me? You want to stay at my house after being such a bitch when I was looking for your boyfriend last year? Not fucking likely."

Vanessa's face crumpled. "I know. I'm sorry." She sobbed into her hands.

"Why'd you marry that asswipe after all the shit he's pulled?"

"I...I thought if I married him, he would treat me better, that he would finally love me."

"Yeah, because that always works. Time to wake up from the fairy tale, princess. Freddie is no Prince Charming. I tried to tell you that last time."

"Jinx, ease up on the girl." Byrd put a hand on my shoulder.

"Hey, you want to take her in, be my guest."

"I would, but I don't think my pit bull, Peaches, would get along with Jasmine."

My old companion, guilt, tugged at my heartstrings like a toddler yanking on a mother's sleeve for attention. Was it really my responsibility to deal with Vanessa's bad relationship choices?

"Where are you two staying while you're down here?" I asked Shea.

"Hadn't really thought about it. Any suggestions?"

"I don't spend a lot of time at motels unless I'm looking for a fugitive."

"The Desert View Inn's not far from here," said Byrd. "It's not too pricy, and it's clean."

Shea looked at Fuego, who shrugged. "Sounds okay."

"Great," I said. "The three of you can bunk together."

"Do they allow dogs?" asked Vanessa. "I can't go anywhere without Jasmine. She's my emotional support animal."

"Let's hope to hell they do," I replied. "Because that little four-legged tarantula is not coming to my place."

The quiet of the kitchen was disturbed by the sound of a car pulling into the driveway. Vanessa's eyes lit up with fear. "Freddie," she whispered.

"Stay with her," I told Fuego. "Shea, Byrd, let's go say hello."

Freddie Colton opened the front door to see us with our guns drawn. He was tan and tall and had a sexy bad boy look about him. From the bulge on the side of his jeans, I knew he had a gun tucked inside his waistband. And he wasn't alone. Freddie's companion had a Neanderthal look to him—heavy brow, jet-black hair that had been slicked back.

"Who the fuck are you? Vanessa!"

"We're Vanessa's book club," I said. "Unfortunately, you're not invited. Girls only. You'll have to come back later."

Freddie locked eyes with me. I saw the wheels turning in his mind as he worked out where he knew me from. "You're that bitch that dragged me back to jail. Threatened to blow my dick off if I didn't come along quietly."

I pointed my gun at his crotch. "After all this time, you still remember. What a romantic you are."

"You bitches best get out of my house or..."

"Or what?" asked Shea. "You gonna throw us out? I don't think so."

"Vanessa! Get your scrawny ass in here!" Freddie shouted.

"Vanessa," called Byrd, "you stay right where you are, darling. We got this."

"Boy, you best watch yourself. You think I'm gonna let a black man and a couple bitches come between me and my wife?" Freddie's hand hovered over where his gun hid underneath his shirt.

Byrd shook his head. "You and your friend should walk away and cool off before someone gets hurt."

"Don't you tell me what to do, boy. She's *my* wife. This is *my* house. You can't take what's mine."

"And if we do? Whatcha gonna do, dickhead?" I asked. "Call the cops?"

The anger in his face edged up a few notches. "I'll fucking kill you. Every one of y'all. Vanessa, too, that pathetic little bitch."

"Well, I'm terrified. How about y'all?" I asked.

"Absolutely trembling," Byrd said with dripping sarcasm.

"I may just piss myself, I'm so scared," added Shea.

"Come on, man," said the Neanderthal. "We can hang at my apartment for now."

"Yeah, man," I said. "You little boys go have a playdate at your buddy's apartment."

Freddie pointed at me and said, "Y'all gonna regret this." He and his lumbering companion turned and walked away.

I followed him outside with Shea and Byrd on my heels. "You threatened me the last time, numb nuts. How'd that turn out exactly? I can't remember."

He kept walking with his back to me and flipped me a bird. The tires of his Pontiac Trans Am squealed as they drove off. The three of us returned inside.

"They gone?" Vanessa and her overgrown rat both sat trembling.

"For now. I suggest y'all take Vanessa and get checked into that motel. We can reconvene in the morning and refocus on finding James Fitzgerald's murderer."

"Agreed," said Shea, giving a look to Fuego.

"Y'all investigating that Brother James murder?" asked Vanessa. "I thought the police caught the killer. Some black tranny hooker."

My fist tightened at the slur.

"The cops arrested the wrong person," I muttered. "We're tracking down the real killer."

"And she's not a hooker," Shea growled. "She's a member of our club."

Vanessa looked from Shea to me and back again. "Oh, sorry."

"Enough chitchat," I said. "Y'all get checked in to your motel. I'm going home."

"How'm I supposed to take Jasmine and my stuff on the back of a motorcycle?" asked Vanessa.

I wanted to tell her to call an Uber, but we had no way of knowing how soon Freddie and his buddy might return. Possibly with backup.

"You can ride in my SUV. But if that little rat dog of yours pees or poops on the seat, you can fucking walk for all I care."

"Jasmine's very well trained," she replied, even as the dog resumed yapping at us.

Byrd helped Vanessa load her suitcase into the Gray Ghost. On the ride to the motel, the two of them chatted about dogs. Despite my ever-growing attachment to Diana, my appreciation for canines did not extend to yappy ankle-biters like Jasmine. I focused on dealing with the surge of rush hour traffic.

The Desert View Inn was located on the southbound access road off the I-17, just south of Thunderbird Road. The last time I was here, I'd been ambushed by a couple of fugitives fleeing a murder charge and ended up with a nasty concussion.

I pulled into the overhang by the front door. "Goodbye, Vanessa. Don't keep in touch."

"Thanks for your help, Jinx." She leaned over and planted a kiss on my cheek. Jasmine started barking all over again and just missed giving me a nip.

I sat parked while Vanessa, Shea, and Fuego walked up to the front desk. I needed a second to clear my head before driving back into Phoenix traffic.

"What do you think's going to happen to her?" Byrd asked.

"Don't know. Don't care. As my dad says, 'Not my monkeys, not my circus.'"

"Sounds like a smart man, your dad."

"He is." I took a deep breath, let it out, and pressed Play on my sound system. Polythene Pam's "Tall Girl Posse" started playing. "Let's get out of here. I'm exhausted."

"Hold up." Byrd put a hand on my arm.

Shea was racing out of the lobby with Vanessa shimmying behind carrying the dog.

"What now?" I asked.

Shea came around to my side of the truck. I rolled down the window.

"What now?"

"The motel doesn't allow pets."

"Oh for the love of bacon, are you serious? Did he suggest a place that did?"

"He didn't know. Can she stay with you for the night?"

I was starting to think Wilhelm Penzler had the right idea. Just take a flying leap and end it all.

I scowled at Vanessa, who was cradling her dog and looking particularly pathetic. "Get in the goddamned truck." To Shea, I said, "You owe me big-time. I'll call you in the morning."

23

Shadows were getting long when we arrived at my place. I told Byrd to be back there at eight the following morning. "I'll find a way to make this pay for us one way or another."

"Copy that," he replied. "Good luck." I wasn't sure if he was talking to Vanessa or me.

While he drove off in his car, I escorted Vanessa and her dog into the house through the side door. Diana came bounding toward me. After showering me with kisses, she turned her attention to Jasmine, sniffing warily. The Yorkie yapped and growled at the much larger puppy. Diana replied with a couple of playful barks that seemed to say, "Nice to meet you! Let's play."

"You didn't tell me you had a dog," Vanessa said quietly. She tried to turn her body to keep the two dogs separated, but Diana was determined to get to know the little beast better.

"You didn't ask. But if you'd rather not stay, I'd be happy to call you a taxi."

"He won't bite her, will he?"

"It's she, and no, she probably won't. But if your little rat keeps growling like that, all bets are off."

Vanessa gave Jasmine's behind a gentle swat. "Hush or that giant dog will eat you."

If only. "Let me show you to the spare bedroom."

I led her to the room I used for a home office. There was a double bed, a weight bench, and a dusty set of free weights, with a window that was shaded outside by a shrub I couldn't identify. Some plant that grew red berries in the winter.

She set down Jasmine, who ran off to play chase with Diana.

"So what's the deal with you and the bikers?" Vanessa sat down on the bed.

"One of their members is being framed. I'm helping them get the charges dropped."

"I thought you only went after people who jumped bail."

"Me too," I admitted. "Look, I'm planning on ordering delivery. Your choice, pizza, Chinese, or Greek."

"I've never had Greek before. What do they eat?"

"I'll order a couple of gyros. It's like a gordita burrito but with a mixture of lamb, beef, and a cucumber-sour cream sauce."

"Sounds okay."

I placed the order, then went to my room to get cleaned up. The bruises looked darker, but my face was less swollen than it had been. A hot shower helped wash away most of the day's tension, though it still felt like a giant emptiness inside me was sucking out all my happiness. By the time I returned to the living room, the gyros had arrived.

After dinner, we were watching the latest news story about the string of fatal stabbings attributed to the Valley Slasher when a burst of gunfire erupted on the street.

"Get down!" I pushed Vanessa onto the floor as countless rounds plinked against the Lexan windows. Ducking under the coffee table, I grabbed the .44 Magnum revolver, holding it ready to fire, in case the shooter came through the front door.

As quickly as it started, the gunfire stopped, and the shooter's car roared off down the street.

"Stay put," I told Vanessa.

I raced out the front door and caught a fleeting glimpse of red taillights blazing into the night and around the block.

"Shit!" I hunched over to catch my breath. My heart thundered in my chest. The soles of my feet burned. I realized I was barefoot. I hobbled home to survey the damage.

My next-door neighbor, Adam, came rushing out of the house he shared with his husband, Steve. He was dressed in a T-shirt and shorts with his cell phone to his ear.

He stared at the large revolver in my hand. "Were you shooting at someone?"

"Not me. Some asshole just shot up my house. Y'all okay?"

He nodded. "I called the police. They're on their way. We were watching the *Game of Thrones* finale when we heard the shots. You think they'll be back?"

"Probably not. When the cops get here, send 'em my way. Oh, and thanks for taking care of Diana for me."

"Yeah, sure. This shooting—is it connected to why you were out of town?"

I shook my head. "Don't think so." The bottoms of my feet began to throb. "Have a good night, man."

"Yeah," he said nervously. "You too."

When I returned to examine the damage to the house, my nose twitched at the sharp smell of burnt powder in the air. A line of two-inch-wide snowflakes stretched across the impact-resistant polycarbonate windows, but none of the bullets appeared to have penetrated. Chips in the brick walls revealed a few more rounds had hit. They stopped just short of the door.

Had I been living in my old house, my houseguest and I would have been toast. Conor's renovations paid off yet again. "Thank you, Conor, wherever you are," I whispered to the night.

A trail of bloody footprints led up the walk to where I stood. I lifted my right foot. A smear of blood and grit covered the sole of my foot. Probably stepped on broken glass in the street.

I hobbled inside, trying to avoid bleeding onto my floor.

Vanessa lay on the floor, curled in a fetal position around her whimpering dog.

"You can get up now. Show's over."

"Wha...what was that?"

"A drive-by." I limped to the bathroom and washed the cuts on my foot with a soapy washcloth.

Vanessa followed me. "Who...who?"

"If I had to guess, I'd say that asshole husband of yours. Sounded like his Trans Am. He have any guns?"

"A few. But just for protection."

"Yeah, right. Protection."

I pressed a gauze pad against the wound and taped it in place, then pushed past Vanessa into my bedroom and slipped on a pair of ankle socks and my sneakers.

Vanessa continued to shadow me like a frightened child. "Maybe...maybe we should call the police."

"The neighbors already have." I sat on my bed and took a cleansing breath to clear my head. "Shit. Where's Diana?" I hadn't seen her since before the shooting.

"Who?"

"My dog." I ran down the hall, looking for her. "Diana! Where are you, girl?"

I checked under the bed, in the guest bedroom, the bathrooms, all the places she liked to hang out, but turned up nothing. *Shit!*

My heart started pounding again as worry set in. *Please be outside. Please be okay.* "Diana!"

I grabbed the Smith & Wesson again, along with a flashlight from my kitchen drawer, and rushed out the back. "Diana! Diana!"

The backyard was dark beyond the glow from the kitchen window. A security light on the patio wall had gone out a month ago, and I hadn't bothered to replace it.

"Diana!" Fear crept in my voice. "Where are you, baby?"

A shadow moved in the darkness near the six-foot block fence. Was it her? Or another threat? I raised the revolver as I approached.

Her sudden bark sent my stomach lurching into my throat. It was a miracle I didn't pull the trigger. My night vision sharpened enough to spot her outline patrolling the edge of the fence. She looked at me and gave another bark, then fast-trotted over, tail wagging.

"You okay, baby?" I checked her over but didn't feel any blood. In the distance, sirens wailed. Right on time. "Come on inside."

She followed me into the house. Just as I returned the revolver to its holster under the coffee table, someone pounded on my front door.

I opened it to two uniformed officers. I answered their initial battery of questions. Twenty minutes later, a female plainclothes detective came in. She looked vaguely familiar. Her amber eyes matched the suit she wore, contrasting beautifully with her dark-brown skin. I wondered if we'd met before I quit the force.

"Ms. Ballou?" she asked. "I'm Detective Nicole Clifford from Phoenix PD's Gun Enforcement Squad. I understand you and your guest had some excitement this evening."

"Yeah, you could say that."

Vanessa was in the guest bedroom, speaking with one of the unis. I ushered Detective Clifford inside the living room.

"You have bulletproof windows?" From the armchair she was sitting in, she gestured to the pockmarked windows.

"I inherited the house from my fiancé," I said. "He was a cautious man, both of us professional bail enforcement agents."

She wrote in her notebook. "And where is he?"

A punch of emotion caught me off guard. Tears stung my eyes. "The Piestewa Freeway bomb." I didn't feel like elaborating any further than that.

"I'm sorry for your loss, ma'am." A grave nod of recognition. "Any idea why someone would shoot at your house?"

I put the finger on Vanessa's boyfriend. When pressed for other people with a motive, I provided her names and contact information for the past few fugitives I'd recovered, except for Penzler. Most of the fugitives I'd returned to jail weren't happy about it. But I explained to Clifford that I'd had my skip tracer scrub the Web of my home address. The shooter had to be Colton.

Maybe he had a way of tracking his wife's phone. He was enough of a control freak to do something like that. Or maybe he tailed us without me noticing. I was certainly pissed off enough when I drove her back here that I could have missed a car following me.

"I saw blood on the porch," said the detective. "Was anyone injured during the shooting?"

"I ran outside barefoot to try to see who was shooting. Probably stepped on some glass."

She wrote my answers in her notebook, then had me go through my story again, backward and forward, looking for inconsistencies. When she was satisfied, she told me to stay put while she coordinated with the rest of the investigators.

A peek outside my window revealed that the crime scene unit had pulled up. Intense floodlights lit up the yard like a Broadway stage, while techs scoured the scene, placing markers, taking photographs, and placing evidence in bags.

Three hours later, the circus left with all of the evidence they had found.

Detective Clifford stepped back inside. "We've recovered the brass from the street. Looks like the shooter was using a ten-millimeter semiautomatic handgun."

"Ten mill? That's an unusual caliber."

"Uncommon, but there are a number of models out on the street. Two of the six rounds embedded in the polycarbonate may be clean enough to compare ballistics, but no guarantee we'll find a match in our database."

She gave me her business card as well as the name and number of a local window repair company. I'd most likely call my brother, Jake, anyway, since he renovated houses for a living.

"You're going to pick up Colton, right?" I asked the detective when I walked her to the door to leave.

"Please," begged Vanessa. "Before he comes back and does something worse."

"We'll bring him in. If he's the shooter, we'll take the appropriate action. I promise. I'll let you know what we find out."

"Thanks." I shut the door behind her and collapsed on the couch. "Shit."

Part of me wanted to tell Vanessa to get the hell out of my house and my life. But even if she did, Freddie still might make an encore appearance. Underneath my frustration, I caught myself feeling sorry for her.

I grabbed a bottle of tequila and two glasses from the kitchen. When I returned to the living room, Vanessa was watching a cheesy Christmas movie on the Hallmark Channel. I would've told her to change it to something less insipid, but I was too exhausted to care.

"I'm sorry I got you into this," she said out of the blue, barely touching her tequila.

"Yeah." I didn't know what else to say.

"I'll pay for the damage. Somehow."

"I have insurance. I just want you gone tomorrow. Don't care if you're with one of your little girlfriends, at a motel, or on a park bench."

I drained my glass, enjoying the burn in my throat. After a couple of refills, I shuffled down the hall and collapsed onto my bed. Diana curled up near my feet, tail swishing back and forth. At least someone still loved me.

24

Despite my need for sleep, the incessant yapping and whining of Vanessa's rat dog kept me awake the rest of the night. On the rare occasions I did drift off, I was haunted with nightmares about drive-bys and intruders.

At four o'clock, I gave up the effort. I planted myself at my desk and pored over the case documents—criminal background checks, financials, phone logs, and news stories. On my laptop, I had links to online videos showing Fitzgerald in heated confrontations with passersby. The sick fuck knew how to push people's buttons.

I compiled a list of the most viable suspects for his murder. At the top was Wes Hancock, the father of the girl Fitzgerald had raped.

Below that I added Deneisha Love, the sister of Tamika Love, a trans woman who was murdered a few months back. Deneisha blamed Fitzgerald and his violent rhetoric for inspiring the murderer.

I also listed Gabby Tyson, a woman who claimed Brother James was the deadbeat bio dad of her special-needs child. There were dozens of others who might have murdered Fitzgerald, but I had to start somewhere.

The sky outside was showing morning's first light. I shuffled into the kitchen and started the coffee maker. While it gurgled and hissed, I poured myself a bowl of cereal and perused the news headlines on my phone.

The usual nonsense was going on at the federal level—legal wrangling between the White House and Congress, calls for impeachment, rumors of a potential war with Iran, and two more white men I'd never heard of had announced they were entering the 2020 presidential race.

I scrolled down to the local scene. More stories speculating about the Valley Slasher. One about a family of four killed by a wrong-way driver on the 101. The City of Phoenix was cracking down on dirty swimming pools after six more West Nile virus cases were discovered. And of course, a proposed bill in the Arizona state legislature to allow businesses to discriminate against LGBTQ customers. Same shit, different day.

I tossed the phone aside and realized the house was quiet. No more yapping. Rat dog must've finally worn itself out and gone to sleep after keeping me awake all night. *Mission accomplished, you little shit.*

Diana padded into the kitchen carrying her leash, her claws clicking on the Saltillo tile floor.

"I suppose this means you want to go for your run."

She gave me a look that seemed to say, "Yes, please, Mom." The soulful eyes of a puppy are more powerful than the Borg any day. Resistance really is futile.

I put my dishes in the sink, slipped on my running shoes, and took off with Diana toward Seventh Avenue. Leaving Vanessa alone in my house felt weird. But I needed to get out and burn through all the shit in my head, replacing it with some exercise-generated dopamine.

As my heart rate and breathing fell into their usual rhythm, my mind focused on the Fitzgerald murder. The more I thought about it, the more Wes Hancock, the rape victim's father, seemed the most likely candidate.

He had more motive than anyone. Not that I blamed him, if he'd done the deed. I half wondered if there was a way to get Indigo acquitted without sending Hancock to jail for his service to the community. Probably not.

I arrived home after seven thirty, sweaty and winded but mentally in a better place. Vanessa sat at my kitchen table spoon-feeding canned tuna to Jasmine.

"I hope you don't mind. You weren't here when I got up." She nodded at the empty tuna can.

"I'll just add it to your bill."

She gave me a confused, concerned look.

I shook my head to indicate I was kidding. "I gotta take a shower. You get ahold of your friend yet?"

"I called her again and left a message."

I shook my head in disgust. *How the hell do I get myself into these messes?*

Diana looked at rat dog nibbling the tuna, then at me with a wounded look on her face. I had a strict rule against feeding her people food. Sets a bad precedent. I reached into the pantry and offered Diana a few of her favorite treats, which she carried to her doggy bed in the living room.

The doorbell rang as I was drying off from the shower. I quickly pulled on a T-shirt and jeans. By the time I reached the living room, Vanessa was already letting Shea and Fuego inside.

Diana rushed in to meet the new houseguests. Shea knelt and made baby talk while scratching Diana's ears.

"She's such a cute dog. How old?"

"Nine months. You have one yourself?"

"Nope. Got a twelve-year-old cat named Ninja."

"You live with your niece, too, right?"

Shea turned and gaped at me. "How'd you know that?"

My face warmed from embarrassment. "Don't worry. Not a stalker. Just came up in my background research when I was looking for Indigo."

"Right. Sorry. That makes sense."

"What happened to the front of your house?" Fuego's brow furrowed. "Looks like someone's been using it for target practice."

I jabbed a thumb at Vanessa. "Someone's unhappy husband."

Vanessa hung her head, looking like a kid who'd been sent to her room.

"Anyone hurt?" asked Shea.

"No, but I'm done playing referee in someone else's domestic violence shit." I turned to Vanessa. "You're not staying here any longer. There are motels that allow dogs. I suggest you find one."

"Actually, while you were in the bathroom, my friend Emma called back. I can move in with her for the time being. Problem is...I don't know how we're going to move all my stuff before Freddie gets home at four. So unless he's been arrested..." She clutched Jasmine closer to her chest.

"We can help with that," said Fuego. "We've done a lot of clandestine moves for women in abusive relationships."

"Hold on. Time out." I formed a T with my hands. "I agreed to prove your buddy Indigo innocent provided the Athena Sisterhood helps out. So far, all you've done is put me further in danger by dragging me into this little side drama. And now you're helping her move?" I glowered at Shea. "Maybe I should tell Pima Bail Bonds to revoke the bond and take your house."

Fuego exchanged a glance with Shea. "You're right.

We're here because of Indigo. Shea, go with Jinx to find the murderer. I'll put the word out to the club to come down and help Vanessa with the move."

Shea turned to me. "Does that work for you?"

"I suppose so." To Vanessa, I said, "Grab your shit."

The doorbell rang. I checked the peephole and saw Byrd in full gear on my doorstep. With all the chaos, I'd almost forgotten he was helping out. I let him in.

"Uh, did you know that someone—"

"Shot up my house? Not at all."

"Do I want to know?" Byrd looked concerned.

I shook my head. "Not really."

"So what's our game plan?"

While Vanessa packed up her stuff in the guest bedroom, I led Byrd, Shea, and Fuego to the kitchen and laid out the case paperwork. "Wes Hancock seems our most likely suspect. Fitzgerald raped his daughter. Over Hancock's objections, the county prosecutor accepted a guilty plea for misdemeanor assault. No jail time. Didn't have to register as a sex offender. Hancock was furious."

"Can ya blame him?" asked Shea.

"Hancock has made a number of veiled threats on social media while ranting how the legal system protects rapists and does nothing to protect victims."

"How do we prove he killed Fitzgerald?" asked Fuego.

"It comes down to means, motive, and opportunity. He obviously has motive. Did he have the physical means to kill Fitzgerald? Possibly. Fitzgerald's official cause of death was a GSW to the head, but the crime scene photos show he was severely beaten and had his dick chopped off prior to the fatal shot. Fitzgerald was a big guy. Maybe Hancock is too. We won't know until we meet him.

"As for opportunity, he provided an alibi for the day of the murder. I don't see in the discovery documents that the police verified it. They arrested Indigo so quickly, they may not have investigated Hancock as thoroughly as they should."

Shea replied, "Sounds like a solid lead. Where do we find him?"

I pulled up his contact information. "Off Forty-Fourth Street and Camelback in Phoenix."

"Not far from Scottsdale," Byrd added.

"Exactly. Let me give him a call, make sure he's home. If so, we'll pay him a visit." I dialed the number, and Wes Hancock picked up on the fourth ring.

"I have no more comments to the press on that goddamned preacher's death."

"I'm not a reporter, Mr. Hancock. My name's Jinx Ballou. I'm a fugitive recovery agent working on a case related to your daughter's assault. I need your help tracking down a fugitive." I felt bad about dancing around the truth, considering what his family had been through.

"My daughter was *raped*, not just assaulted!"

"Of course, I'm sorry. But I could really use your help. The person I've been hired to track down has connections with James Fitzgerald. And the case is possibly tied to Alexandra's rape."

"Who are you looking for?"

"Unfortunately, I'm not at liberty to say. But I'm hoping you might provide me with some information that could lead to his capture. Could I stop by your home and ask you some questions?"

"You have questions, ask them now."

I didn't want to ask them on the phone because as soon as he got wind of my objective, he could just hang up. "Because of the sensitive nature of this investigation, it would be better if we met in person. And if at any time you want to end the interview, you say so, and I will leave."

There was silence on the line for a moment before he answered. "All right. I'm just sick of all this crap. Bad enough that sick son of a bitch raped my daughter. Then the whole pathetic excuse of a plea deal, not to mention being harassed by the media every time I turn around."

"I understand. You and your daughter have my sincere sympathies."

"I'll be home until ten this morning. Then I have to go to work. You have the address?"

"I do. I'll be there shortly. And Mr. Hancock, I greatly appreciate this."

25

Fuego and Shea convinced a half dozen of their fellow bikers to drive down to the valley and help Vanessa move to her friend Emma's place. Shea would stick with Byrd and me to solve Fitzgerald's murder.

Byrd, Vanessa, her dog, and I piled into the Gray Ghost and drove to Emma's, while Fuego and Shea followed behind on their motorcycles. The house wasn't far from Vanessa's but looked better maintained.

"Thanks for your help," said Vanessa as she climbed out with the dog under her arm. "Sorry about your house."

"Just stay out of my life, okay? And if you still got a brain in your head, you'll stay out of Freddie's." Without another word, I drove off.

The Hancocks lived in east Phoenix's Arcadia District in a white wood and brick ranch-style house trimmed with black faux shutters. A white picket fence with brick posts every ten feet encircled a perfectly manicured yard that was lush and green. A cobblestone walk led from the street to the front porch, where small flowering plants bloomed in ceramic pots.

Byrd and I got out of the Gray Ghost, leaving our gear inside but sporting our bail enforcement badges around our necks.

Shea parked her motorcycle just past the truck.

"Ditch the biker vest and sidearm," I told her. "I want to keep our talk with Hancock low-key and professional."

"What if he's the killer and realizes we're onto him?"

"Then concealed only. I don't want to further traumatize him if he's innocent."

Shea's expression told me she wasn't keen on the idea, but she stashed her vest and gun, holster and all, in a trunk on the back of her bike. "So what's the game plan, madam bounty hunter?"

"I want to establish a rapport with him if I can. Gain his trust before I start asking questions related to Fitzgerald's murder."

I felt out of my element. It had been nearly ten years since I was a cop. Even then, my experience looking into homicide cases was limited to canvassing areas near crime scenes and taking witness statements. No in-depth interrogations pressing suspects for confessions.

After I rang the bell, Mr. Hancock opened the door. According to his file, he was thirty-eight. But from the bags under his eyes, he looked ten years older.

"You Agent Ballou?"

"I am. These are my associates, Jubal Byrd and Shea Stevens. May we come inside?"

Hancock glanced at us. "Come on in."

The interior of the house was furnished with mid-century modern furniture and an abundance of metallic and glass artwork. He led us to a couch and matching chairs.

"Can I offer you some water or coffee?"

Byrd and I declined. Shea agreed to some water.

"Mr. Hancock," I said when he returned with a bottle for Shea, "let me say how sorry I am for what happened to your daughter, Alexandra. When I was a teen, I was brutally assaulted. The perpetrator fled the jurisdiction before he could be brought to justice. So I appreciate what y'all have been through."

"Thank you," he said, staring at his hands.

"Did James Fitzgerald know Alexandra prior to the rape?"

His body tensed at the mention of Fitzgerald's name. "No. He showed up one day outside her high school, shouting the most disgusting things and carrying hateful signs."

"He was protesting outside a high school?" Byrd asked. "How is that legal?"

"Parents complained, but the police told us that as long as he was outside the fence, there was nothing they could do. He was there for three days, shouting how girls who wore makeup were asking to be raped. Alex could hear him in her classroom."

"Disgusting pervert!" Shea muttered.

"When Fitzgerald was protesting, did Alex engage with him in any way?" I asked. It wasn't strictly relevant to our investigation, but I was curious.

"I don't know. Nothing to deserve being raped."

"Of course not. I just wondered why he targeted her."

"Who knows? When Alex..." Hancock's voice shook with equal measures of sorrow and violence. "She said he followed her home from school in his car. We don't live far, and ever since she turned thirteen, my wife and I agreed to let her walk home, provided she's with at least two of her friends."

His face darkened. "But that day, one of her friends stayed home with the flu. The other had an after-school activity. Alex was supposed to call me when she didn't have anyone to walk home with. But she...she didn't want to bother me at work." Tears ran down his face. I grabbed a tissue from a nearby box.

"Thanks." He took a deep breath and let it out. "Alex walked home alone. She was in the neighborhood when he pulled alongside her in his Volvo. He apologized for the things he'd said in front of the school and offered to drive her to Cold Stone Creamery to discuss their differing viewpoints. Despite our warnings about strangers in cars, she got in."

His fists were so tight, his knuckles were bone white. "He slipped Rohypnol into her drink. She woke up in some sleazy Scottsdale motel where he...he hurt her." His head shook violently, and he rubbed at his eyes as if trying to clear the horrific images in his head. "He'd taken pictures of her...nude pictures. Said if she told anyone, he'd post the photos to the internet for all her friends to see."

"What a wicked thing to say," Byrd grumbled.

"How did she get back home?" I asked.

"He drove her. When her mom and I got home, we knew right away something was wrong. After a lot of encouragement, she told us what happened." He pounded a side table so hard a couple of knickknacks fell over.

Now we were getting somewhere. "What did you and your wife do, Mr. Hancock?" I asked.

"My wife took Alex to the hospital. I...I drove to the motel, but he was gone. I managed to get a home address from the little twerp in the front office. Fitzgerald's house wasn't far from the motel. I pounded on his front door till he opened it. God knows, I...I'm not a violent man, but..." He shook his head, clearly writhing in emotional pain.

"We understand, Mr. Hancock," said Byrd. "Any loving father would feel the same way."

Rage rolled off of Hancock in waves. I could almost taste it in the air. "I wanted to kill that man right then and there. Got in a few punches before the cops showed up. They took me to the Scottsdale police station. That damned Sam Elliott look-alike they call a detective kept asking ridiculous questions. Was Alex sexually active? What was she wearing? Did she ever drink alcohol or use drugs? Like getting raped was somehow her fault.

"When they finally found him guilty, I thought finally we'd get some justice. But no, that idiotic judge didn't send him to prison. Six months of probation, for God's sake. Didn't even have to register as a sex offender. After what he did to my daughter and who knows how many girls before that."

"I can imagine how that made you feel," I said. "I felt the same way when my attacker made bail and then disappeared."

"Pardon the profanity, but I wanted to fucking kill them all. Brother James, the cops, the judge."

I knew the time had come to ask the ugly questions. "Where were you the night that Fitzgerald was killed?"

"What?"

I could tell from his expression that the question had caught him flat-footed. "You think I killed that monster?"

"No, I don't. But for my paperwork, I need to put down something, or my boss will think I'm slacking off."

"I...I don't know where I was...I think the three of us went to dinner and then a movie."

"What movie did you see?"

"What difference does it make?"

"It doesn't, I just need it for my report."

"Um...that female superhero movie."

"*Captain Marvel*?" I asked.

"Yeah, that was it."

"Good. That helps. I know it sounds stupid. Where'd you have dinner?"

He gave me a quizzical look.

I held up my hands apologetically. "I know. I don't believe you killed him. My boss is a hard ass for details."

"Pei Wei, I think. Indian School and Forty-Fourth Street."

"And just so I can tell my boss I officially asked, did you kill James Fitzgerald?"

"No. I did not. But whoever did deserves the goddamn Medal of Honor. I heard the police arrested someone. Some hooker, I think."

"She's not a goddamned hooker," growled Shea. "And she didn't kill him either."

I put a hand on Shea's knee and gave her a look that told her to keep it together.

Hancock narrowed his gaze at Shea, then turned back to me. "All I know is what I heard on the news. I'm glad he's dead, but I didn't kill him."

I figured we'd gotten as much out of him as we were going to. I stood up. Shea and Byrd followed my lead. "Thanks for answering our questions, Mr. Hancock."

Hancock walked us to the front door. "I still don't understand why you're here. You mentioned a fugitive. What's this have to do with what happened to Alex?"

I stepped out into the warm sunshine. "I wish I could tell you, but I can't reveal the details for legal reasons. I can assure you, this will help bring them to justice."

"Well, good luck, I guess."

When the three of us reached the Gray Ghost, Byrd asked, "So, what do ya think? Did he do it?"

"Possibly," I replied.

"What about his alibi?" asked Byrd.

"I plan to check it out," I said. "If he's telling the truth, he probably charged the dinner and the movie. All we got to do is check his bank statement. If the alibi checks out, he's off the hook, and we'll move on."

I called Becca and told her the story. She agreed to double-check the alibi and get back to us within the hour.

"I found the two other people on your suspect list. Deneisha Love was the sister of Tamika Love, the trans woman whose murderer was inspired by Fitzgerald's rants. She moved to live with her father in New Jersey two weeks before Fitzgerald bought the farm. Also, she's only seventeen. I'm guessing she's not your killer."

"What about the mother of the special-needs child?"

"I did a little more digging into her. Gabby Tyson was in jail the night of Fitzgerald's death for possession of a controlled substance. Apparently, she has a heroin addiction. Right now, she's in a treatment center in Albuquerque and has been for the past forty-five days."

"All right. Thanks for the info. Let me know when you can confirm Hancock's alibi."

"Will do."

I hung up, frustrated. My list of prime suspects was getting short, but I wasn't any closer to finding the murderer.

"So where to now?" asked Shea.

"I want to see where Fitzgerald lived. I'm sure the cops already went over it with a fine-toothed comb, but as much as they were gunning after Indigo, maybe they missed something. Or more accurately dismissed something that might've led to the killer."

"How will we get in?" Byrd asked.

I grinned. "We'll find a way."

"Can we do that?" asked Byrd. "Legally, I mean."

"With Fitzgerald dead, who's going to complain if we pop in and look around?"

Byrd shook his head. "Maurice hired us to return Pearson to custody. Doing a little investigating is one thing, but you're talking breaking and entering. I don't know if I'm comfortable with this."

"Says the man vandalizing a perfectly good motel room wall."

I could have sworn he blushed, but with his dark skin, it was hard to tell.

Shea put a hand on his shoulder. "Look, Mr. Boy Scout, a friend of mine is being steamrolled for the murder of a piece-of-shit rapist. And you're uncomfortable looking through his house?"

"Fine," he replied. "How do we get in? Break down the door with the battering ram?"

"Too noisy. I got a better solution." Shea pulled a narrow leather case from her biker vest. I had a similar set of picklocks in the Gray Ghost. I was beginning to like this woman.

I gave Fitzgerald's address to Shea in case we got separated, then Byrd and I piled into the Gray Ghost.

26

Fitzgerald had lived in an upscale neighborhood near Pima Road north of Chaparral Road. The trees were mature, lawns manicured and green, the houses well-kept. Like something out of *Leave It To Beaver*, only in this scenario, Eddie Haskell was a pedophile rapist.

The house sat on the corner with a driveway and garage on one street and the front door on the other. The mailbox was shaped to look like a church. What a joke!

A late-model Buick sat in the open garage. Someone was home. My hope of sneaking in unnoticed evaporated. I parked past the driveway, next to an orange tree covered with star-shaped white blossoms.

"Did Fitzgerald have a roommate?" asked Byrd.

"Nothing in the paperwork mentioned it. I guess we'll go say howdy."

My phone started playing the *Game of Thrones* ringtone.

"Anything on Hancock's alibi?" I asked Becca.

"According to his bank records, he did purchase three tickets last month to see a movie at the Esplanade AMC Theater on the same day he purchased a meal at Pei Wei."

"So his alibi checks out."

"Not exactly. The dinner and movie tickets were charged two days *after* James Fitzgerald's body was discovered."

"So the alibi's bogus."

"So it appears."

"Okay, thanks for the 411. One more thing. I need you to run a plate for me." I read her the license plate off the Buick.

"Okay, let me log in to the database." I heard some key clicks. "The Buick belongs to Michael Andrew Wilkes."

The name sounded familiar. "The head of Fitzgerald's church of hate?"

"Yep." More key clicks on her end. "Let's see, ah, here we are, Michael Andrew Wilkes. Born in 1949, height five five, weight one thirty. Blah, blah, blah. What else do you want to know?"

"What's his background?"

Her fingers clicked away. "Checking NCIC. He has a sheet. Michael Wilkes, aka Elder Michael. A laundry list of misdemeanors—trespassing and harassment mostly—though he did a nine-month stint for assault back in the 1980s."

"Imagine my surprise."

"Currently listed as the head pastor of the Evangelical Light of the Messiah Church. Served in the Marine Corps during Vietnam. Ho, ho! Dishonorable discharge. Doesn't list why. Bummer. Registered owner of Colt .45, a Beretta 92, and an AR-15. Geez, what is it with Evangelicals and firearms? Let's check out his social media accounts... oh, wow! This guy is completely off his rocker."

"Why?"

"Wilkes's page is filled these dark, poorly Photoshopped memes depicting demons, torture, and hellfire but with provocative captions. Like Dante's *Inferno* meets the *National Enquirer*. He repeatedly calls women whores, refers to African Americans as mud people and jungle bunnies, and says queer people are children of Satan that must be destroyed before the Messiah will come again."

"Praise Jesus!" I mocked. "Sounds like a real charmer."

"Man, these memes are horrific. Here's one with a photo of an underwear-clad teenage girl in a suggestive pose. Caption reads 'Evil seductress falsely accused our Brother James of rape.' Misspelled the words *seductress* and *accused*."

"Funny how ignorant and hateful go hand in hand," I mused.

"There's another with a photo of Zia Pearson's face pasted onto a succubus body. Text claims Fitzgerald was murdered by the Negro whore of Babylon. Yowza! This guy takes toxic masculinity, racism, and radicalized Christianity to a whole new level."

"Why has social media not banned this guy?"

"You have to ask?"

I knew the answer. "Okay, thanks for the info."

"Watch your back, girl. This guy is seriously twisted. Old but twisted."

"Don't worry. I've got Byrd and Stevens with me. Wilkes would be an idiot to try anything."

Byrd and I got out of the Pathfinder and met Shea still on her bike, once again wearing her biker vest, a Glock on her right hip.

"So," she said, "I'm guessing breaking in is out of the question."

"The car and house belong to Michael Wilkes, a mental case who calls himself Elder Michael. Fitzgerald's boss, apparently. From what Becca tells me, this guy is like

Brother James on acid." I opted not to share with Shea what he'd called Indigo.

"We going in?" asked Shea.

"Absolutely. I don't know if we'll find anything helpful, but we don't know unless we look." I glanced at the house. "Let's gear up. Wilkes is an old guy, but he's clearly off his rocker and may be armed."

With weapons, vests, and badges in place, the three of us walked around to the other side of the house. I checked the mailbox and rifled through what was there—a couple of utility bills, some Netflix movies, and the latest issue of *Playgirl* magazine addressed to Wilkes.

Now why would an old man get a porno magazine filled with naked men? Another closeted gay man consumed with self-hatred?

I picked up his copy of the *Arizona Republic* on the way to the front door and rang the doorbell.

A few minutes later, an art deco speakeasy grille in the door opened with a wrinkled face peering out.

"What do you want?"

"For starters, here's your mail and newspaper." I held them out to him. "I hear this issue of *Playgirl* has some really hot guys in it. You into hot guys, Mr. Wilkes?"

The speakeasy grille closed, and the door opened. A hunched man with no chin and pouty eyes stood with the assistance of a cane. He was dressed in a sweatshirt and sweatpants.

He snatched the mail and paper out of my hand. "My name is Elder Michael. And for your information, some pervert thought it'd be funny to send me a subscription to this filth. Now why are you people darkening my doorstep?"

I held up my badge. "We're looking into the death of James Fitzgerald."

"I thought the police already arrested someone. That Negro tranny whore."

"Fucking bigot!" Shea muttered under her breath.

I put my arm out to keep her from lunging at him.

"New evidence has come to light that exonerates the African American woman. So we are conducting a further investigation. You were Brother James's boss, correct?"

"I am the pastor of our church. Brother James, God rest his soul, was one of our disciples."

Byrd snorted. "Disciples, right."

I gave him a look that said, *Don't blow this.*

Byrd stood silent, looking like he'd swallowed a turd.

"And where is your church located? I couldn't find an address for it on Google."

"We are a private congregation. The location is kept confidential due to security concerns. We get a lot of death threats."

"Gee, I wonder why," said Shea.

"Brother James used to live here, correct?"

"Yes. Your fellow officers already tore up his room once looking for clues. What more do you people want?"

Impersonating an officer was illegal. But if Wilkes here mistakenly jumped to the wrong conclusion, I wasn't under any legal obligation to disabuse him of the notion.

"Because of recent developments in the case, we'll need to take a second look."

"Do you have a warrant?" Wilkes stood defiantly, or at least as defiantly as he could while using a cane for support.

"You do want Brother James's killer brought to justice, don't you?" asked Byrd. Good to see he was on board.

"Of course I do. What kind of stupid question is that?"

"Seems like you don't want us to look around again.

Like maybe you have something to hide. Makes you look guilty, to be honest."

"Guilty? Me? How dare you!" He crossed his arms and engaged me in a staring match.

After a few minutes, he sighed. "Very well. You two can come in but not her." Wilkes stabbed a bony finger at Shea. "She looks like one of them hooligan homosexuals."

"Her? She's one of our undercover agents." Sounded legit, anyway.

"I don't want her in my house." Wilkes's jaw was set. "She can wait outside."

I took Shea aside. "Poke around the garage. See if you can find anything of interest," I whispered.

She nodded and walked off.

I turned back to Elder Michael. "So, give us the grand tour."

He harrumphed and slowly shuffled away from the front door, his cane clomp-clomp-clomping along the floor. Byrd and I followed him inside.

27

A hallway lined with artwork in gilded frames ran the length of the house. Most were copies of Renaissance paintings with a gruesome Biblical theme—crucified Jesus in agony, saints being martyred in horrific ways, and depictions of hell. I recognized a few from an art appreciation course I'd taken in college—Bosch's *The Garden of Earthly Delights*, Grünewald's *The Temptation of St. Anthony*, and David's *The Judgement of Cambyses*.

One, which was less gruesome, I identified as Rembrandt's *The Return of the Prodigal Son*. I suppressed a laugh as I passed it. It had always looked like a man giving a blow job to another.

An open door on the left revealed an office with an antique walnut desk and matching bookshelves lining the walls.

"This is my office," Wilkes said, shuffling past.

"Mind if we have a look?" Never hurt to ask.

"I do mind. It is private and has nothing to do with Brother James's untimely death."

We continued down the hall.

"He was renting a room at the Cactus Inn twice a month," I said. "Why exactly was he doing that?"

"Brother James conducted Bible studies with prospective members of our church. Part of our vetting process."

"Bible studies?" Byrd asked in a disbelieving tone. "At a motel advertising porn channels and frequented by hookers?"

Wilkes fixed him with a stern look. "We preach to sinners, not to saints."

"We'll need a list of the people he met with there over the past few months, along with their contact information."

"That information is strictly confidential."

"Someone he met with recently could well be the killer," replied Byrd.

"What motive would any of them have to kill Brother James?"

I scoffed. "Oh, let me think. He was a rapist, a homophobe, and a racist."

"Brother James was a godly man. And no one he was meeting with had any motive to harm him. We are very careful in our screening process."

"Nevertheless, I want those names," I pressed.

"I don't care what you want, young lady. I won't do it. Arrest me if you like. I know my rights."

I exchanged a glance with Byrd. "Show us Brother James's room."

We continued slowly down the hall past a spacious sunken living room with large windows overlooking the front lawn. On the other side was a kitchen, then a den with a couch set and an old tube television.

"What's here?" Byrd rapped on a closed door on the right.

"The garage."

I nodded and continued on until we came to an open

door on the left. Elder Michael pointed inside. "This was Brother James's room."

I flicked on the overhead light. A double bed was bordered by a small bookcase on one side and a four-drawer upright dresser on the other. A small desk and a separate three-drawer vertical file cabinet stood at the opposite side of the room.

"Thank you," I said dismissively to Wilkes. "We'll let you know when we're done."

Wilkes glared at the two of us, then slowly clomped back down the hallway.

"Makes me sick the way he's perverted Christ's teachings," grumbled Byrd.

"Let's focus on searching this place. Maybe we'll get lucky and find something that implicates Wilkes." I gave him a wink, but he just frowned.

I opened the file cabinet; it was empty. The center drawer in the desk had also been cleaned out except for two paper clips, a ballpoint pen with no cap, and thirteen cents in change. Atop the desk sat a flat-screen monitor, a pencil cup, and a small framed print of Jesus with long blond hair. No computer, but there was a rectangular impression in the carpet underneath the desk.

"Looks like someone took Fitzgerald's computer," I said.

"Probably the cops." Byrd checked under the bed and between the mattress and box spring.

"There wasn't any mention of it in the discovery files Rebecca Li sent."

"You think Wilkes got rid of it before the cops showed up?"

I shrugged. "I wouldn't put anything past a man like Wilkes."

"I wouldn't put anything past those cops. That guy with the cowboy hat struck me like he was hiding something."

"Maybe he knows his case is full of holes and is afraid we'll expose them."

Byrd and I spent fifteen minutes searching the shelves, the closet, the bathroom, and every nook and drawer of the room. I checked all of the pockets in his clothes for notes. Inspected underneath drawers for clues. I did find a note with a list of what appeared to be computer passwords, but it was useless without the computer itself. I wasn't likely to be getting my hands on it. Still, I tucked the list away, just in case.

Despite our best efforts, we found nothing that might indicate who killed Fitzgerald.

I was about to suggest we wrap up our search when the ratcheting of a pistol hammer caught my attention.

Wilkes stood in the doorway, holding a .45-caliber Colt pistol in his trembling hand. "Who the heck are you people?"

I stood up, my back sore from stooping and snooping. "Like I said, we're investigating Brother James's mur—"

"Don't lie to me. I just spoke with Detective Atkinson. That case is closed. That Negro tranny's still charged with his murder."

"Mr. Wilkes, please put down the gun," said Byrd in a soothing voice.

"My name is Elder Michael, boy! And don't you forget it."

"Elder Michael, I understand you're upset." I shot him a reassuring smile. "We are independent investigators, and we have evidence that exonerates the woman that Scottsdale PD arrested. We are just trying to ascertain the truth."

"The truth is that tranny whore murdered my colleague. Her DNA proves it. I don't know what you people are up to, but you have no business being in my house, pretending to be cops."

"We never said we were cops. Only that we were investigating the murder, which is the truth. But seeing as how you're upset, we'll leave and get out of your hair."

"Oh no you don't. The real cops are on their way. You're not going anywhere. If you try to leave, I'd be within my rights to shoot you."

"Try it, ya little fucker." Shea pressed her Glock to the back of the old man's head. "I'll splatter your brains all over this room."

Wilkes's left eye twitched, and his mouth twisted into a snarl. After several long seconds, he laid the weapon on the nearby dresser. "You people will burn in hell for all eternity. And I will rejoice in your suffering."

"We'll keep that in mind." I grabbed the Colt from the dresser, ejected the magazine, and popped the round from the chamber, catching it in my free hand. I pocketed the magazine and extra round, then handed him back the unloaded pistol. "Until then, we're going to find out who really killed your little buddy and clear our friend."

We walked out the front door and convened between the Gray Ghost and Shea's motorcycle.

"Well, that was a waste of time," Byrd said.

"Not necessarily." Shea opened the top case on the back of her bike and pulled out a folder filled with papers.

"You find something?" I asked.

"A banker box in the garage contained some legal documents. Not sure if they shed any light on what happened or not." Shea handed me the folder.

I flipped through the papers. "There's a nondisclosure agreement and a severance agreement. Fitzgerald was leaving the fold. Wilkes didn't want him spilling any dirty secrets apparently."

"Could go to motive," added Byrd.

"Possibly. No doubt there was some bad blood between

the two. But this parting of the ways seems mutual. Why kill Fitzgerald if he was already leaving? Doesn't make sense."

Shea's face fell in obvious disappointment. "Well, shit."

I clapped her on the arm. "Hey, it's another piece in the puzzle. Right now, Hancock's still our prime suspect, especially since his alibi was bogus. I say we press him, see if he'll crack and confess."

"And if he doesn't?"

"We'll keep digging until we come up with something more definitive. Any word from Fuego on getting Vanessa moved?"

"Yeah, she said a half dozen members of the MC showed up and moved her stuff to her friend Emma Kahn's house. No sign of the abusive husband. Quick and clean and no caffeine."

"Glad to hear it. Because if she spent another night at my place, I was going to strangle her and feed that little rat to my golden retriever. Let's go pay another visit to Mr. Hancock."

28

A green '70s-model muscle car parked on the street started up as we drove out of Wilkes's neighborhood. It was still a few cars behind Shea when I turned left onto Camelback Road.

"Looks like we got company," I said.

Byrd glanced back. "The '71 Nova? You think they're following us?"

"One way to find out." I made an abrupt turn south on Scottsdale Road just as the turn arrow switched from green to yellow. I glanced in my rearview. Shea squeaked through just as the light went red.

"They still tailing us?" I focused on the heavy congestion around Scottsdale Fashion Park. From behind us came a squeal of brakes and a blaring of horns.

"Yup. You think it's the guy who shot up your house?" asked Byrd.

"Freddie Colton drives a Pontiac Trans Am."

"Maybe it wasn't Colton last night. You said it sounded like a sports car."

A chill ran down my spine. "Who else would try to kill me? I haven't pissed anyone off lately."

"Other than the FBI, the county prosecutor, the Athena Sisterhood..." Byrd chuckled.

"I'm working with the Athena Sisterhood," I clarified. "And I don't think the feds or the Maricopa County Attorney's Office shoot up people's houses or drive classic muscle cars."

"The guy at the Cactus Inn."

"Why would he be after us? I paid him for the info and even rented a room."

"Maybe he doesn't like people asking too many questions."

I shook my head and confirmed the Nova was still behind us.

"Old Man Wilkes, perhaps."

"Doesn't track." I turned west on Indian School Road. The Nova stayed with us.

"Someone's interested enough to keep tabs on you. Maybe you have a rabid fan who likes when you dress up as Wonder Woman. Like a stalker."

A chill ran through me. I'd had a stalker once who had left a gift on my front doorstep in the form of a dead newspaper reporter. The stalker turned out to be Milo Volkov, the Chechen gangster whose brother, Sergei, was Penzler's boss. Maybe Sergei was looking to tie up some loose ends. Loose ends like me.

The Nova continued to tail us up Sixty-Fourth Avenue and back onto Camelback. I pulled into the right lane, intentionally getting stuck behind one of the city buses that was stopped while passengers boarded. The Nova sat a few cars behind us for a minute before jumping back into the left lane, cutting off a delivery truck. It happened so fast I wasn't able to catch a license plate.

As the bus resumed its route, my phone rang. I answered it in speaker mode.

"Ballou Fugitive Recovery."

"Is this Detective Ballou?" asked a familiar male voice with a western twang.

"This is Jinx Ballou."

"Well, howdy, Miss Ballou. This is Detective Atkinson with Scottsdale PD."

Aw shit. "How's it going, Detective?"

"Funny you should ask. I just had a most interesting conversation with a certain man of the cloth asking why a couple of my detectives had reopened the case into Fitzgerald's death."

"Is that so?"

"Miss Ballou, there's an old saying, 'Don't dig for water under the outhouse.' Last I checked, you're no longer a law enforcement officer, much less a member of my squad."

"I never told Michael Wilkes we were police officers. I simply explained that we were looking for Brother James's killer and had reason to believe that Zia Pearson was falsely accused."

"Tread softly, Miss Ballou. I don't appreciate people interfering in my cases. Neither does the county attorney's office. I suggest you and your little posse focus on returning Pearson to custody."

"I have a PI license, Atkinson. I'm well within my rights to track down exculpatory evidence that you and your buddy Torres missed."

"Watch yourself, little lady. Hate to see you sharing a cell with your tranny friend." He hung up.

"Goddamn that fucking man," I said when we pulled onto Hancock's street.

"Jinx..."

"Sorry...golly darn that f-ing man." In my mind, it still sounded like *goddamn that fucking man*.

"Better." Byrd sighed. "The more that guy Atkinson talks, the more I want to blow his case out of the water."

"You and me both," I replied.

I pulled into Hancock's driveway.

"You notice that green Nova behind me?" asked Shea after we got out.

"We noticed. May be nothing, but we need to be ready in case they show up again."

I rang Hancock's doorbell. When there was no response after a few minutes, I rang it again.

"Maybe he's not home," said Byrd.

"Should we let ourselves in?" asked Shea.

I pointed at the vertical window beside the door. There was just enough light inside to see a security panel on the wall. The lights told me it was armed. "Place is alarmed. We're here to talk to Hancock, not search his house."

Shea shook her head. "You're no fun."

I called Hancock, listening for a ringtone inside the house. The call rang a few times, but I heard nothing from inside. On the fourth ring, the call went to voicemail.

"Hi, Mr. Hancock. I hate to bother you again, but I do have a few remaining questions. If you could give me a call back, I'd appreciate it." I left my number and hung up.

Had I made a mistake in making the deal with the Athena Sisterhood? Finding fugitives was one thing. Solving a murder that the cops got wrong was a completely different skill set.

"When Fitzgerald was murdered, he obviously wasn't alone," I said to my colleagues.

"No doubt fucking one of the dancers from next door," said Shea.

Byrd looked like he'd been sucking on a lemon.

"Do the dancers at Naughty's moonlight as hookers?" I asked her.

"What do you think?" She smirked. "But I don't see a hooker murdering a john."

"Unless he got too rough," suggested Byrd, "trying to act out his little rape fantasies."

"So we have motive, potentially opportunity. But means?" I wondered aloud. "Brother James was a big man. A woman could shoot a guy like that. Even chop off his manhood. But from the crime scene photos, he looked like he'd gone twelve rounds with a heavyweight champ."

"Maybe her pimp did it. One of the bouncers from the club, perhaps," added Shea.

Byrd nodded. "Seems reasonable."

I looked at Shea. "Y'all spent a few hours at the club that night. Think we could speak to some of the dancers? Find out if any of them were doing sex work on the side? Or would know who might have been meeting Brother James next door."

"I don't know, Jinx. We were there, but honestly, I don't remember any names. Sapphire. Precious. Chastity. After a few rounds, the stage names all sound the same."

An idea popped into my head. I pulled out my phone. "Hey, Amber, it's Jinx."

"Jinxie! Oh my Godiva! How are you, girl? You know, I still owe you that lap dance for helping me out that time."

Amber Chaney and I had been close friends for years, having first met at the Phoenix Gender Alliance. At one point, the trauma and depression of transitioning got the best of her.

I found her after an attempted suicide and took her to the ER. In time, she found the determination to turn things around. She got work as an exotic dancer and earned enough money for her gender confirmation surgery.

For the past few years, she'd been attending Arizona State University during the day and dancing at night. How she found the energy to do both, I'd never know.

"You helped me track down those fascists last December," I told her. "I'd say we're even. How's school?"

"If I pass my finals next week, I'll get my degree and hang up my G-string for good. I already have a job offer from Hilton and Hodge Accounting."

"That's awesome, Amber!"

"You sure I can't interest you in a lap dance? Last chance!"

"I appreciate the offer, but you're like my little sister. It'd be a little awkward."

"Oh, poo! You never wanna play! How about that sweet Irish honey of yours?"

"You didn't hear? He...uh..." A wave of emotion blindsided me like a sucker punch to the solar plexus. "We're not together anymore."

"Seriously? I'm so sorry, sweetie."

"Listen, Amber, I'm calling because I need your help on another case."

"Really? At this rate, you may owe me a lap dance," she said with a chuckle.

"You know anyone dancing at Naughty's Cabaret in Scottsdale?"

"That slime pit? That's one of the clubs run by those Russian gangsters."

A knot formed in my stomach. "The Volkovs?"

"Yep. They own Naughty's and that sleazy motel next door."

"Shit." Not what I wanted to hear.

"Why the interest in Naughty's?"

"I'm working on that case with the preacher who was

murdered next door. I suspect he was sleeping with one of the dancers, and things went bad."

"Wait, that preacher who's always saying queers should be put to death?"

"That's him. Or was until someone shot him. A trans woman is being framed for the murder. Got sent to a men's lockup. You can imagine what happened."

"I remember reading about that. Let me make some calls. I'll be in touch."

"I'd appreciate that, Amber."

"Take care of yourself, sweetie!"

"You too." I turned to Byrd and Shea, who were looking at me impatiently.

"A friend of mine may know a dancer at Naughty's."

"What do we do in the meantime?" asked Shea.

I looked at my watch. "Let's grab some lunch. There's a great place near my house."

29

Shea made a call to Fuego, and we all met up at Grumpy's Bar and Grill, around the corner from my house. It was a regular winner of *Phoenix Living*'s "Best of Phoenix" awards in the Bar & Grill category.

Grumpy Russell, the owner, was a pudgy Vietnam vet with silver mutton chop sideburns and an ever-present unlit cigar stub dangling from his lips.

He wasn't a fan of finicky customers. All those half-caf, no-foam, fat-free latte-type requests would elicit a string of vulgarity from Grumpy that could ignite wildfires. Even ordering dressing on the side was a risky move.

When Fuego, Dragon, Savage, and four other members of the Athena Sisterhood joined Shea, Byrd, and me, I feared Grumpy would have an aneurysm.

"Y'all couldn'ta called ahead o' time?" Grumpy growled, the cigar stub bouncing up and down from the corner of his mouth.

"Kind of a last-minute thing," I said. "Besides, we both know you don't take reservations."

He harrumphed. "Gimme a minute to clear out couple o' tables in back."

When we finally got seated and ordered, I filled in the bikers on our progress or lack thereof.

"I was hoping you'd have some proof by now." A worried expression hung on Savage's face.

"This was your idea," I snapped back. "You want this little whodunit solved faster, you're welcome to hire someone else."

"We're grateful," Dragon replied. "Savage is just worried about Indigo. Keep working to get evidence. Sooner the better, of course."

Yeah, whatever.

I was halfway through my Grumpy Burger and fries when my phone rang.

"Ms. Ballou? This is Detective Clifford. We met last night after the shooting at your home."

"I remember. You arrest Freddie Colton yet?"

"That's why I'm calling. Colton has an alibi for the shooting."

"Whatever he told you, he's lying."

"Unfortunately, his alibi's pretty solid. He was in the ER being treated for a knife wound from a bar fight when the shooting took place. I've confirmed with the attending physician and reviewed surveillance footage. He was not the shooter. We're still waiting on ballistics. If we find a match, I'll let you know."

I thanked her and hung up.

It was midafternoon by the time we paid the checks—which Grumpy agreed to split, though not without complaint. Between the lack of sleep from the night before and the lack of progress on the case, I was spent. Shea, Byrd, and I agreed to reconvene at my house in the morning. Shea headed off with her fellow bikers. I took Byrd back to my place, where he drove off in his Chevy Malibu.

The bullet-riddled front of my house reflected how I felt. I wanted to relax into Conor's arms, to tell him about my crazy day and hear about his own adventures chasing down fugitives. One advantage of dating another bounty hunter was that our war stories didn't freak each other out.

But Conor wasn't here. And it was my fault. If I had run away with him, he wouldn't have turned himself in to the Northern Irish police. I was shit. A shit girlfriend. And a shit bounty hunter who couldn't keep a crew together for more than a few months. One who gave up pursuing a fugitive at the first sign of trouble. Hell, now I was working for the very people who refused to give her up.

Determined to do at least something right, I laid out all of the paperwork on my antique kitchen table. It felt like assembling a puzzle with no idea what it was supposed to look like, half the pieces missing, and others that didn't belong. I arranged the reports different ways, hoping a new perspective might reveal connections I was overlooking. No insights came. Not so much as a tickle in the back of my brain. I was shit at being a private investigator.

At some point, I poured myself a liquid dinner from a bottle of cheap tequila, which I bought on the way home. I followed it up with a little sativa for dessert.

I lay on my bed and thumbed through photos of Conor on my phone, my brain unraveling like a knit sweater in a monsoon. When the phone rang, it slipped from my hand and dropped hard on my forehead. "Ow, fuck!"

I picked it up and looked at the caller ID. Pima Bail Bonds. *Fuck.* I tried to send it to voicemail, but in my impaired state, I hit the answer button by mistake.

"Hel...hello?" I mumbled.

"Jinx, this is Maurice Begay over at Pima Bail Bonds. I'd like a progress report. Where are you in locating Pearson?"

"I...uh...wow, you know." I tried to concentrate, but my thoughts felt like wisps of smoke swirling around me. "I am really, really close, man. So very, very close. Like it's almost inside me. You know? Maurice the man. Man-reece!"

"Jinx, are you okay? You sound...odd."

"No, no, no, I am totally cool. Just chilling out after a hard day of fugitive-ing. Fugitive catching. Chasing. Fugitive chasing. That's why they call it fishing. 'Cause they don't call it catching. Or something like that."

"I've got a lot riding on this job and am paying double the standard rate. I expect results. And regular updates."

"I've...I've narrowed the suspect list down to a few people."

"Suspect list? What suspect list? You mean people who are hiding Pearson?"

"What? Oh yeah, that's what I meant. People who are hiding with person. Pearson. The Pearson person." A giggle snuck out before I could stop it.

"Is this funny to you, Ms. Ballou?"

"No." I guffawed. "No. This is..." An eruption of laughter burst forth so intense I couldn't catch my breath. Tears streamed down my face. The room was spinning, and even that seemed hilarious. By the time I got control of myself, Maurice had hung up. I laughed at that as well. Oh, I was so totally fucked, but at the moment, I didn't really care.

The next thing I remembered, Diana was licking the side of my face. I swatted at her blindly, but she was back a moment later. It took me a few minutes to realize I was lying on the tile floor of my kitchen. My head thundered like a late-summer rainstorm. A sharp beeping pulsed viciously in my ears. *Is this a hangover, or am I getting tinnitus? Or maybe it's a tumor. No, no, it's not a tumor.*

With considerable effort, I used the chair and then the kitchen table to pull myself in a near-vertical position. Baking ingredients, glass mixing bowls, sifters, and other utensils were scattered across the counter. *Have I been trying to bake? While baked?*

I caught a whiff of something burning. The piercing sound riveting my brain wasn't the hangover. It was the smoke alarm. The oven was on. What the fuck?

I turned off the oven and opened it. Smoke billowed into the kitchen. I opened the back door and windows and cranked the ceiling fan to high while coughing like a lifelong smoker.

Using a pot holder, I pulled a rectangular Pyrex dish from the oven and set it on the stove. An inch-thick layer of charcoal lined the bottom of the dish. *Brownies? Shit.*

I ran down the hallway and fanned the smoke detector. It refused to shut up. I tried to pull it off the wall to remove the batteries, but I couldn't figure out how to twist or pull it off. Finally, I grabbed a hammer from the junk drawer. After a few wobbly blows, the beeping stopped.

I collapsed into a chair and rested my throbbing head in my arms until I felt Diana pawing at me for attention. The rising sun was shooting death rays through the haze-filled kitchen straight through my eye sockets, intensifying the pain in my self-traumatized brain.

"Guess you need to go for a run, huh, baby?" I asked her.

Her tail thumped on the floor. She rested her head on my lap. I started bawling and hugged her. "You deserve a better mom. You know that? One who isn't such a fuckup."

More tail thumps. I wasn't sure if she was agreeing with

me or reminding me she loved me regardless. I was still new at this whole dog-mommy thing.

I tumbled down the hallway to my room, pulled on a T-shirt and shorts that were only a little smelly, attached Diana's leash, and went outside into the furious light of morning. A ball cap and my wraparound shades barely sufficed to protect my brain from the golden rays of pain peeking through the trees. I shuffled along the sidewalk, Diana tugging me to go faster, jolting my concussed brain into new experiences of agony. But I couldn't scold her. This was my fault. I deserved to suffer.

As we waited at a light, I pulled my phone out of my pocket from habit. Another text from Maurice. Delete. A text from Vanessa. I was about to delete it as well, but something in her text caught my eye.

You still looking for Bro James killer? Emma thinks Simon knows whos involved. Call me.

Diana barked. The light had turned green, and fellow pedestrians pushed past me to cross the street.

Who the hell is Simon? I stepped into the street. An asshole in a pickup truck nearly clipped me while making a right turn.

Once I was safely across the street, I called Vanessa. It rang six times before going to voicemail. Figured.

"This is Jinx. I got your text. Call me."

30

I was in the middle of showering when my phone rang. "Thank Guinness!" I rinsed the shampoo out of my eyes before tossing the shower curtain back and picking up the phone.

"Vanessa?" I asked without checking the caller ID.

"Um, no. It's Shea. Something's happened."

"What? Where?"

"At Vanessa's friend's house. The police are here. Vanessa and Emma are both dead."

"Text me the address. I'll be right there."

I grabbed my gear and raced over to Emma's in half the time it should have taken.

A dozen police vehicles with lights flashing had blocked off the road, forcing me to park one street over. Crime scene tape stretched across the front yard. I found the Athena Sisterhood huddled just outside the tape.

"What the hell happened?" I asked.

Shea's face was dark. "Got a call a couple hours ago from Vanessa. Freddie was pounding on the front door."

"Fuck!" Another wave of guilt hit me. If I'd let her stay at my place, would she still be alive?

"I told her to call 911," explained Shea. "We drove over quick as we could but were too late. We found them both shot to death."

"Shit. Who's in charge of the investigation?" I asked.

Shea pointed at a group of unis gathered around a plainclothes detective. "Black guy right there. I think he said his name was Hardy."

"Hardin. Detective Pierce Hardin."

"You know him?"

"He was my FTO when I joined the force. My field training officer."

Hardin turned toward us. His eyes narrowed when he spotted me. He shook his head and wandered over. "Don't tell me you're involved in this shitfest, Ballou."

"Vanessa Colton called me yesterday because her asshole husband, Freddie, kept beating on her. I let her stay one night at my place. After that, she moved in with her friend here." I was tempted to tell him about the drive-by, but since Detective Clifford had cleared Freddie, it didn't seem relevant to Vanessa's murder.

"How did you know Ms. Colton?" asked Hardin, taking out his notebook.

"I took her husband to lockup after he jumped bail two years ago on a domestic violence charge. She still had my business card from when I showed up looking for him."

"Anything else you can tell me?"

"That's it." I caught myself feeling angry as well as guilty. I should have done more to protect Vanessa, but so should the cops. This shit between her and her husband had been going on for years. "Hey, what kind of gun was used?"

"Ballou, you know I can't tell you that."

"Come on, Detective. Just tell me. Was it a ten-millimeter auto?"

"Why?"

"It's relevant to a case I'm working."

"No brass was recovered. My guess is it was a revolver, but we won't know the caliber till the slugs are recovered from the bodies."

"What happened to Vanessa's dog?"

"What dog?"

"Vanessa had a little dog. A Yorkshire terrier."

Hardin shrugged. "No one's mentioned finding a dog in the house. If we find it, you want I should call you?"

I shook my head. "No. I've got one. That's plenty for me."

"Well, thanks for the information." Hardin tucked away his pen and notebook.

As he turned to walk away, I asked, "Hey, wait! You ever work with a Detective Atkinson out of Scottsdale PD?"

"Atkinson?"

"Big cheesy mustache. Wears a Stetson."

That actually got a rare belly laugh out of Hardin. "That Wyatt Earp wannabe? Shit. I woulda thought he'd be retired by now."

"So you know him?"

"That white boy done seen too many westerns. Moved down here from Chicago 'bout twenty years ago. Thought putting on a hat and adopting a swagger made him seem like a local. Far be it from me to dis another officer, but I'm glad he ain't on my squad. What's your interest in him?"

"He arrested the wrong woman—a trans woman—for a murder. I'm helping out some friends to get the charges dropped. So far, neither Atkinson nor the prosecutor, Prather, will budge."

Hardin let loose with another belly laugh. "Damn,

Ballou, how many times a fugitive tell you they didn't do it?"

"More than I can count. But this time I believe her."

"Because she's transgender?"

"That's part of it. It isn't the first time she's been falsely charged with something. I think Atkinson has it in for her. And Prather, well, he's not exactly a fan of mine after what happened with Wilhelm Penzler."

"Jesus, you sure know how to step in it, don't you?" The look on his face told me he believed me. "I'm not saying you're wrong. But I'd caution you to watch your step. You cross Atkinson and Prather on this, you damn sure better be right."

"Noted."

"By the way, you remember an officer named Garza?"

"Luis Garza? He was my partner when I worked Patrol. Why?"

He let out a long, slow breath. "He's dead."

"What? How? When?"

"A few weeks ago. Couple of gangbangers held up a liquor store. Garza was there buying beer. Wrong time, wrong place."

"Shit. That sucks." I felt bad even though things between Garza and me had soured after he found out I was trans. "Camila and the kids okay?"

"Devastated. He'd recently made detective, assigned to the Assaults Unit. Jennings is working the investigation. "

"Shit. I'm sorry. If you see Camila, please give her my condolences." I thought about calling her myself, but it would be all kinds of awkward.

"Will do."

I returned to Shea, Savage, and the others.

A whimpering sound caught my attention. Savage was juggling a bundle under her jacket. "Shhh...it's okay."

"You took the dog?" I asked.

"Didn't know what else to do with her," Savage replied. "Poor girl just lost her mommy. Didn't want that murderous bastard to get her or for her to end up in the pound."

A lump formed in my throat. I hated the little rat, but I also felt sorry for her. I hoped they nailed Colton's ass to the wall. For good this time. "Glad she's got someone to care for her."

"You learn anything from your detective friend?" asked Shea.

"Not much." I told them about the text I'd received from Vanessa. "Any idea who Simon is?"

"A guy that Emma's been going out with," said Fuego. "She mentioned him when we were getting Vanessa moved in. Don't know his last name, though."

"All right. I'll see what Becca can dig up on him. He supposedly knows who killed Fitzgerald."

31

As it was only seven o'clock, I texted Becca instead of calling her, telling her what I knew and asking her to locate this Simon person for me.

"The rest of the Sisterhood's heading back up north. Not much else they can do now that Vanessa's dead." Shea's face was solemn. "What's our game plan, boss?"

I stared out at the sky smeared with streaks of thin clouds. "We need to track down Hancock and get a straight answer about where he was the night of the murder. I also want to speak to this Simon, since Vanessa thought he knew something about it. And I'm still waiting to hear back from my friend Amber regarding the dancers at Naughty's."

Becca returned my call. "Emma's Facebook account shows she's in a relationship with a Simon Benedict. Wow, this guy looks like a freakin' caveman. He doesn't have an account of his own, as far as I can tell. Doesn't pop up on any other social media. I've run a skip trace and located an address for his apartment off Northern and the 51. Works nights at a bowling alley on East Glendale Avenue. I'll send you what I have."

"He drive a green Chevy Nova by chance?" I thought about our tail from the other day.

"Let's see..." Keys clicked away like machine-gun fire. "I'm showing a 2007 Hyundai Excel, red, registered in his name. No other vehicles. Sorry."

"Thanks for getting back to me so quickly, Becks." I hung up and immediately called Byrd. "Dude, we've had some developments."

I filled him in on everything. "I want you to go to Hancock's place. If he's home, call me. If not, contact Becca and see if you can track him down. When you find him, let me know, and we'll show up."

"Roger that."

"So what're we doing?" Shea asked when I hung up with Byrd. The rest of the Sisterhood had taken off.

"Becca tracked down Emma's boyfriend, Simon Benedict." I pulled up the photo Becks had sent me. "Look familiar?"

"The guy with Freddie Colton. Vanessa's friend was dating him?"

"Apparently. Emma must've told him that Vanessa was staying over, and then he told Freddie."

Shea's hands balled into fists. "What a pathetic piece of shit."

"Yeah, but one who may know who killed Fitzgerald. What say we go have a talk with the guy?"

She pounded her right fist in her left hand. "I say we do more than talk."

"Talk first. We'll see about anything afterward. Oh, and this time, I'm taking the Charger in case our friend in the green Nova shows up again."

Simon Benedict lived in a faded-yellow apartment complex. Despite a fence enclosing the property, the automatic gate was wide open for anyone to drive through.

Benedict's red Hyundai sat parked in one of the covered parking spaces, not far from his apartment.

When I stepped out of the Charger, I was hit with the smell of garbage and urine coming from an open dumpster. Small weeds poked through the crushed rock that once served as flower beds between the buildings. Everything about the complex was a study in neglect.

I pulled on my gear and met Shea by her motorcycle.

"How you want to handle this?" Her hand rested on the grip of the Glock on her hip.

"We don't know for sure he told Freddie where Vanessa was staying or why, if he did. But be ready. If things go sideways, remember we need him alive to tell us what he knows."

"I'll resist the urge to shoot him," said Shea with a mischievous grin. "But no promises."

We approached the door, and I rang the bell. Simon the Neanderthal opened the door a minute later looking barefoot and bleary-eyed. He reeked of alcohol and body odor. His T-shirt and shorts looked slept in.

"Simon Benedict?" I asked.

"Who wants to know?" Clearly, he didn't recognize us. I considered that a plus at this point.

"You're Emma Kahn's boyfriend, right?"

"Yeah. Why?"

"I'm afraid we have some bad news. Mind if we come in?"

He stood there a moment, as if sizing us up. "You cops?"

I tapped the badge hanging from a chain around my neck. "I work mostly fugitive cases, but this is in regards to a homicide."

Fear seemed to punch him between the eyes. He stumbled back, holding onto the wall for support. "Is Emma all right?"

I took that for our cue to enter. He lumbered to his kitchen table and collapsed into one of the wooden chairs.

"I'm sorry to inform you that Emma Kahn was found dead this morning, along with her friend Vanessa Colton."

He sat there wide-eyed and pale, meaty hands trembling while gripping the table. "No, no, no! Emma can't be dead. I saw her just last night. We were supposed to go out, but Vanessa was staying over."

"You mention seeing Vanessa to Freddie Colton?" asked Shea.

"Freddie? Sure, Vanessa's his wife. Why shouldn't he know?" He looked at Shea, then me. I could see him doing the calculations in his head, however slowly. "Wait, no! No way! I mean, Freddie gets a little rough with her now and then, but he wouldn't...."

"You were in their house a few days ago when he threatened to kill her," I said, dropping my comforting tone.

"But that's just the way Freddie talks. He'd never actually..."

"Oh, he would, and he did," insisted Shea. "Killed Vanessa and Emma both, thanks to you."

His anguish morphed into anger. "That motherfucker!" He knocked a napkin holder into the wall with enough force to shatter it, sending a cloud of paper napkins drifting to the floor like dandelion seeds.

He looked up at me. "Y'all...y'all were at Freddie's. Y'all ain't cops."

"Now he figures it out," Shea said grimly.

"I used to be a cop. Now I'm a private detective investigating a recent homicide. But if you'd like us to call the cops, we'd be happy to let them know you tipped off Colton to his wife's whereabouts. That makes you an accessory to first-degree murder."

Simon's face blanched. "I had no idea what he was gonna do."

"Yeah, right." Shea snorted.

"You're certainly welcome to tell that to the cops, Simon," I replied. "Or you tell us what we want to know."

"Whaddya wanna know?"

"We're looking for the man who killed James Fitzgerald," I said. "Vanessa sent a text saying you knew who did it."

"Fitzgerald? Don't know nobody by that name."

"Sure you do. That preacher who was murdered in Scottsdale a month or so ago. Went by the moniker Brother James."

"Him? Whaddya wanna know about him for?"

"That's our business," replied Shea. "Now spill, or we give your name to the cops."

"Fine. I was down at the Stone Horse Pub a while back. This guy Boris, kind of a regular there, he's drunk off his ass, bragging how he put a beatdown on some loudmouth preacher. A week later, I saw a story on the news about that preacher's body being found. Figured it was Boris."

"Did Boris have any dealings with a man named Wes Hancock?"

"Don't know nobody named Hancock."

"Where does Boris live?" I pressed.

"How the hell should I know? I see him every once in a while at the Stone Horse."

"What's Boris's last name?"

"Geez, I don't know. All them Russkie names sound alike. Starts with a *G*, I think, and ends in *O-V*. Garnov. Gorkov. Who knows? We just call him Boris because he speaks with an accent. Probably not even his real name."

"Any idea where he works?"

"From what he said, he ain't got a regular job. Beats

people up for a living, but I don't know for who. Why are we even talking about him? My girlfriend's dead, man. Boris can go fuck himself for all I care." He broke into sobs. Who knew Neanderthals had such deep emotions?

I put my hand on his arm, remembering how I felt when I learned about Conor and the explosion on the highway.

I wrote down Detective Hardin's name and number on a piece of paper and handed it to him. "I'm sorry for your loss, man. This is the detective working the case. He'll help you out."

I nodded to Shea, and we let ourselves out. A text from Byrd told me that Hancock wasn't home, but he was in touch with Becca to track him down.

"What do you think?" asked Shea.

"Until now, my money was on Hancock, especially with his bogus alibi. But in light of what Simon told us, maybe it was this Boris person, whoever the hell he is."

"Maybe Hancock hired Boris."

"Possible. But that still doesn't explain Hancock's bogus alibi." I looked up the Stone Horse Pub on my phone. "Stone Horse doesn't open until one. I'll have Becca see what she can dig up on Boris Gorkov or Garnov."

I sent Becca a text giving her what little I knew about the guy. I knew it was a needle in a haystack, but it was all I had.

She texted back, "Wasn't Gorkov a Cardassian in *Deep Space Nine*?"

"That was Garak, you goofball," I replied.

She responded with a goofy-faced emoji and a message that she'd look into the name.

My phone rang just as I was putting it back in my pocket. It was Amber.

"What's up, girl?"

"Friend of mine was caught up in Volkov's trafficking operation. Used to dance at Naughty's in Scottsdale. The girls there took interested clients next door to the motel for sex."

Bingo! No doubt Fitzgerald was one of those interested clients. Bible study, my ass!

"How do I get in touch with her?"

"Well, that's the thing. She's a little shy."

"She takes off her clothes in front of strangers, but she's shy?"

"Shy about speaking to strangers. You gotta understand, Sergei Volkov's people keep a tight rein on the girls. My friend was lucky she got out."

"I get it. But one of Volkov's clients was murdered in the motel next door, and a trans woman is going to take the fall unless I can prove someone else did it. I need to talk to someone who's been on the inside."

"If Volkov finds out she talked..."

"He won't, Amber. I swear."

I heard voices in the background. "You remember where I live?"

"Off Olive Avenue and Grand. Near Glendale Community College."

"Exactly."

"I'll be there shortly." I hung up and smiled at Shea. "We got someone who used to work at Naughty's. Follow me."

32

I navigated out of Simon Benedict's neighborhood and pulled onto Northern Avenue. A green muscle car behind Shea's bike caught my attention. Whether it was the Chevy Nova we'd seen earlier, I couldn't tell from the glare off the windshield, but it seemed the same emerald shade. So far, our dogged shadow hadn't made any aggressive moves. Maybe the driver was just keeping tabs on where we were going. Maybe they were biding their time, waiting for the opportune moment to strike. Either way, in light of Amber's concerns for her friend's safety, I didn't want to lead our shadow to her place.

At the last second, I turned hard onto the northbound I-17 on-ramp and floored it. Shea followed on her motorcycle, having no trouble keeping up. The Nova followed suit.

"Okay, girl," I said to Conor's old Charger. "Let's see what you can do."

Back in 1968, the 440 R/T was a helluva car, I was told. But after she'd had more than a half century of use in the dry heat of the desert, I wasn't sure she still had it in her.

I forced my way through the post-rush-hour traffic to

the car pool lane. I put the pedal to the metal, the engine growled, and the speedometer climbed...60, 70, 80, 90. I checked my rearview. The Nova was behind me. Where was Shea?

I looked right and saw her next to me, crouched down to reduce wind resistance. She shot me a thumbs-up then ducked into the center lane to dodge a utility truck and put on a surprising burst of speed. The Nova changed lanes, clearly attempting to follow Shea.

When the Nova was next to me, I tried to catch a glimpse of the driver but couldn't see through the tinted windows. I turned the wheel to the right, gritting my teeth at the sound of metal crunching against metal. The Charger shoved the Nova, then the Nova shoved back. We swapped paint a few more times before the traffic thickened as we approached the Loop 101 interchange. I was forced to move back into the carpool lane or risk losing the Nova completely.

Shea was about a quarter mile ahead of us. Maybe she was trying to lead him off and lose him. She had mentioned that her bike had a high-performance motor. But I didn't like the thought of leaving her to deal with the asshole in the Nova by herself.

Once past the 101, my speedometer wobbled to a hundred miles an hour, then one ten as I took after the Nova that was pushing hard to catch Shea. The car shook with the increased speed. The world around me became a blur, leaving only the Nova in focus.

I jerked the wheel hard, barreling into the Nova's crumpled side panels and driving it onto the shoulder. I hoped that was the end of it, but the Nova swerved back onto the road, cutting behind me and ending up on my left.

I glanced over in time to see the passenger window rolling down. The barrel of a gun appeared. I rammed the car. My rear window shattered when the gun went off. I rammed again, even harder this time. Metal scraped. Tires screamed, but I kept pushing, driving it from the left lane, into the carpool lane.

Ahead, an RV was cruising along in the carpool lane. Some snowbird probably headed back to Canada or Minnesota. We were going a hundred and twenty. The RV zoomed toward us almost as if it were going the wrong way. At the last second, the Nova slid onto the left shoulder. The RV vanished behind us.

An idea popped into my head. A memory from the police academy's defensive driving course. I eased off the gas a hair. The Nova pulled ahead. I drifted into the right lane. The other car followed.

An arm emerged from the passenger side, holding a gun. I pulled in behind the Nova and rammed it as hard as I could from behind. The gun dropped from the shooter's hand and disappeared behind us.

I moved back into the right lane, then swerved into the Nova's rear quarter panel. The Nova spun around out of control in front of me as I jammed the accelerator to the floor. The combination of speed and rotational forces sent the Nova catapulting end over end in a flash of green paint, chrome, and smoke.

My heart was hammering faster than the pistons under my hood. A smile crept across my face. "See ya later, alligator."

I recognized the tiny dot in the distance as Shea. I floored it to catch up. The distance between us narrowed until she was on my left. I gave her a thumbs-up. She returned the gesture. I slowed to 80 miles an hour, then took the Carefree Highway exit and pulled into the Chevron and sat there.

"You all right?" asked Shea. I could hear the concern in her voice as she appeared outside my door.

"Think so." The door groaned when I got out. My knees were wobbly, and I leaned on the car for support.

"You should've let me lead them off," she said. "I could've lost them and doubled back."

"They had a gun. They could've shot you." I held her gaze for a moment. A lot of things passed between us, things I didn't have words for. "One thing's certain. It was the same Chevy Nova. And now I have a plate number."

I texted the info to Becca to pull up on the Motor Vehicle Department's database. She replied she'd pull it up when she could, but at the moment, she was tied up with a client whose entire network had been hacked and brought down. She hoped to have an answer within the hour.

I was tempted to tell her that our situation was also time critical, but she'd often put me ahead of her better-paying clients.

"I don't like this." Shea gazed south at the highway.

"Me either." I followed her sight line. A column of black smoke was rising in the distance, too far away to know if it was the Nova or something else on fire. "Hopefully, that's the last we see of them."

I walked around the Charger. The body panels looked like the car had been through a giant pinball machine. Green paint streaked across the dented black body panels. The front grille was cracked, though the radiator seemed intact. The bullet had punched though the backseat window and into the upholstery. I found what was left of the slug embedded in the spare tire in the trunk. I was glad Conor didn't have to see what I'd done to his beloved sports car.

"Let's go meet this former dancer."

33

The streets in Amber's part of town were cracked and riddled with potholes. Dollar stores outnumbered Starbucks. All of the buildings had a tired, dingy look to them, as did the pedestrians cruising down the weed-strewn sidewalks. Sprouting from street corners were homemade signs promising free cable and cash for houses.

A couple of streets south of Northern, Amber maintained a cute little three-bedroom, which she shared with a gay man named Ace and a single mother named Rebel and her two-year-old daughter, Sage. Only Amber was home at the time.

Amber was tall, sinewy, and tan. Her voice was husky but sultry in a Miley Cyrus sort of way, and the only hint of her being trans. She hugged me when she opened the door to let us in.

I introduced Shea. Amber introduced us to her friend Maricela Ramirez. She was shorter than Amber but busty with bronze skin and burgundy hair. Her eyes were large and lips full. She looked like she was hiding a basketball under her shirt.

We settled in around the coffee table in Amber's living room.

"Thanks for agreeing to talk to us," I told Maricela.

She looked worried, like she was on trial for her life. And maybe she was. The Volkovs were ruthless, as Shea and I already knew. The last thing I wanted was to put someone else's life in danger, even to save Indigo.

"If word gets out that I talked..."

"We know. We've dealt with Milo Volkov in the past. I'm sure Sergei's not much better."

"Not better but different. Milo treated girls like meat. He let his men rape us. Some women, he kept chained like animals. Sergei...he has a different approach. More businesslike. Only paying clients could have sex with us. And if a client gots too rough, Sergei's men put a stop to it. More protective, in a way, unless..."

"Unless what?"

"Unless we tried to escape."

"What happens to those who try to escape?" There was fire in Shea's voice. I felt it too.

"Bad things. Very, very bad things. Most girls were from other countries. Honduras. Nigeria. India. Sergei's men promised great jobs in America. But when we got here, we learned it was a lie. They kept our passports. Forced us to dance and have sex with clients. Some tried to escape. One lost an eye. Another..." She blinked back tears.

"But you left, anyway. Despite the risk."

Her arm wrapped protectively around her enlarged belly. "I discovered I was pregnant. It happen before. They forced me to get abortion. I don't want that again. I want this baby. I heard about a group who helps women like me, women who are forced to be prostitutes."

"The Human Trafficking Resource Center," Amber added. "I sometimes volunteer for their helpline."

"I called and talked to Amber. She helped get me out."

"Did you tell the police or the FBI about Volkov's operation?" I asked both Maricela and Amber.

"She's undocumented," Amber replied. "Volkov pays cops to look the other way. The feds would've turned her over to ICE and stuck her in a cage before eventually sending her back to Honduras. Best if we keep quiet."

"You said when a client got too rough, Sergei's men put a stop to it. How?"

"Yuri would send his men to have talk with him. Andrei or one of the other bouncers at the club."

"Who's Yuri?" asked Shea.

"He is in charge of Naughty's and of the prostitution business."

"Just talk?" said Shea.

She shrugged. "Maybe not just talk."

"Would they kill a john who got too rough?" I asked.

"Never heard them do that. Usually just..." She made punching gestures in the air.

"Beat him up a bit?" asked Shea.

Maricela nodded. "Tell him to play nice, or he no longer a client. Sergei is more businessman than Milo was. Smart. Police look the other way for prostitution. But killing a client can bring the feds. Bad for business. Also drives away other clients. Easier to beat up a bad client or tell him not come back."

"You ever meet James Fitzgerald? The preacher?"

"Brother James? Yes, a few times." She stared down at the floor. "He got rough. Yuri sent Andrei to talk to him."

Shea's posture stiffened. "What'd that piece of garbage do?"

"He liked to pretend to rape us girls. Tie our hands and feet." Maricela rubbed her wrists. "Then he slap, punch, kick. Very rough sex. Broke my wrist and cracked two ribs. I could not work for weeks. I was afraid Yuri would do something bad to me, but he let me rest and get better."

"How long ago was this?" I asked.

"A year."

"What did Yuri do to Brother James?" Shea sounded angry.

"I do not know exactly. I never saw Brother James again."

I was getting a good picture of what went on. Shea and I continued to probe Maricela's knowledge of Sergei's operation, asking how clients approached dancers for sex work, how money was handled, anything that might help clear Pearson. Unfortunately, what little Maricela knew didn't shed much light on the situation. And she had escaped long before Fitzgerald was murdered.

"You ever hear of a guy named Boris working for Sergei?" I asked finally. "I think his last name is Gorkov or Garnov."

Maricela's brow crinkled. "I do not know a Boris."

"Who took your place with Brother James after he hurt you? He was obviously sleeping with someone else."

"I don't know. I was happy it was not me."

"What are you doing now?" I asked. "For work, I mean."

"Amber helped me find a job working in a restaurant. At least till the baby comes."

"Amber's good people." I gave my friend a wink. She blushed.

My phone rang. Caller ID came up as Arizona Mutual Life Insurance. No doubt Pete Stansfield wanting to chat about Conor's life insurance policy. No thanks. Bigger fish to fry. I sent it to voicemail.

"Jinx, Maricela's looking a little tired," said Amber. "Think we can wrap it up?"

"Of course. Thanks for talking with us, Maricela. I hope everything goes well with your baby."

"*Muchas gracias.*"

Amber walked us to the door. "You get what you needed?"

"Hard to say. I appreciate your setting this up."

"Hope it helps."

Back at the vehicles, Shea asked, "What do you think?"

"Some good background on Sergei's operation. But nothing she said points to him or one of his minions being the killer."

"Not yet. But we both know what psychos the Volkovs are, no matter how 'businesslike' she said Sergei is. I'm sure they're mixed up in Fitzgerald's death somehow. Maybe not for beating up a ho. Maybe some other shit they had going on between them."

"Could be." I checked my watch. "Let's grab some lunch and then head to the Stone Horse Pub. Maybe we'll get lucky and find this guy Boris."

34

While we chowed down on a couple of burros at Filibertos, Becca called back.

"Sorry to put you off, Jinx, but this client was seriously shitting bricks. She runs a chain of sporting goods stores, and getting hit on a Friday..."

"I get it. You find anything out on this Boris fellow or the Chevy Nova that's been tailing us?"

"Nothing on Boris yet. No one named Boris Gorkov or Garnov that I can find. As for the Nova, it belonged to an eighty-year-old woman named Consuelo Silva."

"Eighty?" That caught me off guard. "Was it reported stolen?"

"Not at this time. You want a photo? She's cute. Reminds me of my *abuela*."

"I'm sure she's lovely, but I don't think she's the one who's been tailing us. She have any grandkids with a record?"

"Entirely possible. I'll run some face-recognition algorithms and see if a relative has posted family photos on social media. I can also run a search on her address. Maybe she's got family living with her."

"Thanks. Let me know what you find."

I hung up. Time to find Boris.

The Stone Horse Pub had seen better days. The illuminated sign on the street was so yellowed with age, I wondered if someone had scorched it with a flame. The building's plaster facade was made to look like flagstones, but the years had left the surface pockmarked and chipped.

A life-sized concrete horse stood outside the front door. It had been tagged with graffiti and patch-painted so many times, it made the poor beast look like a pinto. A jagged stub remained where the lower jaw had been.

Shea and I stepped inside the bar, geared up in case Boris was here. It took my eyes a moment to adjust to the low-lit interior. Not all that charming inside either. The barracks in the police academy had more character than this dive.

A bar with an oaken top ran the left side of the room. The bartender was a white woman with a bulldog face and crooked teeth. The Statue of Liberty had been inked on one of her arms and an M-16 along the other.

Four patrons sat at the bar, nursing drinks, occasionally glancing up at the baseball game on the TV above the bar. The Diamondbacks were pounding the Giants 10-1 in the bottom of the fifth. A handful of tables, all filled, and a jukebox with a cracked glass cover sat along the right wall. Welcome to Barfly Central.

"What can I get you ladies?" Bulldog the bartender asked when Shea and I approached.

"Information," I replied. "I'm looking for Boris. Speaks with a Russian accent. I hear he's a regular customer."

"Boris, huh?" The bartender had a deadpan expression.

"You seem to know a lot about this guy. I hope you find him."

"He was here bragging about killing a guy a month or so ago," Shea added.

"Guys are always shooting their mouths off in here, bragging about one thing or another. How tough they are. How fast their cars are. How big their dicks are. It's the nature of the beast. I just sling booze. I don't keep track of who says what. You want booze, I'll line 'em up. You want information, try the library over by PV Mall."

Great, a tight-lipped bartender with a snarky attitude. Just what I needed. I set three twenties down on the bar. "Does this refresh your memory?"

She shrugged nonchalantly. "Not really."

The man on the stool next to me slurred something and slumped over. He would have face-planted on the floor if I hadn't caught him. I shoved him back up and flopped him onto the polished bar, toppling his glass.

"This guy's plastered." I took a photo of him with my phone. "I do believe over-serving is a great way to lose your liquor license. Maybe I should send this to the Department of Liquor Licenses."

"Leave Sam alone. His wife just died of ovarian cancer, for Chrissakes. You okay, man?" she asked him.

Sam mumbled something that sounded like "Okeydokey."

Bulldog shot me a stern look. "I've already called him a cab, all right?"

"Tell us what we want to know, or I report this."

She narrowed her gaze, perhaps gauging whether I was bluffing.

"Look, Boris comes in every so often. Drinks Stolichnaya. Talks a lotta shit. Claims to be some tough guy, but if you ask me, he's full of hot air. That's all I know."

"What's he look like?" Shea asked.

"Big guy. Short brown hair. Dark eyes. Kind of a body-builder type. Has some tattoos on his arms and hands. Skulls and stars, I think."

"He got a last name?" I inquired.

"Everybody does, but I don't know what it is. Starts with a *G*, I think."

"Garnov? Gorkov?" I pressed.

"Garnov sounds right. His first name's really Alexei. Boris is more of a nickname on account he's Russian."

"When's he usually here?" Shea asked.

"Do I look like I keep a schedule of my customers?"

"Fine." I held up my phone again, tapping on the screen. "Ah, here we are. Report a liquor license violation."

"Stop! I don't know when he's here. I honestly don't keep track. Best guess, middle of the week but late at night. Maybe ten or so. I could be wrong."

"You are useless," Shea told her.

Time for plan B. Crowdsourcing. I pulled a few twenty-dollar bills from my wallet and faced the rest of the room. "Good people of the Stone Horse, can I get your attention, please? I have sixty bucks to anyone who can tell me where to find Boris or Alexei Garnov. Has a Russian accent. Lots of ink. Likes to brag about killing people. Sixty bucks."

"You're wasting your time," Bulldog said with her arms crossed.

The people in the bar ignored me. I pulled out a few more twenties. "One hundred. One hundred bucks. All you gotta do is tell me where Boris is."

A couple of people looked up from their drinks but remained silent. Sam the Puddle mumbled something, but it was a slur of syllables.

Shea held up a C-note. "Make that two hundred dollars."

"Two hundred dollars," I echoed. "Easy money. Just gotta tell me where we can find Boris."

"Make it three!" said a guy nursing a glass of whiskey at a table.

Shea pulled out another. "Fine. Three hundred dollars."

"You know where we can find Boris?" I asked him.

"Your mama's house." That got a round of laughter from his fellow patrons.

"Good one, Joe!" said Bulldog, clapping.

"Last chance, gentlemen! When was the last time a woman gave you three hundred bucks?"

"Last time I fucked your mama," Joe retorted.

"That's real classy," Shea said, strolling up to him. "Last time I saw your mama, she was licking my pussy. I guess your father didn't interest her no more."

"Fucking dyke!" His face turned the color of a rotten tomato. He threw his drink at her. She popped him in his face with a quick jab. The back of his head smacked the jukebox like a gunshot. He collapsed to the floor, blood trickling down his face.

In the span of a heartbeat, the stale air in the bar crackled with anger. Men at both ends of the room jumped from their seats and converged on us.

I blocked the punch from one man and drove the heel of my palm into his nose. A second attacker swung a chair. I dodged left, feeling the breeze as it brushed my ear. My hand caught the chair, ripping it from his grasp, and I brought it down on his head.

Bulldog reached beneath the bar. I drew my Ruger before she could pull out whatever was under there. "Drop it! Now!" I demanded.

I heard the resonant clunk of a baseball bat hitting the floor.

Another man rushed at me from the side but stopped

short when I glared at him. He held up his hands and took a step back.

"Get out of my bar," growled Bulldog.

"Tell us what we want to know, and we will oblige," I replied.

"We don't know where Boris is, all right? No one does."

"Fucking pigs," grumbled the guy Shea had punched. The other combatants were picking themselves up and returning to their duly appointed booze.

"Come on. Let's blow this joint. These people don't know shit." Shea grabbed a bar rag and held it to her bleeding nose, wincing when she pressed it to her face. Somebody must have gotten in a lucky punch, but from the looks of things, she'd had three guys to contend with. "The smell of bullshit and cheap beer's turning my stomach."

I tried to think of a clever parting remark to tell Bulldog off but drew a blank. Instead, Shea and I backed out without another word.

My phone rang. The caller ID revealed it was Byrd. "Yo, man, what's up?"

"I tracked down Hancock. He's working in the sales office of an equipment rental place."

"You there now?"

"Yeah, parked in the CVS lot next door. You want me to go in and press him on his bogus alibi?"

"Stay put. We'll be there shortly."

I hung up and turned to Shea, who still held the rag to her nose. "You okay to ride?"

"I'll manage. Just wanna get the hell outta here."

"Good. Byrd tracked down Hancock."

35

Hancock did not look happy to see the three of us crowding into his cozy equipment rental office. "I told you everything I know. Why can't you leave me and my family alone?"

Shea plopped her butt on his desk, glaring at him with her arms crossed. "Seems there's a discrepancy in your story, dude."

"What are you talking about?" From the look on his face, I thought he might bolt. I nodded at Byrd, and he blocked the door.

"Your alibi is bullshit," I said.

"Do you own a gun?" Shea pressed.

"No, I don't own a gun. I hate guns."

I glared at him. "Then where the hell were you that night?"

"I told you, my family and I went to the movies!"

"Two days *after* James Fitzgerald was murdered. We checked your bank records."

"You went into my bank records? What gives you the right?"

I tapped my badge. "A man was murdered, and a

woman has been framed. No more lies, Mr. Hancock. Where were you the night of the murder?"

"None of your business."

"I beg to differ. Right now, you're our prime suspect. You had means, opportunity, and a helluva motive. So if it wasn't you, then you need to prove where you were."

"I could call my lawyer."

"And I can call *Phoenix Living*. They'd love to do a front-page story about the man who took revenge against his daughter's rapist. You'd still go to prison, but at least you'd have the support of the reading public as an avenging father."

His tough-guy act folded. "Look, I...I was at an AA meeting. Court-ordered."

"Can you prove it?"

"It's Alcoholics Anonymous. Emphasis on anonymous."

"How does the court know you went?"

He reached into his pocket and pulled out an aluminum coin. I examined it. The AA emblem appeared on one side with "60 Days" embossed in the middle. On the back was printed the Serenity Prayer.

"Doesn't prove anything," Shea said. "I have lotsa friends in recovery. You can buy one of these for less than a buck at the Sobriety Bookstore on Seventh Street."

"I also had the chairs at the meetings sign a sheet. After thirty days, I turned it over to the drug court clerk."

"You have a copy?"

He pulled out his phone, tapped the screen a few times, and held it out to me. An image of a document was on the screen. I zoomed in. The sheet had a list of signatures with dates and times and locations of meetings attended.

The night of the murder, he attended two meetings. One at eight p.m. in Central Phoenix and another at nine thirty p.m. in Glendale. According to the ME's report,

Fitzgerald was killed sometime between nine and ten o'clock that night. Assuming the sign-in sheet was legit, Hancock would have either been at the meeting in the west valley or traveling to it. The complete other side of town.

"Can you forward a copy of that to me?" I gave him my business card again.

He snatched his phone out of my hand and tapped on the screen. His phone made a whooshing sound. Ten seconds later, my phone dinged. I forwarded the image to Becca to look into.

"Before you quit drinking, you ever hang out at the Stone Horse Pub?" I asked.

"This really is beyond the pale. I proved I was nowhere near Scottsdale when that piece of shit was killed. I don't need to answer any more questions."

"You lied once," replied Byrd. "Your credibility is shot."

"Just answer the damn question," insisted Shea.

"Yeah, I've been there once or twice. So what? It's not a crime."

"Is that where you met Alexei Garnov? Sometimes goes by Boris?" I asked.

"Garnov? I don't know anyone named Garnov."

"Come on," said Shea. "Russian accent. A regular at the Stone Horse. What I hear, he likes to tell tales when he drinks. He was heard bragging he killed Fitzgerald. Maybe you hired him. "

There was no recognition in his eyes. "I don't know anyone with a Russian accent. I didn't kill that goddamn rapist, nor did I pay someone to do it for me. I'm just glad someone did so no one else has to endure what my daughter did. Now get the hell out of my office."

"Gladly," I said.

"And if you harass me any more, I am calling my lawyer and suing you for harassment. How do you think *Phoenix*

Living will write that headline? Cops harass father of rape victim."

"Cops?" I smirked. "No one said we were cops."

His jaw dropped, and his face flushed red. "Then who the hell are you?"

"Don't worry. If this thing about the AA meetings checks out, you won't see us again," I promised.

We stepped out into the parking lot, where tractors, lawn equipment, and hydraulic pumps were waiting to be rented.

"I was so sure it was him," said Byrd.

"I'm still not convinced it wasn't," replied Shea.

"I don't know much about these sign-off sheets," I added, "but Becca will let me know what she thinks."

My phone dinged. "That's probably her."

I unlocked my phone. I had a message. *Back off or you die.* It wasn't from Becca but from an unknown caller ID.

I glanced around the CVS and equipment rental parking lots. No sign of a green car.

"We seem to have ruffled some feathers." I showed them the text.

"Any idea who it's from?" asked Byrd.

"Not a clue. From what I've learned from Becca, a text message can be sent via an SMS service and completely anonymized."

Byrd hooked a thumb at the rental office. "You don't think it's Hancock, do you?"

I looked toward the office. "I wouldn't rule out the possibility, but my gut tells me no."

"Then who?" asked Shea. "Someone working for Volkov? This Garnov dude?"

"Quite possibly. First the drive-by, then the green Nova tailing us, now this. The question is, what do we do about it?"

"Rally the troops and go into lockdown," Shea replied.

I raised an eyebrow. "Meaning?"

"I grew up around my father's motorcycle club. Whenever the shit really hit the fan, such as a war with a rival club, they gathered everyone together at the clubhouse. Members, old ladies, and kids. Kept everyone protected until the threat could be neutralized. We've done that once or twice with the Sisterhood, too, as needed."

I thought about it. We weren't a motorcycle club, and we didn't have a clubhouse, but we did have the Bunker.

"You're both welcome to stay at my place. Safer than staying at a motel."

"Thanks for the offer," replied Byrd, "but I should be all right at my place."

I nodded. "Suit yourself, but watch your back. And keep your eyes peeled for a green Chevy Nova."

"You want me to get members of the Sisterhood back down here?" asked Shea. "A little extra firepower."

"I'd rather not turn my neighborhood into a war zone."

Concern hardened Shea's face. "Whoever sent that text may plan to do just that, whether you want it or not."

"Let's hold off for now." I turned to Byrd. "Meet back at my place tomorrow morning at eight."

"Tomorrow's Saturday, Jinxie."

"Yes, and we only have till Tuesday to either get the charges against Pearson dropped or get her back in custody."

Byrd nodded and gave me a half hug and a pat on the back. "For my cut of that sixty grand, I'll be there."

Shea followed me to the Willo District. The streets were clogged with afternoon rush hour traffic, which always seemed worse on Fridays. A block from my neighborhood, I pulled through a Culver's for a couple of butter burgers and vanilla malt shakes.

When we finally pulled into my driveway, the pockmarked window reminded me I hadn't called my brother, Jake, about repairing the damage. The Lexan had held up to the bullets from the drive-by but wouldn't take much more abuse.

Shea stared at the front of my house. "If Freddie Colton didn't do this? Who did?"

"Probably one of his buddies."

Diana greeted us when we walked in the door, nearly knocking the tray with the milkshakes out of my hand.

"Such a sweet baby," Shea cooed. I couldn't help smiling. Anyone who got along with my dog was okay in my book. And even with her face busted up from the bar brawl earlier, she looked sexy as hell.

We settled into the kitchen and dug into dinner.

"Tell me something," I said. "If the Athena Sisterhood is so gung-ho on protecting women, how come y'all were at Naughty's?"

"We weren't all there—just those of us who are into women. 'Course, if we'd known the club was owned by the Volkovs, we woulda taken our business elsewhere."

"Makes sense."

She hooked a thumb in the direction of the living room. "I notice you have a lot of comic books stuff. Movie posters, dolls..."

"Action figures, not dolls. But yeah, I'm kinda into the whole superheroes thing. You?"

"Not so much. You go to those conventions where people dress up in costumes?"

Embarrassment warmed my face. "Yeah."

"You dress up?"

"It's called cosplay."

"You're avoiding the question."

"Because you think it's stupid. I can see it in your eyes."

"Hey, we all have our own kink. I was curious. No judgment."

"I cosplay as Wonder Woman. Sometimes as Xena. I even won an award last year."

"That spiky thing on the table in the living room? Impressive. I'd like to see you in costume sometime."

I took a deep breath and tried to let go of my embarrassment. "I'll be at San Diego Comicon in July. Maybe you can come along."

"Maybe."

"Now it's my turn to ask questions."

"Shoot."

"How come your niece lives with you? The background check didn't say."

"Annie moved in with me after my sister and her old man were killed." Her voice took on a somber tone. I was curious to learn more but didn't want to pry.

"Shit, I'm sorry. Must be tough."

"Never saw myself as the mommy type. But somehow it's working. The Sisterhood's helped a lot. They're like an extended family of aunties. Annie's staying with my friend Whiplash while I'm down here."

"How old's Annie?"

"Eleven."

"Almost a teenager."

Shea chuckled. "Yeah, so not looking forward to it. I was a hellion at that age."

"Me too."

An awkward silence settled in the room. I found myself endlessly fascinated with this hardcore biker woman. Strange considering two days earlier, we were trying to beat each other's brains out.

"Well, I better see about getting these windows fixed." I wiped the grease from my face.

"I need to check in with Annie. Make sure she's doing her homework."

Shea disappeared into the guest bedroom, while I dialed Jake's number.

"Wow, who is this?" Jake asked in a snarky tone.

"Very funny."

"Is this my long-lost sister? The one who hasn't shown up to Sunday brunch in forever?"

"All right. You made your point. I need to hire you to do some repair work on my house."

"Which one?"

"Conor's place."

"The Bunker? Why?"

"Someone thought it would be funny to redecorate the front of my house with bullets."

"You're kidding, right?"

"I need you to replace one of the Lexan windows and patch the holes in the brick."

"You're serious. Geez, Jinxie. What the hell are you into?"

"Just the usual. Tracking down somebody that doesn't want to be found. Not something you have to worry about." I hoped, anyway.

"I can stop by tomorrow morning and take a look."

"Thanks, bro."

"Provided you show up Sunday to Mom and Dad's."

Sunday brunch was a big deal at my folks' house and had been since we were kids. Last December, I'd missed once and got hit with major Catholic guilt from my mother. After I lost Conor, my attendance grew more sporadic until they stopped asking about me. But I knew my family. Just because they weren't guilt tripping me didn't mean they weren't concerned.

My mother especially was a worrier. My job as a bounty

hunter didn't help.

"I'll try to get over there Sunday."

"Do or do not, there is no try," said Jake in a very poor Yoda voice that sounded more like Pee-wee Herman.

"I'll be there. Okay? Now will you fix the damage to my house?"

"I'll be there." I hung up.

Shea and I spent the next few hours going over all of the documentation we had, looking for our next lead. Time was running short. All we had were bits and pieces, none of which connected into solid proof that someone other than Indigo had killed Fitzgerald.

36

The doorbell rang at six o'clock. Diana rushed off the bed to the living room, barking excitedly.

I grabbed my phone from the nightstand and pulled up the security video feed for the front door. It was Jake, thank goodness, and not some eastern European mobster. Then again, assassins didn't usually ring the doorbell.

I pulled on a bathrobe and shuffled out of my room but not before Jake rang another couple of times and pounded on the door for good measure.

"Jesus Christ! I'm coming!" I shouted.

"Who is that?" asked Shea, coming out of the guest room in a black T-shirt and boxers. Her short spiky hair was flattened on the left side. My heart fluttered, and my face warmed at the sight of her. Even with her hair a mess, something about her made my pulse race. "It's my brother. Sorry to wake you."

I hustled into the living room. "Morning," I mumbled when I opened the door.

"Shit." Jake stared at me like I was something the dog threw up. It had been months since he'd seen me. "You look like crap. You're nothing but skin and bones. And your face is all bruised. What happened to you?"

"Gee, thanks. You sure know how to make a girl feel pretty."

Regret crossed his face. He gave me a gentle hug instead of his usual hearty embrace, as if he thought I'd break. "I'm worried about you, baby sister."

I pulled back, and our eyes met. "I know. I'm doing better than I was. Working again, for starters."

He glanced at the snow flurry of pockmarks on my front window. "I can see that. You expecting whoever did this to return anytime soon?"

"No."

"Whose motorcycle's in the carport?"

"Mine." Shea stepped into the room, her hair once again perfect. Hubba hubba.

"Jake Ballou," said my brother, shaking her hand. "Pleasure to meet you. You a bounty hunter like my sister?"

"Shea Stevens. Jinx is helping a friend of mine out with a...a case."

"A member of Shea's biker club is being framed by Scottsdale PD," I explained. "I'm working as a PI to get the charges dropped against her."

Jake shook his head. "Looks like things are getting pretty crazy."

"Nothing I can't handle. When can you do the repairs?"

"Depends. Are we talking cash or labor?"

I occasionally helped him renovate homes he planned to flip when work was slow for me.

"Cash this time. Family rates, right?"

"Fine. I'll put together an estimate. Let me go outside and assess the damage." He stepped out the front door.

Shea and I retreated to the kitchen, where I poured each of us some coffee. Before sitting down at the table, I looked through the pantry. "Don't have much in the way of food. Cold cereal, okay?"

"It's fine."

I opened the fridge and remembered the milk was sour. "No milk, though. Sorry. I suppose we could go out."

"I got a better idea. Tell me where the nearest supermarket is. I'll get some groceries and make us some breakfast. It's the least I can do for all the trouble we've been putting you through."

"You cook?" I asked a little too earnestly.

Shea shrugged. "Not like gourmet. But I can do a decent breakfast. Whaddya like? Bacon, eggs, French toast, waffles? I can even do an omelet if you want."

"All of that sounds good. Whatever you feel like making." *But what I really want to eat is you.* I hoped I wasn't drooling. "There's a Safeway on McDowell just past Third Street. North side of the road."

After she finished her coffee, she pulled on her shades, boots, and biker vest. "Be back in a jiffy."

Moments after she roared off on her motorcycle, Jake stepped inside. "She's cute. You two...uh..."

Heat poured into my face. "We're just...working together." I swallowed hard.

A devilish grin curled the corner of his mouth. "Uh-huh. Right. I know things didn't work out with that prison guard, but I'm not blind. I can see you two have the hots for each other."

"You think she has the hots for me?" I was at once terrified and elated.

"Duh. Are you kidding?"

I poured him a cup of coffee as he sat down at the kitchen table, totaling his estimate. "How are things between you and Rodeo?" I asked. "Will we be hearing wedding bells anytime soon?"

"Geez, you sound like Mom."

"So, spill. Since he started working for Deez's crew, I don't seem him around very much."

"Things are good. Not talking about wedding bells, but he's helped me work through a lot of my...issues."

"Like holding hands in public?" I asked.

Now it was his turn to blush. "Among other things. That stunt you pulled last Christmas in the restaurant was the push I needed. Embarrassing as it was."

"Glad I could help."

He handed me the estimate, and I gasped. "What about the family discount?"

"Babe, that is with the family discount. It'd be thirty percent more otherwise."

It wouldn't have been a problem if I didn't have that damn insurance adjuster demanding I return Conor's life insurance money. I might be all right if we got paid on the Pearson job, but even that wasn't a sure thing.

"Okay," I said between gritted teeth. "When can you start?"

"I'll check with my suppliers to see if they have this grade of polycarbonate in stock. If so, I can get started this afternoon."

I hugged him. "Thanks, bro. I appreciate it."

"I better see your scrawny ass on Sunday. I'm telling Mom you'll be there. You don't show, she will be crushed." From the look in his eyes, I knew he meant it.

"You're as good at this Catholic guilt shit as Mom."

"I learn from the best. See ya later this afternoon."

"If I'm not here, you have a key and the security codes, right?"

"I do."

Shea showed up twenty minutes later with bags of groceries, including eggs, cheese, milk, and vegetables that didn't come out of a can. While she was whipping up something delicious, my phone rang. It was Becca this time.

"Hey, Becks. Whatcha got for me? You find Garnov?"

"Still nothing on this mystery man. But I have learned some interesting tidbits about the not-so-dearly-departed Brother James Fitzgerald. Turns out he had put down a deposit on a condo along the Central Corridor. One of those fancy high-rises."

"Are you serious? Those places are fucking expensive. Like mid six figures. How could he afford that? Especially since he and Wilkes were parting ways."

"I found an alternative email address he was using. According to *Publishers Weekly*, he signed a seven-figure deal with Little, Brown a couple months ago."

"Who's Lil Brown? A rapper?"

"Little, Brown. A major book publisher. He was writing a nonfiction book on his experiences with the Evangelical Light of the Messiah Church. He also exchanged emails with an Olivia Sullivan at *Phoenix Living* about an interview."

"A tell-all book?"

"Looks like it. Not sure what all he was going to tell that was so scandalous. That's what I'm trying to find. So far, I haven't been able to track down any details."

"How did the cops not know about this?"

"The money from the publisher was wired to an account in Turks and Caicos. I just happened to stumble on it when I came across the other email address. Maybe once the cops found Pearson's DNA link, they stopped looking elsewhere."

"If Wilkes knew about this book deal, that might be motive to take out Fitzgerald. But I don't think he could have done it alone. Any evidence that Wilkes hired a hit man?" I started wondering about Alexei Garnov.

"I've looked into it but haven't found anything definitive yet. Wilkes's finances are a maze of shell corporations. Lots of money coming in from extreme right-wing organizations and individual donors, then getting shuffled around. The money trail is so convoluted, it makes my head spin."

"Keep looking. We need some solid evidence, and fast."

"Will do. Talk to you soon."

Shea brought a couple of plates to the table, each loaded with a beautiful omelet and two strips of perfectly crisp bacon. "Find out anything?"

"Fitzgerald was writing a tell-all memoir about Wilkes and his little church of hate. He's been talking to a reporter, Olivia Sullivan at *Phoenix Living*. I have a feeling she's getting ready to write an exposé on Wilkes. I want to talk to her about this conflict between Fitzgerald and Wilkes."

Becca had texted me Sullivan's email address. I sent a message to Sullivan telling her I knew she was writing an article on Fitzgerald and that I, as an investigator looking into the murder, had information she might want to include. I stipulated I would only give it to her in person and it had to be today. Time was running out to resolve this case one way or another.

37

By the time Byrd arrived at eight o'clock, I'd received a response from Sullivan asking to meet at the *Phoenix Living* office downtown.

Despite its battered appearance, I opted to drive the Charger over the Gray Ghost. I had no reason to believe that whoever was chasing us before wouldn't do so again. I invited Shea to ride along with Byrd and me, under the premise of saving gas. Really, I just wanted to be closer to her.

"Thanks, but I'd rather follow on my bike. Not a big fan of riding in cages."

I tried to hide my disappointment, but it was probably for the better. I needed to focus on the task at hand. Having my head in a pink cloud over my newfound romance with Conor was what got Deez shot so many years ago. I didn't want history to repeat itself.

We drove down Central Avenue to the Sun Glow Building and parked in the underground garage. We geared up and hit the elevator. I didn't think we'd be ambushed, but I wanted to send a message that we meant business.

It wasn't the first time I had visited *Phoenix Living*. A year earlier, I had confronted Brian Hensley, one of their senior reporters, on a hit piece he'd done on me, outing me to their readers and getting me fired in the process. The problems didn't end there.

We took the elevator to the seventh floor. The glass doors to *Phoenix Living*'s office were locked, as Sullivan had told me they would be since it was Saturday. *Phoenix Living* was a weekly paper. I pressed the call button on a nearby intercom.

"Can I help you?" asked a staticky female voice.

"Jinx Ballou to see Olivia Sullivan."

"Be right there."

A moment later, a woman in her midforties wearing a sleeveless dress pressed a button to release the lock. Her lavender chalcedony earrings matched a pendant that hung from a gold chain around her neck. Sullivan had a tan face and a smart, above-the-shoulder haircut.

The lobby's style was understated elegance. The name of the paper was mounted in brass letters on the wall behind the receptionist's desk. A stack of the latest edition stood on a small table surrounded by comfortable armchairs.

"Jinx Ballou." Her eyes narrowed. "The transgender bounty hunter, right? I thought the name sounded familiar when you called."

"And you're Olivia Sullivan. Cisgender reporter. Now that we've established professions and gender identities..."

"Let's speak in my office, shall we?"

She led us down the hall, grabbed an extra chair from a conference room, and pulled it into her office. She took a seat behind her cluttered desk. The three of us sat down in front.

"So, Ms. Ballou. You're the one Jim Hensley wrote that

story on. Right before he turned up dead on your doorstep."

"Milo Volkov killed Hensley. Probably pissed about the exposé Hensley did on his sex trafficking organization."

"Why did Volkov dump Brian's body on your front porch? Wrapped up in plastic like a sack of garbage."

My face flushed with heat. "Volkov was a psychotic stalker. He developed a twisted obsession with me thanks to Hensley's article. I wanted nothing to do with the sick fuck. And when push came to shove, I killed Volkov and several of his men. Think of it as avenging Hensley's death despite him getting me fired. You're welcome."

We held each other's gaze for what felt like an eternity. I hadn't anticipated getting blindsided like this, but I wasn't going to put up with the bullshit.

"Very well," Sullivan said at last, taking out a notebook and pen. "You have information about the James Fitzgerald murder. How'd you know I was working on a story about him?"

"I'm a bounty hunter, remember? Finding out information is my job."

"And what information can you tell me about Fitzgerald's murder?"

"The woman charged with the homicide is being framed. I suspect Fitzgerald's boss, Michael Wilkes, hired someone to kill him."

She leaned back in her chair, rotating slightly from side to side, twirling a pen in her hand. "Interesting. You have evidence to back up this theory?"

"Fitzgerald was moving out and leaving the cult they call a church. He also signed a major book deal with a whopper of an advance. A tell-all exposé. Clearly, Fitzgerald and Wilkes had a major split over something explosive. Something big enough to have him killed over. I was hoping you could tell us what it is."

Her eyes registered a hit, but she quickly regained her composure. "So you're here looking for answers, not providing them."

"We're looking to free a woman being framed for murdering that scumbag rapist," said Shea.

"But you're a bounty hunter," Sullivan said. "Did someone jump bail?"

"I'm also a licensed private detective. The defendant's attorney hired me to look into the case."

She studied us for a moment. "Since it comes out Thursday, anyway, I might as well tell you. Wilkes is gay. Fitzgerald caught him in bed with a man hired from Pool-Boy, an online male escort service. Thus the rift."

Shea snorted. "Fitzgerald raped a teenage girl but got his panties in a wad when he found out his boss is gay? That's one fucked-up religion."

Byrd shot Shea a look. "Don't paint all of Christianity with the same brush."

"Fitzgerald didn't just rape the Hancock girl," continued Sullivan. "Since his death, several girls have come forth alleging they were assaulted by Fitzgerald."

"Did Wilkes know about Fitzgerald's book deal?" I asked Sullivan, trying to get the conversation back on track.

"Possibly. I don't know."

"You might want to hold off on publishing that story, then."

"Why?"

"In the past week, someone has shot up my house. A green Chevy Nova has been tailing us. And yesterday, someone sent a text threatening to kill me if I didn't back off. Clearly, someone doesn't want us to expose the truth. Whoever killed Fitzgerald may go after you as well."

Sullivan shrugged. "We get threats all the time here at *Phoenix Living*. I think we can handle whatever Wilkes is capable of."

"I'm sure Brian Hensley thought the same thing about Volkov."

"We suspect Wilkes may have connections with Sergei Volkov's organization," Byrd said.

"Sergei Volkov?" Sullivan looked from Byrd to me. "Milo's brother?"

"Sergei runs the motel where Fitzgerald was killed, along with the strip club next door. We've talked to a woman who used to dance at the club. He doesn't like people interfering with his business."

Sullivan wrote furiously. "The dancer's name?"

I shook my head. "Confidential. Her safety's at risk if Sergei's people find out."

"So you think Wilkes hired one of Volkov's people to kill Fitzgerald? Any evidence to back this up?"

"Not yet. A Russian named Alexei Garnov was heard bragging about killing Fitzgerald at a Phoenix bar."

"How does that connect back to Wilkes?"

My phone dinged with an incoming message from Becca, asking me to call her. I slipped it into my pocket. "Wilkes had motive. Sergei's people have the means and opportunity. I have one of my people looking for a solid connection between the two."

"When you find it, let me know. I'll put it in my article. Could be some good publicity for you."

"I'd prefer to remain an unnamed source, if it's all the same to you. Considering what happened the last time I was mentioned in a *Phoenix Living* article."

I turned to Shea and Byrd. "I think we're done here. Let's go."

While waiting for the elevator, I called Becca. "What'd you find?"

"Turns out Wilkes is a closeted gay man. Fitzgerald found out about it and decided to move out."

"So we learned from Olivia Sullivan. He was hiring escorts from PoolBoy."

"Not just PoolBoy. ManSlave, Indiscreet, and several other escort services. But there's more. He was banned from PoolBoy after Wilkes offered five grand to an escort to kill Fitzgerald."

"That's it! We got him! Good work, Becks."

"Not so fast. According to a forum on PoolBoy, the escort, who uses the nickname Rodman, declined the offer. I don't think he killed Fitzgerald."

"But if Wilkes tried with one guy, he probably tried with someone else and got results. Any luck finding Garnov?"

"No Garnovs. But there are approximately eight hundred people with the last name *Garinov* living in the valley."

"That's got to be it."

"Only one Boris Garinov. He's an orthodontist working in Sun City. Originally from St. Petersburg."

"Russia?"

"Florida, actually."

"Don't think he's our guy. The Garinov we're looking for is from Russia, lots of prison tats."

"There is an Andrei Garinov who's a Russian permanent resident working for...wait for it...wait for it..."

"Just tell me already."

"Naughty's Adult Entertainment in Scottsdale, Arizona."

"That's got to be our guy. Think you can find a financial transaction that shows Wilkes hired Garinov to kill Fitzgerald?"

"I've been looking but so far haven't seen one. No financial transactions between Wilkes and Garinov, nor between any of Wilkes's business entities and Volkov's. I've checked all US banks, PayPal, even several offshore banks. If there's a payment for a hit, it's hidden deep. Possibly using cryptocurrencies, but Wilkes doesn't strike me as the type."

I blew out a breath in frustration. "Keep looking. It's got to be there."

I hung up and turned to Byrd and Shea as the elevator doors opened. "Time to pay another visit to the Right Reverend Wilkes."

On the ride down to where we'd parked, I shared what I'd learned. I felt a certain satisfaction knowing we were finally connecting some dots.

The instant we stepped out of the elevator and into the parking garage, the air exploded with a deafening barrage of gunfire.

38

I glimpsed a couple of figures wearing yellow bandanas across the way, between a white Ford passenger van and a black Pontiac Grand Prix.

The three of us ducked behind a concrete pillar as the shots echoed through the parking garage. My ears were ringing from the deafening sounds.

I pulled my Ruger. Byrd and Shea both drew their weapons as well.

"Cover me," Shea shouted above the din. She dashed past a couple of cars.

I stepped out from behind the column and fired a few rounds at one of the gunmen. My shots went wide and hit the van next to him, shattering a window and mirror.

He turned toward me. I ducked. Chips of concrete exploded in my face as bullets hit the pillar.

Gunshots with a different pitch punched through the air. Shea was five cars down, apparently trying to outflank our assailants. Byrd had worked his way in the other direction, returning fire.

I pulled off another series of shots and hit the first

gunman in the shoulder. He vanished from view, his screams adding to the ungodly noise.

The second gunman ducked out of view. I stepped from the safety of the pillar and cautiously duckwalked toward them. The driver's-side door on the Grand Prix opened. The second gunman reappeared and raised his weapon.

I pulled my trigger first, but the firing pin hit an empty chamber. A bullet screamed past my ear. I hit the magazine release on the Ruger to reload. Pain exploded in my chest before I could grab a replacement magazine.

The garage spun. I slammed into the ground on my side. More shots ripped through the air.

"*¡Hijo de puta!*" someone screamed.

I struggled to get up, trying to ignore my throbbing rib cage.

A vehicle roared to life. The Grand Prix loomed toward me. I rolled out of the way while more gunshots thundered through the garage. Glass shattered. Tires squealed. The Pontiac raced up the ramp toward the exit. More gunshots followed and then a deafening silence.

My body trembled with pain and shock. I reached to my chest and felt three hot lumps embedded in the fibers of my ballistic vest.

Byrd and Shea appeared above me, their faces flush and anxious. Byrd's hands were all over me, no doubt checking me for wounds.

"Anybody hit?" I squeaked out.

Shea burst into laughter. "Just you, Wonder Woman. You hurt?" She helped lift me to my feet.

Awkwardly, I fumbled with the Velcro straps on my vest. Shea reached over and helped pull it off my aching torso. I reached under my shirt. Damp. I pulled out my hand, expecting a stain of scarlet but found only sweat, not blood. "I…I think I'll live."

I tried to cock my jaw and jiggle my ear canal with my finger to stop the ringing from the gunfire. Didn't help.

"Thought we lost you for a second," Byrd said.

"I'm harder to kill than I look." I shuffled to where the Grand Prix had been parked. Bright-red blood stained the dirty white pavement littered with spent brass. "Looks like we got at least one of them."

"I hit one of them in the chest," said Byrd. "But he could've been wearing a vest."

"They're Latino." I glanced around looking for witnesses but saw no one. "One of them cursed in Spanish."

"They were Jaguars." Shea's eyes had a haunted look. "A drug gang."

"How do you know?"

"Yellow bandanas."

I nodded. "Why are they after us?"

"No idea." Shea squatted down and stared at the blood. "They used to run heroin and weed up in Cortes County. Worked with the Confederate Thunder back in the day. But then one of the Jaguars kidnapped my niece. It got…ugly. A lot of folks died including my sister and her old man. The few Jaguars that survived moved down to Phoenix."

"Maybe they're after you." Byrd pointed an accusatory finger at Shea. "That why the Nova's been following us?"

"I don't know how they'd know I was here." But there was guilt in Shea's expression.

"Anybody get the license plate on the Pontiac?" I asked after an awkward moment.

"I did." Byrd rattled it off.

"Good. I'll have Becca run the tags. It's time we have another talk with Wilkes. If the Jaguars come at us again, we'll deal with them."

I sent a text to Becca, then glanced around looking for

security cameras but didn't see any. "Let's get out of here before the cops show up."

We were driving north on Central when a couple of police cruisers with lights and sirens raced past us, heading toward the Sun Glow Building.

My phone dinged. I handed it to Byrd.

"Becca says the plate is from a silver Mercedes S55 AMG belonging to Sandra Levy," he said while I drove east on the I-10. "She's a fifty-two-year-old investment banker."

"The car we saw was a black Pontiac. You sure you got the plate number right?" I asked him.

"Absolutely. Becca says Ms. Levy reported her plate stolen yesterday while parked in the parking garage at Scottsdale Fashion Park."

"Scottsdale, again. Are the Jaguars and Volkov's organization working together?"

"No idea." He let out a harsh breath. "Speaking of working together, I don't like working with Shea."

"Why? Because she insulted your religious beliefs?" I asked.

"Not just that. After she and her biker gang refused to surrender Pearson, I had Deez do a little more digging. A few years ago, the Athena Sisterhood were suspected of dealing drugs and burning down several buildings including a bar popular with the Confederate Thunder. Now these Latinx gangbangers show up. And surprise, surprise, this chick has a history with them too. This is not the job I signed up for, Jinx. Not by a long shot."

I thought about it. Part of what drew me to Shea was her sexy bad girl biker image. "I hear what you're saying. Hopefully, we can get a confession from Wilkes, clear Pearson, and somehow get paid. You'll never have to lay eyes on her again."

Byrd didn't say anything, but the air between us rippled

with tension. He wasn't wrong. The situation was getting way out of hand.

Thirty minutes later, we pulled up in front of Wilkes's house. When we got out, I handed Shea a walkie-talkie. "Go around to the rear of the house in case this little turd blossom decides to sneak out the back door."

"You got it, boss." She gave me a two-fingered salute. "Won't be hard to catch if he does. He moves kinda slow."

I turned to Byrd. "Keep an eye on the garage door. Don't need him driving away either."

He shot darts at Shea with his eyes as she walked away, then turned on his walkie-talkie. "Roger that."

I strode up to the front door and waited for everyone to get into position. "Y'all ready?" I asked into the walkie-talkie.

"Back door ready," replied Shea.

"Garage door ready," said Byrd.

"Showtime, kiddos." I rang the doorbell. When there was no response after a couple of minutes, I rang it repeatedly until I heard a shuffling on the other side.

The speakeasy grille in the door opened with a familiar face peering out. "What do you want now?"

"We need to talk, Wilkes."

"I'm not interested." The speakeasy grille snapped shut.

"You can talk to us," I shouted loud enough for him to hear me through the door, "or you can explain to the police why you hired someone to kill Fitzgerald."

"I...I don't know what you're talking about" came his muffled reply.

"It's why you got banned from the PoolBoy escort service, isn't it? You really think you could keep that secret? What are the police going to say when we tell them? Or maybe *Phoenix Living*? I'm sure they'd love to do a story on you."

"Someone must have stolen my credit card information."

"Is that what you're going to tell your Christian Coalition donors? You think they'll believe you? We have your posts on PoolBoy's forum. Should make for interesting reading."

"You wouldn't."

"Exposing a purveyor of homophobic hate as a closeted hypocrite? In a heartbeat."

"What do you want?"

"I want inside to talk."

"I don't believe you. I think you're here to kill me."

"If I wanted to do that, tempting as it may be, you'd already be dead. I'm here as a courtesy."

The dead bolt slid free with a snick. The door opened. "Where's your cohorts?"

"Coming." I keyed the walkie. "Everyone please report to the front door. Over."

I stuck my foot in the doorframe, making sure he didn't try to shut it on me again. Byrd and Shea arrived momentarily.

Wilkes led us into the kitchen. Swirling reflections of light from the backyard pool gleamed through the French doors, painting patterns on the ceiling. He slumped into a chair. The three of us stood around him.

I pulled out my phone and set the audio memo app to record. "You hired someone to kill Brother James, didn't you?"

"Yes."

"Why?" asked Shea.

"He...he found out I...I have an affliction."

"An affliction?" I asked. "What kind of affliction?"

"Sexual attraction to men."

"Being gay isn't an affliction, you twit," replied Shea.

Wilkes shook his finger at her. "It's an abomination. It says so in the Bible. You! I can tell you're a homosexual. Short hair, dressed like a man. The penalty for this evil is death and everlasting fire."

Shea grabbed him by the collar and drew back to punch him, but Byrd held her arm. "No."

"You think your God's going to forgive you for killing Brother James?" I asked. "Or don't the rules apply to you?"

"I...I didn't kill him."

"No," said Byrd. "You hired someone else to do it. Blood's on your hands. The sin is the same. So is the punishment."

"The guy I tried to hire, he refused. Said he doesn't do that kind of thing."

"But you hired someone else," I pressed. "A Russian named Andrei Garinov."

"No, no, I didn't. I repented of my sinful anger, and God has forgiven my transgressions out of his ever-flowing mercy."

"He's lying," Shea replied.

"Brother James and I came to an agreement. He was moving out. I agreed not to tell anyone about him raping those girls if he didn't tell anyone about my...my affliction."

"Affliction, my ass." Shea popped him in the face before I could stop her.

39

"You protected a rapist so your holier-than-thou sponsors would keep sending in the Benjamins," Shea screamed while she pummeled Wilkes.

He collapsed on the floor, pleading for Shea to stop and shielding his face from further blows.

Byrd pulled her off him and tossed her across the room. "Stay off him. We may not like the things he preaches, but that don't give us the right to physically assault the man."

"He's a fucking murderer, a bigot, and a liar," Shea growled. "He deserves a lot more than a beatdown. He deserves to be dragged behind a motorcycle until he's nothing but roadkill."

"Enough, you two!" I stepped between them. "Shea, back off. This isn't the way we do things."

Fire burned in her eyes. I knew that look and felt it too. The urge to kill.

I looked down at the pathetic little man while Byrd helped him back into his chair.

"I didn't have Brother James killed," Wilkes sobbed. "It

was wrong of me to try, but I didn't. I swear upon the Holy Scriptures."

"For once, I think he's telling the truth," I said.

"Seriously?" Shea scoffed.

"Did you hire anyone to come after us?" I asked him.

He wiped his face with a tissue. "No, I did not."

"He's lying, Jinx. Let's just do what we came to do."

"We came to get the truth. Not kill a man, no matter how despicable or pathetic he is."

"You think we're going to get the truth out of him?" Shea kicked his chair leg. He bellowed, cowering and covering his head with his arms.

"Shea, stop."

I tried to think. This was all going off the rails. I had no reason to believe Wilkes about not hiring Garinov. But my gut told me he was telling the truth.

"I really should let her kill you," I said.

"No. Please, God, save me! I am your good and faithful—"

"Shut the fuck up!" I said. "And listen."

He shut up. His entire body trembled. I almost felt sorry for the little fuck. Almost.

"Who else would have killed Brother James?"

Wilkes looked at Shea. "That tranny Negro—"

"Wrong answer." Shea drew her Glock.

"No, please!" Wilkes wailed.

I put my hand on her gun and pushed it away. "Don't."

"Who else?" Shea shouted at him.

"I...I don't know who else. We get lots of death threats."

I stared at him. It would be so easy to look the other way and let Shea end his miserable life. For all the anguish that assholes like him had caused marginalized people. Encouraging rape, assault, and suicides. Wouldn't the world be a better place without him? But was it worth risking my own freedom?

"We're not going to get any more answers out of him." I locked eyes with Shea. "And we're not going to hurt him."

Shea holstered her pistol with a grunt. "This is such bullshit."

"If anyone asks, we were never here. Got it, Wilkes?"

He nodded vigorously. "I promise."

"And one other thing," said Byrd, who pulled the guy up by his front collar before tossing him back into his chair. "Stop preaching that women should be raped and queer people should be killed."

"I have a mission to preach the gospel."

Byrd leaned down into his face. "You do and we share everything with the press and the police. Your male escorts, your attempts to hire a hit man, everything. We will ruin you. All your donations will dry up when they discover what a hypocritical little cockroach you are. From now on, you preach only love, unity, and forgiveness like Jesus did. Understand?"

"I have the right to free speech," he said in a shaky voice with all the self-righteousness he could muster.

"So do we," I replied. "So does *Phoenix Living*."

His face clenched as if struggling with tremendous pain. "Fine. I will...tone things down a bit."

"See that you do." I looked at Shea and Byrd. "We're done here."

"You're going to let this piece of shit live?" Shea looked aghast.

"For now."

I led them out of the house.

The second I closed the front door, Shea turned on me. "That little shit weasel murdered his rapist buddy."

"Now listen here..." said Byrd.

I held up my hand to him and tossed him the keys to the Charger. "Go start the engine and get the AC going. Shea and I need to talk."

Byrd exchanged a tense glance with Shea then walked to the car.

"You and me, we want the same thing here," I told Shea. "I don't trust Wilkes any farther than I can throw him. But we need solid evidence to clear Indigo. And putting that asshole in the hospital, much less the morgue, won't accomplish that."

Shea blew out a harsh breath. "Maybe you're right."

I put a hand on her shoulder. Electricity crackled at the touch. From the look in her eyes, I thought she felt it too. I found myself falling into her gaze. Fear and excitement sizzled through me in equal measures. I wanted to feel her body close to mine.

"I need to know I can count on you, Shea."

"You...you can count on me." Her hand clasped mine.

It took every ounce of self-control I had not to kiss her.

I called Becca and asked her to look into the Jaguars street gang and also told her about Fitzgerald's other rape victims. This job was going to cost me a lot with all the skip tracing she was doing. I hoped I got paid somehow, which was looking less and less likely.

While I drove home, Byrd kept his eyes peeled for tails, in case the Jaguars decided on a rematch. But so far, there were no signs they were following us.

"I'm thinking we should handle this case just the two of us," said Byrd.

"Meaning without Shea."

"She just...she's not a professional. You saw what happened with Wilkes. That can land us all in hot water."

I pulled onto the Loop 202 headed to downtown Phoenix. "She knows she stepped over the line. Shouldn't be a problem going forward."

"Why even have her along? What does she contribute?"

"She's an extra set of eyes for starters. And I didn't mind having her when we were ambushed at the Sun Glow Building."

"For all we know, she's the reason we were ambushed."

On the ramp where the Loop 202 merged onto the I-10, an asshole trucker refused to let me over. I tried to get ahead of him, but he sped up. I slowed to get behind him, but he stayed in my way.

"Your objection has been duly noted, but I want her on the team. That was the agreement. That at least one member of the Athena Sisterhood would work with us to locate Fitzgerald's killer."

"We should've just found some other way to bring in Pearson. It ain't right to let a fugitive suspect evade custody and then work with the people protecting her."

I forced my way in front of the semi and was rewarded with a long blast from his air horn. *Right back atcha, buddy!*

"Byrd, I appreciate what you're saying, but I'm in charge of the team. For now, she stays. If that doesn't work with you, you're welcome to leave."

Byrd didn't reply, but I felt his anger coming off him in waves.

I turned on my stereo and hit one of the playlists without looking. Lily Allen's "Fuck You" started playing. I stabbed at the Next Song button, worried that Byrd would think I was trying to tell him off. Tegan and Sara's "Goodbye, Goodbye" cranked up. *Next!* The Pink Trinkets' lead singer Wicked burst into a repetitive chant of "You so stupid! You so stupid!" at the beginning of the title song of their *Orange, You Stupid* album. I turned off the stereo.

"Sorry," I mumbled.

He didn't say anything until I exited onto Seventh Street. "You sleeping with her?"

"What? No!"

"Jinx, don't lie to me. I see how you look at each other."

"I'm not lying, Byrd, and I don't appreciate the accusation. Sure, maybe she's…she's interesting."

"Interesting…uh-huh. Yeah."

I pulled into a Filiberto's drive-through. Shea pulled through behind us on her motorcycle.

"You want anything?" I asked. "My treat."

Byrd shrugged. I ordered a few of their torpedo-sized burros, anyway, in case he changed his mind.

When I got to the window, I asked if Shea had put in an order. A teenage gal with a thick ponytail and a cheerful voice assured me she had. I paid for both orders. When the girl handed me the bag of food, I leaned out the window and shouted to Shea that I had her order. Shea responded with a thumbs-up.

As we drove the final half mile to my house, the aroma of meat and spices turned my hunger into a deep primal need so strong the saliva glands in my mouth ached.

By the time we got inside, I grabbed a burro and dug into it without bothering with a plate. Byrd reached into the cabinet and distributed plates and napkins, then took one of the burros and some chips and salsa for himself.

The burn of the spicy meat was equal parts pleasure and pain. The more it burned, the faster I ate with the ferocity of a piranha. I'd inhaled two full burros before I slowed down enough to grab us some drinks from the fridge.

40

When my ravenous hunger was sated, the fire lingering in my mouth, I grabbed my laptop. I ran a search, looking for links between Wilkes, the Volkov crime family, and the Westside Jaguars street gang, as they were officially known. Nothing definitive came up. The two organizations tended to stay in their own territory, with the Westside Jaguars' drug operation in the west valley, Volkov and his human trafficking ring in the east. No direct connections between Wilkes and either group.

Maybe the Jaguars' attack had nothing to do with Fitzgerald or Wilkes. Maybe Byrd was right in suggesting they were after Shea. I searched for news stories that showed connections between the Athena Sisterhood and the Jaguars. Even that was a bust.

Maybe I had arrested a bail-jumping member of the Jaguars without realizing his affiliation to the gang. Usually, something would have come up in the background check, unless the guy didn't have any priors. So many possibilities. Not so many answers.

"Goddamnit! It's gotta be here," I said, pushing away the

laptop. I took a long pull on a soda. I craved tequila, but after my last meltdown, I'd poured the last of it down the drain. I'd also tossed the last of my weed. I needed a clear head if I was going to work this shit out.

"Don't worry, Jinx. You'll figure it out," said Shea. "Sometimes when I'm working on a custom bike and it's not coming together, I focus on something else until inspiration strikes."

"Except we're running out of time. And I'm not building a motorcycle. I'm trying to solve a murder."

Shea shrugged. "I'm just saying, give your mind a break."

Byrd glanced at her, then at me. "Hate to say it, but Shea's right. You got to unplug."

I sat staring at the laptop, trying to let my mind go blank, using the meditation techniques my dad was always talking about.

"Don't fight the monkey mind, *chère*. Embrace it," he'd told me once. "It's part of the meditation process. We allow the junk into our consciousness. We acknowledge it. Only then do we let it go so more productive thoughts have room to flourish."

I still had no idea what he was talking about, but he was a psychologist, and I wasn't. I let the memory float away like a helium balloon.

Out of nowhere, I remembered Hardin telling me Detective Garza had been killed by a couple of gangbangers robbing a liquor store.

I pulled up a news story from a local TV station that included video from the liquor store's security footage. The anchor at the beginning of the video warned that some viewers might find the images disturbing. *No shit, Sherlock.*

I stared at the screen, my finger poised above the play

button. Like a coked-out drummer, my heart pounded out a rapid rhythm in my chest.

Garza and I hadn't been all that close. For months, he was always flirting with me. Hell, he flirted with anyone with tits who came within ten feet of him. But when he learned I was trans, the innuendos and double entendres stopped abruptly.

I took a deep breath and clicked Play. Garza walked into the store, gave the cashier a wave, and strolled to the refrigerated case at the back of the store. Another camera shot showed a white woman with long dark hair and a black male companion in one of the aisles, apparently debating what to buy.

Two men wearing yellow bandanas—one bald, the other with spiky, dark hair—rushed into the liquor store with guns raised. The spiky-haired gunman stopped at the counter and pointed his weapon at the cashier, who raised his hands. There was yelling in Spanish, but the audio wasn't clear enough to make out.

Meanwhile, Baldy stalked deeper into the store. A second camera showed him searching the aisles, presumably for potential witnesses. When he spotted Garza, he immediately fired two shots. Pop, pop. The first hit Garza in the face, blowing out the back of his head. The second hit his chest.

Spike made threatening gestures. The cashier opened the register and handed him a stack of bills. Spike stashed the money in his pocket, then both gunmen rushed out of the store.

The burros I'd eaten felt like rocks in my gut. Garza was a womanizer, but he was good police and didn't deserve to be gunned down like that. He truly cared about the community we served.

Something about the video nagged at me, but I couldn't say what.

"Jinx, you all right?" asked Byrd.

"What's wrong, girl?" Shea put an arm on my shoulder.

I realized I was crying. "My partner...back when I was a cop." I swallowed hard. My throat felt like someone had a noose around it.

I turned my laptop so the two of them could see it.

Byrd furrowed his brow. "Jinx, I'm sorry."

"Yeah, that fucking sucks. And I don't like cops all that much," said Shea.

"Something's wrong..." I managed to squeak out.

"That's for sure," said Shea. "Fucking Jags. I hope whoever we shot in the parking lot dies."

I managed to get a handle on the anger and grief tearing at my insides. "Something's not right about the video."

"Like someone tampered with it?" asked Byrd.

It came to me. "No. The gunmen. Why shoot Garza but not the cashier or that couple?"

"Maybe they knew he was a cop."

I turned the laptop toward me and watched it again. It still felt like a punch in the gut, but I forced myself to study the interaction between Garza and the second gunman. Garza looked up as the gunman approached. Without a word, the gunman fired two shots and walked away.

I watched it again. And again. And again. I grew more and more convinced this was not a case of wrong time, wrong place.

When I managed to pull myself together, I called Detective Hardin. "It...it's Jinx Ballou." My voice felt raw, like a coyote's growl.

"I'm kinda busy at the moment."

"It's about Garza."

"What about him?" The change in his tone told me I had his attention.

"The gunmen, members of the Westside Jaguars. They weren't there to rob the store."

"What the hell you talking about?"

"I watched the security footage from the liquor store holdup. The bald gunman went right after Garza. No words, just shot him on sight. But they didn't shoot the cashier or the couple in the store. Not only that, the gunman up front didn't ask for the money in the drawer until after Garza was shot. It was a hit, Pierce, not a robbery gone bad."

"Goddamn. You sure about this?"

"Look at the security footage. Was Garza investigating the Jaguars for anything at the time?"

He let out a sigh full of frustration and bluster. I heard typing on his end. He must've been at his desk, working late on a case.

"At the time of his death, he had four open cases. Two domestic disputes. One sexual assault of a minor. One road rage incident. The only Latin name in any of the cases was the sexual assault victim."

"Who?"

"I'm not giving out the victim's name. She was a minor."

"What about the suspect in the case?" Could it have been Fitzgerald? Was that the connection?

"Barry Fields. The case has been turned over to the Maricopa County Attorney's Office."

"Had Garza investigated James Fitzgerald for anything?"

"Fitzgerald? Not that I...wait, hold on a minute. He was a suspect in a sexual assault case, but the status is listed as cleared by exceptional means. No arrest made."

It was a status that was supposed to be used only in rare

cases, such as when the suspect was dead or there was another reason the suspect couldn't be charged despite strong evidence of guilt. But it was too often used to juice clearance rates on rape cases, even when no charges were filed.

"Exceptional means? Are you serious? He was already found guilty once for sexual assault on a minor. Why was he not charged again for this rape?"

"I don't know the details, Ballou. I'm telling you what I see in the system. I don't have the casebook in front of me."

"Who was the victim?"

"She was a minor. I can't divulge that information."

"Just tell me this, was she Latina? Could she have any connections to the Jaguars?"

"Ballou, I…aw, shit."

"I'm right, aren't I? Who was the victim, Hardin?"

"I can't give you that. All I can tell you is Garza interviewed Fitzgerald, as well as the victim and her father."

Something clicked in my brain. "The father got a rap sheet?"

More keyboard clicks. "Multiple convictions for aggravated assault and possession with intent to sell. Spent several years in Perryville. Suspect in several homicide cases but never charged.

"Who is he, Hardin? Who's the victim's father?"

There was silence on the line. I feared we'd been disconnected. Then Hardin said, "Juan Alfonso Cabrera. He's an enforcer for the Westside Jaguars."

"When did the rape take place?"

"March second."

"A few months after Fitzgerald got probation for raping the Hancock girl. And Garza refused to charge him?"

"Getting prior convictions admitted as evidence is

tricky. You know this, Ballou. And when the victim's father is a violent gangster..."

"So you're saying the teenage daughter of a violent gangster can't be raped?"

"That's not what I'm saying, and you know it. The legal system's messed up. Rape cases are tough to prosecute, especially with a victim with family ties to a criminal organization. I'm not going to sit here and second-guess Garza's decision."

"Garza's decision got him killed, Detective."

"You don't know that."

"Yes, I do. And so do you. Can you send me that information on the Cabrera sexual assault case?"

"Are you kidding me? I shouldn't have even told you about it. I could lose my job."

"Hardin, I'm the one who clued you in on why Garza was really shot. It's looking more like the Jaguars killed James Fitzgerald as well. I'm trying to make sure an innocent person doesn't go to prison for that crime."

"I'm sorry, Ballou. I can't help you. Goodbye."

"Wait, wait, wait! At least tell me what caliber weapon was used to kill Garza."

Hardin let out an exasperated breath. "Ten millimeter."

"Thanks, Detective."

I hung up and grabbed Fitzgerald's file to check the ballistics report. He'd been shot with a ten mill as well.

"What are you thinking?" asked Shea.

"I think the Westside Jaguars murdered James Fitzgerald after he raped the daughter of one of their enforcers. They also killed my partner Garza because he didn't arrest Fitzgerald."

"Holy fuck!"

I repeated what I'd learned from Hardin. "I also think Cabrera shot up my house. Same caliber handgun was used in all three shootings—a ten-millimeter auto. I'd be willing to bet that's why they attacked us this morning. They don't want us looking into Fitzgerald's murder."

She looked at me. "How would the Jags know we were looking into the case?"

"Someone must have told them," replied Byrd. "Question is, who?"

"The other thing that's bothering me is this Garinov fellow. He was supposedly bragging about killing Fitzgerald. And he works for Volkov. Is he also connected to the Westside Jaguars?"

Shea shook her head. "The pieces don't exactly fit together, do they?"

I grabbed the police reports for the discovery of Fitzgerald's body. "The 911 caller used a pay phone at the liquor store next door to the motel and refused to give a name. Police interviewed a motel housekeeper named Camila Morales. She reported seeing a tall African American female with long braids leaving the room shortly before the body was discovered. Everyone assumed that woman was Pearson. But it wasn't."

I looked at Shea. "When you and the Sisterhood were at Naughty's, did you see a dancer who resembled Indigo?"

Shea let out a deep breath. "Shit, I dunno. We were there for a few hours. I got a little drunk. Hold on..."

Shea made a call. "Savage, that night at Naughty's, did any of the dancers look like Indigo? Yeah, yeah. I vaguely remember that. You get her name by chance? Oh, well, thanks." She hung up. "Savage said a couple of the sisters were teasing Indigo because one of the dancers looked like she could be her twin."

"So maybe that's who the housekeeper saw leaving the motel room right before they found Fitzgerald's body." I stood up. "Grab your gear. We're going back to Scottsdale."

41

It was three in the afternoon when we reached the Cactus Inn.

"We need to find this housekeeper, Camila Morales." I scanned the area, looking for a housekeeping cart or an open room door.

"We don't even know if she's working today," said Byrd. "You going to ask the guy at the registration desk?"

"Nope."

"Then what's the plan?"

"I'm going to talk to her." I pointed at a heavyset Latina woman stuffing bedsheets into a laundry bag attached to her cart. "Wait here."

I stepped out of the Charger and sidled up to Shea. "Sit tight. I want to talk with the housekeeper over there."

"I can come with you."

"I don't want to spook her."

"Spook her?" Shea smirked, giving her biker vest a tug. "Nothing spooky about me."

I figured she got my point and sauntered over to where

the woman was pulling fresh sheets from a stack on her cart.

"Excuse me! Miss!" I said, trying to sound worried and desperate.

"*¿Si?*"

"I'm hoping you could help me," I said in Spanish, hoping that would put her more at ease. "Do you recognize this man?" I held up a photo of Brother James on my phone.

Fear glimmered in her eyes. She waved her hands, shook her head, and backed away. "*¡No se! ¡No se!*"

I knew she was lying. "Please, I need to know what happened to him. It's important."

"Front desk say I no talk to police," she said in English.

"Not police. Private investigator."

She pointed at the bail enforcement badge hanging on my chest. "*¡Policía!*"

She glanced toward the office. "I should not talk to you. I don't know anything. I never saw him," she insisted in Spanish.

I realized I was going about this all wrong. "I'm sorry. My name is Jinx Ballou. What's yours?"

"Camila. Camila Morales."

Bingo! "You are the person I need to speak to. You told the police you saw a woman leave this man's room."

"I...I was mistaken." She shuffled into one of the rooms and tried to shut the door, but I held it open.

"Please! A friend of mine is in trouble." I pulled up Indigo's photo. "She's being framed for that man's murder. She's a good woman. Do you think she should go to prison for someone else's crime?"

With some effort, she looked up at my phone. I offered it to her, and she held it. Tears glistened behind her eyes. "I...I saw that man. He was with a girl but not this girl."

"Who was he with?"

"I could get in big trouble."

I pointed at where Shea was leaning against her motorcycle. "You see her? She's a part of a group of women who can protect you." I didn't know if the Athena Sisterhood would help, but I was running out of options. "That's what they do. They protect women in trouble. Keep them safe." Most of the time.

Her face cycled through a series of emotions—fear, guilt, possibly anger. At last, she set the sheets in her hand on the bed. "I saw him with Scarlett. She dances at the club next door. She is also a prostitute."

"What does Scarlett look like?"

"Like your friend—black skin, long braids. But Scarlett has..." She gestured around her mouth.

"A more prominent jaw?"

"Yes, that is it."

"Was Scarlett with the man when he was killed?"

Sweat trickled down her dark face. "I cannot. I cannot say." I could tell she knew more.

"Please. Don't let my friend go to prison. We'll protect you."

"Yes, she was with him but ran out of the room screaming. She was bleeding. A man ran after her."

"A man? Who? Andrei Garinov? Did he kill Fitzgerald? Or someone else? Was he Russian? Latino?"

Her eyes grew larger. "I did not get good look."

"Was he tall? Short? Skinny? Fat? What color hair?"

"I do not remember." She was getting flustered. I was losing her.

"Is it common for housekeeping to work so late?"

She blushed. "Most customers stay only an hour or two. We must get rooms ready for the next customer. So we work sometimes at night."

"Was Fitzgerald still alive when Scarlett left?"

"I do not know." She looked away and gasped. "You must go now! Mr. Ivanov is coming!"

I turned toward where she was looking. Lenny, the skinny little pissant from the front desk, was striding toward us. *Shit.*

"Don't worry." I turned back to Camila and put a hand on her shoulder. She was shaking like a dog in a thunderstorm. "We will protect you."

"Not me I worry about. It's my daughter."

"Get the hell away from her," said Lenny. "Camila, get your fat ass back to work!"

"Camila," I pleaded, "come with us. I won't let them hurt you."

"Stay out of this, bitch. Camila, you know what'll happen if you don't shut your mouth and get back to work."

Shea and Byrd ran toward us.

I stepped between Camila and Lenny. "What's going to happen, asshole? You going to hurt her? Her daughter?"

"She knows." His voice was pure venom.

"It's okay, senorita," said Camila in a shaky voice. "I go do my job. I say nothing. I promise."

"No, it's not okay. You leave her and her daughter alone, you piece of shit. Or you'll wish you had."

He smirked. "You don't know who you're dealing with."

"Oh, I know exactly who we're dealing with. Sergei Volkov. Am I right? You can tell Sergei to kiss my ass. I kicked his brother's ass. I have no problem kicking Sergei's too. Now go back to jacking off behind the registration desk."

"What the hell's going on?" asked Shea.

"None of your goddamned business," said Lenny sharply.

"This little pissant's threatening this hardworking woman."

"Is that so?" Shea shoved Lenny back a step. "You like threatening women?"

"No, Miss Jinx," pleaded Camila. "Everything okay. I go back to work. You go now. Don't come back."

"See? Camila doesn't want you around. That means you're trespassing." Lenny had a smug expression that begged to be punched. Only question was whether Shea or I would do the honors.

"You gonna call the police?" I asked.

"Come on, Jinx," said Byrd. "Let's not make things worse than they are."

"Listen to your man, lady," Lenny replied.

It took all my self-control not to deck him. "If I learn you hurt Camila or her daughter, you will regret it."

"You won't hear nothing, bitch. If you come back, you will regret it."

I turned away from him only because Shea had grabbed one arm and Byrd the other. I shrugged them off and continued to the car. "I'm going."

When I climbed in the Charger, I made a call.

"Special Agent Lovelace. How can I help you?"

"It's Jinx Ballou. How's life at the FBI?"

"Ms. Ballou. I'm really surprised to hear from you after what happened to Wilhelm Penzler. We were counting on his testimony to bring down Sergei Volkov."

"Not my fault he jumped bail," I replied. "Nor was it my fault he threw himself off a three-story balcony rather than testify against Volkov."

"Why are you calling me, Ms. Ballou?"

"Trying to help you nail Volkov. I'm down at the Cactus Inn and just had a very interesting conversation with a woman from housekeeping named Camila. Sergei's people are holding her daughter hostage. The little turd bucket in the front office really doesn't like the staff talking to people with badges. You might want to send someone down here to investigate and maybe protect this poor woman."

"Okay, thanks."

"Just thanks? Are you coming down to investigate?"

"We will look into the matter."

"When?"

"Ms. Ballou, I appreciate your assistance in this matter. We will handle it."

"Don't you even want a description of Camila or the little shit running the registration desk?"

"We have it handled."

"Handled how?"

My phone beeped as the call dropped. "Shit."

"We should probably go," said Byrd. "We got enough trouble dealing with the Westside Jaguars. We don't need Volkov's men coming after us too."

"Not yet. Camila said the woman she saw leaving Fitzgerald's room was named Scarlett. She's a dancer at Naughty's. Looks like Indigo but with a more prominent jaw."

"What are you proposing?" asked Byrd.

"We go next door and try to find her."

"Into the dragon's den," said Shea with a wicked smile.

Byrd looked pale. "Volkov doesn't like people interfering with his business. If we get caught..."

"Relax, man." Shea slapped him on the arm. "We're just gonna have a drink and enjoy the entertainment. I'll even buy you a lap dance."

"That's the other thing. This isn't the kind of place I should go into."

"Why?" asked Shea. "Will Jesus send you to hell for looking at naked women?"

"Shea, ease up," I warned her. "Byrd, we're just going in there to locate Scarlett. This is the job. If we see her, we'll ask a few questions. Very low-key." I pulled off my vest and my tactical belt, then stuffed my Ruger in the concealment holster at the small of my back.

He let out a long sigh but didn't say anything.

"Or you can stay in the car. Your choice." I figured I might as well give the poor guy an out.

"And let you two ladies go in by yourselves? What kind of man would I be then?"

Shea rolled her eyes. "I think we can handle it, big guy."

"So you're in?" I asked him.

"I'm in."

42

I don't hang out in strip clubs very often. Not because I'm a prude or have a problem with women doing what they choose with their bodies. It just feels too much like window-shopping. You can look, but you can't touch. What fun is that?

But I needed some strong evidence to impeach Indigo's DNA. If Scarlett witnessed Fitzgerald's murder, I needed to find her.

I paid the cover charge for the three of us, and we stepped inside. The place smelled of booze, cheap perfume, and sex. The music was loud and bouncy. A dancer who looked all of sixteen spun around a pole on stage, leaving nothing to the imagination. Topless women with drop-dead gorgeous bods, in all sizes and colors, were giving lap dances and serving drinks. Middle-aged guys with an out-of-town-salesman vibe filled the tables crowded around the stage.

Shea pointed at an empty table. No sooner had we sat down than a woman with large, hypnotic eyes and olive skin offered to take our order. I asked for a bottle of water, Shea a Dos Equis, and Byrd nothing.

"Hey," I shouted to our server, trying to be heard over the music. "Is Scarlett dancing this afternoon?"

"Scarlett?"

"African American, long braids down her back."

"I think she's off today."

"When will she be back?"

Our server shrugged.

I nodded. "Okay, thanks."

After she walked off to fill our order, Shea leaned over. "What now?"

"Let's keep asking. Maybe we'll get lucky."

Shea eyed the new dancer on stage, who seemed a bit older and more busty, discarding piece by piece a sequined outfit inspired by the stars and stripes. "Maybe we will."

I sat staring blankly at the onstage entertainment as I contemplated our next move.

A different server brought our drinks. A flowering vine tattoo ran up her leg, around her torso, and out her left arm, with red hibiscus blossoms every six inches or so.

"You asking about Scarlett?" She handed me our drinks.

"Yeah. You know her?"

"She disappeared about a month ago. Right after that man was killed next door." The server looked around nervously.

"You know her last name? Or a phone number for her?"

She shook her head. "Sorry. I hope you find her. She was nice."

"Thanks for your help." I turned to Shea and Byrd. "I think this is a dead end."

"I told you," replied Byrd. "Let's get out of here."

"Aw, come on, guys. I'm thirsty. At least let's finish our drinks."

"Do what you want," I told her. "Byrd and I are leaving."

I gestured to Byrd, and he nodded. As we stood up, Shea took a long pull on her beer and followed along. We were almost to the door when a bouncer the size of a bulldozer stepped into our path. "Someone wants to see you." His accent was definitely Eastern European.

"You got the wrong person, pal." I tried to push past, but Bulldozer was hard to get around. I reached for my Ruger at the small of my back, but someone grabbed my arm and whirled me around.

The big guy holding me had a long face with lips like Mick Jagger's. He relieved me of my Ruger, phone, and wallet, then smiled, showing off his horse teeth.

Byrd and Shea were similarly disarmed by two hefty guys who reminded me of Hans and Franz, the comical bodybuilders from *Saturday Night Live*. It would've been funny if they didn't look so hostile. Four steroid-swollen bouncers against the three of us were not good odds.

Bulldozer pointed toward a hallway at the back of the room. Every cell in my body told me not to go wherever they were herding us. But now that they had our weapons, we didn't have much choice.

The bouncers frog-marched us across the room and down the hallway. Bulldozer led the way, followed by Hans pushing Shea. Franz drove Byrd a few steps behind her. Me and my buddy Mick Jagger brought up the rear, with him holding my arm tight enough to leave a bruise.

When a dancer emerged from the dressing room ahead of us, Bulldozer shouted, "Get back in room!"

She squeaked like a mouse and dove inside the dressing room.

Bulldozer turned right up a staircase. If we went up there, odds of us coming down alive were slim.

I pinwheeled with my free arm, breaking the bouncer's grip. Jagger returned the favor by driving his mallet of a fist into the side of my head. I dropped to my knees as the room spun like a carnival ride. He jerked me to my feet.

"Do that again, I snap your skinny little neck." He shoved me into Byrd, who helped steady me.

"You okay?" asked Byrd.

"Just peachy." I tried to shake away the cobwebs while being half dragged up the narrow staircase.

At the top, the bouncers led us down another hallway, where the doors were secured with large padlocks on the outside.

Bulldozer unlocked one of the rooms. Before I knew what was happening, Jagger tossed me inside like a sack of flour, crashing into the far wall. The door slammed shut followed by the snick of the padlock.

My temple throbbed. I rubbed it with my hand, and it came away wet. I didn't think it was sweat this time, but the room was near pitch dark. The only light came from a narrow slit under the door.

The stale air reeked of urine and fear. A quick search by touch told me it was empty and about the size of a small closet. *Fuck!*

I pounded on the door. "Let me out of here!"

"Shut your face, bitch, or I put bullet into your girlfriend."

"Shit!" I leaned against the back wall and slid down to the floor. *How the hell am I going to get out of here?*

My mother was right. I should have switched to something safer. Like being a bomb disposal technician, a stunt person, or a window washer for skyscrapers.

I lost track of time. All that was left was the darkness, the pain, and a highlights reel of reasons the world was better off without me. The thrum-thrum-thrum of the music downstairs was interrupted only by the occasional footsteps in the hallway.

Why do I even bother trying? I'm a goddamn failure. Bad enough I'm probably going to die. Now Shea and Byrd probably will too. I was a horrible girlfriend to Conor, only letting him get so close. I was a horrible daughter, a disappointment for a sister, a lousy best friend. A pathetic excuse for a bounty hunter, much less a private investigator. No matter what I do, people around me are hurt and killed.

The snick-clack of the padlock being unlocked caught my attention. When the door opened, a blaze of light ripped through the room. I shielded my eyes with my arm.

A meaty fist wrapped around my arm and yanked me to my feet. "Someone wants to see you," Bulldozer muttered in a gravelly voice.

He dragged me down the hall and practically threw me into a large office. Jagger stood between Shea and Byrd, a pistol in one hand and my Ruger still stashed in his waistband.

A man with a rectangular face sat behind a wooden desk. Didn't look like the photos of Sergei Volkov that Becca had sent me, though his features were definitely European. He wore a black suit that looked a little heavy for this time of year in Phoenix. Our wallets and phones were on the desk in front of him.

"I hear you question my employees," he said in a thick Russian accent.

"Yuri Barayev," I guessed, recalling my conversation with Maricela.

"Impressive. And you are Jenna Ballou," he replied using my legal first name. "But you go by Jinx. Curious name. It means cursed, yes?"

"Only for people who get in my way."

"Why you poking nose where it does not belong?"

"You're going to have to be more specific. Poking my nose where it doesn't belong is what I do for a living."

"Why you look for Scarlett?"

I shrugged. "I heard she's a great dancer. Thought we'd come check her out."

Barayev nodded to Jagger, who punched Shea in the gut.

"Leave her alone, you fucking pig." That came from Byrd. I was shocked to hear him curse.

"Tell me what I want, or my friend here will do worse."

Jagger pressed the muzzle of his gun to Shea's temple. I needed a way to change the power dynamic and fast.

"All right! Here's the deal. Scarlett witnessed a murder we're investigating," I replied.

"The preacher man. Why you looking into murder? Police already make arrest someone."

"The wrong someone. We're looking for the right someone."

"Scarlett is not here," Yuri said. "She is gone missing. No answers here. Only trouble for you."

He glared at me, but I caught his gaze drifting down to my chest. My shirt was damp with sweat, making the outline of my nipples visible even through my bra. Fine. He wanted to look. I'd give him something to look at.

"You know, Yuri, I think we all got off on the wrong foot. I'm a woman. You're a man. This doesn't have to be an adversarial relationship." I took a step toward the desk.

Bulldozer aimed his pistol at me.

"Easy, big guy. I'm unarmed." I held up my hands and flashed Yuri a seductive smile.

He nodded. I stepped around the desk, pulling off my T-shirt. Yuri's eyes widened with want.

"I think we can come to a more amenable agreement."

I pushed him back in his swivel chair and straddled his

lap. His dick was hard and pressing into my ass. "You know, back when Milo ran things, he and I…" I traced his jawline with my finger. "We had a little thing going. But now that he's gone, I haven't had anyone to entertain me. No one to… fill my emptiness. You think you could do that? Fill the empty hole inside me?"

He started to grind against me. "Da," he said in a breathy voice.

I leaned my chest against his. He stared down at my breasts peeking above my bra. I wrapped my arms around his waist and found exactly what I was looking for.

In a flash, I pulled the pistol from his waistband, pivoted off of Yuri, and pressed the gun against his head while using him as a shield. "Drop your guns, assholes!"

When Jagger looked at me, Shea snatched the gun out his hand and kneed him in the crotch. The floor shook when he hit the ground, groaning. "Fucking asshole!" she said.

A bullet zinged past my ear. Bulldozer! Before I could return fire, Byrd twisted the gun out of the bouncer's hand and leveled it at him. "Don't shoot at my friends, please."

I stepped away from Yuri. "SIG Sauer. Nice. Always liked these. Thanks for the gift."

Yuri's eyes blazed with anger. "You just bought large trouble, bitch. You think you clever. Not so clever when you are dead."

"Don't threaten us, Yuri. We're just trying to solve a murder. Now where the hell is Andrei Garinov?"

"I am Garinov," said Bulldozer.

"I'm told you killed Fitzgerald."

The confused look on his face looked genuine. "I not kill goddamn preacher."

"Don't lie to me, asshole. You were heard bragging

about it at the Stone Horse Pub. Guess you get blabby when you've had a few Stolis, huh?"

Garinov glanced at Yuri, a jolt of concern in his eyes. "I did not kill. I teach preacher lesson after he hurt our girl. But he was still alive. He come back, sleep with other girls."

"Including Scarlett, who just happened to go missing right after Fitzgerald turned up dead," replied Byrd. "Maybe you killed them both."

"Andrei did not kill preacher. We do not kill client, even when they are problem. Dead client is bad for business."

"You threatened to kill us," Shea snorted.

Yuri glared at her. "You are not client."

If Andrei didn't kill him, then who? Cabrera? I would need some sort of proof to get Indigo off the hook. But I wouldn't find it here.

"Well, I'm glad we got that cleared up. Listen, boys. It's been a lot of fun, but it's time we take our toys and leave. Stay out of our way, and we'll stay out of yours. Okay?"

"Not okay," growled Yuri. "You find Scarlett, you bring her back to me. Or we will..."

"Yeah, yeah, you'll kill us. Blah, blah, Russian blah. Here's the deal, Big Red. Come after us again, you'll wish you hadn't." I grabbed my wallet and phone from the desk, then handed Shea and Byrd theirs. "Let's go."

"Yeah, let's get the fuck outta here." Shea gave Jagger another kick.

We raced down the staircase and ducked out the back door, setting off a security alarm. We hustled into the dark alley outside and around the building to the front parking lot.

The alarm had dancers and patrons pouring out of the building like ants from a disturbed mound. Several of the men still held their drinks, looking around trying to figure out what was going on.

Shea, Byrd, and I filtered through the crowd, working our way to the Charger and Shea's bike.

"What now?" asked Shea.

"Back to my place. I've had enough of Scottsdale for one day."

Shea pulled on her helmet and threw a leg over her bike. Byrd and I hopped into the Charger.

The tension in the car was thick as butter. Every time we stopped at a light on Scottsdale Road, I pounded on the wheel and yelled at the light to turn green, then screamed at the cars in front of me to go.

Byrd silently stared out the window.

I started to settle down as we turned onto McDowell, passing between the wind-carved hills known as the Papago Buttes. As we crested the rise, the lights of Phoenix glittered in the night off to our left.

"You were right," I finally admitted. "We shouldn't have gone in there."

"I wasn't going to say anything."

"I know you weren't. That's why I did. You were right. I'm sorry."

"Sorry won't do us much good when the Russians track us down and kill us."

"I think they got the message to leave us alone." I hoped I wasn't wrong again.

"You think Garinov was telling the truth? That he didn't kill Fitzgerald?"

I turned left onto Fifty-Second Street, then right onto the Loop 202. "Simon heard Garinov brag about putting a beatdown on the preacher. Didn't specifically say he killed him."

"Because Fitzgerald got abusive with one of the dancers."

"If we track Scarlett down, maybe we can get the proof we need and wrap things up."

But clearing Indigo was only one of our problems. We had the Jaguars and Volkov's people after us. Our chances of getting out of this with our hides intact were looking slim.

43

It was eight thirty by the time we reached my house. To my surprise, the damaged window had been replaced. When we walked in the door, Shea's phone rang. She rushed off to the guest room for some privacy.

"You want to stay here, or you headed home?" I asked Byrd.

"After what we just went through, I'd just as soon stay at my own place to Netflix and chill. I need some serious decompression."

"You want Shea or me to escort you home?"

"I'll be okay."

"All right, but keep your head on a swivel."

"Will do."

"See you tomorrow?"

"Sunday? I got church and...to be honest, I think I'm done playing private detective. Between the Russians and the Latino gangsters, this is a little more than I bargained for."

"Well, take care."

"Thanks." He gave me a hug. "Watch your back, Jinx."

I closed the door and called Maricela. I needed more information.

"*Bueno.*"

"Maricela, this is Jinx Ballou. We spoke yesterday about your dancing at Naughty's."

"*Sí.*"

"Did you know a dancer named Scarlett?"

"Yes, I liked her. Long braids. Very pretty. We used to talk a lot about our life before. She was from Haiti originally. Barayev found her, told her he could get her started in a modeling career."

"I think she was assigned to service Fitzgerald after he hurt you. She witnessed who killed him."

"*¡Ay, Dios mio!* Is she okay?"

"I don't know. She's disappeared. Do you know any way to reach her? A phone number? Her last name?"

"I…I have nothing to do with that world anymore. Too painful. Too risky." From her tone, I got the impression she was holding back. "I'm sorry."

"Please, Maricela. I understand you're scared, but I'm worried about her. Do you have any way to reach her?"

Silence filled the line, and I wondered if she'd hung up. "Yuri did not allow us phones. But Scarlett got one from a client. Before I escaped, she gave her number. Hold on. I will find it." She paused, then read me off the phone number. I wrote it down.

"Thanks. Could you call her? If I call, she might not talk to me, because I'm a stranger. But if you call…"

"I…I can't. Too risky. Yuri is smart. He might learn about phone. Track her down, then find out where I am. It is too much risk. I am sorry. Goodbye."

She hung up.

Shea walked into the living room with a smirk on her face.

"What's up?" I asked.

"Nothing."

"Nothing? You look like the proverbial cat who ate the canary."

"Club stuff."

I ordered us a pizza and turned on the TV for background noise. Shea and I talked about everything from motorcycles to her adventures growing up in an outlaw biker family. My own life, even as a trans kid, seemed pretty vanilla and privileged by comparison.

She got me to talk about my decision to leave the police force to become a bounty hunter. We compared notes on our experiences with Milo Volkov.

"Kinda weird," said Shea before she finished the last slice of pizza.

I took a long pull on my soda. "What's that?"

"Me an ex-con, you an ex-cop. Opposite sides of the law, and yet here we meet in the gray, murky middle."

"Yeah, I suppose that is kind of weird."

"I heard about your ex-boyfriend, the Irishman who's on trial in the UK. What's his name? Colin?"

"Conor. It's...I don't know what it is. He was caught up in some bad stuff when he was younger. The Troubles, they call it. Ironic that he nearly died trying to stop a bomb here."

"The one that blew up on the Piestewa Freeway. Yeah, I heard that."

I felt the well of grief starting to open beneath me, calling me back into the all-too-familiar darkness. "I don't know if the Northern Irish cops tracked him down or he simply turned himself in, but now he's sitting in a cell somewhere in Belfast. I feel like it's my fault. If I'd..."

"Not your fault. He made his choices—both when he was a teenager and after the bomb blast here. We all make choices. I've made plenty of shitty ones. Spent seven years down in Perryville as a result."

"But then you turned everything around."

"Sometimes I wonder how much."

Something Byrd said popped up in my memory. "I heard that the Athena Sisterhood was involved with drugs and arson. What's that about?"

Shea's face darkened. "Who told you that?"

"Not important. Is it true?"

"Few years back, a couple of our members were involved with some bad shit. It wasn't a club thing. When we learned about it, well, we shut it down. I can't say any more. Not allowed to talk about internal club business. The Athena Sisterhood is a law-abiding club. We don't allow drugs or any other criminal activity."

"Good to know." My phone rang. "Yello."

"Jinx, it's Max." He sounded out of breath.

"Who?" The name sounded vaguely familiar, but I couldn't place it.

"Max Alexander. I'm a trans guy living at your old house with Ciara. We met a few days ago when you were..."

Flashes of memories flitted through my brain. Me arguing with someone about whose house it was. "Yeah, I remember. I was a little...confused. Sorry about that."

"This isn't about that. It's Ciara. Someone...someone took her."

"Took her? What do you mean 'took her'?"

"These big guys with accents. They showed up asking for you. We told them you didn't live here anymore. When Ciara refused to give them your new address, they kidnapped her."

"Did you call the police?

"They arrived a little while ago. I told them what happened. They want to talk to you."

"Sit tight. We'll be right there."

I hung up and looked at Shea. "We gotta go."

Five minutes later, we pulled onto my old street and parked a few doors away from my house. Patrol vehicles and unmarked cars, all lighting up the night in flashes of red and blue, blocked off the street. As we approached, I noticed uniformed officers canvassing the neighbors, no doubt looking for witnesses.

We found Max sitting on the curb outside the crime scene tape. He was wrapped in a foil survival blanket, holding an ice pack to his forehead and looking hopeless.

I introduced Shea, as we sat on either side of him. "What happened?"

"I was..." He swallowed hard. "I was taking a shower when the doorbell rang. Ciara answered it. That's when I heard shouting."

"What were they saying?"

"I couldn't make out the words at first. I turned off the water and pulled on a shirt and shorts..." Max's androgynous voice cracked with emotion.

"There were three of them. Big, scary guys. Thick accents. Russian or Ukrainian, I think. They were looking for you and a woman named Scarlett."

"Assholes!" Shea said.

"Ciara tried to calm them down and explain you didn't live there. When she refused to say where you lived now, they punched her. I tried to save her, but there were too many of them. They punched me in the head. When I came to, the door was wide open, and they were gone along with Ciara."

"Shit."

A woman in a dark suit approached, carrying a small notebook. The shield on her waist told me she was a detective. "How you doing, Mr. Alexander?"

He shrugged again.

"These friends of yours?" she asked.

"Jinx Ballou." I offered my hand, which she shook. "I own the house."

"Detective Cooper, Violent Crimes Division." She glanced at her notes. "Ah yes, Ms. Ballou. Mr. Alexander stated the assailants were looking for you."

"Based on Max's description, the guys who took Ciara are part of Sergei Volkov's human trafficking ring. They're looking for a former sex slave named Scarlett who disappeared. They think I know where she is."

"And why would they think that?"

"Because I'm looking for her too. She witnessed a murder that I'm investigating."

Cooper raised an eyebrow. "You're a detective?"

"Private. Normally I work as a bail enforcement agent, but I'm also a licensed PI."

"Does Scarlett have a last name?"

"I'm sure she does, but I don't know it."

Cooper cocked her head. "Why would they look for you here?"

"We were at the club earlier this evening looking for Scarlett. They...uh...detained us briefly. Probably looked through our wallets. This address is still listed on my license."

I suggested she get in touch with Special Agent Lovelace at the FBI, since Lovelace was already working to shut down the human trafficking ring. Cooper asked several more questions, having me go back through my story repeatedly, before thanking me for my time and returning to the house to continue her investigation.

"What am I going to do now?" asked Max.

Guilt hung heavy on my shoulders. This was my fault.

Again. "You're welcome to sleep on my couch until the situation gets resolved." I wasn't sure what *resolved* meant.

"He can have the guest room," Shea said. "I'll take the couch."

"Is it safe?" He looked at me the way a frightened child would.

"The place I live in now is very secure and not far from here."

"What about Ciara?"

"Sounds like Detective Cooper has a handle on things."

My phone rang, but the caller ID on the screen was blank.

"Ballou Fugitive Services."

"I have your friend." The Russian-accented voice was familiar. Yuri! A blood vessel throbbed on my temple.

"Motherfucker! You let her go. She's got nothing to do with any of this."

"Perhaps. Once you bring what we look for. You know of whom I speak."

"Look, man, I got no idea where Scarlett is. She's long gone."

"Find her. Return to me what is mine."

"She's not your property."

"Return her or your little friend dies. And not quick death. No, it will be slow. We take her apart piece by piece. She seem very healthy. Will last a long time before she dies."

"Hurt her, and you'll regret it. That, I promise you."

"Your little threats do not scare me. And do not involve police."

"Too late, dipshit. They were called right after you kidnapped Ciara."

"That is unfortunate, but maybe salvageable. This conversation stays between us. You deliver property back to us, we return friend. You have until two o'clock tomorrow. Or will not be much left for us to return."

I was about to say something when the line went dead.

"Who the hell was that?" Shea held my gaze.

"Take a wild guess."

"Yuri. That sick motherfucker!"

"We can discuss this later." I turned to Max. "See if the police will let you inside to pack a bag. Then we'll head back to my place."

Max hailed one of the unis, who escorted him inside the house.

"Yuri wants Scarlett back," I said once Max was out of earshot.

"Even if we find Scarlett, we can't turn her over to Yuri," Shea replied.

"I know." I wasn't sure what options that left us. "We still need Scarlett to testify on behalf of Indigo. I've left voicemail messages, as has Maricela. We only have another day or so before Indigo's bond is declared forfeit. That's serious."

"This is so messed up. I had no idea protecting Indigo would turn into such a clusterfuck."

Max returned fifteen minutes later dragging a black suitcase. I led him to the Gray Ghost, and we returned to the Bunker, where I set up the sofa with a pillow and sheets for Shea. I thought about inviting her to share my bed but didn't want to seem too forward.

44

What sleep I managed to get was haunted by nightmares of being pursued by men with rifles. I was a coyote.

I woke at six the next morning to Diana pawing at me, whining to go for a run. It felt like such a mundane task in light of all of the craziness going on. But I couldn't think of a more productive thing. Perhaps it would jiggle loose a solution for the problems we were facing.

I pulled on shorts and a shirt and quietly stepped out the front door and past a snoring Shea. At least someone was getting some sleep.

The ground was damp from an overnight rain. The cool air smelled sweet with the fragrance of palo verde blossoms and free of its usual cocktail of desert dust and car exhaust.

Diana insisted on stopping every hundred feet or so to smell a tree, a mailbox, or a street sign, and raise a leg to make her mark, the canine equivalent of graffiti, I supposed. While she did her thing, I sent a text to Becca asking her to put a trace on Scarlett's phone since calling and leaving messages wasn't getting us anywhere.

When I returned home, I found Shea and Max helping themselves to French toast and hot coffee.

"There's another couple of slices next to the stove," said Shea. "You didn't have any vanilla, so I had to make do without."

"I'm sure it's great. Thanks." I fixed a plate and turned to Max. "Any word from the cops?"

"The detective called. They searched that strip club, Naughty's, and the motel next door, but no sign of Ciara. The man who runs the place—Yuri somebody—had an alibi for last night, so they couldn't hold him. Jinx, you gotta do something. She's in trouble because of you."

"I know. Don't worry. We'll find her and bring her back," I assured him.

"How?"

"We'll find a way." Shea patted Max on the back. "We've got the Athena Sisterhood to provide backup if need be."

"I hope it doesn't come to that," I replied. "But we'll get her back, Max."

"Mind if I use your shower?" asked Shea.

"Go ahead. There's fresh towels in the linen closet in the hallway."

"Thanks."

I was halfway through my own breakfast when Becca called back. "I pinged the number you gave me. I got a hit."

"Where?"

"The Salt River wash just off Nineteenth Avenue."

"The Salt River wash? Why would she be there?"

"I don't know, but the phone hasn't moved in the twenty minutes I've been watching it. Jinx, I have a bad feeling about your girl."

"Yeah, me too. Last night, Sergei Volkov's goons kidnapped my friend Ciara from my old house so I would bring them Scarlett."

"Oh my Goddess, are you serious?"

"Seriously serious."

"That's going to be hard to do if my suspicions are correct."

"Only one way to find out. Shea and I'll drive to the wash."

"One more thing I thought you'd want to hear."

"What?" As if I wasn't dealing with a big pile of shit already.

"You were talking about Freddie Colton, the husband of that woman you were protecting."

"Trying to protect, anyway. He murdered her. Why?"

"Saw on the news that he was found dead."

"Freddie Colton is dead? How?"

"Shot twice in the face. Body found in his Trans Am parked behind Llantera Ruiz, a used tire shop on Hatcher Road."

"I swear this whole town's gone crazy. And it's not even summer yet." I wondered if Simon Benedict got his revenge for Colton killing Emma.

"Jinx, maybe you should walk away from this one."

"Too late. I'm already in too deep. Only way out is through. But thanks for the info, Becks. I'll be in touch."

"Please watch your back, Jinxie. You've been my bestie since sixth grade. I don't want to lose you."

"I'll be extra careful. Promise. You got anything fun planned now that Easton's back?"

"There's a farmers market they've been wanting to check out, and then we're meeting some friends of theirs for brunch at Queen Mary's. I'd invite you along, but it sounds like you've already got plans."

Queen Mary's was a restaurant on Seventh Street, known for its über-campy drag shows on Friday and

Saturday nights and their elaborate buffet brunch on Sunday mornings.

"No worries! Have fun."

I hung up and called Byrd. When he didn't pick up, I left a voicemail asking him to call.

Max rinsed his dishes in the sink and excused himself to the guest bedroom. I got the impression all of the business talk was worrying him more. Not that I blamed him. Sometimes I forgot how crazy my work could get.

Shea walked in, her hair still damp from the shower. She smelled delicious. A surge of attraction crackled through each of my nerve fibers. I forced myself to focus on the situation. No room for distractions.

"We have a possible location for Scarlett. Or at least her phone," I told her.

She poured herself another cup of coffee. "Where is she?"

"Down on the Salt River, near the Durango Curve."

"That doesn't sound good."

"No, it doesn't. I learned something else from Becca. Our buddy Freddie Colton was found shot to death."

Shea stared out the back window, sipping her coffee, but said nothing.

"You knew, didn't you?"

She sighed but wouldn't meet my gaze. "Savage called me. The guy was a menace, Jinx. So don't expect any tears, all right?"

A chill ran down my spine. "Did the Athena Sisterhood murder Colton? Is that what that phone call was about last night?"

"We didn't kill him. But if we had, would it be the worst thing in the world? The man murdered two women in cold blood. Someone did the world a favor by taking him out of the picture."

"There's something you're not saying. I can hear it in your voice."

"The Athena Sisterhood did not kill Freddie Colton." She turned and faced me. "At least not directly."

"What's that supposed to mean?"

"Fuego, Savage, and Rah-Rah tracked him down to a dive bar on Dunlap Avenue, then passed the info on to Simon Benedict. But that's it. We didn't touch him."

"Why didn't you call the police?"

"All the times the police were called when he beat up Vanessa, and she still ended up dead. A different solution was called for."

A sick feeling formed in my stomach. I hated that she thought that was okay. And yet I wasn't entirely sure she was wrong. Fitzgerald had raped two teenage girls and didn't spend a day in prison. Was vigilantism the only option when the legal system routinely failed vulnerable women? I didn't want to believe it.

"We'll talk about this later. We need to see about Scarlett and somehow get Ciara back from Yuri. Let's grab our gear."

"What about me?" asked Max, walking into the kitchen.

"Stay put and keep Diana company. We'll be back shortly." I hoped.

45

When we stepped out my side door to the carport, I noticed a black sedan parked across the street in front of the Hendersons' house. The hairs on the back of my neck stood up.

"What's wrong?" asked Shea as she pulled on her motorcycle helmet.

"The car across the street. Something about it looks wrong." From the Gray Ghost, I pulled out a pair of binoculars I often used for surveillance.

The sedan was an old Crown Vic police interceptor model with a searchlight by the side-view mirror. But this one had gold-plated spinners on the wheels and dark-tinted windows. I had just enough of an angle to read the license plate—LDWENDE. Patrol cars didn't have custom plates. Someone had bought it at an auction and added the bling.

The Hendersons were a white couple with two young kids. Mrs. Henderson was the proverbial soccer mom with the requisite minivan. Mr. Henderson was an accountant who drove a used Volvo. A Crown Vic with tinted windows and spinners was not exactly their style. My gut told me the driver was a member of the West Side Jags.

I sent a text off to Becca to get the registration info on the driver when she had the chance, even though the last two I'd had her trace had been a bust.

She replied that she would run the trace as soon as she got back from Queen Mary's. I thanked her and said the sooner the better.

"You want me to draw them off on my bike then lose them?" asked Shea.

"If it's the Jags, I don't want you dealing with them alone. Dividing us up works in their favor, not ours."

Shea slapped the side of the damaged Charger. "I doubt you'll lose them in this old thing. No offense. She's fast, but a refurbished patrol car like the one out there has arguably more power and better handling. Better if we ride two-up on the bike. I got an extra helmet in my trunk."

"Never ridden on a motorcycle before." The thought sent a thrill of fear through me, coupled with a daring sense of curiosity.

She stepped into my personal space, making my heart flutter. "Then today's your lucky day, girlfriend."

I looked into her eyes, inches from mine. "While you go all Steve McQueen trying to lose them? Yeah, what could go wrong."

"Don't you trust me?" Her grin deepened.

"I...yeah, I trust you. It's just..."

"Don't tell me the badass Jinx Ballou is afraid of a little motorcycle."

I was still upset about the Sisterhood's involvement with Colton's murder. The thought of putting my life in her hands was a little unsettling. And yet...

"I...I'm willing to give it a try."

She unhooked her full-face helmet from the back of her bike and handed it to me. "Try it on."

I squeezed my head into it. My skull felt like it was being compressed in a vise. "It's a little tight."

She jiggled it. "Good. It's supposed to be." She pulled a half-dome helmet out from the trunk. "I'll make do with the party lid. Let me get the bike turned around so we can race straight outta here."

Using the Gray Ghost as cover from our stalkers in the Crown Vic, she turned the bike around to face the street and threw a leg over it. "Use the rear pegs to lift yourself up onto the bitch seat."

"The what?"

"Sorry. Old habit. The passenger seat."

With a hand on her shoulder for balance, I awkwardly hoisted myself onto the narrow cushion between her and the backrest. My body pressed against hers, as if we were spooning. I could smell the rich leather of her vest and the vanilla scent of her shampoo.

"What now?" I asked.

"Keep your feet on the pegs and hold onto me. When I turn, lean the way I do. And watch out for the pipes. They get fucking hot when the engine's warmed up. They'll burn you, even through your jeans."

My pulse raced as the engine roared to life beneath me. She gave me a thumbs-up. I returned the sign.

With a jolt, the bike accelerated onto the street and past the Crown Vic. My heart thundered in time with the rapid chut-chut-chut of the engine. I dared a glance back. The Crown Vic was making a U-turn.

"They're coming!" I shouted when we reached the Central Avenue intersection. A large pickup truck rumbled toward us on our left. An instant before the truck reached the intersection, Shea pinned the throttle and jumped out in front of it.

Brakes screamed and tires squealed. I pitched left, struggling to hold on to Shea's waist while we raced down Central. I felt like I was on the back of a roller coaster, while Shea nimbly wove between vehicles, splitting the lanes at times.

We leaned a hard right onto McDowell. The pavement loomed up toward us in the tight turn. I thought we would fall over until she straightened it up and accelerated further.

At Fifth Avenue, we hit a red light. Shea pulled into the left turn lane. The Crown Vic's horn blared somewhere behind us as it fought through traffic to catch us.

"Dammit, they're still following us," Shea growled. "Hold on!"

Despite the red light, Shea gunned the motor and turned onto Fifth Avenue. A light flashed. Stoplight camera. A ticket was better than getting killed, I supposed.

I chanced a look back when we turned onto the I-10 on-ramp. The Crown Vic was back a few cars but still in pursuit. Shit! With the velocity of a fighter jet, we surged down the ramp. The front wheel lifted and dropped.

Once on the highway, we whizzed past the other vehicles, the wind a thunderous rocket in my ears.

This must be what flying feels like. I realized I was laughing even as tears streamed down my face. My vision narrowed at the expanse of highway ahead of us. *Oh fuck yeah!* This was better than booze or weed or sex. Like an orgasm that wouldn't quit.

I'm Daenerys Stormborn soaring on the back of a dragon. If I survive this shit, I am definitely getting a motorcycle.

We merged onto I-17 South, taking the ramp at over a hundred miles an hour. My soul screamed with excitement, adrenaline coursing through my veins. I squeezed Shea tighter, pressure building in my groin. My face warmed at the thought of me with this ex-con biker chick.

It wasn't until we pulled off onto the Nineteenth Avenue exit and stopped at the light that I remembered we were running from the West Side Jags.

"I think we lost 'em," said Shea, sparing a glance in her side mirror.

"Thank goodness."

On Nineteenth Avenue, she returned to a reasonable speed. Shortly before we reached the bridge over the Salt River wash, she pulled into a small parking area on the side of the road. A hiking trail led down to the riverbed.

I shakily climbed off the bike and pulled off the helmet. My heart still thundered in my chest. My knees had turned to jelly. I put a hand on the backrest to steady myself.

The seat must have been pressing on a nerve because my clit tingled with a pins-and-needles sensation. One look at Shea, and my pulse accelerated even more. Maybe it wasn't a pinched nerve after all.

Shea hopped off the bike, took one look at me, and burst out laughing.

"Wh-what?"

"You should see your face." She slapped my shoulder and guffawed. "Like you just got your cherry popped."

"I...uh...feel like I did."

"And?"

"I think I...it's..." I almost said, *I think I'm in love*. "Helluva ride."

"Hells yeah." She put an arm around my shoulder. Her scent of vanilla and leather set my senses ablaze.

Unexpectedly, her mood turned somber. "Let's find Scarlett."

Using an app on my phone, we trudged down the trail

to the coordinates Becca had provided for the phone's location.

Our boots crunched underfoot on the sandy ground. Aside from the road, the terrain was barren scrub desert. A few hearty shrubs—brittlebush, creosote, and tumbleweeds—dotted the landscape. Along the wash itself, green-barked palo verdes rose up, their yellow blossoms in full bloom.

When we reached the banks of the riverbed, the trail turned left following the Salt upstream. Large pools of water remained in the wash from the overnight rain.

"According to the coordinates Becca gave me, Scarlett's phone is on the other side of the bridge." I pointed past a fence with a No Trespassing sign.

"Then that's where we go."

We hopped the fence and continued on. I looked in the distance along the water's edge and spotted a figure on the ground. As we drew closer, the cloying scent of death hit us followed by the disquieting buzz of flies. I pulled the top of my T-shirt over my nose and mouth, but it didn't keep the stench away. Nor did it fend off the sense of failure that hit like a sledgehammer to my chest.

The remains were those of a dark-skinned woman. The body was so bloated and discolored, I couldn't begin to guess age. She was dressed in a crop top and cutoff jeans. The gunshot wound above her left eye served as a gateway for insects seeking the decaying delights inside.

A halo of jet-black hair was matted with blood. Her hands were bound with wire. A weathered piece of duct tape clung loosely from her blistered lips.

A metallic glint in the sand to the right of the body caught my eye. A shell casing. I inserted a twig into the open end and lifted it up. The dimpled back of the spent round was stamped with the words "P M C 10MM AUTO."

Same caliber used in the drive-by and to kill both Fitzgerald and Detective Garza. I eased the casing back into the same spot I found it.

"Shit. I had hoped..."

Shea's hands around my shoulders steadied me both physically and emotionally. "I know. Me too."

I gave myself fifteen seconds to grieve this poor woman's fate, then took a deep breath through my mouth and blew it out. I needed answers.

46

Was this Scarlett? If so, where was the phone? I pulled on a pair of latex gloves I carried in a Ziploc bag in a cargo pants pocket. On more than one occasion, I'd apprehended bail jumpers with open wounds, others covered in vomit, piss, and feces. Always best to be prepared.

Carefully, I searched the deceased's pockets, but they were all empty. *Where the hell's the phone?*

I reached into her bra and pulled out a flip phone. It was a pre-pay from the looks of it. When I opened the phone, the screen revealed three percent battery power remaining. I scrolled through the calls received and recognized my own number.

"No ID, but this has to be her." I stood and peeled off the gloves one into another, then stuffed them inside out into my pocket.

Shea's left arm wrapped around her face to fend off the odor of decay. "She doesn't really look like Indigo."

"Other than the fact that she's dead and Indigo isn't?" The dark sense of humor I'd developed as a cop emerged, a coping mechanism for situations like these.

"Indigo's more slender."

"Well, the body's bloated. Hard to really gauge."

"This woman's too short and doesn't have braids or dreads. Her hair's not even that long."

"What are you saying? That this isn't Scarlett? She has her phone."

"Scarlett could've tossed the phone, and this woman picked it up."

"You think Scarlett may still be alive?" I swallowed hard, trying to keep down the bile that threatened to rise up my throat. "Suppose anything's possible."

"What now?" Shea asked.

My mind searched for a solution. "Yuri wants Scarlett in exchange for Ciara. So let's give him what he wants."

I brought up the call history on the phone and deleted Maricela's calls. The former cop in me chaffed at my evidence tampering, but I had a life to save and didn't need anyone, cop or gangster, tracking down Maricela. Lastly, I used the phone's camera to take a picture of the dead woman.

"Jinx, what are you doing?"

"You're probably right. She isn't Scarlett. But she's bloated enough that it's hard to tell from a photo. Plus, we have the real Scarlett's phone, which shows I called her a few times. Maybe it will convince Yuri to let Ciara go."

"I fucking hope so."

I dialed the number from Yuri's recent call.

"Ms. Ballou. Do you have what I requested?"

I glanced at the woman's body lying on the sandy ground. "Yeah."

"This is good. Meet me two o'clock. Niko's Greek restaurant. Grand Avenue. Peoria. You can find this?"

"I know where it is." I had driven by the shuttered restaurant countless times. "Why wait? Let's meet now."

"I have other business to attend thanks to your friends in FBI. Be at Niko's when I say. And no police, or your friend pays bigly. We are clear?"

"Crystal."

"Excellent." He hung up.

I called Byrd again but again got his voicemail. I left a second message, more urgent this time, to call me. He was probably at church, but I couldn't help worrying something had happened to him.

What about her?" Shea nodded toward the deceased woman after I hung up.

"I'll call 911."

Thirty minutes later, the place was crawling with cops, evidence techs, and people from the medical examiner's office. Patrol officers had escorted Shea and me back up to the main road and questioned us.

The story we told was that Shea and I were hiking along the trail when we spotted the body. I didn't mention Yuri, Ciara, the West Side Jags, or the phone I'd taken off the remains. No need to complicate things further.

When Detective Hardin showed up and took charge of the investigation, I gave him the same story.

"I wasn't aware you were such an outdoorsy person, Ballou," said Hardin.

"What can I say? I've let myself go these last few months. I figured, what with the nice weather, it'd be a nice day to walk along the Salt River."

"Do you always go hiking dressed like you're getting ready to knock down doors?" He nodded at my vest and gear.

"The weight of the gear is good training for the job."

"Uh-huh." He looked at Shea. "So this DB has nothing to do with the case you've been working. That dead preacher over in Scottsdale?"

"Scottsdale's, like, twenty miles away. Why would this have anything to do with that?"

"Don't you bullshit me, Ballou. I ain't got nearly the patience for this."

"I got an anonymous tip that the body of one of Volkov's former sex slaves was down here."

"Anonymous tip, huh? This girl got a name?"

"She went by Scarlett," I said. "Probably just a stage name."

"And why is this particular woman of interest to you?"

"She witnessed Fitzgerald's murder."

Hardin spit on the ground. "Dammit. I knew you were involved."

"Any progress on Garza?" I asked, desperate to change the subject.

His suspicious scowl softened. "Jennings is working the case. I filled him in on your theory. We'll see where that goes."

My phone rang. "Ballou Fugitive Services."

"Hi. Maybe you can find my sister. She's about five six, skinny as a rail. Supposed to show up at our parents' Sunday brunch, but there's been no sign of her. Think you can find her?"

"Aw, shit, Jake. I'm sorry." I looked at the time. It was ten thirty. "Things have been crazy. I'll be there in a bit, okay? And tell Mom and Dad I may be bringing a few guests."

"I'll tell them. Just get your butt over here. That was part of the deal with me fixing your fancy bulletproof windows. Remember?"

"I'll be there. Give me an hour." I hung up and locked eyes with Hardin. "My brother. I'm expected at my folks' place."

"Anything else I oughta know about the decedent?" Hardin asked.

"That's all I know, Detective." *Aside from the phone in my pocket.*

"Y'all get on out of here. I got any other questions, I know where to find you."

I called Max as we walked to Shea's motorcycle.

"Any updates from the detectives looking for Ciara?" I asked.

"No. You find the woman you were looking for?"

"Sort of. In a few hours, I'm supposed to meet with the people who took Ciara. With a little luck, I can get her back safe and sound. In the meantime, you're invited to my folks' place for Sunday brunch. You game?"

"Why not rescue her now?"

"If I could, I would."

"Guess it beats sitting around here all alone waiting for something to happen."

"Do me a favor. Look out the front window. Do you see any cars parked on the street? In particular a black Crown Vic."

"Hold on. Let me check," Max replied. "No, no cars parked along the street. Why?"

"Good. Take my SUV to my parents' house in Mesa." I gave him the address. "The spare key's in the drawer just left of the dishwasher. And lock the front door behind you."

"Thanks, Jinx," he said glumly. "For everything. You're not as bad as I thought you were."

"I'll see you in a little bit."

"You want me to have the Athena Sisterhood back us up when meeting with Barayev?" asked Shea.

I had thought about it. What I wanted was for Byrd to call me back. Someone who had experience in tight situations. Someone who I could trust to not lose their head when the shit hit the fan. After what happened to Colton, I wasn't keen on getting them involved.

"Let's hold off for now. I don't want this to turn into a bloodbath. If we can convince Yuri that Scarlett's dead and that we're not a threat to his business, we may be able to walk away with Ciara."

"Who says we're not a threat to that scumbag's business? I got nothing against consensual sex work, but this is human trafficking, Jinx. Nothing consensual about this. We can't let him continue to exploit those women."

"I hear you, but right now, our objective is rescuing Ciara. We can worry about shutting him down another day."

I was about to pull on the borrowed helmet when my phone rang again. Byrd calling.

"You're alive," I said.

"Yeah, why?"

I updated him on the situation, including finding the phone and our scheduled meeting with Yuri to rescue Ciara. "I need you, man. You in? I'll even treat you to Sunday brunch at my folks' house beforehand."

"Good food?" he asked with curiosity in his voice.

"You like Cajun and Southern home cooking?"

"Girl, you're playing my song."

I gave him the address, and he agreed to meet us there.

I pulled on the helmet and hopped onto the motorcycle behind Shea. We took the 17 north to I-10, then picked up the 202. Shea zipped along between cars with the grace of a ballet dancer.

Arriving in my parents' working-class neighborhood in Mesa was a time warp back to my childhood. Such a concentration of intermingled cultures—Native American, African American, Mexican, and Anglo. Brilliantly colored murals decorated the sides of buildings with urban flair and Aztec designs. Panaderías huddled between New York–style delis and galleries selling Navajo and Hopi artwork.

On the back of the motorcycle, I discovered the air was rich with the aromas of spices from around the world. Rap songs and Mexican love ballads played from the open windows of cars, evoking memories both joyful and painful from my childhood.

We passed the clothing store where I'd been caught shoplifting a dress at age eleven, back when I was still deeply closeted about my gender issues.

We turned the corner onto my parents' street. I recognized my friend Mirabella's house. As eight-year-olds, we played dress up with a box of her mother's old clothes. Such a whirlwind of fear, excitement, and joy that had been.

At last, Shea parked in front of my parents' house, a salmon-colored stucco structure my mother described as Mediterranean rose. To the rest of the neighborhood, it was the Pink House.

My brother's work truck, which was almost as battered and scratched up as the Gray Ghost, sat in the narrow driveway.

"Should we wait for Max and Byrd?" Shea asked.

I was a little concerned that Max wasn't already there, but then Shea hadn't exactly been heeding the speed limit on the highway.

"They know where we are. I need to say hello to my folks. Haven't seen them in a while."

The front door was unlocked. I ushered Shea inside. The air was filled with the sharp bite of cayenne and the indulgent aroma of bacon.

47

A conglomeration of Cajun, Italian, and Mexican artwork gave my parents' living room welcoming and comfortable style.

I led Shea into the kitchen, where the table was covered with dishes of strawberry crepes, poached eggs, grits, paella, French toast, boiled shrimp, beignets, and fresh fruit. A carafe of chicory coffee stood in the center of the table next to a spray of fresh-picked roses from my mother's garden.

My mother's eyes welled up with tears as a hand clapped over her mouth. "Oh...oh my dear sweet girl."

She was a petite woman with long graying hair that was once jet-black. She launched from the table and wrapped me in a hug so tight I could barely breathe.

"Oh, just look at you." She released me and planted kisses on my face.

"I've missed you too, Mom." I said when our eyes met once again.

I could see the hurt and sorrow roiling inside her. "Why

have you stayed away so long? Did I do something to hurt you?"

I tried to hold back the tears pricking at my eyes. "No, Mom. It wasn't you. It was...I just needed some time after what happened with Conor."

She smoothed my hair and gripped my face in her wrinkled hands. "I have missed you so much. Every morning and every night, I prayed the Virgin Mother would send you back to me. I called so many times, but you..."

"I'm sorry." The dam broke, and tears streamed down my face. "I was messed up for a while, but I'm doing better."

"Truly? You're skinny as a stray dog. Are you eating?"

"I'm eating. More than I was, anyway." I caught my father striding toward the two of us. "Hey, Dad."

Tall and lanky, he hugged me and kissed my cheek. "Missed you, *chère*."

"I missed me too."

"You gonna introduce us to your friend?"

Shea stood next to me, looking awkward. "This is my friend Shea. She's helping me out with a case. These are my folks. And you remember my brother, Jake, over there stuffing his face full of cornbread."

"Mmmph," said Jake. "'Bout time you got here."

Shea gave a two-fingered salute. "Pleasure to meet y'all."

"Well, you two sit down and help yourselves," said my mom, wiping her face, a smile having replaced her grief. "And don't be shy. There's plenty more."

"I'm expecting a couple more, if that's all right."

"The more the merrier."

The doorbell rang. I opened the door to see both Byrd and Max on the front porch. I led them back to the kitchen and introduced them to my family.

After a few extra chairs were squeezed around the table,

I fixed myself some grits topped with a poached egg, but I just picked at it. Max didn't look like he had much of an appetite either.

"What's with all the picky eaters? Something wrong with the food?" asked my dad. "Jenna, you really oughta eat something. You, too, Max. No need to be shy."

"The food's great, Dad. We're just worried about...stuff."

"Oh? What pray tell?"

"Not exactly table talk," I replied.

My dad gave an understanding nod. He knew I didn't talk about work here if I could help it.

"Someone kidnapped Ciara," said Max, staring down at his plate, a strip of bacon hanging limply in his hand.

"Who's Ciara?" asked my mother.

"My roommate. We live at Jinx's old house."

"Kidnapped?" Worry deepened the wrinkles of my mother's forehead. "Jenna, what are you involved in?"

"Just a case, Mom. It's okay. We got it handled."

"Why would they kidnap her?" replied my father. "Do you need money for a ransom? Is this because of the life insurance money you got?"

"No. Just a misunderstanding. We just need to find the folks who took her and...talk to them."

The worry returned to my mother's face. "I wish you'd go back to school and get a law degree. You're smart. You'd make a great lawyer."

"And I'd hate it. I hate lawyers."

"But people wouldn't be trying to kill you."

"People aren't trying to kill me, Mom."

"Honey, she can handle things." My dad put an arm around her. "She's got Byrd and her friend Shea."

"Jinx is good at what she does," Shea added.

Byrd glanced at her then at me. "When she's going after fugitives."

"I hope so. If something were to happen to you..."

"Nothing will happen, Mrs. B," said Shea, clapping me on the shoulder. "Your girl can handle herself."

"What's that mean?"

"Nothing, Mom."

The conversation died, and we spent the rest of brunch in awkward silence. The grits sat like cement mortar in my stomach. I hated to see my mom all worked up.

When I couldn't stand to stare at my plate any longer, I helped my dad clear the table. Shea, Max, and Byrd followed Jake into the living room to watch the Diamondbacks game.

"Your mom's not the only one who worries." He dried the plate I'd just washed.

"Like Shea said, I can handle myself."

"I'm not as worried about your work as I am your mental health." My dad, ever the shrink. "You don't look well."

"I know I've lost weight. I was having a rough time of it, I won't lie. But that's behind me."

"You go to a grief counselor or a support group?"

"I tried. Not a good fit. Getting back into work helped."

"You still drinking?"

"You knew about that?"

"I'm a trauma therapist. I recognize the signs."

"I'm not drinking."

"Have you heard any more about Conor?"

"All I know is he's being held in jail in Belfast. I tried to get word to him but haven't heard anything back."

"Did you know he was alive?"

"Not till after Christmas. I went down to Mexico and saw him."

"Jenna, if the police or the FBI found out..."

"Dad, I needed closure."

"Conor was a good man. I admit, I was surprised to learn about his past. Sounds very...complicated."

"Yeah."

He took a bowl from me, dried it, and put it in the cabinet. "This case you're working...do be careful. And if you need help..."

"What?" I said with a laugh. "You going to show up on a white horse and rescue me?"

"I was going to say, call the cops."

"I will. I promise."

He hugged me. "You're irreplaceable, *chère*. You know that, don't you?"

"So are you."

The *Game of Thrones* ringtone played on my phone. "It's Becca, Dad. I gotta take this."

I stepped into my old bedroom for some privacy. "What's up, Becks?"

"I ran that plate. The Ford Crown Victoria is registered to Juan Cabrera. I ran a background on him. He's an enforcer for the Jaguars. His nickname is *El Duende*."

"What's *El Duende* mean?"

"*El Duende* is a goblin-like creature from Latin American mythology. When I misbehaved as a kid, my mom would warn me that *El Duende* would bite off my toes if I didn't behave."

"Ugh. How horrible."

"Cabrera has a brutal reputation, Jinxie. He once hacked off the hands and feet of someone from a rival gang."

"That's who's following us? Shit. His daughter was raped by Fitzgerald."

"And Fitzgerald was found with his junk chopped off. Be super careful. These guys are freakin' psychos."

"I get the picture. Thanks for the 411."

I looked at my watch. It was one fifteen. Time to get moving.

Back in the kitchen, my father was putting away the last of the dishes into the cabinet. "Everything okay?"

"Yeah. We gotta head out. You mind if Max hangs out here until...Shea, Byrd, and I can get back?"

"He's welcome to stay as long as he likes. But shouldn't you let the cops handle this?"

"I used to be a cop, Dad. I can handle it." I kissed his cheek.

He hugged me and held on for a long moment. When he released me, he looked me in the eyes. He was fighting back tears. "Don't be a stranger, *chère*."

"I won't. I'll see you soon."

I walked into the living room, and the place erupted in cheers. The Diamondbacks had just scored a three-point home run.

"Hate to break up the party, but we gotta go. Max, hang here until we get back."

"You need any help?" asked Jake.

"I think we got it, bro. But thanks."

48

I pulled on my Kevlar vest and slipped my Ruger and Rossi into their respective holsters. The two of us climbed onto Shea's bike and took off down the road. Byrd followed in his car.

My mind marinated over how to convince Yuri to let Ciara go. I hoped telling him that the Jaguars had murdered Scarlett would give him someone else to direct his anger at. I wasn't sure it would work, but we were low on alternatives.

It was just shy of two when we pulled into the Niko's parking lot. The restaurant had remained vacant for a couple of years. The surrounding strip mall had similarly suffered from urban blight. Weeds grew through cracks in the parking lot. Signs for the stores had either been blacked out or flipped backward.

A black Lincoln Town Car sat by the restaurant's back door.

I stepped off of Shea's bike and adjusted the straps on my ballistic vest. My adrenaline was surging from the ride.

Now, as I faced the daunting task of rescuing Ciara, my mind and body were firing on all cylinders.

"We ready for this?" I looked from Shea to Byrd.

Shea racked the slide on her Glock. "Time to kick some Russkie ass."

Byrd nodded. "We got some sort of strategy?"

"Tell Yuri that Scarlett's dead. Show him the photo and her phone. Point him to the West Side Jags as the ones responsible. Hopefully, he will give us Ciara alive. They are businessmen, after all."

"And if he doesn't?"

I took a deep breath. "Then we go with plan B."

"What's plan B?"

I drew the Ruger and chambered a round. "We take her by force."

Byrd didn't look convinced this was a winning strategy. "God help us."

I opened the rear door of the restaurant. The kitchen had been stripped of appliances, shelves, and equipment, giving the place an eerie, abandoned feeling, like the photos of post-meltdown Pripyat, Ukraine. The lingering aroma of Mediterranean spices was faint compared to the more prevalent stench of blood, sweat, and urine—the reek of cruelty and torture.

Andrei Garinov appeared across the room, holding a chrome-plated .50-caliber Desert Eagle.

"No weapons. Put on ground." Garinov pointed at the tile floor.

Three-to-one were odds I could live with. "We'll hold on to them this time, thank you very much."

Hans, Franz emerged from the office on our right, holding large-caliber pistols. Mick Jagger stepped out of the restroom on our left, carrying an AK-47.

An ugly sneer split Garinov's face. "No weapons or you and your friends die."

Déjà vu really sucked sometimes. "Fuck!"

I set my Ruger on the floor. Hans snatched it up and stuffed it in the front of his waistband. He frisked me and relieved me of the Rossi revolver in my ankle holster. Byrd and Shea were similarly disarmed.

"Where the hell's Ciara?" I tried to keep the anger out of my voice.

"Where is whore Scarlett?"

"That's between us and your boss."

"Bitch" was all Andrei said before he lumbered out of the empty kitchen. The three other Russian trolls prodded us to follow into what had once been the dining room. Plywood covered the plate glass windows. The only light came in from the glass doors. The carpet had been ripped up, exposing the bare concrete slab drizzled with dried glue. Wooden strips with exposed carpet nails ran along the edges.

Ciara sat slumped in a chair, a layer of plastic sheeting beneath her. She was topless and gagged, hands bound behind her back. Her face was swollen and bruised. Blood oozed from dozens of wounds across her body.

Yuri stood behind her, arms crossed, a displeased look on his face.

Ignoring the guns at my back, I rushed to Ciara's side. "You still alive in there?"

Ciara moaned and partially opened one eye. "Jinx?"

"Just hold on," I whispered. "We'll get you out of here."

I stood and glared at Yuri. "You fucking monster. Beating up a defenseless woman? Does it boost your fragile male ego, you fucking Russian snowflake?"

"I told you no police. And yet police and FBI show up at

club. Question me for hours. Interfere with business. Try to shut me down."

"You don't like cops? Try not breaking the fucking law. Now let her go."

Yuri shrugged. "You say you find Scarlett." He spread out his arms and glanced around the room. "Yet I do not see her. This does not please me."

"We found her." I reached for my pocket.

Jagger and the boys swiveled their guns on me. I raised my hands. "Relax. Just getting a phone." I pulled out the phone we'd found on the dead woman, pulled up the photo I'd taken of her, and handed it to Yuri.

"What is this?" he asked.

"Scarlett's phone. That's her body in the photo."

His eyes narrowed. "You kill her? Why?"

"Wasn't us. It was the Westside Jaguars. We found her body in the Salt River wash."

"Fucking dirty Mexicans. Why they kill Scarlett?"

"Your former client, James Fitzgerald, raped the daughter of Juan Cabrera, an enforcer for the Jags. After the cops refused to prosecute Fitzgerald, Cabrera went on a killing spree. Killed the preacher, the cop, and Scarlett. Guess they didn't want any witnesses."

"How do I know this not trick? This black woman." He pointed at the photo on the phone. "She could be anybody."

"That phone was on her. Look through the call log. Some of those calls are from me trying to get her to call. It's Scarlett, all right, and she's dead."

He clicked through the call log, then said something in Russian that sounded like a curse. "Dirty Mexicans think they can interfere with my business? Kill my girls?"

I wanted to argue that Scarlett wasn't his, but it didn't

seem like the right time. Getting out alive with Ciara was our priority.

He stood up and got into my face. He smelled of dollar store cologne and vodka. "I do not like people snooping at my club, talking to my people." He looked like a bull threatening to charge. "But I am businessman, Jinx Ballou. We make deal. You find this Juan Cabrera. Bring to me. Then we let your friend go."

"We already had a deal, man," said Byrd. "We're taking Ciara with us."

"No. Old deal is Scarlett for friend. No Scarlett, no friend, no deal."

"She's dead, you dipshit. D-E-A-D! Dead!" shouted Shea. "What're you? Stupid? Your mother drop you on your stupid commie head? We're not bringing you nobody."

Yuri snatched Hans's gun from his hand, grabbed Shea by the collar, and pressed the barrel against her forehead. "Maybe I kill you all. Right here, right now."

At this point, we were down to plan F—fucking out of plans. I thought about my mother. I saw her tear-strewn face. Deep within me, a fire erupted. I was not going down without a fight.

From outside the restaurant came a deep, rolling thunder. But it wasn't a storm. Monsoon season was months away.

"What is that?" shouted Yuri. "What is going on outside?"

Andrei stood next to me, peering out one of the side doors. An endless stream of motorcycles roared past in flashes of chrome and leather. Jagger disappeared into the kitchen. Hans and Franz turned to the other side door, guns raised.

While Russians scrambled, Shea, Byrd, and I exchanged

a split-second glance. I grabbed my gun, still in Andrei's waistband, and squeezed the trigger. A spray of blood exploded between his legs. He collapsed, bellowing in pain.

In the same instant, Shea disarmed Hans and finished him off with a double tap to the chest. Byrd grappled with Franz over his gun. Byrd drove his heel into the Russian's instep. Franz released the gun and fell to one knee. Byrd pressed the pistol to the man's head.

"I surrender," said Franz. Byrd lowered his weapon, but as he did so, Franz reached for it.

I raised my Ruger, but Shea was faster and pulled off two more shots, dropping the guy to the floor.

I turned my gun on Yuri. His narrow face colored with rage. "You stupid bit—"

Another pull of my trigger sent his brain splattering across the room.

A series of shots echoed from the kitchen, and the Athena Sisterhood charged in, guns raised. Jagger was no doubt dead.

"We're good! It's over," Shea told Fuego, who led the charge. The dining room filled with leather-clad women.

"Damn." Fuego shook her head as she surveyed the carnage. "We missed all the fun?"

At my feet, Andrei muttered frantically in Russian while blood oozed between his fingers pressed against his crotch. I'd hit his femoral artery. His eyes were wide with terror. I was tempted to finish him off but decided not to.

"Die slowly, asshole."

His muttering dissolved into moaning and then silence.

I moved to Ciara and cut her bonds. She collapsed into my arms. Savage appeared next to me and helped lower her to the floor.

"She's in shock," said Savage. "We need to cover her up."

I looked around for something to use—a blanket, a tablecloth, anything—but came up empty. Shea retrieved a jacket from the back of her motorcycle and draped it over Ciara. I pulled off my ballistic vest and used it as a pillow for her head.

"How'd you know we were here?" I asked Savage.

She nodded toward Shea. "She gave us a call. Sorry we were late."

"911 is on the way." Byrd turned to Shea. "Thanks for the save."

Shea snorted. "And I thought only Jesus saves."

I knelt down beside Ciara. "You're safe. Ambulance is on the way."

Her sobs were the only response.

As I studied the faces of the women bikers, I recognized one and approached her. "Zia Pearson, right?"

Her eyes narrowed. "Yeah?"

I slapped my cuffs over one of her wrists and then the other. "Jinx Ballou. Friendly neighborhood bounty hunter."

"Hey, wait a minute! Help!"

Savage, Fuego, and Rah-Rah turned toward me, weapons in hand. "Let her go!"

Dragon stepped between us and gestured for the others to lower their guns. "Jinx, do we have to do this now?"

"That was the deal. I find the real killer. Indigo turns herself in."

"These people?" Dragon indicated the dead Russians. "They killed Fitzgerald?"

"No," said Shea, joining us. "Juan Cabrera, aka El Duende, of the Westside Jaguars did. Jinx has the evidence we need to prove it. I'm no lawyer, but it should be enough to get the charges against Indigo dropped."

Approaching sirens screamed in the distance.

Indigo looked at Dragon, her face filled with terror. "I

don't want to go back to jail. Not for another night. Not after what happened last time."

"I understand your fear," I said. "But I can keep you safe. A friend of mine's a CO in Scottsdale. She can put you in protective custody. No one will get to you."

Her fear turned to rage. "But I didn't do nothing wrong. Why should I suffer for what some *cholo* did?"

Our eyes met. She was right. If I took her in, knowing what she'd already endured, I was no better than that cowboy cop Atkinson who'd railroaded her. I uncuffed her.

The back door slammed open. Four uniformed officers from Peoria PD burst into the room, guns raised. "Police! Everyone down on the ground!"

I complied with their instructions to lie on the floor while the officers snatched up our weapons. "Oh, goody. The cavalry's here. We're saved."

"Just when things were getting fun," replied Byrd.

EMTs arrived and transported Ciara to the hospital. More unis arrived by the dozen, along with FBI Special Agent Lovelace and detectives from Peoria's homicide squad. I was allowed to call my attorney, Kirsten Pasternak, before Shea, Byrd, and I were herded into squad cars and taken to the precinct for questioning.

Kirsten arrived shortly after I was put in one of Peoria's interview rooms. After a brief consultation with her, I told Agent Lovelace and the Peoria detectives assigned to the case that I'd been contacted by Yuri Barayev and told to show up with Scarlett. We'd shown up with the phone as fictional proof that Scarlett was dead, whereupon Yuri threatened to kill all of us. Byrd, Shea, and I had consequently acted in self-defense.

Neither Agent Lovelace nor the detectives were happy about me removing evidence from the dead woman's body in Phoenix. I surrendered the phone to Lovelace, who agreed to forward it to Detective Hardin for his investigation into the dead woman's murder. I had no doubt I'd be hearing from Hardin and would get a thorough ass chewing. Whether he'd charge me with evidence tampering and interfering with a murder investigation was uncertain.

After several hours of questioning, I was officially released, though Lovelace warned me the investigation was still open pending ballistics and autopsy. She informed me that Ciara had been transported to Boswell Medical Center in Sun City.

While being escorted to the precinct lobby, I sent Max a text letting him know about Ciara and offering him use of the Gray Ghost so he could drive there from my folks' house.

Byrd, Shea, and members of the Athena Sisterhood were waiting for me in the precinct lobby.

"Thanks for your help," I told Kirsten.

"Try to stay out of trouble, Jinx." She gave me a hug. "Though if trouble finds you, you know who to call."

"Hey!" said Byrd. "How'm I supposed to get back to the restaurant to pick up my car?"

"I can give you a lift." Kirsten turned to me. "You coming?"

I looked at Shea, and she nodded. "Naw, I'm good. Watch out, Byrd. See that she doesn't charge you for the lift. Her rates are outrageous."

"Very funny." Kirsten stood in the doorway. "For that crack, I should charge you double for dragging me out on a Sunday night."

Me and my big mouth.

"So who's up for a victory celebration?" I asked the group.

Shea and her fellow bikers seemed in a rather somber

mood considering we'd avoided multiple murder charges. "I think we'll pass," said Shea.

"We just rescued my friend from Russian gangsters. I'd say that calls for some sort of celebration."

"They took Indigo into custody," said Dragon.

Only then did I notice Indigo wasn't with the group. My enthusiasm fell. "Why? I let her go."

"A bench warrant had been issued," Dragon explained. "Peoria PD will be transferring her to Scottsdale lockup later tonight. I'm going to try to get her bail reset, but considering the circumstances, I'm not hopeful. At least she's being sent to the women's unit this time."

"I'll contact my friend at the Scottsdale jail. She'll make sure Indigo's kept safe until we can get the charges dropped."

"We'd appreciate that, Jinx." Dragon managed a weak smile.

"I wish I could have done more."

"You did enough." Shea's eyes met mine. "You risked your life. Several times. We couldn't have asked for more."

"Thanks. I'll—" My phone rang. The caller ID was unfamiliar. "Hold that thought." I answered the call.

"Hi, I think you've been trying to reach me," said an accented voice. "My name is Sophie Dujardin. I used to go by Scarlett."

~

Sophie agreed to meet with me the following morning. I made another quick call to my ex-girlfriend, Toni, at the Scottsdale jail and let her know about Indigo. It was an awkward conversation, both of us still regretting how our brief fling had ended, but she agreed to keep Indigo safe.

Apparently, two COs had lost their job over what had already happened to Indigo.

I hitched a ride on the back of Fuego's bike, while Shea doubled up with Dragon to pick up her bike at the old Greek restaurant.

When we arrived, the parking lot of the blighted strip mall was dark except for the motorcycle headlights. All of a sudden, I felt very alone. The thrill of rescuing Ciara and avoiding arrest had faded.

"You heading back up to Sycamore Springs?" I asked Shea.

"Not yet. We want to stick around until Indigo gets arraigned and hopefully released."

"Where you staying?"

"Desert View Inn." The corners of her mouth curled in a wistful smile. "Unless I get a better offer."

"Well, there's a cute little house down in the Willo District. Owner's not much of a cook, but it's homey, and there's a very friendly dog."

"I do like dogs," she added. She reached for my hand, and a jolt of electricity ran up my arm.

There was no sign of Juan Cabrera or any of his gang-banger friends on the street when Shea and I arrived at the Bunker. It was nearly nine o'clock when we walked through the door. I was beat and wanted to collapse into a coma for the next six months, despite a desire to get to know Shea on a more intimate level.

After I made a few quick phone calls, Shea and I tumbled into my bed, kissing, cuddling, and drifting in and out of sleep. Both of us were too exhausted for anything more.

49

On Monday morning, Dragon called and informed us that Indigo's new hearing was set for Tuesday morning at ten. Indigo was miserable being in custody but safe for the time being.

I felt bad for her, but there wasn't much I could do except provide Dragon with what I had uncovered about Juan Cabrera and the trail of bodies he left following his daughter's rape.

"What's our game plan?"

"Sophie Dujardin, aka Scarlett, has agreed to meet with us this morning," I told Shea over coffee and cold cereal. "I'm hoping we can convince her to testify."

"Fingers crossed," she said. "How's Ciara?"

"Stable, but the doctors at Boswell Medical Center are still checking her for internal injuries."

"What are we going to do about the Westside Jaguars?"

"I spoke with Detective Hardin last night before we crashed. There's a statewide BOLO out on Juan Cabrera and Chuy Rodriguez, another member of the Jaguars. The ballistics from Garza, Fitzgerald, and the woman we found in the wash all matched, as did the ones from the drive-by. Hardin will provide Dragon with copies of the reports."

"He mad about the phone?"

"Can't you tell one of my ass cheeks is missing?" I joked. "Trust me, I got an earful. But he's not going to charge me with anything."

"So Cabrera and this other guy are still on the streets?"

"As far as I know. Hardin agreed to have a patrol car cruise by my house every couple of hours in case Cabrera shows up."

"How the hell did Cabrera know we were looking for Fitzgerald's murderer?"

"I don't know."

"Maybe that cowboy cop in Scottsdale and/or his partner are on the Jaguar payroll. Maybe that's why they railroaded Indigo—to cover up for Cabrera."

As a former cop myself, I didn't like to think of other cops as being corrupt. Assholes, yeah, but actively working with felons to throw a murder case? "So long as Phoenix PD puts Cabrera and Rodriguez away for killing Garza, I don't care how they knew." I stood up and set my dishes in the sink. "Before I meet with Dujardin, I want to visit Ciara. You care to join me?"

"I got nothing better to do." She smiled, and my insides melted.

Getting ready took longer than anticipated. Turns out, taking a shower with someone you're sexually attracted to doesn't save time or water. But it was enlightening. Turns out, Shea had very strong hands and knew how to use them for more than building motorcycles.

Once dressed, I pulled on my ballistic vest. Peoria PD had seized my Ruger and Rossi for evidence. Fortunately, I still had the SIG I'd taken off Yuri Barayev, which I tucked in a conceal holster at the small of my back, and a snub-nosed .38, which I tucked in my ankle holster. I offered Shea my spare vest.

She replied, "Nah. When it rains, I just run between the drops."

I gave her a look. "You serious? Cabrera's still looking for us, remember? Your bike may be fast, but I doubt it will outrun bullets."

"Kevlar vests are heavy, hot, and make it hard to move out of the way. Thanks for the offer, but I'll pass."

I looked out the front window. No cars on the street as far as I could see. Maybe they'd caught Cabrera after all.

Shea helped me onto the back of her bike, and we cruised toward Seventh Avenue. I spotted Cabrera's Crown Victoria parked on Fifth Avenue. The headlights flickered on as the car roared to life.

"That's them," I shouted to Shea.

"I'll lose them." She poured on speed, and we flew past Cabrera's car.

I hung on as best I could while Shea navigated through the labyrinth of streets in the neighborhood—up Fifth Avenue, onto Granada, twisting onto Third, around the island where Holly Street split with Monte Vista, then back west, headed for the ever-bustling traffic on Seventh Avenue. Cabrera bore down on us the whole way.

I felt the impacts a microsecond before I heard the triple crack of the gun. They hit like a sledgehammer to the spine. I slammed into Shea, smacking our helmets together.

"Jinx?" shouted Shea.

"All right," I wheezed through gritted teeth. "Kevlar."

More gunshots followed. Shea put on a burst of speed just as I reached for the SIG Sauer. I slammed hard against the backrest, another explosion of pain rippling through my body. The pistol slipped from my hand and disappeared behind us.

Shea wove sharply back and forth down the road, trying to make us harder to hit but forcing me to cling to her for dear life. The busy Seventh Avenue intersection rapidly approached. There was no way to make the turn without either getting creamed by oncoming traffic or stopping and letting Cabrera catch us.

"Hold on," Shea shouted.

Without slowing, Shea pulled a hard Hail Mary right turn. An air horn bellowed behind us followed by the wail of screeching tires, screaming people, and the sickening crunch of metal and glass.

Shea whipped onto a side street and stopped so suddenly that I tumbled forward and landed on my back. I was so stunned I barely noticed the asphalt scorching my arms and legs. Every breath felt like a power drill to my spine.

Shea rushed over to me. "Jinx, you okay?" The concern on her face nearly broke my heart.

"I'm...alive." I gritted my teeth and, with her help, wobbled into a standing position. I ripped off my vest and found three rounds mushroomed in the back.

Shea pulled up the back of my shirt. "Didn't break the skin, but you're gonna be feeling those hits a while. Guess I didn't do so well at driving between the drops, huh?"

I turned and caught her gaze. "Not your fault. And I'm not so easy to kill."

An unexpected chuckle escaped from her throat. "So I see."

I took a deep, painful breath and looked at what had become of our pursuers. Cabrera's car lay crushed between a cement truck and a bus shelter.

“Let’s finish this,” I growled, pulling the .38 from my ankle holster.

Fueled by adrenaline and rage, we pushed through a crowd of people gathered around the crash site. The cement truck had pancaked the driver’s side of the Crown Vic through to the center console. Somewhere in the tangle of twisted metal, plastic, and glass were the flattened remains of Juan Cabrera. *El Duende* was now *Una Tortilla*. I approached the car’s passenger side.

A man with a shaved head and an elaborate neck tattoo sat dazed with the door halfway open, one foot on the ground, a .45-caliber held loosely in his right hand. Blood trickled down his face. He looked up at me with glazed eyes and tried to raise his gun.

I pressed my revolver to his forehead. “Drop it, or I’ll put one through that ugly face of yours.”

The pistol clattered to the ground. I kicked it away.

“Who are you?” I asked.

“*¿Que?*” he asked in a deep growl.

“Cómo te llamas, pendejo?” I repeated.

“Chuy.” A fine mist of blood sprayed from his lips as he mumbled his name. “Chuy Rodriguez.”

“Who told you we were investigating Fitzgerald’s murder, Chuy?” I asked in Spanish.

His eyes were dull and glassy. “*Pinche puta*.”

I pressed the barrel of the .38 harder against his skull. “*¡Digame! ¿Quien?*”

“*¡Chingáte!*” He started to cough up more blood.

With Shea’s help, I dragged him out of the car and tossed him onto the sidewalk. I took a photo of his face with my phone, then cuffed him. “Fuck you, too, asshole!” I whispered into his ear.

The heavyset driver of the cement truck huffed into view. There was an abrasion and a dusting of white powder on his face from where his airbag had hit him. "I tried to stop, but that car, it just came out of nowhere. You gals police?" he asked, looking at the handcuffs on Rodriguez.

"Not exactly," I said. "But this man's wanted for murdering a cop."

"I...I called 911 and my corporate office. Geez, I sure hope I don't get dinged for this. I'll lose my job."

When the patrol officers and ambulance arrived, I explained that Chuy Rodriguez and the now deceased Juan Cabrera had murdered several people including Detective Garza. I suggested they contact Detective Oliver Jennings, who was assigned to the Garza case. He arrived not long after.

Detective Jennings always reminded me of a chunky Tom Skerritt. His salt-and-pepper mustache was bushier than the last time I'd seen him. The guy must've been pushing sixty at this point, and I wondered if he'd ever take his pension and retire.

"Ms. Ballou," he said genteelly, shaking my hand. "Getting yourself into a little dustup with some gangbangers?"

"Something like that."

I introduced Shea and gave him the rundown on the situation, filling him in on Cabrera's involvement in the murders.

"He shot at you?" Jennings asked when I told him about our most recent narrow escape.

I held out my vest and showed him the three hollow point rounds still embedded in the Kevlar fibers.

"I'd like to take that in as evidence, if you don't mind." Jennings was always polite. It was his friendly, I'm-your-best-buddy style that got him so many confessions from suspects.

Giving up my vest felt like surrendering my wallet or phone. I felt naked without it. But with Yuri and his guys in the morgue and Cabrera soon joining them, my need for it was less critical than it had been. I watched him put it in a large evidence bag.

By the time Jennings allowed us to go, I'd received a text from Max that Ciara had been released and was home resting. I replied that I'd check on her later. We didn't have much time before we were due to meet with Scarlett.

50

Shea and I pulled into my neighborhood, where I found the SIG still lying in the street. Maybe my luck was changing. Last thing I needed was one of my weapons ending up in the hands of one of the neighborhood kids.

At ten o'clock, we arrived at a small brick building on Thomas Road that served as the office for the Human Trafficking Resource Center. We parked in a small lot behind the building and left our weapons in the top case on Shea's bike.

A sign by the back door read Entrance, but when I turned the knob, it was locked. I rang the doorbell.

A large black man with the physique of a bodybuilder opened the door. A semiautomatic pistol hung from his left hip. "Can I help you?" His voice was deep and gravelly but polite.

"Jinx Ballou and Shea Stevens. We're here to meet with Ms. Acevedo."

"Can I see some ID?"

We handed him our driver's licenses. The man inspected them, looked us over to make sure our faces matched the photos, and handed them back. “Right this way, ladies.”

He led us past a break room into a reception area with couches and overstuffed chairs. The shades were all drawn.

A woman dressed in a tan summer-weight business suit sat on a sofa that looked like it had been picked up at Goodwill. She stood and shook our hands. “Welcome to the Human Trafficking Resource Center. I’m Mariana Acevedo, the senior coordinator. I see you’ve met our security officer, Lewis Jackson.” She nodded at the man who’d let us in.

Shea and I introduced ourselves.

“I really appreciate you meeting with us,” I said.

Mariana’s smile faded into formality. “Please sit. Would you care for something to drink?”

We both shook our heads and sat in armchairs across from Mariana.

“Do you know about the rescue center? What we do here?”

“Perhaps you could tell us,” I said.

“I like to think of ourselves as an underground railroad helping people escape modern-day slavery. We operate a loose network of volunteer service providers and shelters. On occasion, we work with law enforcement, but many human trafficking victims are also undocumented immigrants. We often find ourselves having to protect clients as much from the federal government as from the criminal organizations.”

“Makes sense,” I said. “Wouldn’t make sense to rescue a woman from human traffickers only to have ICE stick her in a cage.”

“Exactly.”

“We’re here because a woman is being wrongfully put in a cage,” I explained. “She’s being framed for a murder she didn’t commit. She’s transgender and has already been raped once in jail because the idiots in Scottsdale stuck her in a men's facility. If she's found guilty, it could cost her her life."

"Yes, our client told me you are investigating the murder of that preacher." Mariana's face revealed a laundry list of emotions.

"Scarlett is the only eyewitness to the murder," Shea replied. "We need her to testify."

"That is out of the question. She is an undocumented refugee from Haiti. Not only would she risk deportation if she testified, but she would face reprisals from the men who trafficked her and from the men who murdered that preacher."

"Yuri Barayev and the men running the sex ring are dead," I replied. "Juan Cabrera, the man who murdered Fitzgerald, is also dead. She doesn't need to fear reprisals."

"If you already know who's responsible, why do you need her to testify?"

"If she doesn't, my friend will die in prison. Police found her DNA under the victim's fingernails." Shea's voice crackled with emotion.

When Mariana gave us a quizzical look, I added, "The two of them had a...scuffle earlier that day. She didn't kill him. But when juries these days hear DNA, they think guilty. Scarlett's testimony is crucial to prove our friend innocent."

Mariana appeared to process the information for a few minutes, then nodded at Lewis. He vanished down a hallway and returned with a woman dressed in a loose-fitting sweatshirt and jeans. She had dark skin, long braids, and a very nervous look. She could easily pass for Indigo's sister.

"Jinx Ballou, Shea Stevens, this is Sophie Dujardin,

whom you know as Scarlett. I leave it up to her whether to assist you."

I shook her hand. "Thank you for calling me back."

We all sat down, and I explained Indigo's predicament to Sophie. "We really need your help."

Sophie shook her head. "I…I just want to live my life. Nine years ago, much of my family was killed in the earthquake near Port-au-Prince. Then my mama and brother Pierre died from cholera. I was alone. A couple years ago, a man told me I could be a model and actress in America. But he lied."

"He turned you into a sex slave," I said.

"*Oui.* I lost hope of ever being happy. The men were like animals. And then that horrible night…"

"I'd like to show you a couple of photos. Could you tell me if you recognize them as the men who murdered James Fitzgerald?"

Mariana looked to Sophie, who nodded. I pulled up a photo of Juan Cabrera that Becca had sent me, and handed my phone to Sophie. The moment she looked at the photo, she shuddered, then nodded before squeezing her eyes tightly shut. A tear streamed down the side of her face. "He's one of them." She handed me back my phone.

I pulled up the photo of Chuy Rodriguez I'd taken at the car crash a few hours earlier. "How about him?"

She took a deep breath and let it out. "*Oui,* he was the other."

"Thanks. That helps. Now if you could testify to this in court…"

Sophie's face tightened like a fist. She clutched her chest but couldn't tear her gaze away from the photo on the phone. "I…cannot. I am sorry."

"Please, Sophie," Shea begged. "You can't let my friend go to prison."

"I think we're done here," said Mariana. "You've made your case, but clearly—"

"Can I show you one more photo?"

Sophie wiped the tears from her face. "Okay."

I pulled up another photo and gave her the phone.

She gasped and covered her mouth, handing me back the phone as if it were too hot to hold. "I do not know this person."

"Her name is Zia Pearson. Her friends call her Indigo."

"What happened to her?"

"She was brutally assaulted at the Scottsdale jail. The men's jail," said Shea. "She's transgender, and those bastards stuck her in with the men. Didn't care that she's post-op. She, too, has been traumatized for a crime she didn't commit. And unless you help us prove she's innocent, they're going to send her back. She'll probably be raped again and eventually murdered. Even if you don't want to testify, we need to know exactly what happened in that motel room."

She closed her eyes, both arms now wrapped around her. "Okay, I will tell you."

51

Sophie went through her story. Yuri had ordered her to service Fitzgerald. She had no idea he had been violent with Maricela. Shortly after she entered the motel room, Fitzgerald got verbally abusive with her, calling her an ugly whore.

At first, she thought this was just playacting. But then he struck her with his fist. She tried to escape, but he was too big and powerful. He forced her onto the bed and was about to rape her when Cabrera and Rodriguez burst into the room. Both had guns. Cabrera had a machete stuck in his belt.

Fitzgerald yelled at them to get out, but Rodriguez pulled Fitzgerald off the bed and held his arms while Cabrera pummeled him, screaming at him for raping his daughter. Then Rodriguez dragged him into the bathroom while Sophie cowered in the corner. She heard a thunk followed by a bloodcurdling scream.

Sophie grabbed her clothes and headed toward the door. Cabrera spotted her and yelled, "Where you going, *puta*?"

Blood dripped from the machete in his hand. He lunged at her, but she managed to escape. She recalled hearing a loud bang like a gunshot as she raced across the parking lot.

She took refuge in the liquor store next door. Turned out that Marco, the old man who owned the store, was an HTRC volunteer. He hid Sophie in the storage room. When Cabrera stormed in moments later, Marco claimed she had run out the back.

After Cabrera left, Marco contacted the HTRC hotline. Mariana picked up Sophie and brought her to an HTRC-affiliated shelter.

Sophie buried her face in her hands as she finished her story.

"Thank you for sharing this, Sophie," I said. "Is there any way I can convince you to talk to my friend's lawyer? No judge. No jury. Just the lawyer."

"I am sorry for your friend, truly I am. But I cannot risk going back to Haiti. And the man with the machete, he was part of a gang. They would come after me."

I nodded. "If you change your mind, please give me a call. Thank you both for your time."

"No, you have to testify!" Shea rose to her feet, the scars on her face deepening with emotion. "You want to be an American? Well, that means standing up to injustice."

"Shea!" I reached for her, but she swatted my hand away.

"No, I understand you're scared. We were scared, too, but we risked our lives to rescue a woman that Yuri Barayev and his goons kidnapped. We nearly got killed by Cabrera and his *cholos* because you refused to tell the cops what you witnessed."

Lewis Jackson, the security officer, reappeared in the room, looking very stern.

Mariana stood. "Ms. Ballou, Ms. Stevens, I'm going to have to ask you to leave now. Sophie has given you as much information as she is comfortable providing."

"No, you can't do this," insisted Shea.

"Shea, we got to go." I put a hand on her shoulder and steered her toward the back door. "We tried our best."

Shea began walking, but her rage continued. "I swear, if Indigo gets convicted, I will find you."

"Shea, stop," I whispered.

Mariana and Lewis stood stone-faced. Sophie sobbed on the couch.

Shea's shoulders slumped as we stepped outside into the parking lot. The dead bolt on the door clacked shut behind us.

"It's not right." She tossed me my borrowed helmet.

"I know. But we know the whole story now. We can piece together the evidence because we know what we're looking for. We'll have the ballistics and police reports to tie it all together."

"What if it's not enough? You know how juries are with DNA."

"Trust the process," I said.

"What the hell's that mean?"

"Something my father says. All we can do is what we can do. Then we have to trust that things will somehow work out the way they're supposed to."

"The way they're supposed to," Shea repeated derisively. "The way they worked out for my mother when my father murdered her? The way they worked out for your fiancé? The way they worked out for Vanessa Colton?"

I put a hand on her shoulder. "Let's talk to Dragon. She's a smart lawyer. With the information we have, she'll figure out a way to get the charges dismissed."

We left the HTRC office and met Dragon in her room at

the Desert View Inn. I provided copies of my report that connected the dots between Fitzgerald raping Cabrera's daughter and the murders of Fitzgerald, Cabrera, and the woman found in the Salt River wash, as well as the drive-by at my house. I referred her to Detectives Jennings and Hardin for copies of reports from ballistics, autopsy, and whatever else she needed from the Phoenix Crime Lab to prove her case. I also gave her a copy of the audio file of Sophie's statement I'd secretly recorded on my phone.

"It's too bad Ms. Dujardin won't testify. I can try to get the audio file admitted into evidence, but it's iffy. We may have to make do with the other information you provided. I'll file for a dismissal first thing. Thanks for your work on this."

I glanced at Shea. "It's been interesting."

My phone rang. It was Maurice at Pima Bail Bonds. I stepped outside Dragon's motel room and answered it. "What's going on, Maurice? How come they issued a bench warrant for Pearson a day early? I was about to turn her in."

"Ms. Ballou, when I call you or text you for a progress update, I expect a response."

"Well, things were—"

He kept going as if I hadn't said a word. "I brought you in as a favor to Deez. But I expect a minimal level of professionalism."

"For which I—"

"Dodging my calls or telling me you're close when you aren't is not acceptable."

I stepped outside, and Shea joined me. The sunlight glittered in her eyes.

"Maurice, to be fair, I—"

"Now I hear you teamed up with the people hiding Ms. Pearson so you could play private eye? What were you thinking?"

I waited, not wanting to be cut off again. Plus having Shea so close to me all of a sudden felt very distracting. Images of the two of us in my bed doing more than cuddling played through my mind.

"Ms. Ballou, are you there?"

"Uh, yeah. I'm here."

"Did you partner up with the Athena Sisterhood to locate Fitzgerald's killer?"

"I did everything I could to bring Pearson in. It wasn't going to happen. Deez's crew couldn't do it either, by the way. So I gathered exculpatory evidence as an incentive for her to surrender voluntarily."

"I nearly lost my shirt on this deal."

"Look, Maurice, I—" The call dropped.

Shea stepped in close, sending a jolt of electricity through my body. "Everything all right?" she asked in that sultry alto voice of hers.

"Just the usual. Me getting fired. It's kinda my thing."

Looking into her eyes was like taking a hit off a joint. Waves of euphoria washed over me. A deep fire I hadn't felt in months blazed to life inside me. Before I knew what I was doing, I was kissing her.

After what felt like an eternity, I came up for air. "I...uh, you want to...um, head back to my place?"

She looked so deep into my soul I felt naked and yet unafraid. "Yeah."

We said goodbye to Dragon, then hopped on the back of her motorcycle. We blazed down the Black Canyon Highway, weaving between the cars, roared onto the Thomas Road exit, squeaking through yellow lights, and it still wasn't fast enough. We hooked a left so hard onto Central I literally saw sparks flying when her foot peg scraped the pavement.

While racing past a light rail train, I caught myself

waiving at the passengers like a goofy teenager. I didn't care how silly I looked.

We stepped inside my house. Diana rushed up to greet me like I hadn't been there for a thousand years. The way she always did. I loved that about her.

"Hey, baby!" I said as she showered me with sloppy doggy kisses. "You keep the place safe from intruders?"

"She loves her mommy. That's for sure," Shea said.

I gazed into the furry face, reflecting over the past few months. "She's been my North Star ever since I got her. Even when everything went to shit, she was always there for me. Always loving me no matter how broken I got." Tears pricked my eyes.

I stood up and turned to Shea, mustering a smile for her.

She caressed my cheek. "What say you and me go to your bedroom and tear each other's clothes off."

I pretended to be appalled. "What kinda girl do you think I am?"

"The kind who needs someone to tear her clothes off."

"Okay, you got me there."

"And who hasn't been properly fucked in a good long time." A sly smile crept across her face.

My knees almost buckled from anticipation. "Aw, shit, I'm in trouble."

We meandered down the hallway, hand in hand, looking at each other like a couple of shy, lovesick schoolgirls. I flopped down on my bed and winced in pain.

"What's wrong?" she asked.

"My back," I replied through gritted teeth.

"Lemme take a look."

I sat up, and she helped me off with my shirt.

"How bad is it?"

"Shit, girl, you got a lot of scars."

"Hazards of the trade, I'm afraid. What about from today? Where I got shot."

"Got yourself some hellacious bruises and a bit of swelling. Wait here." She stepped out of the room.

Diana started nudging my hand, wanting me to pet her and scratch her back.

"Diana, go lay down in the living room."

She gave me a pouty look that tugged at my heartstrings. But right now, my heartstrings would have to wait. "Lay down and we'll go for a run later." She whined, then hustled off, wagging her tail.

"This should help." Shea returned with a bag of frozen peas, pressing it to my bare back.

I gasped and sucked in a pain-riddled lung full of air. "Fuck. That's. Cold."

"Sorry." She nuzzled close so that I could feel her breath on my ear. The icy chill of the frozen peas suddenly didn't bother me so much. Her free hand slipped over the inside of my thigh. The words "fire and ice" took on a whole new meaning.

"I...I'm not...huh...not complaining," I managed through breaths as she nibbled on my earlobe. Shivers that ran down my spine had nothing to do with the bag of frozen peas. A needful ache grew between my legs.

I lay on my side, facing her. In the afternoon light filtering through the security blinds, I studied the scarred landscape of her face, softened by the warm glow of her eyes. I was still trembling—not from the improvised cold pack on my back but from the thrill of opening myself up, allowing this person beside me to see my most vulnerable self.

I traced the lines on her face. "You're so fucking beautiful, you know that?"

"You sure you didn't hit your head when you fell off my bike?" She chuckled. "Clearly, your judgment is impaired."

"We both have scars. Do my scars make me less attractive?"

"Fuck no." She pressed her forehead against mine. Waves of heat rippled between us.

My deepest fear bubbled up. I couldn't avoid it. "Does it bother you that I'm trans?"

She kissed me deeply. The pack of peas dropped with a smack onto the hardwood floor. I cradled her face in my hands, our tongues teasing and probing and caressing each other in a dance.

I rolled onto my back. She positioned herself on top of me, our legs intertwined.

"I'm not hurting you, am I?" she asked. The concern on her face was almost heartbreaking.

"No. I'm okay." I could barely register the throbbing in my back.

She bent down and kissed my breasts, gently sucking and teasing at first, and then grew more insistent. For the next hour, we explored each other's bodies, tracing war wounds and battle scars and bringing each other to much-needed climaxes over and over.

52

The next morning, I felt lonely and confused about the situation with Shea. Where the hell was this going? She lived up in Sycamore Springs, easily an hour's drive away. Maybe less the way she drove. But still, it wasn't like we could see each other on a daily basis. Things were crazy enough when I'd dated Conor, and he'd lived only a couple of streets over.

Was I even ready for a relationship? Was I making more of it than it was? Maybe it was just a friends-with-benefits situation. A friendly fuck between comrades in arms who'd survived some harrowing events. Suddenly, I jumped out of bed. Shit! I'd totally forgotten about Ciara.

I called Max. "Hey! How's Ciara doing?"

"Jinx. Hey." He sounded sleepy. The clock read six twenty. Shit. I'd woken him up. "Let me get her. Hold on."

A moment later, a raw, tired voice I barely recognized as Ciara came on the line. "Jinxie?"

"I'm sorry. I shouldn't have called so early. It's just, I meant to stop by yesterday, and well, things kept getting in the way."

"It's no problem. I'm...I don't know how I'm doing. Physically, docs said I should be okay. Mentally, I'm still trying to process everything."

"Yeah, I get it. I've been through some similar stuff."

"The hospital staff recommended some therapists who specialize in trauma. Your father was on that list."

"Not surprised. He knows his shit."

"Would it be weird if I went to see him? At least with him, I don't have to rehash all the transgender stuff."

"Not at all." I sighed, trying to push through the guilt. "Ciara, I'm so sorry for all of this. If I had known..."

"Not your fault."

I felt like it was. "If there is anything I can do, just ask."

"You rescued me, Jinx. You killed those bastards. I'm... I'm glad they're dead. Is that a bad thing to say?"

"No, I'm glad they're dead too. Not even sorry I killed some of them. I'd do anything to protect you. You're a good person."

"I'm gonna go back to sleep now. They gave me these meds. Just so tired."

"Sleep. We'll talk again soon."

"Hey, lover," Shea said when I put my phone back on the nightstand.

"Hey." I kissed her, soaking in the bliss of whatever the hell this was.

"You hungry?"

"For you or food?" I asked.

She shrugged. "Either."

Forty minutes later, we pulled ourselves from the sheets. I took Diana for her morning run while Shea showered.

The air was warmer than it had been. The cooler-than-usual spring was giving way to the first hints of the fury of summer. I didn't care. I felt whole in a way I hadn't in a very long time. Not just because of whatever this was between Shea and me. I felt like I'd broken out of the swamp I'd been living in for so long. I felt powerful.

An hour later, I was dressed in a blouse and slacks, even put on some makeup and did something with my hair other than pull it into a ponytail. I tried to convince myself that I wanted to look professional in court, especially if Dragon needed me to testify that Indigo should be released again on bail. Deep down, I knew why I was really going full femme. Shea.

She packed her stuff into her motorcycle's top case, and we drove separately to the courthouse. After all the time I'd spent getting ready, I didn't want to show up with helmet hair. I offered Shea a ride in the Charger, but she declined.

"Not a big fan of riding in a cage," she reminded me with a twinkle in her eye. "Besides, look at that thing. You drive like a maniac."

I arrived in the courtroom to see two dozen women sitting in the gallery, dressed in Athena Sisterhood biker vests, which I had since learned were called cuts. Guessed if I was going to become a biker, I needed to learn the lingo.

Byrd was there, too, looking quite dapper in a charcoal-gray suit. When I sent him the details for the hearing, I wasn't sure if he'd show up. I was glad he did.

The Honorable Alice Gwinnett, a woman with graying hair, walked in, her black robe swishing as she walked, and called the room to order. Wayne Prather started the proceedings by claiming that Indigo was a flight risk and should be remanded without bail. I wanted to smack the hell out of his smug little face.

Dragon objected, calling for the charges to be dismissed, explaining that she had ballistic reports that tied Fitzgerald's death to other murders in the valley. She further offered to have detectives from Phoenix PD testify that Juan "El Duende" Cabrera, recently deceased, was believed to be responsible for the murders of James Fitzgerald, Detective Luis Garza, and Bisi Awojobi, a Nigerian-born sex worker whose body was found in the Salt River wash.

Objections, counter objections, and all kinds of legal wrangling ensued. One reason I decided not to go to law school. Justice was more like a high school debate than the pursuit of truth, all about cleverness and procedure. For all its risks, I much preferred my work as a bounty hunter.

After listening to all of the arguments and counter arguments, Judge Gwinnett issued a ruling. "After consideration of your motions, I—"

My phone rang. I had meant to silence it but forgot. The caller ID showed it was Sophie Dujardin.

"Whoever's phone that is needs to silence it immediately," demanded the judge.

"Hello? Sophie?" I whispered.

"Ma'am, you are disrupting this proceeding. Either—"

"Ms. Ballou, I have changed my mind. I...I will testify."

"Ma'am, do you hear me? Hang up that phone this instant or leave the courtroom. Otherwise—"

"I cannot let another innocent woman suffer because of what happened."

"Thank you, Sophie. Hold on just a moment." I squeezed past the other people sitting in my row and strode up the aisle toward Dragon.

"Ma'am, if you do not sit down this instant, I will hold you in contempt."

I ignored her.

"Bailiff! Please take that woman into custody."

I was almost to the defense table. Dragon looked at me as if I'd lost my mind. The bailiff charged toward me like a linebacker. I tossed the phone toward Dragon. She fumbled it, and it clattered to the floor the same instant the bailiff tackled me.

I was cuffed and frog-marched downstairs to a holding cell, which I shared with three other women, all wearing DOC coveralls. I ignored them.

For two hours, I sat there. Periodically, a bailiff would escort one of the other women out of the cell for her court appearance. I couldn't believe I'd come so close to getting Indigo free. My phone was smashed and useless. I might never get back in touch with Sophie, and even if I did, she'd probably have changed her mind. Indigo would spend the rest of her life in jail suffering who knew what horrors.

"Comfy?"

I looked up to see Dragon outside the bars, her briefcase in hand. A bailiff stood beside her.

"I've had better days."

"That was a bold move in court. Not necessarily smart but bold."

"What can I say? Not smart but bold is how I roll."

"I've got some good news and bad news. Which do you want first?"

"Rip off the bandage. Hit me with the bad news."

"You are being fined three hundred dollars for disrupting the court and ignoring Judge Gwinnett's demands. You will also have to personally apologize to her."

"So what's the good news?"

"The prosecutor and I met with the judge in chambers. She listened to Sophie's statement over your phone. The prosecutor didn't want her testimony admitted, but the judge heard her out. The charges against Indigo have been dismissed."

I took a deep breath and let go of a boatload of tension. "That is good news."

"Also, I spoke with Maurice Begay at Pima Bail Bonds and explained that you were instrumental in returning Indigo to custody. He's agreed to pay you your bounty and to keep you in mind for future jobs."

"Thanks, Dragon. You didn't have to do that."

"You really went above and beyond. It was the least I could do."

The bailiff let me out and escorted Dragon and me to Judge Gwinnett's chambers. She spent ten solid minutes chastising me for my disruptive behavior and schooling me on courtroom protocol. I stood there and took it, and when she was done, I apologized.

After paying my fine to the court clerk's office, I met the members of the Athena Sisterhood in the downstairs lobby.

Dragon handed me her business card. "If Mr. Begay doesn't hire you for any more bounty hunter work, look me up. I can always use a good investigator."

"Jinx," said someone behind me. I turned to see Indigo, arm in arm with Savage. "Havoc told me what all you did to help me. You put your life at risk multiple times. I...I don't know how to thank you."

"I got paid. I'm good." It sounded more mercenary than I intended, but I didn't know what else to say.

"I know I shoudn'ta run, but..."

"You don't have to explain," I said. "I probably would've done the same thing if I'd been put in men's lockup. I'm glad it all worked out."

"We got to celebrate!" insisted Savage. "Is it too early to drink in this town?"

I looked at my watch. It was just after noon.

"I'm sure it's beer o'clock somewhere," said Fuego.

"Let's head to Naughty's," Rah-Rah suggested.

"Let's not," said Shea, giving me a wink. "Jinx, you know this town better than we do. Where do you suggest?"

"I'm kinda in the mood for Grumpy's. And they have beer for those who want it." I thought about it. "'Course, he'll probably have a heart attack when he sees all of us show up at once."

My phone dinged. Ciara had sent me a text. *Please meet me at your house.*

I replied. *Which one? Old or new?*

New came the reply

What's up? I asked.

Not over the phone.

Meet you there shortly.

"Hey," I said to Shea. "I got to take care of something real quick at home. But I'll meet you all there."

"Everything all right?" she asked.

"Yeah. It's Ciara. Probably dropped the Gray Ghost at my place and wants a ride back. Shouldn't take long."

"You want me to come with?"

I wanted to say yes, but everybody was in such a celebratory mood. "Naw, I'll be along soon enough. Just save me a seat."

Shea gave me a peck on the lips. "Don't take too long, gorgeous."

I didn't see the Gray Ghost when I pulled into the carport. Aside from a black BMW parked down the block, there were no cars in sight.

I unlocked the door and found the security system wasn't armed. In my haste to get to the courthouse, I must have forgotten. But then I stepped inside, and immediately, something felt wrong.

"Diana?" Where was she? She always came running when I walked in.

"Dog is here," said a thickly accented male voice.

Fuck. Having just come from court, I didn't have any weapons on me.

I stepped into my living room. Two men sat on my couch. One, I guessed to be in his fifties with a long chin-beard but no mustache or sideburns. I recognized him from his photo—Sergei Volkov.

The other looked to be in his thirties and was built like a linebacker. Both had guns stashed in their waistband. Diana sat between them, getting her head scratched by Volkov.

53

"Fine guard dog you turned out to be," I told Diana. She gave me a confused look. I pointed toward the hallway. "Bed." I didn't want her getting hurt when the shit hit the fan.

After Diana had disappeared into the bedroom, Volkov gestured toward a stuffed armchair opposite the coffee table. "Sit."

"Why are you in my living room, Volkov?" But I had a good idea of the answer to my question. "And what are you doing with Ciara's phone?"

"You know of me. This is good. And this is Anatoly. He doesn't say much."

"Pleasure. Now get the fuck outta my house."

"You are Ballou, yes? Jinx Ballou, famous bounty hunter."

"That's me."

"Ballou is French, yes? *Parlez-vous français?*"

"*Nyet!*" I replied with a sneer.

"Oh, you speak Russian."

"'Fraid not, wise guy. Spanish and English only. Pretty much all I need in these parts."

"I am impressed you speak Spanish. Most Americans only speak English. Stupid, lazy. This is why you have clown for president. Me? I speak Chechen, Russian, German, French, and of course, very good English. I am polyglot. Because Russians are not lazy like Americans."

"I thought you were Chechen."

"My family moved to Chechnya when I was child. But we are still proud to be Russian."

"Well, goody for you."

"Please sit. We discuss."

I stared at the gun in Sergei's waistband and complied. As I sat, my hand casually slipped into a pocket on the side of the chair.

"We relieved you of gun in chair pocket," said Sergei.

Anatoly held up the Glock I usually kept stashed there and pointed it at me.

My eyes drifted to the coffee table, where I kept the Smith & Wesson, but I had no way to get to it before Anatoly filled my body with lead.

Sergei pulled my .44 Magnum out of his waistband and aimed it at me. "Also this found under table. You have good taste in weapons."

"How'd you get in here?" I was sure now that I had set the alarm.

"Anatoly look dumb as bull, but he is good with technologies. Especially good bypassing security alarms."

"Fine. Anatoly's a fucking genius. What. Do. You. Want?"

"Several of my men are dead. Yuri Barayev. Andrei Garinov. You know of them?"

"Maybe if Yuri hadn't kidnapped my friend, your guys wouldn't be chilling in the morgue right now."

"Yuri could be a little..." He turned to Anatoly and said something in what I assumed was Russian or Chechen.

"Aggressive," said Anatoly.

"Yes, aggressive. But you show up looking for missing girl. I tell Yuri, have you bring her."

"Scarlett's dead. Murdered by Juan Cabrera of the Westside Jaguars. Same asshole who killed James Fitzgerald, one of your clients at the Cactus Inn. I tried to explain this to Yuri. He still wouldn't release my friend. Left us no choice but to get...*aggressive*. As far as I'm concerned, the slate's clean."

"Slate is clean. What means this?" Sergei asked Anatoly in whatever language. Anatoly replied.

Sergei nodded. "Ah, now I understand 'slate is clean.' Like balancing accounts, yes? I am businessman. I understand business language. But no. Slate is not clean. Accounts not balanced. I see on news Scarlett still alive. And my men are dead." He leaned forward. "But don't worry. I not kill you. Not yet. You want clean slate? You work for me now. First job, bring Scarlett to me."

"I don't think so. I don't work for human trafficking scum like you."

"I am scum? Your government, they lock up people looking for American dream. Put little childrens in cages. Me? I give women opportunity to work in America. Make money. Live American dream. But I am scum?"

"Don't bother giving me the sales pitch, asshole. I'm not buying. Just because our government is doing evil shit doesn't make what you do any better. You can take your job offer and shove it up your Chechen Russkie ass.

"And for the record, I told the feds all about your sex trafficking operation. They're going to shut you down—your club, the motel, and everything else you got going. If you were smart, you'd be getting the hell outta Dodge instead of stinking up my living room."

"You not hear? Club burned down. Many girls die. Very sad." From his exaggerated pout, I could tell he was behind it. "As for you, Jinx Ballou. You are not in position for to bargain."

"Let me give you a little history lesson, Sergei. Your brother, Milo, made me a similar offer. When I turned him down, he got aggressive too. I put him down like the rabid dog he was, along with several of his men. And now I've killed Yuri, Andrei, and those steroid-swollen sides of beef he used for bodyguards. So don't threaten me, unless you want the same."

"I see. Perhaps I kill you now." Sergei raised the .44 Magnum.

Out of nowhere, Diana lunged, sinking her teeth into Sergei's meaty hand. The gun went off right before he dropped the revolver, sending a bullet into my newly replaced window. The gunshot sent Diana bolting out of the room.

My ears ringing from the gunshot, I hurled my spiky cosplay trophy at Anatoly, nailing the silent security genius in the eye. He clutched the injured socket while blood trickled down his face.

I snatched my Glock from his hand and put two rounds in his chest. His chest bloomed scarlet. Sergei reached for the revolver. I kicked it away, pressed the pistol to his head, and pulled the trigger.

"Jesus fucking Christ." Shea stepped into the room, followed by members of the Athena Sisterhood, all with their guns drawn. "What'd I miss?"

I hugged Shea and realized my heart was racing. "How'd you know?"

"Know what? Grumpy's was closed. Gas leak of some kind."

We kissed. I barely noticed the hoots and hollers from the other members of the Athena Sisterhood.

Detective Jennings showed up, along with the uniformed crime scene circus. I was thoroughly interrogated, swabbed for GSR, and eventually escorted out of my home. It would be hours before they were done gathering evidence and I would be allowed back inside, even though it was a clear case of self-defense.

I was not looking forward to cleaning the ick off my wall. I would probably need to repaint and get another new window and a new couch. But knowing Sergei and his crew were gone forever made it worth it.

Was I a sociopath for not feeling bad about killing evil people? Would a sociopath worry about not feeling bad?

Shea and the rest of the Athena Sisterhood were getting ready to head north. A sense of dread, loneliness, and loss hung over me.

"Damn, I'm gonna miss you." I pressed my forehead against hers.

"Likewise. But I gotta get back to Annie and the motorcycle shop. Clarence, my business partner, probably thinks I fell off the face of the earth."

"Yeah" was all I could think to say.

"Jinx, I don't know where this thing between us is going, but I'd like to give it a chance. I know we can't see each other every day, but we got weekends. Take a vacation from this fucking heat and spend some time up in the bustling metropolis of Sycamore Springs. The *Cortes Chronicle* says we're getting a Tastee Freez soon."

I met her gaze. My insides turned to jelly. "I'm told there's a fancy shop up there that makes custom motorcycles for women."

"Come on up. I'll teach you to ride."

"I'd like that."

I pulled her in for a deep, slow kiss that sent the world tumbling. I came up for air only when my phone started playing the *Game of Thrones* theme. Becca.

"I probably should take this."

Shea pulled on her helmet. "I'll call you when I get to Sycamore Springs."

"Please do. I really want to see where this goes."

The Athena Sisterhood mounted their bikes. The air shook with the thunder of two dozen motorcycles. It was so gloriously fucking loud I had to wait until they were out of the neighborhood before returning Becca's call.

54

"Hey, Becks. What's up?"

"I found it."

"What?"

"The smoking gun. Wilkes didn't pay for a hit man. He posted a message on a website run by the Westside Jaguars."

"The Jags have a website? That's rather bold."

"No kidding, right? Even the drug gangs are going high tech. Thing is, Wilkes posted a comment on the site that he knew Fitzgerald raped Cabrera's daughter and told them where Fitzgerald would be on the night he was killed. He totally set him up."

Even though Indigo was already cleared, there was still some reckoning to be had. I suspected he was the one who sent the Jags after us as well. "Send me what you got. I want to see Wilkes's face when I tell him he's busted."

"Will do."

I hopped in the Charger and raced like a madwoman to Scottsdale. I wished I already had a motorcycle so I could split lanes and get past all the slow-moving cars. But finally

I pulled up to Wilkes's fancy house, swelling with joy. I put a call in to Atkinson, got his voicemail, and left a message that Wilkes was an accessory to Fitzgerald's murder. Maybe he could get a win out of this after all.

I waltzed up the walkway and found Wilkes's front door ajar. "Hey, asshole!" I called into the house. "You left your front door open." I walked in past the fancy paintings and sculptures.

"Guess what, dipshit? I got proof you had your buddy Brother James killed. You're going down, you piece of shit."

He wasn't in his office. Not in his bedroom. Something wasn't right. A metallic scent hit my nose.

I stepped into the kitchen and drew my pistol. Wilkes lay on the floor, blood pooling around him from two knife wounds in his back. A teenage girl with a buzz cut stood over him, a bloody kitchen knife in each hand.

"What the fuck?" I aimed the gun at her chest, in case she made a move toward me. But she simply stared at me like a deer in the headlights.

"You stabbed him?" I asked.

"He was always posting videos saying queer people deserved to die." Her voice was soft and raspy but with a resilience. "My friend Rainey was murdered by one of his devoted fans. I had to stop him."

"Yeah" was all I said.

"You gonna shoot me?"

"You planning on stabbing me?"

She shook her head.

"Then I'm not going to shoot you." I lowered the gun but didn't holster it. "What's your name?"

"Maggie. Friends call me Knife."

"You're the Valley Slasher, aren't you?" When I got no reaction, I said, "Well, uh, Knife, my name's Jinx Ballou."

Her eyes widened in recognition. "Jinx the bounty

hunter?"

"You heard of me?" I must be getting a reputation in vigilante circles.

"You're trans. Rainey was too." She looked down at blood dripping from the knives in her hand. "You here to arrest me?"

"Nope." I looked at Wilkes. "He killed one of his associates. I was coming for him."

"Huh."

She turned and nonchalantly rinsed the knives in the sink, then dried them, and slid them into sheaths in her waistband. I should have stopped her. But instead, I let her walk past me and out the front door.

I stood there looking at Wilkes's body. "I hope there's a hell. And I hope you're in it."

I stepped outside and called 911.

Soon Detectives Atkinson and Torres arrived. I told them I'd found Wilkes already dead, then showed them the proof of his involvement with Fitzgerald's murder.

They battered me with questions and even checked my pistol. They were disappointed to find it had not recently been fired.

"You didn't see anyone hanging around the house when you pulled up?" Atkinson asked in a disbelieving tone.

"Not a soul."

"Looks like the same MO as the Valley Slasher," said Torres. "Fucking brutal."

"Huh," I said.

I drove back to my old house to see if I could crash with Max and Ciara. It had only been two hours, and I ached physically to have Shea beside me in the Charger. I was tempted to drive up to Sycamore Springs to surprise her, but after what I'd just witnessed, I needed time to get my head straight.

55

Two months later, I arrived back in Phoenix on my Iron Goddess 1100cc cruiser motorcycle. She had black panels, shiny chrome, and indigo-blue accents. I had named her Storm, after the character from X-Men comic books.

The Athena Sisterhood had invited me to join them on a loop ride through Payson, up along the Mogollon Rim. Riding in the middle of a convoy of two dozen motorcycles was a thrill I never thought I'd experience.

The group ride ended at Gertie's in Ironwood's Downtown Square, where Shea presented me with a leather cut with a patch on the back that read Havoc's Old Lady. The recovery jobs I'd been doing for Pima Bail Bonds allowed me to keep my schedule flexible enough to spend a few days each week with Shea and her niece, Annie. Shea had even joined me at a few of my therapy sessions, which were helping me process the trauma of the past several months.

The only downside to riding with the Sisterhood was returning to the furious August heat of the valley all alone. A monsoon storm was rolling in from the southeast. I hoped to beat it home.

The first fat drops were hitting my visor when I pulled onto my street and spotted a figure sitting on my front porch. A nervous chill ran up my spine until I recognized the eyes twinkling in a ginger-bearded face. I didn't even pull into the driveway. I just parked on the street, scrambled off the bike, and raced up the path to my front door, tearing off my helmet as I ran.

"Are you really here?" My hands grasped his arms, wondering if I was dreaming or hallucinating.

"I am, love. In the flesh, such as it is." His warm hand cupped my cheek.

"But how?"

"The Honorable Mr. Justice O'Rourke found me not guilty, if ya can believe it," said Conor.

"I...I..." My head was doing somersaults. My heart felt like it was trying to tear itself in two.

"Ya just gonna stand there gawking, or ya gonna give your fiancé a hug?"

JINX RETURNS IN *TERF WARS*

A fight for justice has become a battle for truth.

Bounty hunter Jinx Ballou is hot on the trail of Blair Marshall, a fugitive who brutally murdered a transgender woman in a public restroom. As a trans woman herself, Jinx is determined to bring this bigoted killer to justice.

But at every turn, Jinx's attempts to apprehend Marshall are thwarted by the ruthless transphobic hate group her fugitive controls. A series of high-speed car chases, brutal fights, and unsuccessful takedowns leave Jinx and her team frustrated and empty-handed.

When an undaunted Jinx presses on, she finds herself embroiled in a war of media manipulation, disinformation, and deep-faked videos that paints a target on her back and puts loved ones in grave danger.

Will Jinx successfully bring Marshall to justice before more innocent people are killed?

As one of the only openly transgender authors in crime fiction, Dharma Kelleher delivers a heartfelt tale that delves deep into the issues of identity and intersectionality, oppression and accountability.

TERF Wars *is the fourth thriller in the highly acclaimed Jinx Ballou Bounty Hunter crime fiction series, although each book in the series can be enjoyed as a standalone.*

Curl up with TERF Wars and join Jinx on an action-packed thrill ride that will leave you cheering for more.

ABOUT THE AUTHOR

Dharma Kelleher writes gritty crime thrillers including the Jinx Ballou Bounty Hunter series and the Shea Stevens Outlaw Biker series.

She is one of the only openly transgender authors in the crime fiction genre. Her action-driven thrillers explore the complexities of social and criminal justice in a world where the legal system favors the privileged.

Dharma is a member of Sisters in Crime, the International Thriller Writers, and the Alliance of Independent Authors.

She lives in Arizona with her wife and a black cat named Mouse. Learn more about Dharma and her work at https://dharmakelleher.com.

20240214010721